WARNING

This book contains scenes that some readers may find disturbing,
including graphic depictions of rape and sexual assault, and is
intended for adults only.
Reader discretion is advised.

Reading this book... will be like entering the dark web.
ENTER AT YOUR OWN RISK.

REAPER'S SALVATION

ROAD TO SALVATION: A LAST RIDER'S TRILOGY #3

JAMIE BEGLEY

Young Ink Press Publication
YoungInkPress.com

Copyright © 2021 by Jamie Begley

Edited by C&D Editing & Hot Tree Editing
Cover Art by Cover Couture
Photo (c) Wander Photography

All rights reserved.

Connect with Jamie,
facebook.com/AuthorJamieBegley
JamieBegley.net

I dedicate this book to

Terry Deisley,
Randie and her daughter,
& Christopher Fleming.

G inny numbly stared out the window of the private jet that she and Hammer boarded after leaving Silas's house. Sightlessly staring at the grey clouds floating below, she replayed the image of Gavin walking toward the waiting car that would take him to Taylor.

In her bedroom upstairs, she had heard the rumble of his voice as he'd talked on his cell phone. She'd dressed quickly and had gone downstairs to start breakfast to hear Gavin ending his phone call the moment she entered the kitchen. The sound of him starting the shower had her slapping several slices of bacon onto the sizzling skillet.

Blinking back tears of fright from what she had gotten herself into, compounded with her fear of Gavin's reaction to the story she was determined to discuss with him, had her hands shaking. She knew she should have told him about her past the previous night, before her brothers arrived back home, but the precious moments with him had gone too quickly.

She promised herself as she flipped the bacon that as soon as Gavin got out of the shower, she would tell him her history.

However when the sound of the shower stopped, she revised her plan, deciding to wait to tell him anything until after he told her about Taylor being at the clubhouse. The time would also allow her the opportunity to settle the mounting trepidations as the minutes ticked by.

"Where's all the jelly I saw sitting on the counter yesterday?"

Ginny looked up from the frying pan. "I gave it to Viper. Silas is going to bring more from storage when he comes back this afternoon. There's some grape jelly in the refrigerator."

"It's store bought. You took all those jars to the storage building? Why didn't you leave one here?"

"Actually, two were meant for here, but when I asked Viper to take a couple to Lily, he asked if he could take another couple for the club."

"You gave them *my* jelly?"

Ginny's brows rose. Gavin was making no effort to hide his irritation. "Technically, those jars are *mine*. I don't understand what the big deal is. I have ten more jars in—"

"The problem is I don't want Shade eating your jelly. It's mine."

Ginny watched as he plopped down on his chair at the table and then stared sullenly at the plain toast.

Ginny placed a plate of bacon in front of him. "You could make yourself a bacon sandwich," she suggested, trying to hide her amusement at his jealousy. She wondered if it was because she made the jelly or if it was an ongoing rivalry between Gavin and Shade.

"You made some to send to Shade."

Rolling her eyes at him, she turned around, but then found herself being pulled down onto his lap.

"I'm sorry."

Ginny could tell he didn't mean his apology, so she

wound her arms around his neck and called his bluff. "You don't look sorry."

"I'm not."

"Didn't your mother teach you to share?"

"All the women in the club cater to Shade."

Ginny frowned. "When I worked there, I didn't see anyone catering to him."

"I'm not talking about the wives."

"Oh ... I see. The women who live there?" Ginny never paid any attention to the men in the club, so she couldn't say if the women had or hadn't.

"Yes."

Goosebumps rose on her skin when Gavin began tracing imaginary circles on her arm with his thumb.

"Don't give any more to him. Please?"

When he touched her like that, she was willing to jump off a cliff if he asked—though even under extreme torture she'd refuse to admit it ... but God knew she would.

"I won't make him any more jelly. Satisfied?"

Agreeing so easily to his request, she saw the suspicion in his eyes. What could she say? She had bigger fish to fry than dealing with Gavin's ridiculous jealousy over Shade.

"What are your plans for the day?" Unable to resist taking the opportunity to touch him as well, Ginny carefully gauged his reaction as she waited for him to tell her that Taylor was at the club. She promised herself she wouldn't react to the mention of Taylor's name on his lips.

"I'm going to the clubhouse to have a talk with the brothers. They want to return a few of the gifts I gave them."

As Gavin spoke, Ginny realized he wasn't going to admit his ex-fiancée was at the club.

"I bet," she said with a heavy heart. "That's one gift I'm glad I wasn't on the receiving end of."

He lifted her off slightly, then slid a small box out of his pocket and held it out for her to take. Ginny stared at the box, as two separate fears cut her to the quick. Was Gavin still contemplating taking his life, or was this a good-bye gift before he reunited with Taylor?

Seeing the reaction she was unable to hide, despite for her best efforts, Gavin shook his head at her. "This gift is not like the ones I bought for the brothers. I bought this because ... I know the bracelet means a lot to you, and I wanted you to have a piece of me, and because I was missing you."

His explanation didn't erase the fear of Taylor, but it did give her precious seconds to regain her composure.

"Then I'll accept your gift." Pressing a kiss on the corner of his mouth, she jiggled the present in front of his face, pretending to be excited.

Ginny didn't tell him her closely guarded secret—she hated presents. Most of the presents she'd received in her life had been given as a replacement for the person being there. In reality, the only present she ever wanted was to be surrounded by the people she loved.

"Let me guess." She jiggled the small box again, hoping the gift was a sign he was beginning to care about her. "They're charms."

"Good guess."

Ginny could see his eyes watching her nervously, waiting for her reaction, despite him trying to joke.

"Aw ... they're beautiful." She kissed him, and as it spun into a passionate haze she plastered herself against his chest.

Please, God, don't ever let the kiss end, Ginny silently begged.

Her prayer was short-lived and bittersweet. Gavin pulled back from their embrace to straighten her on his lap. "Behave. Viper will be here in five minutes."

Her face fell at the reminder of how fast time was getting away from her. She had yet to confess her past. "So soon? I thought we had at least an hour. Silas just left, and I was—"

"You thought you'd get a little nookie after Silas left?" He gave her an unapologetic, I-told-you-so smirk. "You should have taken my suggestion and snuck down to my room after he went to bed last night."

Ginny's breath caught in the back of her throat as she stared at Gavin. God, he was beautiful. Even though she'd only met him year ago, she could see a glimmer of the man he probably had been, before life irrevocably changed him. Laughter warmed his expression, and she saw the devil-may-care attitude that could attract both men and women like fish to bait.

"Your room doesn't have a door," she reminded him, wanting to continue the banter, hoping to catch another glimpse of the carefree man he used to be.

"Which is one of the chores I have to take care of today, but you need to open my present first."

Ginny stared at the unopened present in her hand, knowing precious minutes were ticking too quickly, mirroring the rhythm of her heartbeat. "If I don't open it, will you please stay here with me?" she whispered.

Gavin took her chin in his hand and lifted her eyes to his. "The most I'll be gone is a couple of hours. I wouldn't go if I didn't have to." Releasing her chin, he took the box, then he placed a star, a moon, and a pair of diamond angel wings charms into her palm. Closing her fingers around the charms, he lifted her fist to his lips. "The next charm I'm going to buy you is a four-leaf clover, to remind you of our first date."

None of his gifts gave her a sense of elation, since she'd been on the receiving end of too many presents which represented good-byes. Gifts had never represented a future together, such as the ones that Trudy had given her; they were a more of appeasement to make them feel better about leaving her.

"Our first date?" Ginny stared at him in confusion. They never had a first date. Then it dawned on her. "I refuse to think of Dirty Dan's as our first date." She wouldn't count it as a first date; she'd left him no choice that day but to accompany her into the restaurant.

"You'd rather be reminded of us having to sneak out before morning to bury a mirror?" That had been another situation she dragged him into.

"Yes, I would. I'd prefer to forget about Marty, and you're going to help me do that by not mentioning he's moving to Treepoint."

"But—"

"No buts… unless it's yours." The last thing she wanted to talk about was Marty.

Hearing Viper's car pull up outside, she knew she'd run out of time to tell him her secret.

Gavin tapped the side of her bottom to get her to stand and together they went to the front door. She'd expected Gavin to tell her about Taylor being at the club, but it was clear to her he wasn't going to. And while he kept that secret, she had to admit she'd kept her own. She wanted to throw herself into his arms and confess who she was and the arrangement she'd made with the FBI to keep everyone she loved, including The Last Riders, safe. *Was it too late?*

Gavin raised her wrist and stared at her bracelet, looking at the dangling charms. "When did you get this one?" Gavin touched the fragile gold sand dollar Trudy had given her when she returned from her honeymoon.

"T.A. gave it to me." Ginny didn't lift her eyes to meet his.

"Why'd T.A. give you a charm? It looks expensive."

It was the perfect opportunity to confess, yet she held the words back.

Gavin hadn't told her about Taylor. Was that why he looked so happy? Was she willing to destroy his chance of happiness with the woman he loved? If Ginny told him the deal she'd made, she knew he'd stay to protect her, and he would be dragged into another mess—this one of her own making.

"She gave it to me for singing at her wedding."

"That was nice of her."

"She's a nice person." Only her iron will kept her voice from cracking.

The loud honk from the yard had them going outside.

Apparently uncaring of Viper watching, he placed a kiss on her lips. "When I come back, I'll be bringing that door."

"You going to tell Silas why you're wantin' to put that door up?" she teased, despite her heart breaking. He wouldn't be coming back once Taylor and he made up. If his feelings for Taylor were over, he would have mentioned her being at the club. The internal debate going on in her head had the question sounding uncharacteristically "Kentucky twang" that would come out when her emotions went haywire.

"I'll leave that up to you," he said, going down the steps.

Turning at the bottom of the steps, Gavin must have seen her expression, because he walked back up the steps. "I'll talk to him, okay?" Rubbing a thumb over her trembling bottom lip, he pulled her into his body. "If it's going to make you uncomfortable, when I come back, we'll talk it over and find another place for us to stay. Now, will you behave, or am I going to have to shove that horn up Viper's ass?"

Hearing him talk of their future and finding another place to live, she smiled and yet her heart still broke. "I'll behave."

Hugging him closer to her, Ginny memorized every detail from his tattoos to his smoldering eyes and the incredible strength she felt emanating off him. She had known the deal with the FBI was going to be hard, but she hadn't expected it to feel as if a lung was being ripped out of her. Having Gavin confess he no longer felt like a man the night before had broken the line of what she should or shouldn't do; however, making love with him was a decision she would never regret. She loved him and wanted to reassure him he was exactly the man she needed. While he promised he would return to her, she knew he loved another woman, but for that moment in time, he had been hers. Ginny had to atone for many mistakes in her life, but making love with Gavin wasn't one.

Ginny stifled her plea to come back as Gavin waved to Matthew and Isaac before he got inside Viper's SUV.

It was too late to back out of the deal she made with the FBI; it would endanger the people she loved. Any hurt she felt over Gavin not telling her about Taylor was inconsequential. He deserved to be with the woman he spent years loving—just as she deserved to face the consequences for stealing from Gabriel Allerton.

Hammer, however, didn't deserve the position she'd put him. By taking the DNA ancestry kit, she wound up using him to help broker the deal with the FBI. Though, she'd been secretly relieved he not only agreed but demanded to accompany her back to Clindale Island.

His steadying presence was the only reason she was able to sit calmly beside him while terror of facing her past twisted her stomach into knots. Every dip and bounce of the plane had her gripping the arms of her seat, expecting it to either explode or plunge toward the ground beneath them.

The FBI had promised to keep her safe, yet Ginny knew Allerton's tremendous wealth would make it easy for him to accomplish the goal of removing her from existence, regardless of how many lives he would take in the process.

"Are you regretting the deal?"

Ginny looked away from the small window to Hammer. "Are you regretting wanting to come along?"

"Regrets mean I messed up in the first place, so no."

"I wish I could say the same. I have too many to count."

"I'm not going to let him hurt you."

"I'm more worried about you getting hurt." Ginny stared at Hammer's rock-hard features. She would never describe Hammer as being a father figure to her, not even a big brother. He had been her protector. Even after she passed the age when he could have washed his hands of her, he hadn't. She'd always known he was only a phone call away, and he would risk his life to protect her. Hammer was an oddity, a man who no longer existed in this day and time. A knight.

Feeling guilty, she looked away from him. "I shouldn't have let you come. You have Mika and Jonas."

"Shut up."

Ginny turned back to face him. "You know I love you, right?"

Hammer's face turned harder. "Nothing is going to happen to you."

"One thing I've learned in life is you can't make promises that are impossible to keep." She had learned promises were as useless as a two-dollar bill—no matter how much people wanted to keep them, life ultimately took what it wanted.

"I've kept every promise I've ever made."

"Then I want you to remember the one you made to me. If this goes bad, I want you to do whatever you have to do to get yourself out without me."

"Don't remind me."

"You swore to me." Ginny had no intention of letting him off the hook from his promise. "I expect you to keep your promise." He might not be able to keep his promise about her safety, but she would make sure he protected his own life. "Jonas and Mika would be devasted if anything happened to you," Ginny emphasized, reminding him why it was so important he survived.

"You're just as important."

Ginny didn't respond. She would be missed by T.A. and her brothers if anything happened to her, but she wasn't *important* to them. T.A. had Dalton and her friends, and her brothers had each other. She wasn't so important that losing her would make a difference in their lives. It was just one of the reasons why she made the deal with the FBI—she was expendable. Gavin wasn't. And even though Viper had Winter and Aisha, he needed Gavin to make him whole.

"You're important to me."

Ginny stared at him ruefully. "No, I'm not."

"Believe me; you are. If anything happens to you under my watch, Reaper will kill me."

"No, he won't. I know Gavin," Ginny assured him.

"You might think you know Gavin, but where Reaper is concerned, you don't know jack shit."

"They're the same man."

"Tell yourself that all you want, if it makes you feel better." Hammer gave her a rueful look. "You're going to find out the truth for yourself."

"When?"

Hammer's expression turned into one of determination. "When I bring your ass home."

CHAPTER ONE

Waving at Matthew and Isaac as they headed inside their shop, Reaper got inside Viper's SUV.

"We're late," Viper snapped before Reaper could even shut the door.

"I got that message two honks ago," Reaper snapped back.

"When I talked to you this morning, I told you we couldn't be late to the meeting with the FBI. Now we're not going to have time to meet with Diamond beforehand."

"We already know what she would have said—be quiet and let her do the talking. I plan to follow her advice, even though she didn't have time to give it."

"You're in a good mood." Viper looked at him suspiciously.

"Do me a favor; if I swear not to off myself, will you quit looking for signs that aren't there? At least not anymore. I feel good. Actually, I feel fucking great."

"You back on your antidepressants? If so, pass me a couple. I had to listen to every brother in the club offer to pack Taylor's shit back into her car. Then Knox called and told me the FBI were waiting for him when he came in this morning. They want us brought in for questioning."

"I'll bring Taylor's shit out to her car myself after our meeting, and we can let Diamond do the talking to the FBI. They have to build a case against us. They have to prove we're responsible for Slate's disappearance. That's going to take time."

"What about Memphis? They have the tape to prove what happened to him." Viper parked in the police parking lot.

"I think I have a plan for that. We'll talk after the meeting. Then I'll go see the brothers and get Taylor out of your hair. At least Ginny doesn't know about her being at the club," he said, getting out of the car and then caught Viper's expression. He knew when he was fucked. "She knows Taylor's at the club?"

"Yes."

"Fuck. Thanks, big brother." He slammed the car door shut.

"I was worried about how you would react. I thought Taylor was part of the reason you wanted to kill yourself—" Viper snapped his mouth shut. "Okay, I fucked up."

Gavin laughed, slinging a brotherly arm around Viper's shoulders. "Welcome to my world."

Any visage of a smile disappeared before walking into the sheriff's office where the desk clerk sent them to the courthouse. "Knox and your lawyer will meet you in Room 2, in the lower level. They are waiting for you."

Reaper and Viper shared speculative glances as they went back out the door, then headed for the courthouse.

"We're fucked."

Reaper's good mood rapidly disappeared hearing Viper's worried curse.

Viper had been mired in the shitstorm Memphis had created. The betraying bastard deserved the death he had been dealt after the greedy fucker was about to blow the whole fucking club up before thankfully being caught.

Finding Room 2, Reaper saw a state trooper guarding the door. Another state trooper was stationed outside another door farther down the hall. The trooper checked their IDs before opening the door. "Make sure you keep several feet apart." Motioning them inside, he then shut the door behind them.

Knox and Diamond were waiting inside.

"Thank God you two finally showed up. They were threatening to issue warrants for your arrests if you didn't show in the next ten minutes."

"Time got away from me." Reaper took the hit for being late. "If they're so anxious for our arrival, where are they?"

"The commonwealth attorney is speaking with the special agents. They'll call us in when they're ready."

Diamond stared at Knox worriedly as time passed and no one came for them.

Cognizant of possibly being recorded, they didn't discuss any of the variety of reasons they could have been pulled in for questioning. Assuming they were there to discuss Slate, everyone was wary to mention his name. The longer it took, the harder it was to keep silent, which Reaper took for a stalling tactic.

"Is this even fucking legal? Keeping us waiting this long?" Viper asked.

Diamond, just as frustrated as everyone else in the room, went to the door to pull it open.

The officer broke off from speaking into the radio on his shoulder, telling Diamond, "I was just informed to bring you to a larger room upstairs. If you all will follow me."

The four of them filed out of the room.

Reaper's gut clenched as they went up the steps, preparing himself to be arrested. Weeks ago, he couldn't have cared less, still having felt as if he belonged in jail, but Ginny changed him—even before he realized it was her voice that had strengthened his will to survive while in captivity.

She had kept him so busy falling for her, he had lost the desire to end his life—she'd made it worth living again.

They entered a courtroom, but there was no judge sitting on the bench, only four suited men waiting for them in the front of the judge's bench.

"Please, take a seat and keep a safe distance apart," an older agent directed them to the seats in the front row.

"I made my clients available at the FBI's request, despite no advance warning. Since you're now playing games, we're leaving." Diamond firmly stood in front and blocked the men from going down the aisle.

The older man, who must have been the lead agent, spoke up. "I'm sorry for the wait. Unfortunately, it was unavoidable. We were waiting for two more people to arrive. I was just notified they arrived at the airport and will be with us within the next five minutes. The FBI appreciates your cooperation."

As he finished speaking, the doors behind them opened again.

Reaper turned to see Sex Piston, T.A., and Dalton step inside, looking just as surprised to see them.

"What are you doing here? You get lost paying a ticket? This is a private meeting," Diamond snapped at Sex Piston as they came farther into the room.

"I don't know why the fuck I'm here, and neither does T.A. nor Dalton. We were dragged here an hour ago," Sex Piston argued back.

"Why didn't you call me?" Diamond asked, her eyes on the group of men waiting for them at the front of the courtroom.

"I fucking tried!" Sex Piston yelled at her sister.

"Ladies, if you take your seats, we will be ready to get started as soon as the other two we've been waiting for arrive."

Ignoring the agent's directive to keep a distance, Knox and Diamond sat together, as well as Sex Piston, T.A., and Dalton.

When the agent asked them to move apart, Sex Piston opened her mouth. "Mind your own fucking business, and I'll mind mine. I've had my temperature taken by three people today—I'm good. How many fucking times has yours been checked today?"

The agent was saved by the opening of the door.

Turning around, Reaper was shocked.

Shade, Jonas, and Shade's father, Will. This shit went deeper and deeper.

Reaper didn't know why they were there, and from Viper and Knox's expressions, they didn't know either.

"Gentlemen, if you will have a seat, we can begin."

The new arrivals sat down in the row behind them and seeing their faces, it was obvious Will and Jonas knew what was going on.

"Do you know what this is about?" Reaper heard Viper ask Shade.

Shade shook his head. "Dad called me five minutes ago and told me to get here quickly."

The lead agent held his hand up. "I'm sorry about the delay. Now that everyone's here, I can explain."

Out of the corner his eye, Reaper saw T.A.'s color had paled and she was shaking. Dalton placed an arm around his wife's shoulders. Sex Piston looked shaken too.

The lead agent came forward. "I haven't introduced myself. I'm Special Agent Corey. I want to explain why the FBI is here and—"

"Then fucking explain already!" Sex Piston yelled.

"Very well." Agent Corey stepped in front of Viper. "Mr. James, the FBI's case on the death of Last Rider member, Memphis Mills, has been dropped. The file has been sealed and closed. The video provided to us of the alleged crime was inadvertently destroyed." The agent handed him a folder. "Within that folder, you will find a document stating that no charges will be filed and will never be linked in connection with Mr. Mills or the witnesses who provided the information."

"Not that my client is guilty, but why has the State decided to be so forgiving?" Diamond asked.

"If you'll allow me to continue, all your questions will be answered."

Agent Corey moved to stand in front of Reaper. "Mr. James, this is the approval for the vaccine trial that Pharm-FYOU was seeking consent to begin. The government extends its apologies in the delay and will ensure Pharm-FYOU gets the highest priority available. We have also begun an investigation into the disappearance of the lab technician and will keep both you and her boss apprised of the situation.

"Furthermore, our agency will no longer offer the man who kidnapped you federal protection. He willfully disappeared, and so the FBI is no longer interested in his location. If, for some reason, he is found, we are aware of the criminal elements with whom he associated and will research only if we deem necessary."

The agent opened a second folder and took out two envelopes. After handing the first to Reaper, he handed T.A. the second. "Mrs. Andrews and Mr. James, these letters are from Miss Evangeline Bellamy."

Reaper looked up as T.A. began sobbing and asked Viper, "Who's Evangeline?"

"Mrs. Andrews and Mr. James, Evangeline wanted me to

make sure you knew she didn't make this decision under duress and wants you to respect the decision she has made. She told me six times to tell you that she is safe, and Hammer will be assisting her on her journey home."

Tearing the envelope open, Reaper began reading the letter as T.A. began wailing in grief.

D*ear Gavin,*
This is the hardest letter I have ever written. I have a past I haven't told you about. I've wanted to tell you so many times, but I was afraid, not for my own life, but for my T.A., for Hammer, and for Will.

Trudy is my biological sister. Freddy adopted me when I was four years old. The Colemans gave me a new life, and I will always be grateful for being a part of their family.

Please don't hate me for not telling you. I love you, and the thought of you hating me would make what I'm about to do so much harder. Hammer and I made the deal for me right after Killyama told me Slate disappeared. I knew he would come for you. He was smart enough to know you wouldn't stop looking for him. He had no choice but to try to kill you first, and I couldn't let that happen. My brothers leaving me alone that day was a trap for him, but I nearly lost you in the process. I hope his death gives you the peace you deserve.

Viper told me yesterday that Taylor is at the club to see you. I kept hoping you would tell me she was there, but you didn't. I know you still love her, and I love you enough to want you to be happy. The hardest part today was not leaving my family but watching you walk away to see her.

Even if you decide not to get back with Taylor, I have to settle my past before I can have a future. I learned that lesson from you. I won't watch my new niece or nephew grow up without me being in their lives like I had to do with Trudy.

. . .

I wish you well, wild man.
    With all my love,
  Evangeline

Reaper stormed to his feet. "Knox, give me the keys to your cruiser!" he shouted over T.A.'s terror-filled screams.

"He'll kill her! Jonas, tell them," T.A. sobbed out, holding onto Dalton.

After Knox gave Reaper the keys, he started running out of the room.

"Mr. James, it won't do you any good to look for her in Treepoint. Her plane left twenty minutes ago to an undisclosed destination."

Fuck, fuck, fuck!

Still, Reaper ran toward the doorway. With his hands held out, he slammed through the second set of doors without stopping. He had seen Knox's cruiser parked outside when they arrived at the courthouse.

Pressing the unlock on the fob as he exited the building, he was in the cruiser and pulling out of the parking spot before Knox, Viper, and Shade came running out. His heart racing as fast as he was driving, Reaper flipped the sirens on, screeched through traffic on the main drag, and drove up the mountain toward the Colemans' home.

As he drove past The Last Riders' clubhouse, he saw the men running down the steps and toward their bikes. Flying past them, he started slowing so he could make the sharp turn into the Colemans' driveway. Hitting the steering wheel, he had to wait until an oncoming car slowed to a stop before he could dart across the lane.

Driving up the steep hill, he didn't have to be told that Ginny was gone. Even if the agent hadn't told him, it was written on all eight of her brothers' faces as he jerked the car to a stop.

Leaving the door open, Reaper ran directly to Silas. "Tell me you know where she is," he begged.

Silas nodded. "I know where she's going."

"Thank God!" Reaper took deep breaths at Silas's confirmation, his hands on his thighs as he tried to catch his breath. He hadn't taken a deep breath since he'd heard Ginny had left. "Tell me. I'll go right now." As he straightened up, his breathing stopped again at Silas's expression. "What's wrong? You said you know where she's going."

The loud rumble of motorcycles coming up the driveway almost drowned out his question.

"She's going back to Clindale Island."

"I'll get a plane." Motioning for Viper to hurry toward him, he was already planning to get Train and a chopper in the next hour; he didn't give a fuck about whatever stumbling blocks Silas was about to tell him.

"That won't work." Silas shook his head. "No one can fly or sail in without the permission from the island's owner."

"Then I'll get his fucking permission! Who is he?"

"The man who wants to kill Ginny."

CHAPTER TWO

Reaper took out his cell phone and pulled up Google maps. Searching for the island, he unconsciously switched into military mode. Emotions would have to take a back seat in order to strategize a way to intercept Ginny, because if he let the mixture of emotions running tumultuously through his brain rule him, he would lose Ginny, and that wasn't acceptable.

Finding the location, he shoved the phone back in his pocket. "They flew out of Treepoint's airport?"

"Fifteen minutes ago," Silas confirmed.

"Then we still have time. Our airport only allows for small planes, so they won't have enough fuel to make it to Clindale Island. They'll have to switch to a bigger plane or stop somewhere to refuel."

Reaper saw Silas give his brothers a questioning look. At their nods Silas offered, "I can track her for you, but I don't know which airport they'll land at until I can hear or see the name."

Reaper knew the sacrifice the Colemans were making. By discussing his gift in front of The Last Riders, they were breaking the secret code that had kept their family safe for decades.

Turning to Train, who stood silently next to Viper, Reaper barked out his first order. "Use every contact you have and find out where they're going to refuel or to switch planes. I don't care if you have to call in every favor owed to you; just get it done. Get your chopper ready to fly. I want to be airborne as soon as possible."

"We won't make it in time, especially if they're switching planes. Refueling will take a few minutes, and that still wouldn't give us enough time to stop them from taking off," Train told him.

Reaper moved out of earshot from the group of men and motioned for Silas to join him. "Are you capable of doing more than tracking someone or lifting a leaf?"

Silas wasn't offended by the way Reaper bluntly asked if his gift could be used for more than lifting a leaf or using the wind as a transmitter. The secrecy of his gifts could be used to their advantage, if Silas was willing to expose the entirety of what he was capable of doing.

Based on his answer, Silas's concern was only for Ginny. "What do you need?"

"If the wind's speed is too fast, they won't be able to take off until it slows down."

"I've never tried something from so far away, but yes, I can."

Reaper nodded, moving back to Train, who was now talking on his phone.

Train lifted his head in question.

"We'll make it. Go."

"Get me that info pronto," Train said into his phone, taking off at a run to his motorcycle.

"It won't matter if you reach the plane in time or not." Jonas moved around the others. "The FBI won't let you get near her. Even if you convince them to get close to Ginny, they won't let you board the plane to Clindale Island with her."

Jonas was right. *Fuck*.

Reaper raked his hands through the sides of his long hair. Then a thought occurred to him. It was crazy as fuck, but if it worked, the island's owner would be hard-pressed to deny him entry.

"The FBI will agree … if we're married."

Everyone looked at him like he was crazy.

"But you're not," Viper stated the obvious.

"Not yet, and the FBI and the owner of the island won't know we aren't."

"How are you going to accomplish that? The FBI will want proof."

"I'll have proof. It will be legal," he stated determinedly. He wasn't going to let Ginny go into danger without him.

"How …?" Viper started to ask.

"A judge in Ohio isn't above using his power when his wife needs a new car. Let's find out what a brand-new Porsche can get out of him."

CHAPTER THREE

A car pulled into the driveway as Gavin gave Knox the name of the officer who had pulled him and Ginny over on their way back to Treepoint.

"Ask him the name of the judge he was talking about, then get the judge's cooperation."

"You're wanting me to bribe an officer of a court?" Knox asked.

"Yes. If you have a problem, then—"

"I don't have a fucking problem with it." Knox stared at him in anger. "I just want to know how high to go if the Porsche isn't enough."

"Just get it done. I don't give a fuck about the cost. I want the marriage certificate in my hands before Train and I take off. Make sure it's backdated to the day the officer pulled me over."

"It's going to take some time. Do you know how many people we're talking about—"

"I don't care how it gets fucking done." Reaper gave Knox an icy glare to get him moving as Viper and Rider shifted closer to him. When he gave an order, Reaper only gave it once. The brothers knew what would happen if Reaper had to repeat it a second time. Knox took off, passing the occupants from the car walking toward him as well as The Last Riders.

"This is all your fault."

Reaper flinched at T.A.'s emotionless voice. The tears and fear she'd shown at the courthouse were gone, now replaced with an eerie calm he knew wasn't normal. Reaper became even more worried for Ginny. T.A. was in shock, as if fear had overtaken her, and her mind was blanketing her from the terror she was experiencing.

"Matthew, get T.A. a chair," Reaper directed, concerned for the visibly shaken woman. "Silas, get her something hot to drink."

The Last Riders remained at a distance while making an aisle between them for T.A. to walk through. Dalton, however, stopped her within six feet of him.

Sex Piston, close by T.A.'s side, drilled him in place with her accusing and furious eyes. While T.A. looked numb, Sex Piston looked like a volcano ready to erupt.

"I know I'm responsible," Reaper said before Sex Piston could let her anger loose. "Ginny must have come to an arrangement with the FBI and got them to rescind their offer of witness protection to Slate and to remove the roadblock for PharmFYOU to start testing. Arin and I have been trying to get their help to find her technician...not one fucking word from them until today. Reaper let out an angry huff of air. "Ginny fucking did this for me. By her taking off to Clindale and the FBI excusing The Last Riders of any wrongdoing, she is sacrificing herself in exchange. What I don't fucking understand is how she knew what shit was going down."

"I told her," T.A. confessed. "She wanted to know how you were doing when you went back to the club house."

T.A. burrowed her head in Dalton's shoulder, her whole body shaking. Matthew brought back a wooden chair for her sit on, while Silas was still inside the house presumably getting her something to drink.

Reaper felt helpless watching Dalton help T.A.; he whispered in her ear, "I know you hate me, but I swear to you, I will get Ginny back."

T.A. shook her head at him. "You don't even know who you're dealing with."

Reaper ran a hand through his thick hair in frustration. "To tell you the fucking truth, you're not the only one who's in shock. I have no fucking clue of any of this shit, but we're no help to her if we don't hold it together." Reaper wasn't going to blow smoke up her ass. "I'm behind the eight ball here, and I really hate to sound like a dick, but T.A., I need you to quit thinking like Ginny is already dead and tell me exactly why the FBI was willing to make a deal with her."

T.A. gave a shuddering breath, taking the mug that Silas handed to her before he moved out of sight.

Reaper recognized Silas' behavior and wanted to ask what he was doing, but right now, he had to focus on T.A. and the information she knew. There was little time, but going into a mission blind could be deadly for Ginny.

"My parents used to work for various charities to develop clean water systems and build schools in underdeveloped countries." T.A's gaze looked as though she had gone back to another place and time.

"When I was eight, I met Gabriel. He wanted my parents to come work for his charity. They were in awe of him. My mother was gung-ho, but Dad kept refusing to sign on even after several offers. Dad wanted to work with populations most in need, and if he signed on to Allerton's organization they would be the ones dictating who would benefit from his skills. He had earned respect from many countries for his work; there'd even been a documentary on one of the projects he'd done.

"But Dad refused to be swayed, despite Mom and Gabriel trying to change his mind. Gabriel wasn't about to take no for an answer; he'd wined and dined my parents—until the fighting started.

"Mom didn't stop pressuring Dad. She'd invited other members of the charity over for dinner. They were good. They sucked my mom into the Goody-Two-shoes spiel that even had me begging my dad to go. They were good ... so good." Self-loathing filled her voice, betraying the blame she held for the past. "I have to give them credit. When they visited, they would bring me toys and they showered me with attention. What little kid wouldn't want to be around them?

"'Daddy, don't you want to help the children? I can help Mom read to them ...' That's what I said to him." T.A. looked sick as she stared down at her stomach, replaying the memories for them. Then she took a sip of her drink before beginning again. "Finally Dad gave in to both Mom and me. And when we arrived on Clindale, we all fell in love with the island and the people. Clindale was just as beautiful as we were told. Every day was a new adventure. I thought the fighting between my parents would stop, but it didn't. Then, one day, my parents told me that mom was pregnant, that I was going to have the brother or sister I had been begging for.

"I was excited, and even though I loved Clindale, I thought we'd go back to the States and Mom and Dad would change back into how they were before we got to the island. But we were still there when Mom went into early labor. There wasn't even time to get her to the hospital on Sherguevil Island. Two women came running from the village to help her when they heard she was in labor. Mom kept

26

shouting at us to take her to the hospital, that she had been labor with me for two days." T.A. laughed, shaking her head at the memory. "Evangeline arrived less than five minutes later. She never did what she was supposed to do … even then." T.A.'s voice hitched at the beauty of her recollecting Evangeline's birth.

"From the moment I saw her, I knew she was special. She barely cried. Evangeline was too busy looking around at us. She gurgled and smiled when anyone came near her. Not only did she wrap me around her finger, but she had everyone else on the island wrapped around her fingers as well." A tear slid down T.A.'s cheek as talked.

"She started walking when she was eight months old, driving our parents nuts. Evangeline was fascinated with the ocean and constantly tried to get into the water, despite our parents taking her out to the ocean several times a day. Dad joked that she was like a little mermaid, trying to go home. Mom and Dad thought it was cute, until a couple of times when she got away from them. Luckily there was always someone around, so Evangeline wasn't able to get too far."

"Dad was busy directing the workers to build the water system, while Mom taught the children and adults who wanted to learn to read and write in English. Then one day Mom put Evangeline down for a nap, and all four of us fell asleep. I was sound asleep when a young man came to our cabin carrying a wet Evangeline in his arms. His name was Manny, he was one of young men whom Mom had been teaching. After nearly losing her that day, I was sure my parents were going to take us back to the States, but we stayed. It would have been an idyllic life if only my parents hadn't continued to fight." T.A.'s expression became tortured.

"Evangeline began escaping more often when Mom was busy working with her students and Dad was gone building the water systems, so they trusted Manny to babysit her; he'd become like a big brother to Evangeline. Our father had taught her the basics of swimming, but Manny had taught her to swim like a little seal and he took her exploring the island. What time they didn't spend in the water or running through the jungle, they spent with his family in the village. "It was the best and worst mistake our parents could have made. Mom and Dad spent less time with us, and I was always hanging out with another family who had children more my age. Mom said it would help me learn the language faster. I grew close with that family, while the whole island fell in love with Evangeline.

"I kid you not, when you saw Evangeline laughing and playing—actually, from the moment she was born—it was weird … there was an aura about her. She seemed to sparkle with happiness. It was like one of those filters on your cell phone." T.A. closed her eyes tightly, as if to shut out the memories.

"What the island children did, she wanted to do, and Manny took advantage of the trust our parents had given him and taught her a skill he'd taught the children in the village."

Giving a bitter laugh, T.A. opened her eyes to stare at him. "We thought it was cute when Manny taught her to sing the island songs; first in their language then in English. That was before we found out he was teaching her to keep other secrets from us."

Reaper wanted to tell her to hurry. He needed to be on the chopper, yet he remained silent, captivated by Ginny's childhood. Every detail T.A. was sharing could be useful when dealing with the man who wanted to kill her.

"Manny might have taught Evangeline to sing out of the goodness of his heart, but he wasn't above using it for his gain. I can't blame him; he didn't know the man who controlled the island was so dangerous. None of us did—until it was too late."

"Who was he?"

"Gabriel Allerton." T.A. gave him a wry smile. "You've heard of him?"

Reaper was shocked by the information. Gabriel Allerton was always in the news. He was known as the man with the Midas touch. Whatever business he invested in or developed turned to gold. Twenty-eight years ago, he sold his business with the intention of retiring, but then founded and headed a worldwide charity.

"Who hasn't? He's one of the richest men in the world. You said he was the one who convinced your parents to move to Clindale? I wasn't aware he owned the island. How could he own and control Clindale Island if there are native islanders living there?" That he owned an island had never made the news, as far as he knew.

"He doesn't own Clindale; he owns Sherguevil Island, which is the sister island. If you think they are taking Evangeline to Clindale, you're mistaken. No one gets near Clindale without Allerton's permission. You are taken to Sherguevil Island first, then to Clindale by a boat operated by his men, and unless you have permission, you won't be allowed within ten miles of Sherguevil or Clindale Island."

"He doesn't own the ocean," Viper interrupted.

T.A. shook her head, as if she was dealing with a child. "The government does, and Allerton has them in his pocket. Don't you watch the news?"

Allerton's charity included high profile, wealthy men and women from around the world.

"He's been photographed shaking the hands of the last four presidents of the US, and he's just as chummy with high-ranked officials in governments and regimes from around the world. The officials might not be endorsed members of the charity, but they do his bidding. They use huge amounts of money donated to Allerton's charity for aid, as well as to grease the wheels of the foreign governments where their 'donors' want to build their companies. The governments look the other way when regulations are loosened. The charity might spend a few million to pay the officials, but in return, they're raking in billions in illegal builds and destroying natural habitats and resources. Whatever wealth they are giving away isn't a quarter of what they are getting in return. Evangeline will only be allowed on Clindale Island *if and when* Allerton lets her."

"Give me a second, T.A." Reaper stopped her from going further, reaching for his cell phone. "Train, the plane Ginny is on will be charted for Sherguevil Island, not Clindale."

"Got you," Train said before abruptly ending the call.

Reaper replaced his phone in his pocket. "What else did Manny teach Ginny?" Trying to speed up the gathering of information, he wanted her to get to the point when their idyllic life changed.

"Not only had Manny taught Evangeline to sing, but he had also taught her how to steal. The islanders from Clindale were allowed to take boats over to Sherguevil Island during the day to sell their fresh food and crafts at the market square.

"Manny's father, Gyi, would take a load of fresh fish over to Sherguevil, and he brought Manny and some of the island children along for the ride. Allerton didn't care, and the visitors were charmed by the children and would usually give them money, which they'd take home to give to their parents. In turn, they'd use those funds to purchase supplies from boats docked at Sherguevil. It kept everyone happy on Clindale Island since there was no other source of income, other than bartering with each other. Allerton never hired the villagers to work on his island, and his staff were not allowed to visit Clindale."

"What if an emergency happened or they wanted to leave the island?" Reaper asked.

"Sherguevil has its own hospital with state-of-the-art equipment and doctors and nurses, all of whom are staffed by Allerton. And no, they never left the island, ever."

"Who would want to work there and never be allowed to leave?" Viper asked. "I could see the islanders being content to stay on Clindale, but if you were an outsider, why would you give up your freedom and never leave Sherguevil?"

T.A. sadly stared down at her cup. "People who have no hope of creating a better life for themselves; people who want more for their families. Allerton gives them the money to send home to their families. And even though they will never get to see them again, they're allowing the ones they love better lives. Allerton doesn't only want people willing to sell their souls to work for him, if that's what you're thinking. He hires employees who are willing to sell their souls so they will never betray him, and none of them ever have... or Evangeline wouldn't have spent years running from him."

"Why did she have to run?" Reaper spoke, turning T.A.'s attention back to him.

"She wasn't given a choice." T.A. face twisted in pain. "Sadly, a great deal of Evangeline's life has been spent trying to outrun the perils she found herself in from those she loves. Most of what I'm about to tell you are things we found out after the fact, and the bits and pieces of what Evangeline remembers."

T.A. took a deep breath and Reaper had a bad feeling this story was going to be long. "When Evangeline was three, Manny started sneaking her aboard Gyi's boat; his father only ever allowed the island children. Gyi would never have allowed Evangeline to go.

"Manny had her sing in front of the visitors, who would throw money in the collection box, but what he was really doing was using her to distract them while the other children pickpocketed the guests. The children then gave the loot to Manny, who took his profit, then divided up some for the kids to take home to their parents."

"What went wrong?" Reaper urged her to go faster.

"Evangeline went wrong. She picked up on what the children were doing and wouldn't stop bugging Manny until he taught her how to be a pickpocket too. By then, I think Manny had no choice but to give into her, knowing she'd tell our parents—and Gyi—if he didn't explain it away like a game. So that's what he did. Manny told her all the children were saving to buy a big boat like the ones docked at Sherguevil Island. They'd all be able to play on it while their fathers fished.

"With the money Manny gave her, she bought little trinkets for the other children and herself in the market. He taught her to hide her purchases and made her promise not to tell our parents or me, or he wouldn't take her again.

"She was fascinated with the large yachts that were docked at Sherguevil Island." T.A. gave a small sob but kept going. "If she won the game, Manny told her she would be able to help the other children buy the big boat for the village."

"Fucking bastard," Razer groaned, shaking his head.

Reaper could understand Razer's anger. He had two rambunctious twin boys who would easily have been suckered into doing the same thing.

"Evangeline was a precocious child and wanted to see the boats. She'd always been pointing them out to me. One day there was a large crowd, and she slipped away from Manny. Evangeline told me later that she'd wanted to pick out the best boat for Manny to buy."

"She managed to get on one of the visiting ships, didn't she?" Reaper asked, desperately trying to hurry T.A. along.

"Yes. How she did it without one of the ship hands seeing her, I don't know, but she did ... and she took something. Manny must have found her and taken her back to Gyi's boat."

Reaper took a step toward her, then stopped himself. "What did she take?"

"I don't know, and Evangeline doesn't remember."

"How does she not remember?"

The expression on T.A.'s face became tortured. "Because of what she witnessed afterward, she blocked the whole thing out. What she does remember is hearing shouts from Gyi and Manny, and the children crying.

"She told me she was terrified and didn't made a sound when she heard loud noises, but she didn't know what was happening ... until she heard Allerton demanding they return what they'd stolen. When they couldn't find whatever it was they were searching for, Allerton told Gyi to take the children home, then to come back for Manny. Gyi brought the children back to Clindale, then unknowingly brought Evangeline back to Sherguevil to get Manny. He had no idea Evangeline was on the boat, and worse he had no idea what was waiting for him.

"Evangeline remembers Manny telling her not to come out until he opened the bunk. Even after she heard Gyi and Manny screaming and yelling, she only left the bunk when she smelled smoke. She said Manny saw her and began speaking in his native tongue, but Allerton and his men had just assumed he was begging for his life. He wasn't; he was saving hers. He instructed Ginny to use the cargo net to climb down and swim home."

T.A. started shaking, and Reaper started sweating. Manny telling a three-year-old to swim home by herself rather than letting her expose herself to Allerton showed the level of danger Ginny had been in.

"It was a miracle she survived. If most of her days hadn't been spent in the water, she wouldn't have. If the water hadn't been calm that day, if she hadn't been so terrified ...." T.A. moaned, crossed her arms over her chest, and started rocking as if she was holding Evangeline in her arms.

"Mom came running into our home holding onto a soaking wet Evangeline, telling us that one of the men from the village had found her in the ocean. She was so young and hysterical, I couldn't understand anything she said. Mom dried Evangeline off and put her to bed, making me swear not to say anything. I've never understood why my mom made me keep quiet about what had happened that day.

"The next day, Gyi and Manny hadn't come back, and the whole Island was upset. The islanders came to our house that morning wanting my father to go to Allerton to ask for his help in searching for them. They'd innocently believed something happened on the ride back from Sherguevil. Mom didn't let us leave her side as Dad and the islanders went to the speak to Allerton. When Dad came back, he told us Allerton had sent his men to help the villagers search for Gyi's boat. The boat, Gyi, and Manny were never found.

"A day later our parents came into my room and told me that they were sending Evangeline and me to our grandmother's for Christmas. I didn't want to leave my parents, but they told me I had to pretend to want to go in order to save Evangeline."

T.A.'s voice became whisper-soft as she told them what her mother had told her. "They were afraid Allerton would find out Evangeline had been on the boat that day. They were frightened one of the island children would let it slip that Evangeline had been there. Our parents told me to find out what Evangeline took and where she had hidden it, then they could return it and we could come home and be a family again, but whatever we did, we were not to tell our grandmother what happened.

"Mom and Dad took us to Sherguevil Island the next morning to catch a plane back to the States. My mother had put Evangeline and me on the plane, and it was ready to take off when I looked out the window and saw Allerton arrive just as we were taxing off. I still see his face ... I have never been so scared in my life." T.A. continued rocking, her mind clearly wanting to hold onto Ginny the only way she could.

"The whole time we were with our grandmother, I expected us to go back to Clindale. I was sick to my stomach with fear, because I knew Allerton would be there when we went back. While I wanted to be with my parents, I remember thinking on that trip that something with my mom wasn't right. She'd been withdrawn and used every opportunity to pawn us off, and Dad was gone more often than he was there, and when they were both home all they did was fight. The day Manny saved Evangeline from drowning I saw an expression on my mother's face that made me sick to my stomach. I never told Evangeline, but I never fully trusted my mother after that, and I don't think my dad either.

"Every day, our father would call my grandmother's and ask me if Evangeline remembered anything. Each time, I told him no. Two days before Christmas, our grandmother took us out Christmas shopping. When we were in the store, I was looking at tops for my dad while my grandmother was with Evangeline across the store. A man approached me and said his name was Garrick, and he was there to help me and Evangeline. I was so scared, I didn't know what to do. I looked for my grandmother, but I couldn't see her. Then he said, 'hot coconuts,' and I knew my father had sent him. It was the secret word my dad had taught me.

"The man told me what would happen if Evangeline and I went back to Clindale, and if I wanted to keep Evangeline alive, I had to do everything he told me. Again, I was sworn to secrecy. When our parents called that night, my dad asked if I missed having hot coconuts. I spent Christmas Day knowing that every moment I spent with Evangeline was precious, because she was going to be taken away from me." Tears streamed down T.A.'s cheeks.

"How did they make Evangeline disappear?"

It took Dalton kneeling down next to T.A., gathering her close to his side, to give T.A. the strength to answer.

"A plane crash. We went down in a plane crash in the ocean. I survived, and Evangeline died that day."

CHAPTER FOUR

"Jesus," Lucky muttered, breaking the silence.

Reaper looked to Shade's father, Will, and Jonas. "Why did the FBI fly you two into Treepoint and have you brought to the courthouse?"

Jonas gave voice to the fury that had been brewing on his face since he'd walked into the courtroom. "I was brought in because fucking Hammer knew I would have stopped him if I knew he was going with Ginny without me. I was leaving our house to get a client released on bond when I was waylaid by the FBI. I'm in the dark just as much as you."

Reaper then looked to Will, who made no effort to hide his concern for Ginny.

"I had just gotten out of bed when they came knocking on my door." Will paused as if he was thinking before answering the question. "My guess is Hammer made that part of the bargain for Jonas and myself to be there at the courthouse so we'd be able help if you need us."

"The FBI bringing Jonas into the loop is understandable, but why you?" Rider questioned what was on everyone's mind.

"I was the one who asked Freddy to take Ginny in and raise her as his own." The former sheriff and retired officer had to clear his several throat times as he spoke. "Twenty-one years ago, Hammer called and asked me to meet him—told me to be on the down-low and make sure no one followed me or knew where I was going. When I met him, he had Ginny, who was a little spot of nothing, and told me to find a safe place to hide her. And before you ask, that's pretty much all he told me, other than Allerton would kill her and anyone who knew about her if she was found."

Reaper felt his phone vibrate with a text message. Time was running out.

"Viper, go to the club and pack me a duffle bag with clothes and what you think I'll need," Reaper ordered. "I'll meet you at the airport in ten minutes."

Viper strode over to his bike.

Reaper turned back to Will. "Hammer asked you to hide a child and you didn't ask him any fucking questions?" Reaper asked harshly, his stomach churning at what Ginny had gone through as a child.

When Shade made a move toward Reaper, Will reached out to touch his son's arm. "It's okay." Will shook his head at Shade before turning back to Reaper.

"Hammer wouldn't have asked if it wasn't a matter of life or death for Ginny. How she ended up in Hammer's hands showed me two things: someone important trusted her with him, and they knew him well enough to know that Hammer would give his life to protect her. Hammer pulled my fat ass out of the fire enough times for me to trust him implicitly if shit hit the fan."

Reaper admitted he did too.

"In the years since then, you never discussed Ginny with Hammer again?" Reaper couldn't believe the two men had never connected again.

"Twice. Once when I called to try to convince him to let Rachel and me keep her before I gave her to Freddy."

Shade's usually impassive face turned into one of surprise at his father's answer.

"And the second was when Ginny called me, begging me to make Hammer let her stay with the Colemans. Our conversations were short, and he never gave me any more information than he did the first time I took her, and his answer was the same both times—*no*."

Shade moved closer to his father. "If you wanted to keep her, to raise her yourself, why did you listen to Hammer and give her to Freddy?"

"If it was only me, I would have," Will admitted. "But there was a connection that could be traced between me and Hammer. I had to put Rachel, you, and Penni's safety first."

"Why did you pick Freddy Coleman?"

Reaper was glad Shade had asked the question and not him. The Coleman brothers were glaring at Shade as if he'd insulted their father.

"You ever have the opportunity to see Freddy with his kids when he came to town?" Will asked his son.

"No," Shade answered. He had never met the man.

"Exactly. If you had, you wouldn't ask me that question. Freddy loved his kids, and they loved him back. He didn't have a mean bone in his body; he homeschooled his children and had promised to let me see Ginny once a week."

"You love Ginny," Reaper stated out loud.

Will's face broke, and he had to lift a shaky hand to cover his expression. It took a full minute for him to gather himself before he told them, "She begged to stay with me; called me Papa Will when I took her to live with the Wests. Yes, I love her. She's as much as a daughter to me as Shade is a son. Whatever plan you have, include me. I'm going with you."

Reaper shook his head. "You can't. It'll be a fucking miracle if I can reach her in time."

Another text on his phone came in. "I have to go. Where's Silas?"

"He's behind the shop," Moses told him. "With Fynn."

As he walked away, he heard Shade talking to his father. "You never breathed a word to me, even when she worked for The Last Riders or when she moved away."

"I actually thought one of you boys would be smart enough to snap her up. It's good to see one of you finally got his head out of his ass." Will's voice deepened with emotion. "I always knew Gavin was the smartest one of you."

"Thanks, Dad."

Will didn't miss his son's sarcasm and gave it back. "You're welcome."

Reaper would have laughed at the play between father and son—if he wasn't flying toward a man who wanted to kill Ginny.

Walking around Matthew and Isaac's shop, he came to a stop at seeing what Silas and Fynn were doing. They had their hands lifted toward the sky, making movements in the air.

"Is it working?" Reaper spoke softly so as not to disturb their concentration.

Neither Silas nor Fynn stopped their movements as Silas answered, "Yes, for now. The winds will only do what I ask for so long before they become too bored or angry to listen anymore."

"I just wanted to tell you I'm leaving, and I'll have Lucky keep you informed."

"Before you go, Ginny left you something on the kitchen table." Silas didn't look at him as he spoke, but from the look on his face, Reaper knew what Ginny had left.

Fury had him quickly turning on his heel, and then he

stormed toward the house, ignoring the looks from the men and women outside. Seeing the small package neatly wrapped, sitting on an envelope, he reached for both, gripping them tightly in his hands before turning back around. Ginny leaving him a good-bye present expressed more than words—she didn't expect to see him again.

"Cash, drive me to the airport. Rider, Shade, ride with us."

The four men hurried toward Cash's truck.

Reaper spared a minute to stop in front of T.A. "If you think of anything else I need to know, tell Lucky; he'll get the information to me."

T.A. lifted her anguished eyes to his. "Evangeline was hurt that she wasn't the first to know I'm pregnant. Tell her I just found out the sex of the baby … Tell her … I'm not telling anyone until I tell her first."

Reaper wanted to reach out to give her a comforting hand, which would was a normal reaction at seeing someone in pain—*before* his captivity—and now the action was alien to him. But T.A.'s relationship with Ginny had him wanting to comfort her … just to have a moment's connection to a part of Ginny. Cognizant of the virus, though, he restrained himself. He would not put a pregnant woman in harm's way. Even if the Pegivirus CP-20 was only blood-borne, they were still being extra cautious.

Instead he said, "I can't believe none of us realized you were sisters."

T.A. gave a shuddering laugh. "No one was looking for it. Wait until you see her without her hair dye and contacts."

Reaper shook his head at her. "Do I even know Ginny at all?"

Sex Piston laid a hand on T.A.'s shoulder, preventing her from speaking. "Evangeline never hid the most important part—her heart."

He unconsciously took a step back. "You *all* knew?"

"She knew we would have her back," Sex Piston snapped at him. "Just like we've had T.A.'s. Make sure you bring the little bitch back, or we're going to fuck you up ...." Sex Piston lost the full effect of her threat when she turned her face away.

"I'll bring her back," he swore through gritted teeth, walking back toward the truck. "She might not be able to sit for a week when I'm done with her, but she's coming back."

Reaper hadn't thought the women could hear his threat, but Sex Piston had excellent hearing.

"Save some of that ass for me!" she shouted. "I'm going to—"

Inside the truck, Reaper slammed the door shut on whatever she was saying.

Fuck, now he was going to have to go gentle on her ass, knowing Sex Piston and her crew were going to take their own turns walloping her for scaring the hell out of them.

As Cash backed out the driveway, neatly avoiding the onslaught of motorcycles, Reaper turned around to face Rider and Shade in the back seat. Holding onto the back of the seat as Cash forced his truck down the road, tires squealing, he stared at Shade. "What I'm about to ask is shitty of me," he began. "You've got Lily and kids, and I've been a dick to you since I was freed, but I'm going to ask anyway."

Holding onto the door handle to keep himself from being flung into the front seat as Cash whipped around, blowing through a red light, Shade tightened jaw before he seethed out, "We've got three minutes before we're at the airport; quit blowing smoke up my ass and tell me what you need."

Reaper knew he didn't deserve his friends. He never had.

He shook the morose thought out of his head. He wasn't going back down that fucking road again. He was going to take advantage of what he had available to him, and Shade was more than an advantage; he was the elite in a category of men, who could name their own price to get a job done, and Shade didn't fail.

Reaper was still outlining what he needed when Cash brought the truck to a stop only feet away from where Train's chopper sat on the helipad with its blades whirling overhead. The four men jumped out of the truck. Reaper had been so intent on talking to Shade that he hadn't noticed the rest of the brothers had been following behind on their bikes.

Stopping beside the truck, Viper got out of his SUV, carrying a duffel bag. Reaper was taking it from him when Knox pulled up next to them in his squad car, lights flashing. Getting out of the car, Knox handed him a yellow envelope.

"All the paperwork you need is in there."

"Thanks, Knox." He'd have time later to appreciate whatever strings it took for Knox to get him legal marriage certificates in less than an hour.

Knox held his hand out to him, and Reaper took it, finding himself pulled into a bear hug.

"Make sure you bring your asses home."

"I will," Reaper said, giving the brother a hug back before pulling away.

Looping the strap of the duffel bag over his shoulder, he mimicked Knox's show of affection, pulling Viper close. "Thanks, bro."

"Anytime. That's what I'm here for." Viper hugged him back.

When Viper released him from the tight hug, he took a step toward Rider so he could be heard over the sound of the helicopter. "You once offered to have my back, and when I didn't take it, I paid for my stupidity with ten years of my life. I don't want to make the same mistake twice. I need your help."

"What'd you want?" Rider walked next to him, moving toward the chopper.

"Allerton, I want his nuts in a vice," Reaper yelled over the sound of the blades.

"The Last Riders are comfortable, but we don't have the kind of money to break that fucker. He has billions, and his friends have even more."

"We might not have billions, but we have something he doesn't have. We have Crux." Giving Rider a fist bump on his shoulder, Reaper then got in the chopper, giving Train a thumbs-up as he buckled in. A key to any successful mission was to know when to divide-and-conquer. Crux's and Shade's skill sets couldn't be beaten. Crux would devise a way to get Ginny and him out, while Shade could dispatch anyone who stood in their way going into hell.

Train immediately went airborne.

Looking downward, Reaper saw The Last Riders lift their fists in unison. Seeing the number of men sprawled out on the tarmac below and more motorcycles still arriving, their support for him hit him harder than any punch to the face could have.

Despite everything he had put them through, they were just as willing to support him now as they had been when they had become friends in the service. He deserved the dick award for being the biggest jerk alive, not deserving the loyalty they were showing him.

He had been so locked in his hatred-fueled rage that it seemed insurmountable to get back on an even keel with them, but as Train flew higher, gaining clearance to avoid the looming mountains, Reaper realized he no longer needed to climb out of the depths he had been swallowed in. He was now able to fly because of one person. Ginny.

He had to get her back, and not only for T.A., Sex Piston, and all her friends and family, but for himself. She was his, had always been and would always be until the end of time. He now accepted her term: soul mates. Allerton might be the richest man in the world, making him believe himself invincible living on his fucking island. What the fucker didn't know was, no matter how rich he might be, he could never cheat death, and death was unquestionably coming for the motherfucker.

CHAPTER FIVE

Viper watched the chopper fly away, and every part of his being wanted to be on board with his brother.

Lowering his fist when the chopper was out of sight, he turned to the brothers lined up behind him. "I want *every* Last Rider in Kentucky at the club in one hour," Viper ordered of Cash. "If they can't be there, tell them I want their fucking cuts and bikes. Call Stud and Calder; they've got an iron in this fire."

Going to his bike, Viper was the first to leave the airport, the brothers riding behind him in formation. Reaching the clubhouse, Viper then directed the brothers to wait outside in the backyard as he directed Nickel to organize a Zoom call so the club in Ohio could listen in on the meeting.

He waited for a moment before joining the brothers outside, forcing himself to appear calm while his thoughts were with Reaper. Self-doubt assailed him. He should have gone with him.

Viper needed to think analytically and started making plans to support Reaper and to organize what he could do from here. It was going to be a fucking miracle if Reaper managed to get on the plane with Ginny, and he would need an even bigger miracle to be allowed to accompany her to the island.

During any military operation, it was intrinsic to the plan to have someone on the ground coordinating the attack, and as much as Viper wanted to have Reaper's six, he was equally useful accomplishing their goals here, to ensure his brother returned safely with Ginny.

Most of the brothers were already here, waiting for their orders. One by one, the women began arriving, as well. Lucky had escorted T.A., Dalton, Sex Piston, and the Coleman brothers, except for Silas and Fynn, to the side yard where they could distance themselves and still be able to hear what was being said.

King and Evie were the last to arrive. Evie went to stand with the women while King positioned himself with the brothers, next to Shade.

Taking a final calming breath, Viper walked out to the backyard and recapped what had happened in the courthouse that morning. Then he went on retell the story T.A. had provided about Allerton and Ginny.

Stud and Calder stood in stunned disbelief as they learned that Sex Piston, Crazy Bitch, Killyama, and Fat Louise had known the closely guarded secret about Ginny's identify. Despite Stud's dismay at his wife's secret, he stepped forward. "The Destructors will stand with The Last Riders to provide assistance."

Calder stepped forward when his brother finished speaking. "The Blue Horsemen also stand with The Last Riders. Reaper has our jacket, as well as the Destructor's. We will all stand with our brother."

"Allerton has made it impossible for us to be there to have Reaper's back. What we need is information about him and what the fuck Ginny stole from him or has on him that would make him want her dead. Nickel will take point; funnel any information you can to him. I want to find out everything about him, from how many shits he takes a day, to the last time he ate and with who. Reach out to your contacts and find out what you can. What you might think isn't important could save Reaper and Ginny.

"She was under our protection, yet she has taken on protecting us. She's not a little nobody, and Allerton can't just sweep this under the rug. Reaper went to bring her back safely, and we're going to make fucking sure he succeeds. We let him down before, I'll be damned if we do it again."

Viper shifted his body toward T.A. "You have no idea what Ginny took?"

T.A. shook her head. "No, and she doesn't either."

Viper nodded, turning back to the whole group. "All we know is that she took *something* from a boat that must have been moored at Sherguevil Island before Christmas when Ginny was three. Somewhere, there are records of who was traveling in the area. Knox, see if you and Jonas can get access to old port records and customs' check points near the islands. Let's find out who's been visiting Allerton in the past and present."

He looked at T.A. again. "Did Ginny ever describe the boat to you?"

T.A. bit her lip as if she was thinking hard. "Maybe …." She brought her hand to her belly as if her heightened emotions were affecting the baby.

"I'm taking her home," Dalton announced, gently grabbing T.A.'s arm. "This is too much for her and the baby."

T.A. pulled her arm away. "We're okay. I can do this. I have to." Giving her husband a look of regret, her expression then turned pensive.

"She was fascinated with the larger ones, so it had to be a good size, but not so big that it wouldn't be docked at the island. There was one I vaguely remember. We were sitting at the beach and she kept telling me to look at how pretty it was, but that's all I remember." She gave a frustrated sigh.

"Do you think if I show you different types of boats, you would recognize the type?"

"Maybe. I can try."

"Something is better than nothing. That's a start, then. We can mix and match that type of boat with the old records to discover who Ginny stole from and why in the fuck Allerton wants it so badly. Anyone else have any questions?"

"What was Ginny taught to steal?" Razer spoke up.

"Paper currency, money clips, watches …," T.A. answered.

"Was there anything else that Ginny was fascinated with besides boats?" Razer, being the father of two rambunctious twin boys, clearly understood the inner working of a child's mind better than most of them.

"Anything shiny," Shade's father answered. "She kept stealing my badge," he added gruffly. "And I had to let her pick out a cell—" Will broke off then continued. "Wait— Hammer had her keep a secret cell phone that only he and I had the number to." Will took out his cell phone, but Viper stopped him from making the call.

"Let me have the number. We know she's with the FBI right now, and I don't want to alert them to the fact that she has the phone if they haven't already taken it from her. I'll have Knox see if he can find the location of the signal from it before we make a call."

Viper looked down at his cell phone to make sure he received Will's text with the number before continuing. "Going back to what we were discussing before"—Viper put his phone away—"we have to take in account considering how long it has been, that whatever Ginny took is going to be irretrievable or has been destroyed. Allerton's a smart man. He'll have come to this same conclusion. What it comes down to is why he wants her so bad, even if the item has been lost forever? I think he's wanting to make sure she didn't see him kill her friends. He's never let out a fart in public, so I can see him doing whatever it takes to keep his image intact. The tricky part for him is to decide just how much Ginny knows. He's going to study Ginny. If she's fooled us for all these years, as to her identity, she might be able to convince him that she doesn't remember or know anything and he'll let her go."

"And if he doesn't?" Willa asked.

"Then Ginny and Reaper are on borrowed time," Viper stated the cold hard truth.

"I have money." Willa moved away from Lucky to stand beside T.A., laying a hand on her shoulder. "Tell Dustin what you need, and I'll have it transferred to your account. I want to help Ginny, whatever the cost."

"Same goes for me," Dalton agreed. "I'll also get on the phone to some of my contacts. Several of them have yachts; I'll see what insights I can get from them about Allerton and his island."

"We have to prepare to fight fire with fire, so I won't be saying no to either of your offers. I, as well The Last Riders, will be getting our hands on what cash we can on short notice, but we're going to have to have large sums at our disposal. Anyone else?" Viper asked, wanting to end the meeting so he could coordinate with Rider and Shade.

Looking at the group circled around him, he was met with silence.

"Then everyone get busy."

Turning toward T.A. again, Viper said, "I'll make sure to keep you informed. Go home and get some rest. I'll be sending some brothers to guard your place. If Allerton now knows Ginny is alive and he gets nothing out of her, he might want to use you as a bargaining chip. I want to make sure that isn't going to happen."

Dalton shook his head. "Save your men. I'll make sure she's protected." The movie star, who was famous for his good looks, exuded a dangerous aura that couldn't be mistaken. Dalton could and would take care of his own. "Besides, Ice and Jackal are on my plane now, so they should be here in the next hour."

Viper nodded. "That's one worry off my mind, then."

Viper started walking to where Shade and Rider were standing but stopped when T.A. called out to him. "Viper? If you are able to get a message to Evangeline, could you tell her something else for me?"

"Yes."

"Tell her I'm going to—" T.A. broke off, unable to go on.

Sex Piston didn't have the same problem. "Tell her we're waiting to welcome her ass home."

CHAPTER SIX

Once they were in the air, Reaper tore Ginny's present open to uncover a small, black velvet box. Flipping the box open, he saw a pair of black pearls. He swallowed hard before opening the envelope.

To replace the one I stole. This will suit you much better. You can use the other as a spare if you lose one. I found these when I lived in Clindale. T.A. saved them for me. I meant to make charms out of them, but I decided I wanted to give you a piece of me so you wouldn't forget about me and how much I love you. They are found in the deepest part of the ocean, yet they could never reach the depths of the love I have for you.

Love,
    Evangeline

. . .

Opening the box again, Reaper took out one of the earrings, putting it through the empty hole she'd left after taking his earring. He took the other black pearl and replaced it with another earring. Setting the empty box and card aside, he started reading the information that Knox had put together for him in the short timespan he'd given him.

Sorting through the paperwork inside the thick envelope, he found the marriage certificate, his passport, and his inoculation records. Knox had made sure to include any paperwork that could possibly keep him out of the country he was headed toward. He silently thanked Shade for suggesting he keep his medical records updated in case they had discovered Slate hiding in another country.

Sorting through the remaining papers, he saw that Knox had listed several of Allerton's assets, as well as his known associates. Reaper read through the list before moving on to read the charities associated with his foundation. Giving an internal whistle at the names on the list, Reaper moved on to the overview of Allerton's personal life. He was single and had been linked with a variety, high-profile women. The woman he was currently dating was a high-powered lawyer from D.C.

Taking out the marriage certificate, passport, and his health records, he placed them in the side pocket of the duffel bag Viper had given him. Replacing the rest of the papers in the envelope, he placed it in the storage box next to Train, as well as the empty jewelry box and letter Ginny had written him.

Queuing his mic, Reaper asked Train, "How much longer?"

"Twenty minutes."

Reaper stared out the bubble of the windshield, his gut clenching at the thought of Ginny being gone before he arrived, and the FBI preventing him from seeing her, much less allowing him to go with her. So many scenarios were in play; each with their own measure of him not achieving his goal.

He gritted his teeth when Train hit an air pocket, sending Train expertly fighting for control of the helicopter.

"Hang on." Reaper heard Train's voice come in and out of the headset.

Reaper tightened his harness. They were risking their lives to fly through the turbulent winds that Silas and Fynn created. Just a few weeks ago, death would have been a welcome relief from the mental anguish he had been suffering through. Ironically, he had never wanted to live more than he did now. He had fences to repair—the first and one of the most important was Ginny.

The image of her standing on the front porch consumed his thoughts. The hopeful expression on her face that turned sad when he had walked back up the porch steps was now more understandable. He thought she was too embarrassed to tell Silas she would be sharing his bed. In hindsight, she had been waiting for him to tell her about Taylor. She'd been testing his feelings for her, and he had failed. Miserably.

Static sounded in his ear. "Five minutes away."

The helicopter bounced again. Reaper heard Train's litany of curses, then suddenly felt the jarring movements stop, and the chopper flew smoothly. Five minutes later they were landing on a helipad.

Unfastening his harness, Reaper grabbed his bag and was already taking off at a run toward the small airport while the blades overhead still whirled.

Reaper felt a rush of wind pass him, crazily thinking it was Silas somehow urging him on. He had to blink twice before he realized it was Train running past him in order to hold open the door with his foot; it reminded Reaper of the friendship they had once shared.

"Getting slow, old man." Train laughed, running next to him after they ran through the door.

Reaper stopped, and not because of the joke, but because he didn't know where in the fuck to go. A hard hit to his shoulder had Reaper looking to where Train was pointing to the side of the concourse, five feet away.

Reaper saw three men in suits and Hammer waiting for Ginny as she came out of the women's restroom.

Reaper took a deep of breath of oxygen, then released it in an explosion of air that had everyone staring at him.

"*Ginny!*"

G inny jumped in shock hearing her name called out. Turning toward the voice she recognized, she saw Gavin and Train walking toward her.

Feeling a tug on each of her arms by two of the FBI agents, who were leading her toward the double glass doors that led outside, Ginny was tempted to give in to their silent demands. God help her, though, because she couldn't move a muscle; she'd become frozen in place at Gavin's menacing approach.

"Uh ... I think ... w-we should wait," Ginny stuttered out in fear.

Oh God ....

She had gotten a glimpse of Reaper on the way back to Treepoint after they had stopped to help that couple on the side of the road, but it was nothing like the man who was coming in hot after her.

Ginny began to doubt her sanity for remaining in place and allowing Gavin to catch up with them. "Hammer?"

Hammer shrugged at her plea. "You're on your own, kid." Her childhood protector folded his arms across his chest.

Her hair swung to the side as she quickly whipped her head to face the agent holding her arm. "I'm ready."

None of the agents moved.

"Ginny, come here."

"Just a minute," Agent Flores finally spoke up. "Miss Bellamy is in our custody."

"Come. Here. Ginny."

Frightened by his tone, Ginny tried to shake off the restraining hands and step toward Gavin, but they tightened their grips, refusing to relinquish control.

"Let go of my *wife!*" Gavin's loud voice drew several curious eyes in the airport, then dropped into a lethal growl. "*Now.*"

Two pairs of hands dropped.

Ginny took a faltering step forward, as Gavin tugged her into his side. Staring up at him with her mouth gaping open, she managed to stutter out, "Uh … what are you doing here?"

With furious eyes, he stared down at her, silently communicating to be quiet.

Ginny was wise enough to know when to keep her mouth shut. She felt as if she was knocking on death's door, and if she wasn't extremely careful, it would be answered.

Satisfied his message had been received, Gavin raised his head to face to the FBI agents. "Who's in charge?" he asked authoritatively.

"Senior Agent Collins." Agent Flores looked as if he would rather jump off a cliff than make the admission.

"My name is Gavin James. And you are?"

"I know who you are … I am Agent Flores."

Gavin dismissed the young agent as if he was an irritating fly. "Which one of you is Collins?"

"He's in the restroom. He became airsick during the flight," Agent Garcia reluctantly admitted.

"Then I guess we're waiting for him before going on to Sherguevil Island," Gavin said firmly.

"How did you ...? You're not going." Agent Flores shook his head.

"Are you denying me the right to accompany my wife?" Gavin tilted his head, as if to make sure he was hearing Agent Flores correctly.

"Ye ... No. I mean, yes."

Ginny had to bite her lip to keep herself from bursting into nervous laughter at the agent's confusion.

"My wife is not leaving this airport without me at her side. Isn't that right, *wife*?"

Ginny's amusement vanished as she nodded her head, too scared not to.

"Miss Bellamy isn't married."

"We were keeping it a secret, on a need-to-know basis. The FBI didn't need to know before. Now you do."

"You can take it up with my superior." Agent Flores's voice found firmer ground.

Gavin eyed him disdainfully. "Which is what I just said."

"Oh ... right."

Ginny would have had some sympathy for the agent, but she was too busy being concerned for her own welfare. Waves of fury were rolling off Gavin, as if he was carefully holding himself in check. She was regretting not telling him this morning about the deal she made with the FBI.

Gavin turned his back on the agents, propelling her toward a cluster of chairs in the middle of the room, making sure to keep a distance from other passengers waiting for their flights. Train moved to stand behind them, and Ginny saw Train whisper something in Gavin's ear before going out the glass door to the airfield. Killyama's husband was dressed in a tan flight suit that had several military insignias prominently displayed. She wasn't able to take her eyes away from his authoritative stride until he disappeared out of sight.

"We are going back to the plane," Agent Flores stated.

Ginny found herself pushed down farther on the plastic chair with Gavin's arm placed snugly over her shoulders. Hammer took the other seat next to her, firmly blocking her in between the two large men.

The three agents stared at each other, as if perplexed at what to do.

Gavin stared at Agent Flores unsympathetically. "How long have you been on the force?"

"I have been in training for four months."

Gavin appeared disgusted as he motioned at the other agents. "How about them?"

"The same time. We were in the same training class at Quantico."

Ginny saw Gavin and Hammer share the same dark look before Gavin shot out another question. "How long has the agent in charge been on the force?"

"Agent Collins has served with the FBI for eighteen years. He's due to retire after this assignment."

"Well, isn't that a fucking coincidence?" Gavin's exasperation was evident.

The agents stiffened at Gavin's insinuation.

"What does that mean?"

"You're the FBI; you figure it out."

"If you're insinuating that Miss Bellamy will come under any harm with us assisting her on her journey to Clindale because of our lack of experience, then you're mistaken. She is under our protection—"

"What did you do before joining the FBI?" Gavin interjected.

"I was an attorney."

Ginny could tell from the flush rising in his cheeks Gavin's eye language wasn't complimentary.

"How about them?"

"I'm sure that Agent Flores is very good at his job—" Ginny broke off when Gavin's laser-like glare settled on her. Lowering her eyes, she mumbled under her breath, "Never mind."

"Agent Garcia was a network administrator. Agent Clark was a lab supervisor."

"None of you have law enforcement or military background?" Gavin asked harshly.

"We were given extensive training in the academy, and all of us have passed the requirements needed."

"Except graduating."

The agents couldn't deny that truth and began looking over their shoulders toward the bathroom. Their relief became palpable when their supervisor exited the restroom.

Mopping his brow with a damp paper towel, his eyes widened when he saw his men gathered in the seating area of the terminal.

"Flores, why haven't you escorted Miss Bellamy back to the plane as you were ordered to do?"

The three agents stepped to the side, exposing Gavin's presence.

"I'm Gavin."

"I know who you are."

Gavin gave the men a lethal stare. "Seems like a fucking lot of you know who I am."

As Agent Collins wiped his brow again, Ginny noticed his hand was shaking, despite his demeanor being more assured than the younger agents.

"Escort Miss Bella—"

"*Mrs.* James," Gavin corrected.

Agent Collins' assurance dropped a notch, yet he

continued with his order. "It has no bearing with the job we have been assigned to carry out." Agent Collins used his hand to motion toward the doors. "The pilot texted me that the winds have let up and it's safe for us to fly. Mr. James, your wife may call you once we reach Sherguevil Island."

"My wife isn't going anywhere without me."

"That isn't possible. Miss Be—Mrs. James chose Hammer as her escort. We have no room for more passengers."

"Reaper can take my place," Hammer stated.

Agent Collins narrowed his eyes in anger. "Mr. James doesn't have the required paperwork to travel to Sherguevil Island."

Gavin opened his duffel bag to remove a yellow envelope. "Which paperwork do you need? I have two forms of ID, one of which is a passport; I have our marriage certificate, my health records and inoculations, which are current."

"The owner of the island requires anyone traveling there to have been quarantined for the last ten days." Agent Collins seemed more confident this would stymie Gavin.

Gavin shut it down. "Considering I'm married to Ginny and the intimate nature of our relationship, if she has the virus, so do I."

"I need to call my director." Agent Collins' frustration became more apparent as Gavin threw his objections aside.

"Do that. And if he denies Ginny's and my request, then he can forget any deal she made with the FBI. Believe me; that's what I would rather she do. I have my lawyer on speed dial, and dude, the last fucking thing you want to do is get her involved. Dealing with Diamond will be like poking a hornet's nest—and she won't leave the FBI unscathed."

"The FBI has nothing to hide."

Ginny thought his denial would sound better if Collins would stop wiping his sweaty brow.

"We'll find out, shall we? I find it extremely concerning

that the agents sent to Treepoint to keep Ginny's sister and me sidelined in the courthouse were the more experienced agents, while the ones sent with Ginny haven't even graduated from Quantico. Don't you find that unusual, Hammer?" Gavin asked mockingly.

Agent Collins gave the younger agents a disgusted look at the knowledge they'd shared with Gavin. "If you're trying to say there are any irregularities—"

"I'm not trying to fucking say it. It's a fucking fact," Gavin spat.

"Agent Garcia, Clark, and Flores are embarking on their fieldwork, as every new agent does. They are at the top of their class, and the director approved their part in this assignment, as the situation with the virus has diminished our numbers. Escorting Miss Bell—" Collins corrected himself. "—Mrs. James is a low-risk operation, and it was deemed advantageous to use trainees rather than seasoned agents, as they are needed elsewhere."

"I bet it is more advantageous," Gavin agreed snidely. "Hammer, I can't believe you haven't already pulled the plug on this shit show."

Hammer leaned forward so he could talk to Gavin without her blocking him from sight. "I would have—if Ginny hadn't told me she would go alone without me."

Ginny squirmed in her plastic chair. "I'm going." She mutinously lifted her chin at Gavin's glare.

"I'd like a word with my wife alone."

Ginny was prepared to tell the agents that she didn't want to be left alone with Gavin. Truthfully, she was suffering her own misgivings about what she had agreed to do and was frightened Gavin would talk her out of the plan.

"I'll give you five minutes," Agent Collins warned as he moved away. "If Mrs. James doesn't continue on to Sherguevil Island, our agreement with her will become null and void."

Ginny heard the deep breath Gavin took as he prepared to talk to her when the men moved away.

"Hear me out, Gavin." Bracing herself, she turned in her seat to face him. "I want you to go back to Treepoint and take Hammer with you. I'll be fine. I've given this some serious thought, and this is for the best—"

Gavin moved his face within centimeters from hers. "Then you've got the brain of duck if you think I'd go along with this for a fucking second. All four of us are going back to Treepoint. Diamond can handle any charges brought against me or The Last Riders."

"I'm not only doing this for you or The Last Riders. Helping you and them is a benefit, not the whole reason." Ginny raised truth-filled eyes to his.

"Then what is the other fucking reason are you doing this?"

"For Trudy, Will, and Hammer."

CHAPTER SEVEN

"I can't keep running to make everyone safe. How would you like living every single minute of each day hiding who you are, and if you make a mistake, those people you love could pay the consequences?" Ginny placed a hand over his on the arm of the chair. "Since I was three years old, I've been living with the fact that Hammer, Papa Will, and Trudy's life were in danger because they were protecting me. One hint that I was still alive, and their lives could be forfeited to get to me. It's why I was never able to see my grandmother before she died, why I couldn't let anyone know Trudy was my sister, why I maintained my distance from my brothers, why any time something happens, I have to separate myself so no hint of my past can come to light. I either face Allerton or I'll have to add my niece or nephew to that list. I won't live like that anymore. I won't ask anyone else to pay the price of loving me costs."

"You could have told me."

Ginny heard the slight tinge of hurt and mistrust in his voice.

"When was I supposed to tell you? Last night?" Ginny felt

a blush rushing to her cheeks as she shook her head. "If you're completely honest, you don't know what you feel about me. You couldn't even tell me about seeing Taylor this morning, and yet you sit here, angry at me for keeping a secret from you that could get Trudy, Will, and Hammer hurt."

"I'm not angry you kept your identity from me; I'm angry because even though you say it was to protect T.A., Will, and Hammer I know the main reason you exposed yourself is because of me." He wrapped his free hand around her neck. "Tell me I'm wrong."

Ginny tried to look away from him, but he wouldn't allow it. She knew then she couldn't lie to him. "I can't," she whispered. "It's too late. Allerton knows I'm alive now. There's no going back. I'm going to see this through; take Hammer and leave. Please, Gavin." She fervently tried to get across to him how important this was to her. "I *have* to do this. I can't live with myself if something happens. Trudy and Hammer have families now, and I can't be their obligation anymore. I have to stand on my own two feet. I should have done this a long time ago, but I wasn't brave enough."

"What makes you so sure that you are now?"

"I'm not sure I am. I just can't live with the consequences any longer if I don't."

He tightened his hand on her neck like he wanted to shake some sense into her. Instead, he pulled her closer.

"I'm not going to let you do this alone," he said.

Her protective instincts for Gavin warred with her determination to return to Clindale Island and accomplish what needed to be done. She didn't want to lead him into danger. He deserved more than losing his life trying to keep her safe.

"Why are you here?" She futilely fought herself to remain in his hold. Gathering her self-control, she moved her hands to his chest to push him back. "Taylor is waiting. Go," she gasped out, finally getting some breathing room.

"Either I go with you, or you're not going."

Ginny saw the tendons in his jaw lock in determination and she hated herself for the relief that flooded through her. Before she could stop from exposing the fear she kept hidden when she saw he was scrutinizing her expression, Gavin gave her an abrupt nod. She didn't like the message she read in his eyes.

"Wait." Ginny tried to pull him back down when he started to rise. It was a wasted effort.

Reaching down for her, he tugged her to her feet then went to stand in front of Hammer. "Go home. I've got this."

Hammer stood, his hard features remaining stoic at Gavin's announcement. "I'm trusting you with her. Don't let me down," he finally said before pulling her into his arms.

Ginny was shocked at the gesture. Hammer had never given any indication of his feelings for her. He still didn't ... other than holding her close.

"Kid, if you get yourself hurt, I won't be happy."

This was the Hammer she knew and loved.

"I'm in good hands." Ginny laid her head down on his shoulder, drawing his strength into her body. She was terrified at getting her way, terrified that she wouldn't be the only one hurt by her actions.

Hammer must have felt her shiver in his arms because he told her, "You're the bravest woman I know."

"Killyama would kick you in your balls for saying that." Ginny gave a small laugh against his shoulder.

"Prove me right."

"I'll try."

Hammer released her from his hold. "Trying won't get the job done. You've been wanting to do this for a while, and I held you back until I was sure you could handle this yourself.

You've got this, kid. You do what needs to be done. Reaper will make sure you come out alive."

Gavin didn't acknowledge Hammer's confidence in him, his attention on the FBI agents standing at the doors.

"I served with him on a couple of missions before he left the service. No one is better than him with his particular skill."

Ginny gave Gavin a considering look at Hammer's statement. "What's his skill?" she asked quietly, not wanting to give a forewarning to anyone listening.

"Kicking ass." Hammer held out his fist to Gavin. "Watch your back, brother."

Gavin didn't give him a fist bump back. "Will do. And Hammer, when I come home, we're going to have a talk."

"Brother, *when* you and Ginny make it back okay, you can have the first punch."

I t took a good fifteen minutes for Agent Collins to get the okay from his director in letting Gavin switch places with Hammer. Ginny remained a silent spectator as Gavin and Agent Collins argued back and forth. When Gavin gave the agent an envelope filled with documents, Ginny looked interestedly at the marriage certificate, amazed at the signature written on the bottom. She was going to have a long talk with Gavin about the perils of forgery. She hadn't done the deal with the FBI to get him out of his legal problems for him to spend five to ten in prison for lying to a federal agent.

A phone call to Collins' boss settled the matter, and Gavin was given the okay to board the plane with her. As they walked toward their plane, Ginny saw Train's head buried in the plane's engine before he said something to the pilot before walking over to them.

"Any problems?" Gavin asked as Train neared.

"No, not as far as I can see." Killyama's husband shoved his hands into his flight suit. "Any chance they'll let me tag along?"

"None." Agent Collins motioned her toward the waiting plane. "Mrs. James."

Ginny ignored him.

"Did you see Trudy?" she asked Train instead.

"Yes," Train's answer was short.

"How was she?"

"How do you think she fucking was?"

Wincing from the stinging dart of anger from Train had her going onto the plane without another word. Taking a seat at the back, Ginny stared out the window, fighting back tears. She had known Trudy would be hurt by her decision to return to Clindale Island, yet from Train's short reply, her sister must have been more upset than she expected.

When Gavin took the seat next to hers, she refused to show him how emotional she was. With legs snuggly fit against the seat in front of him, he didn't show any commiseration with Train's displeasure with her.

"Buckle your seat belt."

She numbly fastened her seat belt, keeping her eyes pointed forward. If Train was as angry as he sounded, Ginny was willing to bet it wasn't a quarter of what Gavin was feeling.

"I should have told you," Ginny whispered under her breath as the airplane taxied forward.

Drawing to the side of her seat, away from Gavin, Ginny clung to the armrest under the window as Gavin planted his face in front of hers, so close that she couldn't glance away.

"That's the understatement of the century." His low voice had shivers going up her back.

"I was trying to help everyone."

"You should have stayed out of it. Didn't it fucking dawn on you that you could make it worse for us?"

Her own anger came to her rescue. "No, it didn't," she hissed sharply. "It was damned bad enough that all The Last Riders were about to get arrested for three deaths."

"Who told you that?"

"Hammer, when I asked him to look into Slate being a confidential informant. I didn't want to see you arrested."

"You should have minded your own business."

Ginny quit shrinking away. He wasn't going to hurt her. She was just being silly. Gavin might look like he could crush a can with one of his pinkies, but she was certain he would never lay a hurtful hand on her.

"Anything that could hurt you is my business."

Gavin gave her an astonished look. "You didn't consider that not telling me the truth about who you are and making a deal with the FBI—*where you deliberately placed yourself in danger*—is hurtful to me?"

"I was going to tell you this morning. I already told you all this."

"When?" he said, ignoring her, "I sure as fuck must have missed you trying to start *that* conversation with me. I could swear on a stack of Bibles that I didn't hear anything remotely like, 'Hey, Gavin, by the way, my name is Evangeline.'"

She tightened her lips at his heavy sarcasm. "I will repeat myself again! I had every intention of telling you *when* you told me you were going to see Taylor," she snapped back.

"Me going to see Taylor is irrelevant," he ground out, their noses bumping each other's.

"It was pretty darn relevant to me."

"If Taylor was still important to me, why in the fuck would I offer to find us a place to live where you wouldn't be embarrassed about us fucking under Silas's roof?"

"Lower your voice," Ginny whisper-screamed at him. Then she poked her head over the chair in front of them to see if any of the agents were listening.

Gavin rolled his eyes at her. "You're wasting your time. I'm pretty sure they are recording our conversation."

She swiveled her head toward him. "Why would they eavesdrop on our conversation? They didn't know you'd be here."

An exasperated Gavin made her feel like she had noodles for brains.

"They would want to listen to *any* conversation between you and Hammer or the FBI talking among themselves. This plane doesn't belong to the FBI; it's Allerton's private jet."

"Oh …"

"Yeah … oh," he said snidely.

"You don't have to be so rude."

"*Evangeline*," Gavin mocked, "if you think I'm being rude now, wait until I get you alone."

CHAPTER EIGHT

Ginny was apprehensive when the plane began its descent onto Sherguevil Island. A confusing array of emotions assailed her—dread, fear, even excitement. She wanted to burst into tears at the thought of seeing her mother and father again, but the growing sense of panic at putting Gavin and herself under Allerton's control overcame her.

"Will your parents be waiting?"

"I don't know."

The possibility of her parents waiting for her to step off the plane added another level of turmoil. Her natural instinct was to want to see them; however, Ginny was unsure how she was supposed to react or how she should feel. She was no longer a child or naïve enough not to wonder why her parents had remained on Clindale Island. The way they had washed their hands of Trudy was an unforgivable offense to her; they had basically chosen Allerton over their children. Even if they had left the island and returned to the States when she was grown, she was uncertain if she would have contacted them. It would have placed Trudy in too much danger if her parents realized she was still alive, assuming that information would get back to Allerton. She never wished ill on anyone in her life, but she had hoped age would catch up with Allerton and solve the problem for her. She should have known better. The devil takes care of his own.

"Are they on Sherguevil or Clindale Island?"

"I don't know."

Feeling wistful, she tried to catch a glimpse of Clindale Island from the window, but from her viewpoint, it wasn't possible.

"I guess we're about to find out." Her attempt at humor failed miserably.

"I don't think I've ever seen you nervous before."

"You want to know the truth?"

Gavin made an exaggerated face, practically rolling his eyes. "That would be a first."

Lowering her eyes so he couldn't see the hurt he just inflicted, she was aware she had no one to blame but herself. "I've never lied to you ... I might had withheld certain facts, but I didn't lie."

He brought his hand to his ear to point at the black pearl. "How about this? You stole my earring, let me search around for it, and even waited in the car while I looked in the bar."

"I didn't tell you that you lost your earring; you assumed you had. That's not my fault."

A frown cut deep grooves across his forehead. "I could swear you used the word *lost*."

"You must be mistaken." She shrugged. "I've been nothing but truthful to you." At least she hoped she had. Omitting certain facts wasn't technically a lie, was it?

"Okay ...." Gavin sarcastically went on as if he didn't believe her. "So, what *truth* were you about to tell me this time?"

Thinning her lips into a line, she showed him her irritation. "Never mind. If you're going to be sarcastic, I'll just keep it to myself."

Gavin looked like he was a hairsbreadth from shaking her.

She decided to sit on her high horse another time—when she wasn't already in fear for her life.

"I was just going to say, I'm usually nervous when I'm around you," she admitted, embarrassed.

A soft bump as the plane landed forestalled any further conversation, bringing back the feeling of dread. Even with Gavin here, it was in full force as she uneasily began unbuckling her seat belt as the agents prepared to disembark.

Agent Collins made his way down the aisle toward them.

"Mrs. James, like I told you when we left Treepoint, we'll all have to be isolated to make sure we don't have the virus. Mr. Allerton has assured us that we will be given adjoining bungalows. The FBI doesn't expect any complications and, hopefully, with your help, we will be able to get this charge against you resolved in an expedited manner." Agent Collins then walked away from them to go outside.

Ginny rose to her feet to follow after him but was halted when Gavin refused to budge.

"What charge?"

She sat back down. "Theft."

"You're shitting me?"

"I wish. Gavin, they are waiting for us. We can talk about this in our rooms."

Reluctantly, Gavin stood up. "You don't leave my side, you got me?"

"It's pretty hard not to. You're speaking loud enough they can hear you outside."

Gavin moved out from the seats, taking her arm and holding onto her as they walked down the small aisle.

"It's going to be okay, Gavin. The FBI has all of this

planned out." She didn't know if she was trying to reassure him or herself as they stopped briefly before going outside.

"That's what I'm afraid of." Gripping her arm tightly, he then lowered his head to go through door.

Stepping out into the bright sunlight, Ginny saw the agents already waiting by two pastel-colored vehicles resembling Jeeps. "What are those? I've never seen those before," Ginny asked.

"They're Mokes." Gavin paused, preventing her from going down the steps. "They're military-grade Jeeps. Don't let their cute appearance fool you. They were made to go over any type of terrain."

"I won't." Nodding her understanding that the Jeeps were wolves with sheeps' appearances, Gavin finally let them reach the ground.

Agent Collins escorted them to the first Moke. Taking the back seat while Collins took the front seat next to the driver, they waited for the other agents to get settled in the other Moke before the driver started moving away from the plane. The paved trail wound downward through the jungle, filled with towering palm trees swaying overhead in the salty air.

The overhead T-shaped bars weren't wide enough to provide a shield from the sun, as the palm trees became sparser and the heart of the jungle gradually tamed. Small homes took the place of the dense foliage when the Mokes reached level ground.

The homes were small but designed to fit seamlessly into the landscape. So far, the island gave the impression of a vacation getaway rather than the headquarters of Allerton's charity.

Ginny looked around with interest as they drove along at a slow speed. As they passed the market area, Ginny tried to remember if it was the same when she had been a child. Nothing seemed similar to her vague memories.

Deciding to stop pressuring herself, Ginny was unsure if her anxiety was the root of the problem or if the island had changed that much since she had been a child. But when they rounded a curve to drive along the ocean front, bringing her within sight of the building that she had once begged Manny to go inside of, it was just as she remembered.

The largest building on the island she had seen so far was surrounded by majestic palm trees. Three stories high, the palatial structure was big enough to be a hotel, with a balcony encompassing the top floor. On each side of the building, people were eating at tables underneath a colorful array of beach umbrellas. Waiters in black and white uniforms moved among the tables, serving the guests. It was weird that not one person glanced up to see the Mokes, the guests and waiters overlooking them as if they didn't exist. Her sense of dread increased. Despite only being several feet away, Ginny found it their behavior disconcerting. Her group was being markedly ignored.

Turning her head, she met Gavin's eyes and knew he was just as concerned.

Twisting herself forward in her seat, Ginny looked past Gavin to see the beach. The view before her was also one she remembered. Two rows of large boats were moored at the long dock, while the huge, more expensive yachts rocked on the sea farther out.

"It's as beautiful as I remember." Unaware of the soft sigh that escaped her, Ginny wanted to jump out of the Moke to walk along the pier and get a closer look at the stunning crafts.

Gavin reached out to take her hand, linking his fingers with hers, grabbing her attention. "Nuh-uh. You got in trouble the last time you did that."

Ginny blushed. "I wasn't going to jump out."

"Seemed that way to me."

"You're mistaken," she denied, turning redder as his eyebrows climbed caustically. He wasn't buying her fib for a second. "Some habits are hard to deny," she admitted, shamefaced.

"Nothing to be embarrassed about. I could get a hard-on for a few of those beauties myself."

If she wasn't embarrassed before, she was now.

"I think they're pretty. I want to see what they look like inside, to see if they match the outside." She tried to explain what she felt seeing the sleek, proud vessels.

"You want to get up close and personal." His brow arched even higher.

She wasn't dumb enough to respond to that. Giving him a cold shoulder, she pointedly ignored the boats and Gavin's low laughter as they passed them.

"I bet you were a handful when you were a child."

"I was an angel."

"I think you still are."

Unable to prevent herself, she turned back to him, expecting sarcasm. However, the sincerity she saw would have floored her if she'd been standing. *Had he just said something nice to her twice in a row?*

"Did you take a nice pill when I wasn't looking?"

"I can be nice when I want to be."

"Are you still angry with me?"

The Gavin she knew and loved reappeared. His expression once more turning grim and threatening.

"I didn't say that."

"Then do me a favor, if you did take a nice pill, then take the whole bottle. I have Prime; I'll order you another."

CHAPTER NINE

The Mokes continued steadily on the paved trail around the front of island, winding into a turn to the side of the island that faced Clindale. The majestic palm trees on Sherguevil provided camouflage for the large building, airport, and numerous smaller buildings from the shores of Clindale.

As the Mokes veered onto another trail, they stopped beside an outcropping of small beachfront bungalows. Guessing this was where they would be quarantined, they got out of the Moke.

Ginny frowned as she stared across the water to Clindale Island. Something was different. Frowning, she took a step forward but was suddenly stopped.

"Mrs. James, Mr. James, you have been assigned this bungalow. The four of us will share the other three. I will be in the one closest to you. Two agents will take turns stationing themselves outside yours to ensure your safety."

"Thank-you."

Ginny walked beside Gavin toward the small bungalow that Agent Collins had indicted. Then any relief that she might have felt toward Agent Collins' assurance was dispelled when he held out a hand toward Gavin.

"I need to check your duffel bag. I'll return it to you when I bring Mrs. James' luggage."

Anticipating Gavin's refusal, Ginny was surprised when he held it out without a comment. He might not have said anything, but his disparaging features had Agent Collins walking toward the other agents who had remained by the Mokes. Ginny, relieved he had restrained himself from having a no-win argument with Collins, gladly walked into the bungalow when Gavin opened the door for her.

The bungalow was larger than it appeared outside. It had a medium-sized living room with a cream and white plush sofa, matching chair, and a low glass coffee table that was half the size of the sofa; the table was engraved with birds on the legs. Two ceiling fans made the room feel airy, and with the green palm trees and colorful succulents, the scenery from outside the open window gave the impression of relaxed comfort. A tall vase filled with tropical flowers was centered on a long marble console table one the wall with a television. To the side of the room was a small kitchenette with a bistro-style table with two white cushioned chairs and there was a basket filled with a variety of fresh fruits.

Ginny remained beside the door as Gavin went to the door next to the table and opened it, seeing from where she stood that it was a bedroom. When Gavin went inside, Ginny followed.

The bedroom was lovely with a grey, thickly padded headboard. The full bed took up half the room and was covered in a subdued coral-colored bedspread. The matching curtains framed the patio doors, which had been left open allowing in fresh air. To the left of the room was an en suite bathroom with a diamond-shaped mosaic tiles, as well as a large shower the size of the entire wall. Catty-corner with the shower sat a two-person soaking clawfoot tub that faced a window with a view of the sea. The room had an earthy, sensual appeal that had Ginny feeling uncomfortable.

Gavin was taking off his jacket to hang in the closet. Realizing she was completely alone with him, she decided to go back to the living room. She didn't make it, as his voice stopped her cold.

"Have a seat while I check the room out."

Nervous, Ginny went to sit on the end of the bed, watching Gavin as he took a lighter out of his jean pocket, then lifted the flame to the mirror that was over the dresser facing the bed.

"What are you doing?"

"Making sure it isn't a two-way mirror," Gavin explained, snapping the flame off before he went to the side of the mirror to run his hand along the frame. He removed each of the paintings on the wall, then stacked them inside the closet. He didn't stop there. After removing the paintings, he went through the bedroom, picking up a small, artificial plant and a small clock, placing them in the closet, also. Thinking he was done, Ginny couldn't understand what he was doing when he climbed on the bed to place a towel over the light fixture that was centered on the ceiling, giving the room a purple hue.

"Don't you think that's a little too much?"

Ginny really wished she kept the sarcastic thought to herself when Gavin jumped off the bed taking the comforter with him. He tucked it around the metal frame of the mirror above the dresser. Seemingly satisfied, he pulled the drapes closed over the balcony doors before going to the bedroom door. Her heart went to her throat when he turned the lock, then turned around to face her.

"My luggage should be here any moment," Ginny hastily reminded him.

"They won't be coming anytime soon."

"Why not? It's not that long of a drive from the airplane. Agent Collins already checked my luggage before I left."

Gavin's lips curled in a sinister smile. "I bet it only took him a couple of minutes, too."

"Yes. Why does that matter?"

"I can guarantee nothing will be coming through that door that Allerton doesn't want you or me to have that could be used as a weapon or a way to contact someone off the island. Do you have your cell phone?"

"Yes." Ginny took out her cell phone. "See? We can call—"

"How many bars do you have?"

Ginny pressed the button on her cell phone and then her heart sank with a *thud*. "None."

"Me neither."

"When did you check?"

"When we got out of the Moke."

"I didn't see you."

"You were too busy looking across the water at Clindale. Does it look like you remember?"

"No, and I don't know why …." Ginny still couldn't put her finger on the difference, but then she became sidetracked when Gavin started dragging the chair over to the bedroom door.

"What are you doing now? You need to unlock the door if you're going to put the chair in the living room."

Small tendrils of alarm began filtering through her bloodstream as Gavin tilted the chair back to brace the door. Her eyes widened when he started undressing. Once his shirt was removed, he began unbuckling his belt, sliding it loose from his jeans as he walked toward her.

"What are"—Ginny lowered her shrill voice—"*you doing?* If you lay a hand on me with that belt, I'll—"

"You'll what?" he goaded, moving closer to her with determined steps.

There was a time to reason, and then there was time to run. Now was the time to run.

Ginny hopped up from the bed, but before she could move a centimeter, Gavin reached his palm out to shove her back onto the bed. Finding herself on her back, Ginny didn't miss a beat, rolling onto her stomach and bringing her knees up to begin crawling over the mattress in the direction that was closest to the bathroom. If she could make it there, she could lock the door and reason with him from the other side.

The jerk let her make it halfway before she felt a loop of leather snag her ankle. Astounded, Ginny turned her head to look over her shoulder at him. "Gavin—"

A huff of air escaped her when he tightened his hand on the leather belt and gave a firm jerk, pulling her knees out from under her. With her fingers, she tried to hold onto the bed as he inexorably reeled her toward him, causing her dress to roll upward as she was tugged across the mattress.

"We should talk …." Desperate, Ginny tried to reason with him while being flipped over onto her back.

"You had all the time last night and this morning to talk."

Her awkward attempt to straighten her dress to a more modest covering was hampered by Gavin leaning over her, and it became more imperative to maintain a safe distance from him.

"I should have told you. I screwed up. *Umph.*"

Another huff of air escaped her when Gavin grabbed her upper arms, moving her higher up on the bed, and moving his massive body along with hers.

She brought her hands to his chest to push him away and was relieved when he raised up to sit on his knees between her splayed thighs, giving her breathing room.

"And you're angry."

"Angry doesn't begin to describe how I feel."

The man above her was as unapproachable as the first day she talked to him when he was working on his bike. There was no hint of warmth or understanding on his face.

She frowned up at him when he reached over and started taking her shoes off, throwing them onto the floor.

"Do you know how terrified I was when I read your letter, and the FBI told me you had already left Treepoint?"

"No." Ginny moistened her dry lips.

"I drove like a madman to get to your house, only for Silas to tell me you were coming here, to an island owned by a man who wants to see you dead."

If his intention was to make her regret the decisions she had made, he was achieving his goal.

"I'm *so* sorry."

"As bad as I took the letter, it didn't come close to how awful Trudy reacted."

Ginny turned her head on satin comforter, looking away from him. "Don't ...," she pleaded.

"She fucking started crying and screaming, Ginny. Your *pregnant* sister fucking loves you, and you fucking put me first instead of her in your lamebrained scheme."

She swiveled her head back to shout up at him. "I did what I had to do! What I should have done before, if I had been brave enough. I knew Trudy would be hurt when she found out what I had done, but I also know she has Dalton, Sex Piston, Killyama, Fat Louise, and Crazy Bitch, who will make sure she and the baby are okay."

"What about your brothers?"

"My brothers did fine without me for years after I was taken away. They'll be hurt, but they will move forward ... just as they did before."

"What about *me*? Did you think I would just go on my merry way?"

She had to close her eyes tightly to prevent herself from crying. "Truthfully, yes." Lifting her lashes, she held back the hurt she felt when he walked away without telling her about Taylor. "You don't need me any more than Trudy does. You have Viper, The Last Riders, *and* Taylor. I saved you from having to come back to tell me you and she are together again. I was never going to be more than second-best to you anyway. And," she sighed, releasing the last of her anger, "I'm kind of tired of being in that position. That's all I've ever been since I was three."

"What in the hell does that mean?"

"I was working for the club when Viper and The Last Riders believed you were dead. Did you know I wasn't even allowed to touch your jacket when it was hanging in the closet? You weren't an afterthought, even years after you were gone.

"Did you know your father became a drunk and was constantly in fights at Mick's? Viper would bring him into the diner a couple times a week just to make sure he was eating, and they would do nothing but talk about you, missing you, and how they would do things differently. They might have been surviving without you, yet each of them *clung* to their memories to still connect with you, as if you were still a part of their lives. Neither of them was willing to let you go entirely and to move on without you. You might not have been visibly present, yet you were *there*.

"The few times I was able to see Trudy, I had to pretend we were just casual acquaintances. The same with Sex Piston, Fat Louise, Killyama, and Crazy Bitch. We'd sneak around to hang out in a Lexington in hotel room. When I went back to Treepoint, and they returned to their families, do you think I was a blip on their radars?

"I love my brothers, but they have always had each other. My presence, or absence, has never made a difference in any of their lives, unlike you with Ton, Viper, and The Last Riders. Do you know why?"

"No."

"Because I was never *there*. I'm expendable. If I disappeared off the face of the Earth, I would be missed, but never to the extent you were. I'm tired of being invisible, to only being there when it's safe or if that person makes the effort, because I'm the one who initiated the contact. It's painful to just take up space in their lives and not be a part of the whole picture. I refuse to deny Trudy being my sister any longer, and I'll be damned if I have to pass my niece or nephew on the street and pretend I'm not their aunt. I need to be seen."

As hard as she tried, she couldn't prevent the tears from welling up in her eyes. "I just can't do it anymore. Please try to understand, Gavin. As much as I love everyone in my life, I just can't do it anymore. When I was singing with Mouth2Mouth, there wasn't a night that I didn't go out and think "Is someone going to recognize me? Will this be the moment Allerton finds me?" Every time I spoke with Hammer about contacting the FBI, he kept putting me off because I couldn't remember what I had taken or where I put it. You just gave me the excuse to do what I needed to do."

"*Thanks*," he said snidely.

Gavin started unbuttoning the front of her dress, exposing the light-cream-colored bra she wore underneath.

"What are you doing?" Ginny asked before she sniffed hard to clear her stuffy nose, intent on not breaking down in tears after baring her soul.

"I'm about to show you that you're not invisible."

"I don't want to have sex when you're angry with me." Ginny pulled the two parts of her dress back together to rebutton it. However, Gavin relentlessly lifted her and pulled it out from under her, leaving her in her bra and panties.

"Ginny, I'm so far beyond angry that it's not even in the ballpark of what I'm feeling."

"Then I definitely don't want to have sex."

"Good, I don't either," he said stonily.

If he didn't want to have sex, then why was he removing her clothes? Realization dawned on her when Ginny felt the belt being removed from her foot. Not liking the expression on his face, self-preservation kicked in and she tried to wiggle out from underneath him.

"Nope, you have a lesson to learn, and you're not getting off this bed until you learn it."

Unwisely, Ginny gave him a haughty tilt of her head to jut her chin out at him. "I really don't appreciate this caveman tactic."

She was given a second of satisfaction when Gavin leveraged his body to the side—until she found herself face-planted in the mattress as he flipped her over.

Turning her head to the side, she saw his hand come up. "You wouldn't dar—"

The smart smack to her bottom proved he would.

The thin material of her panties didn't provide any protection as she remained frozen in amazement that he had actually spanked her.

"Oh, hell no …." Ginny started to get to her knees, only to feel another hard smack on her bottom.

"You try to get up, I'm only going to give you more," he warned.

She screeched at him, "My daddy never even had the nerve to—"

"Yeah, well, he should have," he replied, spanking her again.

Red-hot pain flamed across her bottom.

"This is so childish! I will not be treated like this!"

Were the smacks getting harder? she wondered as another steak of fire lit upon on her ass.

"Did you yell at Silas when he spanked you for being on the roof?"

Another whack of his palm landed for her stubborn silence.

"Did you?"

"No," she mumbled. Pride gone out the door after the stinging in her bottom became more pronounced.

"Why not?" Gavin raised his palm from her bottom, keeping it poised in the air as he waited for her answer.

"I scared him."

The palm came down again, and Ginny let his hand connect two more times before turning to curl against his knees.

"I'm sorry! I didn't mean to scare you."

Giving a ragged groan, he lifted her to hold her alongside him. Ginny felt the rough texture of his breath against her throat.

"Gavin, do you *like* me?"

"I'm still deciding."

Her lips curled up in a smile. At least it wasn't a flat-out no. "I think you like me a little." She wanted to wrap her arms around his sides, but she kept her arms pressed between them, not wanting to ruin the tender moment by making him nauseous.

Loving Gavin did have its drawbacks, but damn, when he let his guard down, however small, it was like discovering a whole new universe.

"I'd like you a whole lot better if you quit dragging me into your lamebrained schemes."

"They aren't lamebrained," she denied, rubbing her cheek against his. "They are carefully thought out."

"Really?" Gavin pulled her away from him to give her a small shake. "If the hot cornbread fucking messes you have dragged me into, not once, not twice, but three times now, have been carefully thought out, then I won't live to see what the fuck you get into when you're flying by the seat of your pants."

"You're back to not liking me again, aren't you?" she asked dolefully.

"Ginny, I'm being serious."

"I know you are." Pulling herself out of his arms fully, she laid back down on the bed on her stomach. Then she reached behind herself to lightly spank her bottom, trying to lighten the mood. "Go ahead. I won't stop you. I deserve it."

Gavin frowned down at her, his eyes going half-mast while his expression turned icy. Then, twisting himself off the bed, he removed his pants and shoes.

Recognizing she was clearly out of her depths, Ginny took a gulp of air and started to roll from the bed. A hand on the small of her back prevented her from doing so.

"Oh no, you don't. Clearly, you haven't learned your lesson. Silas must have worn your ass out to keep you off the roof."

A spurt of relief poured through her when he flipped her onto her back.

Women who found it sexually exciting to be spanked was a mystery to her. Obviously, they had never been spanked by Gavin, or they had masochistic tendencies and needed counseling.

"Luckily for you, I never really believed corporal punishment works, especially when someone really wants to deny someone's authority over them."

Ginny really didn't like the direction Gavin was heading. "No one is the boss of me."

Gavin stared at her sternly. "I beg to differ."

Yeah, she really didn't like where this was going.

"Especially where your safety is concerned. You can be cute all day if you want to be, but when you think of placing yourself in front of me because you think I can't deal with the repercussions, then woman, you're barking up the wrong fucking tree."

Gavin moved to the end of the bed while keeping his hand on her abdomen to keep her in place.

"Gavin …" Her eyes widened when he got to his knees on the carpet, then started pulling her along the mattress toward him. "What are you doing?"

"Like I said, I'm not a fan of corporal punishment. Using pain to teach a lesson has proven ineffective. Studies have proven something else works better."

"Like what?"

"Pleasure. Have you ever heard the saying that too much of a good thing can be painful?"

Ginny frowned. "You mean the old saying: too much of a good thing can be bad."

Gavin gave her a smile that had her toes curling in fear. "No. I meant painful."

CHAPTER TEN

"There are different levels of pain," Reaper began his lesson. "Level one is cause—how you brought the pain on yourself."

"The pain on my bottom was caused by your hand. Cause and effect. You mean like that?"

"My *soul mate* would fight to stay with me," Reaper continued his lesson as if she hadn't spoken, pulling Ginny's panties off before placing a leg over each of his shoulders, effectively baring her pussy to him, "because *she* would know how badly it would hurt me to lose her." Throwing her own words back at her, he slid his hands to her hips, lifting her pussy to his mouth. "You fought for me to recognize we're soul mates. Then the day after I do, you desert me, leaving me to find out you aren't the woman I believed you to be." He moved his mouth to the side of her thigh, trailing his tongue upward. Reaper could feel her muscles trembling under his touch.

"I didn't do it to hurt you … I did it so you could have the life you wanted with Taylor," she gasped out when he blew on the curly hairs shielding the pink flesh he wanted to part to allow him access to the glistening fruit that was hidden beneath. "Two weeks ago, you wanted to die because you couldn't have the life you wanted with her."

Pressing her clit between his lips, he gently bit down, holding her still when Ginny would have twisted away. He scooted closer to the bed, releasing her clit to slide his tongue through the crease between her thigh and pelvis.

"Every time someone tries to make life easier for me, it goes to shit. I'm not a fucking cat or dog who needs someone to watch out for them. I've spent the better part of my life proving myself to Viper. I'll be damned if I spend the last part proving myself to you or anyone else."

"You don't have to prove anything to me!" Ginny tried to sit up, but Reaper moved his mouth back to her pussy and took her labia into his mouth.

"Stay still," he ordered, and she froze beneath his touch.

"You wouldn't hurt me."

"No, I wouldn't." Sliding his tongue between her petals, Reaper laved her opening before going to her other petal to lightly bite down. "*But* there are different levels of pain. Some pain can be sweet …." Releasing her labia, he tenderly licked the petal before sliding his mouth over her opening to the other and then he bit down again. Holding the pressure for a scant minute, he then repeated the motion until it became harder to hold Ginny still. "Which brings me to level two— awareness."

After the tenth time, he started stroking his tongue inside of her, each time going higher before retreating to one of her petals.

The night before, when they'd had sex, he had gone slow, aware it was her first time. Today, he had no such hesitation, raising her desire to a fever pitch without allowing her the climax she was straining to reach.

"Gavin …."

"Level three—acceptance."

She was no longer trying to twist away from his mouth, instead arching her hips higher to press her pussy against his mouth harder. Each time she did, he teasingly pulled away to press kisses along her thighs, only resuming when she laid still.

Losing track of time, Reaper was unaware of the room growing darker until he lifted his head when he felt Ginny quivering, showing she was about to come. Using his thumb, he pressed down on her clitoris, stopping her climax cold.

"Gavin … please!" she wailed, her hands falling to her sides to hit the mattress.

"How bad do you want to come?" he taunted.

"I get the message. I won't put myself in danger again!"

"That's good, but that's not the lesson I'm trying to teach you." Releasing her clitoris, he rose, ignoring stiff muscles as he leaned over her to place a hand on each side of her head.

"I'll never let you be the boss of me"—Ginny reached up to cup his cheeks softly, her touch having him turning his face—"any more than I would expect to be your boss. I do promise never to assume what is better or easier for you ever again. Will that work?"

Reaper let her turn his head to face her again. "Are you being sincere, or are you just jerking my chain?"

"I'm being sincere with you."

"Then why are you smiling?"

"Because I think you might like me more than a little."

He leaned onto his forearms and settled more of his weight on her. "I'm going to have to take your word for it then." He groaned into her neck.

"Why?"

He felt her laughing under his chest.

"Because my dick is about to break in two if I don't fuck you."

Ginny's thighs came up to circle his hips, positioning her opening so all he had to do was thrust inside. "Wild man, I've learned my lesson good enough for today. What more do you want?"

Nudging his cock to her entrance, Reaper bit back another groan as he easily slipped inside her warm passage. "There are two more levels I was going to teach you."

"You don't want to overload me on my first lesson, do you?" she pleaded.

"I want you, all of you—Ginny and Evangeline."

"You've always had both. I never hid the important parts of me from you. I wasn't able to." She sprayed her fingers out on his cheeks to touch his ears. "I'm glad you're wearing my present."

Reaper stopped moving over her, wanting to throw himself off her before it was too late. Emotions that he never felt before, even with Taylor, threatened to escape the iron control he kept on his heart. Ginny was the key to unlocking the man he used to be. He didn't want Gavin to come out. He had slipped out a few minutes the night before, but Reaper had been able to lock him back inside before he could gain a foothold in the light.

As if Ginny understood the battle going on inside of him, she lifted her head to kiss him, anchoring him back to the present.

"You stole my earring." Thrusting higher inside of her, he started fucking Ginny as she started rubbing the skin behind his ears.

"No, I didn't." Ginny removed one of her hands to sweep one side of her hair aside, showing the top portion of her ear. "I only borrowed it."

"Then, can I have it back?"

"No."

"I've never seen you wear an earring there before."

"I haven't."

"Then how?"

"I pierced it myself."

"You sterilized the needle?"

Ginny rolled her eyes at him. "Of course, I did. You think I'm an amateur?"

"You did the other two holes yourself?"

"Lisa wouldn't sign for me to get my ears pierced, so I did it myself. I almost pierced my nose just to get her really going, but I was too chicken."

"You really hate being told what to do, don't you?"

"Yes, it's gotten me in trouble more than once." Ginny circled her arms around his neck Mischievous eyes twinkled up at him, overlaid with the desire she was making no effort to hide. She was being adorable and helping him release the last of his anger. Ginny had learned too early in life how to wrap people around her little finger. Her confidence was coming back, and she had successfully skated around the worse of his punishment.

Reaper felt her pussy grip him tighter as she started to climax. Speeding up his piston-like movements, he didn't try to stop her this time, joining her in the tumultuous reckoning that he had started. Still anchored to her, he kept moving inside of her after they both had come.

"I need to shower." Giving him a pat on his shoulder, she wiggled her hips, trying to tell him that she wanted up.

"Level four—submission."

Ginny raised her head off the mattress to give him a dirty look.

"This level takes longer to master." Gavin pressed her back down into the mattress, grinning down at her ruthlessly. "Luckily for you, I'm a very patient teacher. We'll keep at it until you get it … just right."

CHAPTER ELEVEN

Reaper eased out from the covers to go to the bathroom, leaving an exhausted Ginny in the bed. Filling the clawfoot tub, he returned to the bedroom to remove the covers from Ginny.

"I was using that," she complained sleepily, not even opening her eyes.

"I need it."

"Then that's okay … Just ask next time." The woman would be sassy on her deathbed.

Arranging the covers in the bathroom, he returned once again to Ginny, lifting her into his arms.

"What…? I was sleeping," she said grumpily into his neck.

"You can go back to sleep after we take a bath."

Bending down, he placed her in the middle of the tub.

"Wait—I was going to take a shower."

"When? In your sleep?" Climbing in the tub behind her, he stretched his legs out on the outside of her with her butt pushed up against his pelvis. "Should I have asked first which one you would have preferred?"

Ginny rubbed her bare back against his chest. "Nah, this

is good." Reaching for the soap and washcloth, she began to languidly wash her legs.

"Gavin, why is our blanket over the bathroom mirror?"

"Insurance."

"Has anyone ever told you that you have a very suspicious nature?"

Taking the soapy washcloth from her, Reaper moved it between her breasts, meticulously cleaning each one with care. "It's one of the side effects of being kidnapped."

Ginny turned in the water. "You blame yourself for being kidnapped?"

"I made mistakes, and I paid the price. No one else to blame but myself."

Ginny angrily snatched the washcloth away from him to smack his chest with it. "I don't ever want to hear you blame yourself again! Ever!"

Reaper tried to take the washcloth back, and she just whacked him again.

"That's the most asinine thing I've heard out of your mouth! Memphis, Crash, Vincent, and Slate were the ones responsible. Don't you dare—"

"How do you know who was responsible for my kidnapping?" he asked, his eyes narrowed into slits.

She snapped her mouth shut.

"Killyama told you, didn't she? She told you all of it. You and all the rest of her friends." As rage and hurt bubbled inside of him, he placed his hands on the side of the tub to lever himself out.

"Sit back down!" she snarled up at him.

Reaper had no choice but to gingerly sit back down. *Why? Because she was clenching his hair in her fist.*

"Are you fucking crazy? What if I slipped?" he roared, trying to remove her hand.

"Boo-fucking-hoo. Listen up, wild man. Killyama and I

did talk, but that was after she swore me to secrecy. She jeopardized her marriage to tell me, and no, she didn't tell the other girls anything."

"She had no business telling you jack shit!"

Humiliated that she knew the facts of his kidnapping, he was glad that Gavin was still locked inside his heart. Reaper could bear the humiliation; he was stronger.

Deciding he wasn't ready to go bald, he made another attempt to get out of the tub, needing to get away from Ginny and the memories.

He tried to stand, only for Ginny to twist more fully in the water toward him. She moved her leg over his thighs to curl around his waist, laying more fully over him in the tub. His frantic effort had water splashing onto the tile below.

"Fucking move, Ginny, or so help me … *Ow!*" His ass settled back in the tub when the back of his head hit the stone and a hunk of his hair came out. "Are you fucking crazy? You nearly cracked my skull open!"

"Good, maybe then you would see some sense. Listen to me!" she screeched. "I was feeling sorry for myself after I came to the clubhouse the day after Trudy's wedding. I knew you wouldn't be coming to take me up on my offer for coffee. Killyama had come to the church to see me, to check up on me for Sex Piston … but really, it was for Trudy."

"What in the hell does this have to do with Killyama disclosing information that wasn't hers to share?"

"If you'll sit still and shut up, I'll tell you.

"Killyama, Sex Piston—all of the crew—knew I was waiting for my soul mate. When I saw you at the wedding, I didn't know who you were, so I asked Trudy, but she wouldn't tell me. Neither would Fat Louise or Crazy Bitch. Killyama was the only one who told me when I threatened to ask Shade."

Reaper went stone still. "Why wouldn't they want you to

find me?" Then, wounded by her disclosure, he started prying her hand out of his hair, uncaring about the resulting pain.

Ginny whacked his head back on the tub. Any idea Ginny was a gentle, compassionate woman who wouldn't hurt a flea was smashed to smithereens by the volatile spitfire that was determined to be heard. No way was he taking it her easy on her the next time she deserved a spanking. At this rate, though, he would be lucky to get out of the tub without a concussion.

"Are you trying to knock me unconscious so you can drown me?" he accused.

"That little love tap won't knock you unconscious," she scoffed, pressing her breasts against his chest to tilt him backward. "You actually have to ask why they didn't want me chasing after you?" Sliding her fingers from his hair, Ginny started rubbing the spot behind his ear enticingly. "They were protecting you. Each of them knows me well enough to know that I would drive you nuts with my belief we are soul mates. Hell, even Hammer and Jonas know I've been waiting for you. They also knew you wouldn't be receptive to the notion." Ginny huffed at him. "And boy, were they right."

Reaper shook his head at her, trying to stop her enticing movements. "That wasn't all they were worried about."

"Can you blame them?" Ginny settled her free hand on his chest to prop her chin. "You made no secret about Taylor breaking your heart and that you ignored any overture from any woman in town or at the club. They thought, if none of those women could get to first base with you, I didn't stand a chance. They were protecting my heart. They didn't think I had enough courage to fight for you."

He rolled his eyes at her and asked, "So where does the part about Memphis and Crash come in, then, huh?" Just mentioning their names felt like he was sitting in an ice bath.

"You don't believe me? They were right. Everyone felt I never made an attempt to heal the breach between me and my brothers, and I pretty much let crap slide unless it involved me taking up for someone else."

"For instance?" he growled.

"Anyway,"—Ginny went on as on as if he never spoke—"Trudy was on her honeymoon, so she asked Sex Piston, who was at work, so Sex Piston sent Killyama to see me."

"Do me a favor and just finish bashing my head in or *get to the fucking point!*"

"I will if you would try to be more patient."

Reaper spread his legs wider in the water so her ass would sink, and he could propel her off him without hurting her.

"I thought Killyama came to talk to me to put me off you. She wasn't. She wanted me to be prepared so I wouldn't fail."

"Fail at what?"

"At getting my man! She thought I would have better luck landing Kaden's jet than landing you without her help. She's probably right. I'm not the type of woman you usually go for. I love you, but I'm not eating lettuce three times a day just to get rid of my pouch."

What in fuck did this have to Killyama spilling his secrets?

Confusion had him wanting to get her back on track right *after* he assured her that her body was just fine the way it was.

"I don't fucking expect you …."

"You don't have to disagree with me to make me feel better. Killyama told me you work out a lot. We could be workout buddies. What do you think about that idea?"

Instead of trying to get away from her, Reaper pulled her closer to feel the softness of her body. "I think, Killyama's been running her mouth too damn much. I like the way your body feels." His hand swept over the contour of her stomach.

"She told you the details about my kidnapping ...," he prompted her along trying to get her back on track.

"Yes."

"What else did she tell you?"

"Are you going to try to jump out of the tub again if I tell you?"

"No."

"Then she told me everything she knows."

Reaper raised his eyes to the ceiling.

"I love you, Gavin."

"Don't feel sorry for me."

"I've *never, ever* felt sorry for you."

"I should have been the one to tell you in my own time, not Killyama."

"I'm glad she told me. After Killyama told me, I went to the lookout and cried. Not for you, but because I was so angry at God for not helping you. I haven't gone to church or prayed since, except the night you took off with Slate."

Reaper lowered his gaze back down to her.

"I consider myself a strong woman, but hearing the pain and torture you went through coming from your lips first-hand"—tears brimmed in Ginny's eyes—"I don't ... I'm not strong enough. Maybe if I didn't love you so much, I could ... but I'm weak where you're concerned."

Reaper slowly brought his hand to her cheek to wipe the tears away.

Ginny gave a hiccupping sound. "This is exactly what I didn't want to happen. I'm not crying because I feel sorry for you; I'm crying because when you hurt, I hurt."

"Stop crying, baby." His started stroking her shaking shoulders. "I'm not hurting now, so there's no need to cry."

"If God granted me one wish, I'd give up having you as my soul mate ... and die an old virgin, if He would just turn back time and undo your kidnapping."

"You wouldn't use that wish on your dad and sister?"

"No, I couldn't. Besides, it wouldn't work."

"Why not?"

Ginny sniffed back her tears, then said the most beautiful thing that anyone had ever said to him.

"Because you're all I've ever wished for."

CHAPTER TWELVE

Rolling over, Reaper felt an empty space next to him on the bed. Reaching out for Ginny to pull her closer to him, he opened his eyes to find an empty spot on the mattress.

Sitting up, he looked around the room, seeing the chair was still under the doorknob. He slung the covers aside and got out of bed to find the bathroom was empty as well. Going back to the bedroom, he saw the curtains fluttering from the wind in front of the patio door.

Sliding the curtain aside, Reaper saw Ginny staring out at the ocean, lost in her own thoughts. He then found his jeans laying on the floor and slipped them on before going outside barefoot to stand behind her.

"I told you not to leave my side."

"Look around. Each bungalow has its own patio."

Deciding it would be useless to rebuke her when it was his fault she'd been able to slip out while he was sleeping, he took a casual look around, taking in their surroundings.

"I didn't wake up when you got out of bed."

"You were exhausted. Teaching takes a lot of energy," she quipped without turning around to face him.

Moving in front of her, Reaper swept a swathe of her hair behind her ear at the despondent tilt of her lips. "What were you doing out here?"

"Talking to Silas."

"Can he hear you?" The ridiculousness of his query should have raised alarm bells. However, his new normal with Ginny only awoke curiosity.

"Barely. We're so far away it's like talking through a muted phone line."

"At least he knows you're all right." Silas would be able to reassure Viper and the brothers that he was safe, too. He had checked his cell phone several times last night. It was as dead as a doornail without the signal.

"That we both are," she corrected. "Silas cares about you a great deal."

Once upon a time, Reaper would have taken what Ginny said at face value, but the more time he spent with her, he had come to the conclusion that, while she'd discuss her feelings for him at the drop of a hat or answer any question, she wouldn't volunteer information about herself or what was troubling her, using small talk to defer attention away from herself.

It was an unusual occurrence for him. The women he'd been involved with before wanted a sounding board. Hell, even the men he knew wanted someone they could talk personal shit with, either a friend or an intimate partner. As far as he could tell, Ginny didn't. Unless it was T.A., but Reaper didn't think she'd even confided in her sister. T.A. had been too upset at Ginny returning to Clindale without her knowledge. Was it Hammer? He brokered the deal with the FBI and was the one she wanted to accompany her. There was only way to find out.

"What's your relationship with Hammer?" Reaper watched her reaction like a hawk, unaware his breathing had stopped.

Ginny switched her gaze from the ocean to his. "Hammer and I don't have a relationship."

His breathing returned to normal, whereas his jealousy remained. "Then why ask him to come with you? Why not someone else?"

"I didn't exactly ask him. Hammer *told* me he was coming, and I only agreed when he swore to me that, if it anything happened, he would put his welfare first."

"He agreed to that shit?"

"I didn't leave him a choice," she said firmly.

"You didn't make me promise anything." Reaper wasn't sure if he should be angry at the revelation or not, but he knew one thing; his jealousy grew deeper. He should be happy Ginny hadn't tried to continue to protect him, but did that imply she didn't care about him as much as did Hammer?

"I made that a condition with Hammer, and if he was going to join me he had to agree; otherwise, I would have shut him out of the plan with the FBI altogether. I can't use the same leverage with you."

"You could have told the FBI"—Reaper dropped his voice low so only she could hear—"the truth about our marriage. They could have called in manpower to stop me."

"Do you wish I had?" she challenged him, turning it around to question his feelings.

"I wouldn't have let you set a foot on the plane without me."

"You couldn't have stopped me." Ginny folded her arms over her chest as if she were cold.

"I could have delayed it long enough for Diamond to get

there. She would have made mincemeat of the deal you arranged."

"I'm surprised you didn't bring her with you and that you didn't drag me back to Treepoint."

"It was a consideration," he admitted.

"Why didn't you?"

"Because you didn't use your friendship with Sex Piston to involve her sister Diamond, so I figured you had an important reason to want to come back to Clindale."

"Trudy and Sex Piston both have tried to convince me to ask Diamond for help."

"Why haven't you?"

"I knew I'd be exposing myself, which then opens the chance of Trudy, Diamond, and Sex Piston getting hurt. It wasn't worth the risk."

"If it wasn't for me, you would've never admitted to being Evangeline, would you've?"

"It was time."

"Because T.A.'s pregnant?"

"Yes. T.A. and I grew up pretending we didn't know each other. I can't pretend my niece or nephew isn't related to me. I can't erase the past, but I can attempt to move forward with all my cards on the table."

"Are *all* your cards on the table?"

"Yes."

"Sweetie, Silas should have told you to never play your cards."

"Don't talk down to me." The no-nonsense Ginny had come out to play.

Reaper had to give her credit. Ginny had the ability to come across as easygoing, until her anger or frustration dropped her guard.

"I wasn't talking down to you."

"You could have fooled me. I don't like to be called *sweetie*, especially when you think I've done something you don't like."

"You want to bust my nuts? Go ahead. But be prepared. If you want to talk like you have game, you fucking better be prepared to have game."

"What does that mean?"

"It means that I won't watch what I say, especially when you do something stupid as shit."

Ginny made a comical face at him. "Since when have you ever held back what you wanted to say to me? If you want to call me the B word, then call me the B word. I'd rather be called a bitch than sweetie."

"The B word wasn't what I was trying to avoid. Try reckless and irresponsible."

Ginny winced as if he'd struck her, but Reaper was ruthless.

"And I won't be the only one saying the same thing. Sex Piston and Dalton will agree when you come back. T.A.—"

"Stop, Gavin." Ginny buried her face in her hands. "I can't do what I need to do if I'm worried about Trudy."

Taking the opening he finally found, Reaper moved in before she could regroup. "What do you need to do?"

"I have to defeat the monster."

"Allerton is the monster?"

"Yes."

"How do you plan to beat him?"

"I have to turn the table on him, and make sure he can't hurt anyone else."

Reaper reached out to pull her hands away from her face so he could see her. He expected to see tears, but what he saw shook him to his core.

Fear.

He had become intimately familiar with that emotion,

even before his kidnapping, back when he had served overseas in war zones.

Reaper tried not to think of the terror-stricken people he'd come into contact with during his time in service. Many were either running or in hiding when his company moved in, despite the fact the soldiers sought to help.

What stuck out the most was that Ginny wasn't hiding. She made herself a visible target in Allerton's scope.

"Who has he hurt?"

She didn't try to pull away from his touch. Instead, Ginny swayed toward him.

Loosening his hold on her hands, Reaper gathered her shaking body closer, giving Ginny the heat of his body.

"You wouldn't believe me if I told you," she whispered so low that he had to tilt his head down to hear her.

"Try me."

"He hurts *thousands* of people every minute of every day."

"That's a tall order for a man who is retired and lives like a recluse on a private island without any internet."

"Allerton wants to have the entire world at his feet, and he has enough money and power to accomplish his goal."

Reaper took what she said with more than a grain of salt. "No man I know of has that type of power. But if that's true, how in the fuck do you think you can be the one to stop him?"

"I have to find something that will expose him and cohort of others who have been helping him."

That revelation stopped any doubt he had. It explained why Ginny and T.A. were so frightened, and why Hammer pulled himself back into something when he'd just retired from active duty as a Ranger. Hammer believed Ginny was in danger.

"Is this something what you took off the boat when you were three years old?"

Reaper felt her shudder in his arms.

"What did you steal?"

"I don't remember."

"Did you hide whatever it was on Clindale?"

She nodded against his shoulder.

"I think so."

"Is it still there?"

"I don't know," she murmured.

"Is there anything you do know for sure?"

"I know I'm going to find it."

"And destroy Allerton?" Reaper asked, wanting confirmation on the few details she told him.

"Yes."

"Swee—" Reaper started over when she lifted her head from his shoulder. "Ginny, you're fucking bonkers. You started all of this without having what you need to make the plan a success, and you have no idea where it is ... or what it is?"

Ginny smiled happily with his understanding of her bizarre plan. "Exactly."

"We're in trouble."

CHAPTER THIRTEEN

Reaper found himself grasping at thin air when Ginny tore herself out of his arms.

"Are you making fun of me?"

"Does it look like I'm laughing?" Wanting to curse a blue streak would have been a more accurate description of what he was feeling.

Taking two long strides before she could escape inside the bungalow and ignoring her attempts to dodge his arms, Reaper enclosed her in a hug while pinning her arms to her sides. Then lowering his head to her ear, he whispered, "Chill. I believe you. Look around you, little thief. This might be a private patio, but we're being watched." Nuzzling the side of her jaw, he used his chin to turn her head in the direction he wanted. At her withdrawn breath, he nuzzled her jaw higher. "Two at your left and three on your right."

Wanting to keep the appearance of a loving couple to spying eyes, Reaper let her spin in his arms when she sighted the soldiers.

"They were watching me."

"Yes, they want to make sure you don't move without their notice."

"It could also be they're concerned about us sneaking out while we're in quarantine."

"You can think that, if that makes you feel better," he said, reserving the right to keep his own opinion.

"It doesn't."

Rubbing her back comfortingly, Reaper waited for her to stop trembling.

"You think they're listening, too?"

Nodding, he remained silent.

"I should have never let you come."

Reaper heard the despair in her whisper.

"Where's all the anger you had a minute ago?" he asked, trying to get her spark back.

"I lost it when I saw the guns they're holding."

"They're assault rifles. Allerton isn't playing any games."

"No, he isn't. I don't want to do this anymore."

"It's a little late for both of us. Do you trust me, Ginny?"

She didn't hesitate. "Yes, I do."

"Then quit worrying. I'm not going to let them hurt you. Was there anything else in your plan?"

"I was going to find what I had stolen and make him leave me alone."

He had hoped for a better plan, something he could work with. Neither was he was reassured by the simplicity of the plan.

"Did you explain your plan to Hammer?"

"He told me it wasn't much of a plan … Will you quit laughing at me?"

He could either laugh or cry. Laughter won. Something wasn't ringing true for him, however. Hammer and Jonas had been the ones who uncovered his kidnapping. Hammer going along with this asinine plan without a detailed way to accomplish the objective was blowing his fucking mind.

Pulling out of his arms, she placed her hands on her hips defiantly. "I'm open to suggestions."

"Let's go inside and see what food is in the cabinets. I'm starving," he said in a normal tone of voice. Indicating for her to go first, Reaper then followed closely on her heels back into the bedroom.

After removing barricade from the door, Ginny noticed a blinking light on the phone in the small sitting area. She listened to the message, then started for the door. "They placed our luggage outside the door."

"I'll get them," Reaper told her as he went to the door. Looking through the peephole, he didn't see anyone. Opening the door, he brought his duffle bag and Ginny's suitcase inside before closing the door.

"Don't touch anything," he said when he saw Ginny was going through the refrigerator.

"I'm hungry," she said, taking her head out of the fridge.

"I am, too. Let me see what we have to work with." Moving around her, Reaper opened a few cabinets, finding dishes in one and nothing in the others. Going to the refrigerator next, he found neatly packaged microwavable meals.

Could one fucking thing work in his favor? he thought sarcastically. He hated to be at a disadvantage; they were solely dependent on what Allerton gave them.

Reaper moved to the side of the fridge. "Pick what you want, and I'll heat it up."

Ginny immediately picked out a croissant with turkey sausage.

Taking it from her, Reaper chose the same thing for himself, then took out the carton of orange juice before closing the door.

Grabbing a plate from the cabinet, he heated both croissants and poured them both a glass of the juice. Instead of giving her a glass, he took a small sip from his.

Giving him a strange glance, Ginny reached for hers, but Reaper moved it across the counter, out of her reach.

"Wait a few minutes."

Ginny cocked her head to the side with curiosity. "Why?"

"I want to wait until I'm sure it isn't laced." Reaper removed the croissants from the microwave. "A sedative or—"

"Pois ... on?" Her breath hitched on the word.

"Ginny, I'm just trying to be cautious." Reassured the orange juice was fine, he scooted the glass over to her.

"Shouldn't I be the one doing the taste testing? If something happens to you, what am I supposed to do? Carry your big body over my shoulder and take off?"

Taking a bite of the croissant sandwich, Reaper watched her refuse to drink her juice. "What did you plan to do if something happened to Hammer?"

"I would have told them I wouldn't give or tell Allerton what I stole."

He took another bite of his sandwich. "Then stick to that plan." He decided not to disclose that if the soldiers in Allerton's employment were determined to get information, they wouldn't go about it in a particularly gentle fashion.

"Okay, but I still think it makes more sense for me to do the taste testing."

Finishing his sandwich and juice off, he then carried the duffel bag to the table. He rummaged through what Viper had packed for him to see if anything had been removed.

"Gavin?"

"Hmm ...?"

"Why aren't you saying anything?"

"Because you're right. They won't lethally dose the food if they want information from you."

"Then …?"

Reaper spared her a brief glance as he removed the clothes from his duffel to get access to the hidden compartments that Razer had made when he designed the bag. "Drop it. Eat your breakfast; it's getting cold."

Ginny carried her plate and juice over to the table. "You can be very frustrating sometimes, Gavin."

"Same."

Choosing a clean pair of jeans, a T-shirt, and a pair of grey boxer briefs from the now empty duffle bag, he rose from the table. "I'm going to take a quick shower. If someone knocks on the door, come and get me."

Ginny gave him a mocking salute. "Yes, sir."

Pausing, he speared his hand through her hair to tilt her head backward. "Remind me to spank you when we go to bed."

"Dream on, wild man." Taking the last bite of her sandwich, she lightly waved her hand off as if brushing what he said away.

"Are you sure you've only been spanked once in your life?"

"Twice … after last night," she contradicted him.

The few taps he had given her wouldn't be considered a true spanking in any universe, other than the one in Ginny's mind.

Bending down, he pressed a hard kiss to her lips, but Ginny wasn't in a kissing mood and attempted to pull her mouth away. Forestalling her, he used his tongue to part her lips, delving inside to give her something else to think about besides her upcoming spanking.

He gave her a gloating smile when he broke off the kiss. "I'll be back in ten."

"Take your time."

"Tired of me already?" he quipped.

"I could never get tired of you."

The sincerity in her comment had him clutching her hair in his fist, straining her neck back farther. He had been told that by too many women to count, but it was the first time he fucking believed it.

"Gavin?" Ginny wrapped her fingers around his wrist but didn't try to pull out of his grasp.

"Ginny, don't ever try to play me."

"I won't."

"I'm not happy you didn't confide in me about being Evangeline and T.A.'s sister. I'm giving you the benefit of the doubt when I *swore* never to do that shit again. You have no idea what I'm capable of. If I find out you're blowing wind up my ass—"

"I'm not. I swear on my father's grave I would never lie about my feelings for you. Ever. At different times, I might not have been able to tell you the full truth about some things, but never, at any point, have I lied to you about how I feel about you."

Satisfied, he released her hair and started to let his hand drop, but Ginny retained her hold on his wrist.

"You like me more than a little, don't you?"

He wasn't ready to discuss his feelings with her, despite the moment of clarity he had when flying out of Treepoint. He had put his ring on a woman's finger before, called a woman his, but he had never felt as vulnerable as he did with Ginny. Reaper no longer had a heart to place in a woman's hands again, and the vulnerability she arose in him was akin to Achilles wearing boots had he been forewarned about his death. Taylor hadn't exactly betrayed him. She might not have waited for him, but he didn't believe she fucked around on him while they had been together. Even if she had, he didn't think it would have been a deal breaker from marrying her. Sexual faithfulness had never been at the top of his priority list when he decided to get married. Rider and he had been the ones to come up with the club's rules deciding on how women earned votes to become members. They'd been full of youthful arrogance and fresh out of the service, wanting a smorgasbord of pussy rather than having a monogamous relationship.

Reaper jerked his wrist free. "I'm going to get that shower."

"Go ahead. I'll take mine when you're finished." Her back was ramrod straight when she got up to carry her dishes to the sink. "Oh … Gavin, just so you know, and you can't say this is coming out of the blue … my love for you will never be shaken. However, you can only shake a tree so long before it stops giving fruit."

Reaper turned on his heel. "What in the fuck does that mean?"

A hurt look crossed her face. "To me, it's self-explanatory. You can figure it out for yourself since you don't want to answer my question," she snapped.

"Then, since it doesn't make any sense to me, and probably never will—as I will never be able to figure out the way your minds works—I'll just wait until you decide to explain it to me."

"Then I hope that day never comes, because if it does, it won't matter to me anymore."

Inwardly cursing to himself as he went into the bedroom, he strode to the closet instead of the bathroom. Going inside and shutting the door, he dropped the contents in his hands to the floor, then knelt and blindly began skillfully dismantling the duffle bag. He'd expected his things would be searched, and he hadn't been disappointed. Several items had been removed, but he was hoping the fuckers hadn't figured out the hidden features that Razer incorporated in the bag.

The bag had one long strap and two handles, allowing for a shoulder or a handheld carry.

Twisting one of the handles, he rotated it in a series of movements to open it. His heart started beating faster as he unscrewed the endcap. Pressing the button, he felt inside and the other end of the handle lit up. Putting the uniquely designed flashlight in his mouth, he quickly detached the other handle. Unscrewing one end, he held his hand out to catch the contents from within. One of the items was a tiny vial of pills used to counter the effects of a knock-out drug, then shaking the tube again a slender signal detector that was the size of his pinkie slid out. The signal detector was key; it would work to detect bugs as well as send an SOS beacon if necessary.

Next time he saw Razer, he was going to kiss him for his inventiveness. The bag had been designed to get several tiny items to go undetected through X-ray machines. He needed every tool he could find to keep Ginny safe.

Concealing the items in the clothes, Reaper turned the flashlight off before hiding it and stepping out of the closet to go into the bathroom.

Taking a shower, he then dried off before getting dressed and began sweeping the room for bugs with the wireless signal detector. When he was finished, Reaper hung the towel over the nozzle of the shower as he debated his next move. There weren't many options, if any at all. The number of bugs revealed every action they made.

He had a hard choice to make. Either he sent out an SOS to get Ginny and him out of there, or he could wait and give her the opportunity to accomplish the harebrained goal she set for herself. It was almost nil she would remember what she had stolen or where it was. Was he willing to sacrifice her life ... or his, if her plan ended up in the crapper?

Placing his hands on the vanity, he stared down reflectively. Whatever the decision, it needed to be made before he walked out that bathroom door. No amount of should'ves or would'ves had erased the years he had been kidnapped.

The old Gavin would have told Ginny it was a no-win mission and given her a choice of leaving or staying. Reaper wanted to withdraw to safer ground, regardless of what Ginny wanted. His mind flipped back and forth. It boiled down to whether he had the same capacity to be the soldier he once was. Was he as good, or had he lost that cutting edge that had made him such a formidable opponent?

Straightening his back, Reaper placed the signal detector back in his pocket before removing the blanket from the mirror. Then, opening a prepacked toothbrush and toothpaste, he started brushing his teeth. Tearing open the plastic-wrapped cup, he filled it with water, then swirled the water around his mouth. Instead of spitting into the sink, he spat out toward the mirror.

Satisfied the message would be received the way it was meant, he turned the water off and left the bathroom.

For better or worse, he'd made his decision.

CHAPTER FOURTEEN

"He knows they're being watched."

"What gave you that impression? The towels and blankets being placed over most of the cameras or him spitting on the mirror?" Gabriel Allerton ridiculed the man standing next to him as they continued watching the live feed from the computer on his desk.

"Sorry, sir. Can I get you anything else?"

"No, I'll call you when I want something." Gabriel kept his computer screen the center of his attention as Ethan left the room.

"Do you want me to leave?"

Gabriel raised his eyes to Agent Collins, who looked as if he wanted nothing more than to leave as quickly as Ethan. "Did I tell you to?"

"No."

"Then no, I don't want you to leave."

Unlike his assistant, Agent Collins turned an uncomfortable shade of puce. Gabriel didn't care that the man took umbrage at the reprimand. "I told you not to give them their luggage."

"Why? Your men were the ones who checked them. Everything was taken but their clothes."

"Hmm … Then why did Mr. James go into the closet before he took his shower?"

"I don't know. Maybe he wanted to jerk off without the wifey seeing him."

Gabriel raised his piercing eyes from the computer. "They've been fucking for the last nine hours. I doubt jerking off is why he needed that form of privacy."

Collins gave him a caustic shrug. "Then call and ask him. You should have informed me that their status as prisoners was not a secret."

"I don't have to do anything; that's what I'm paying you for."

"Mr. James wasn't calculated into the price I quoted you. If he had been, my price would have doubled."

"Are you raising your price? I would hate to misconstrue your meaning, considering you were recommended for the job from your previous employer, and I haven't used you before. Increasing your rate, when Mr. James now has a signal detector and has found my hidden devices, isn't advisable at this point."

"I'm not asking for more money," Collins hastily backtracked. "I'm merely saying we'll have to be more discreet in how we handle the situation with Evangeline now that we know they're married."

"They aren't any more married than I am."

"The certificate is legit. My director approved Mr. James accompanying his wife."

"The director of the FBI isn't on my payroll. You are." The undercurrent of his statement expressed his disapproval of the agent's job performance. "I'm checking into the legality of their marriage. Until then, all you have to do is keep them contained to the area I designated for them."

"Then what?"

"Arrangements will be made for Mr. James to be flown out, accompanied by your three trainees, if I find out the marriage certificate was fabricated."

"What if they are married?"

"Then I will continue as I would have if her other companion had arrived. Four more casualties of the virus, while tragic, are explainable."

"What's the difference? Both men are highly skilled in combat and training."

Gabriel rubbed the side of his forehead, trying to find patience. "The difference being, it would have been much easier to make Hammer disappear than Gavin James. Hammer has no close relatives, and he's recently retired from the service. The only ones who'd miss him are his partner and the woman they share a relationship with. The pair could easily be dealt with, unlike Gavin who has several groups of men who will demand an explanation after his disappearance."

"They won't want an explanation; they'll be out for blood if anything happens to him."

"Precisely. While Mr. James' affiliations are of no concern to me, there is no reason to become a source of their animosity unless I am given no choice. The legitimacy of their marriage is being investigated. Until then, all you have to do is keep them contained. Are you able to accomplish that task?"

"Of course."

"Very well."

When Collins remained unmoving, Gabriel pointedly flicked his eyes toward the door. "You may leave."

The FBI agent sank further below the expectations Allerton already had for the Federal Bureau of Investigations. Normally, he would never have hired someone as incompetent as Agent Collins. However in this situation, it worked to his advantage.

The door hadn't even closed behind Collins before his assistant walked back inside.

"Desmond Beck is on line two."

Gabriel waved Ethan back out as he reached for the phone, waiting for the door to close before he pushed the flashing button. "Desmond, how are you?" Gabriel deliberately infused warmth into his voice greeting one of his more generous donors.

"Doing well. How about you?"

"Depends on why you're calling." Leaning back casually on his highbacked leather chair, he kept monitoring the computer as he talked. "Are you ready to give me a chance to even the score? I'm getting tired of you bragging to all our friends about how you beat me at that last round of golf."

"Cut it out, Gabriel. We hate golf, and neither of us can name one person we call a friend, even if our lives depended on it."

Gabriel's caution eased slightly, but not enough to chance lowering the guard he placed on every word when he talked to any of his benefactors over the phone, though he was sufficiently confident Desmond's line wasn't being monitored. "Too true. What can I do for you today?"

"It's not what you can do for me, but what I can do for you," Desmond replied curtly. "Whatever spill you're trying to clean up, let it go. You're just going to make it worse and get the rest of us buried next to you." Desmond was a man of few words and got right to the point.

"And exactly how are you aware of my endeavors?" Gabriel replied just as brusquely.

"One of my men is married to the sister of a Last Rider."

"Which man?"

"Jackal."

"I meant which Last Rider is her brother?"

"Gabriel …" Desmond's voice took on a cutting edge. "We've never played games with each other; don't start now. *You* don't make moves unless you know exactly who you're up against. That's why our business together has been so profitable, which is the only reason I'm giving you this suggestion. Send Ginny and Gavin home, plain and simple."

"I'm afraid I can't do that. Nothing about this situation is plain or simple. I'm rather busy at this moment, Desmond. We can talk later."

"If your time is so precious, then I'm coming there. I am not going to be caught up in this without having a safe way out."

"Forgive me if I doubt your motives for coming for a visit. I won't tolerate any interference from you, Desmond."

"When have I ever interfered? I prefer a safe place to stay, where I don't have to worry about getting my throat slit while I'm sleeping."

"You have several estates to choose from that can offer you the same protection."

"That just shows me how much you're underestimating The Last Riders and the Predators."

Being on the other end of the icy disdain, which Desmond was famous for in their elite circle, irked him. Nevertheless, Gabriel took into account the profitable arrangements Beck Industries had at their disposal. Profitable arrangements that Gabriel had been working unscrupulously to have under his own control.

"Very well. Can you arrange for your own transportation, or do you need me to send my private jet?"

"Send yours. I don't want my men to know I'm leaving. Text me when I need to be at the airport."

"I will. And Desmond, please remember what I said about interference. You're really one of the few who doesn't bore me to tears. However, I won't take that into consideration if I have to end our association."

"I understand."

"I hope you do. Good-bye."

Desmond disconnected the call, placing his cell phone on his desk. "Satisfied? Allerton agreed to let me come, but it wasn't without him giving me a stern warning about any interference."

Waving away the curling cigar smoke, Desmond poured himself a glass of brandy before taking the chair next to his former partner. "Must you smoke in my office? The smell will linger in my books."

King pulled his cigar away from his mouth to stare at the glowing tip. "Do you know how long it has been since I have been able to enjoy a good glass of brandy and cigar at the same time?"

"Being a father and being married do have their pitfalls."

"Yes, they do."

"Any regrets?" Desmond asked him curiously.

"No, not one."

"I would count the lack of cigars and brandy as two."

"Evie doesn't make me give them up; it was my decision to make. It doesn't mean I can't enjoy them when the mood strikes me."

"My phone call didn't lighten your mood?"

"Not unless I misunderstood and Allerton is sending Reaper and Ginny back?" King's keen gaze cut through the curling smoke.

"You didn't misunderstand." Desmond gently swirled the brandy in his glass. "I hate to be the bearer of bad news, but whatever he has in store for Ginny and Gavin won't be swayed with my presence on the island, which is what I told you when showed up on my doorstep."

"Gabriel Allerton was raised with a golden spoon in his mouth. He's never had to be afraid of his own protection a day in his life. You're going to send a message that, if anything happens to Gavin and Ginny, there won't be a rock he can hide under."

"Allerton only hires the best. Those who fail to live up to his expectations are never heard from again," Desmond countered. "He is welcome around the globe." He took a sip of his brandy before getting up to refill King's glass. "Allerton only hires the best for his security personnel and has a jet at his disposal. Whatever threat comes his way will be met with force from whichever country he flees to."

"No rock will be able to hide him," King reiterated his words, glancing up as his glass was refilled. "Or you."

Desmond placed the brandy bottle back on the mahogany sideboard. "Are you *threatening* me, King?"

King placed the cigar between his teeth to gently cup the brandy glass. "We go back a long way, Desmond. But if anything happens to Ginny and Reaper, I won't protect you. I walked away from having a family once, and it nearly destroyed my most precious possession. A Last Rider saved her, made her whole again. So, no, I won't step in. I will be right with them, seeking revenge. Unlike Allerton, I wasn't raised with a golden spoon in my mouth. I can go back to using plastic—they both accomplish the same end."

Desmond stiffened, turning back to him. "Using plastic …? That wasn't just a figure of speech, was it?"

"I know where you've buried the bodies on the road to your success. I would hate to use that knowledge against you, but I will if I have to."

"The Predators would never turn against me—"

"Look out the window."

Desmond went to the window beside the sideboard.

"The Predators might work for you, but they are *loyal* to me," King stated implicitly.

"I'm aware. I should have replaced them with those who wouldn't have divided loyalties," Desmond ruminated out loud.

"Ice and Jackal would have slit your throat if you tried to replace the Predators with new blood."

"What's the difference between then and now? My neck is still on the chopping block."

"The difference is you can help Reaper and Ginny. You will also have both the Predators' and The Last Riders' gratitude. That, my old buddy, is worth more gold than Allerton will ever give you."

"My relationship with Allerton goes beyond money."

"Are the connections he provides worth your life?"

Desmond leaned a hand on the side of the windowsill, staring out at Ice and Jackal standing on his front lawn with twenty or so men sitting on their bikes in the private driveway behind them. The high, imposing gates blocking the entrance had a guard station with two men at all times. Desmond was disgusted with his men.

"Allerton has a wide circle of influence. The Predators may slit my throat, but Allerton can make me wish I was dead before he pulls the plug. Like I said before, if my neck is on the chopping block, does it really matter who is responsible?"

"You know as well as I do," King said uncompromisingly from his chair, "that when it comes down to a life-or-death situation, the only option left is to choose the side that will fight dirtier."

"Are The Last Riders prepared for the havoc Allerton can wreck on their lives?"

"They are."

Desmond went to the cigar box on his desk, opening it to choose one. Taking a cutter inside the box, he snipped one end, then reached for an oversized lighter to hold the cigar over the flame. "And you're willing to sacrifice your new family for them?"

"They are a part of my family."

The silent man who had been monitoring the conversation between King and him spoke for the first time. "Take this. Keep it with you the entire time."

Desmond placed the cigar between his lips to take what looked like a stubby cell phone. Having worked with dog-eat-dog thugs for more years than he wanted to count, the man who accompanied King chilled him to the bone.

"Allerton will have my suitcases and me searched when I arrive at the plane. How am I supposed to get this by his security?"

King grinned. "Be inventive."

Desmond didn't find anything amusing with the situation. Visions of the amount of money he imagined raking in from Allerton's greedy manipulations would no longer be possible unless he was able to convince him to return Ginny and Reaper. Desmond didn't hold out hope. However, he had been in dicey situations before and managed to turn the cards over in his favor.

"Seeing the Predators are no longer following my orders, send them away. They've made their point." Leaning back on his desk, he crossed one foot over the other. "Gabriel will send someone on his payroll to make sure I arrive at the airport alone and to ensure no one will be able to sneak on board."

King rose from the chair to go to the window. Moving the curtain aside, he gave Ice a flick of his hand.

Soon, loud motorcycles could be heard leaving from inside the room.

"Feel free to leave with them," he encouraged.

"Wanting to get rid of us so you can disappear? Allerton isn't the only one who has several places to hide."

King's laconic reply had Desmond grinning at him. "I admit I thought about it," he conceded. "Then I decided it didn't benefit me."

"Why not?"

"Because of you, King. You've never been on the losing side."

CHAPTER FIFTEEN

Ginny watched Gavin leave the room, her bravado deserting her without his presence.

Feeling alone even with him in the next room, she folded her arms over her chest. Trudy had been right; Gavin was never going to love her the way he had Taylor. Her sister tried to spare her that pain, but Ginny held both arms open for him to walk inside and she gave him her heart.

"He never asked for your love." Ginny inwardly defended Gavin from her rising disappointment at his failure to admit any feelings for her.

At first, it was like a needle, or like a splinter trapped under her skin, but each day, his lack of giving any positive feedback when she shared her feelings with him grew worse until she felt as if a knife was being plunged into her heart. She thought any emotion he gave her would be enough; however, making love with him had changed her. She wanted more.

"He never promised you more," she reproached herself.

The first night they made love had been miraculous. It was a springboard to her burgeoning hopes. The next morning, she'd gone through a setback when he hadn't discussed Taylor. Then, when he showed up at the airport with proof of a marriage that didn't exist, her hopes rose again, and they had risen even higher yesterday. But having sex with Gavin last night had been different than the first time. What little piece of himself he gave her the last night he retrenched in the bright light of today. Considering her deception, she should have expected it, but it still hurt that he thought she might be playing him to suit her own needs.

Her chaotic thoughts had her uncrossing her arms to link her hands together as if to pray. Then she rubbed her knuckles back and forth over her forehead.

Whereas Trudy had to live with the ghost of Dalton's previous wife, Oceane wasn't coming back to take Dalton away. Taylor would always be one step away, anytime she wanted to place herself back in Gavin's life. His determined presence here could be solely a simple act of gratitude for taking the heat off The Last Riders. She risked her life for Gavin's freedom, and he knew it. If they were lucky enough to return to their normal lives, his gratitude would eventually wane, leaving her in a one-sided relationship—that Gavin could end without warning. Or even worse, he could continue being with her while secretly wishing she was Taylor. Did she love him enough to stay with him even though his heart would never be hers?

She pressed her knuckles harder against her forehead. She honestly didn't know, which is why she told him you can only shake a fruit tree so long before it would quit giving fruit. Ginny considered herself a strong person, but she didn't know if she was strong enough to keep telling Gavin she loved him without even getting an "I like you" in response! She had told him he was chasing after fool's gold with Taylor, and she believed that with her whole heart. If she hung on long enough, maybe Gavin would see it too.

Before making love with her, Gavin told her that he believed they were soul mates. She now clung to the image of his face when he moved the sheet aside—when he confessed that he believed. Did saying it mean he truly believed it in his heart of hearts? *Does he still love Taylor? Does he love me?* She just didn't know.

Was she the one chasing fool's gold?

"Are you praying?"

Startled, Ginny dropped her hands before turning at the sound of his voice coming from the bedroom doorway. "No, I was just thinking," she said truthfully.

"Seemed to me you were praying."

Ginny pushed her hands into the overly large silk bathrobe she found in the bathroom. "I don't pray anymore."

She noticed a subtle shift in his attitude since he left to take a shower. His face was now impassive, and he had a standoffish attitude she could feel over short distance separating them.

"Because of what Killyama told you?"

"Kind of useless, isn't it?" Ginny shrugged, removing her hands from her pockets to pick up the remote from the coffee table. Plopping down on the couch, she turned the television on.

Gavin moved to stand next to the coffee table, alternating between watching her and looking at the television as she switched channels. "Why is it useless?"

"Because I'm still working through some issues with Him."

"Exactly how much did Killyama tell you?" He nodded as if her issue was understandable.

"Are you going to be angry at Killyama if I tell you?"

"Depends on what you're going to tell me."

Ginny decided on not telling him, since one of his eyelids was already beginning to twitch.

"You can pick something for us to watch. I'm going to take a shower and get dressed." Placing the remote down, she started to rise when Gavin sat down next to her and pressed a hand to her thigh, stopping her.

"Were you particularly religious before?"

"Not like Willa—I can't quote Bible verses—but I believed, if you prayed hard enough, that He would protect you."

"You don't believe that anymore?"

"No, I don't. I thought you were dead, because I couldn't feel you anymore. I thought He was taking care of you in heaven. He wasn't. I know you prayed for His help, and He made you wait too long. I'm having a hard time forgiving Him for that."

"How do you know I prayed to Him?"

"Who wouldn't in the situation you were in? Even if you didn't have a ton of faith, you would be desperate enough to pray. Didn't you?" she asked.

"More times than I can count," he revealed.

"See? That's my issue with Him."

"Ginny, your faith in God shouldn't be decided on me."

"Why not? What happens to you happens to me."

Gavin studied her in silence, his remoteness easing. "Why do you have to make everything so fucking hard?" Giving an overly loud sigh of frustration, he stared at her intently. "Every time I make a fucking decision concerning you, you warp my brain with your cockamamie reasoning."

The knife in her heart twisted. "What decision did you make about me?" Was he about to tell her that he regretted having sex with her or coming with her to Clindale Island?

"Nothing. It no longer matters." Removing his hand from her thigh, Gavin reached for the remote. "Go have your shower. I'll find us something to watch."

"Okay." Bending down, she pressed what she intended to

be a quick kiss on his lips, only to find herself pulled down until she was straddling his lap.

Opening her mouth with his lips, Gavin boldly thrust his tongue inside. As a kisser, he had what it took to make her mind turn to mush. As the kissee, she didn't want it to ever end.

Wrapping her arms around his neck, she gave into the demands his mouth made on hers. A rush of warmth repaired the damage her thoughts of Taylor and him together had caused. Ginny knew the relief would be short-lived before more doubt would slice a larger hole.

Easily rising with her weight, Gavin carried her into the bedroom before slamming the door closed with his foot.

"What about my shower?" she murmured against his jawline.

"We can take one together when I'm done."

"You just had one."

Laughing when he tumbled them to the bed, she sensually rubbed her palms down his sleek back.

"I'm about to get real dirty." Reaching between them, he tried to pull her robe free. "Why isn't it coming off?" he groused.

"It's tied."

"That would have been good to know."

Ginny playfully took little nibbles on his collarbone as he maneuvered her out of the housecoat. Then, one second he was there, and the next, he was jackknifing himself off her and the bed.

"Wha …?"

"Take your shower." He even sidestepped her when she tried to pull him back down.

Stopping midaction, she saw the pale pallor of his skin. "What's wrong?" Sitting up, she placed her hands on the mattress where he could see them.

"Nothing. Just take your fucking shower and leave me alone," he snarled, fumbling with the doorknob to get out of the room.

Ginny quickly bounded off the bed, reaching out to help him open the door. He winced away from her as if he was suddenly afraid of her. Trying not to be hurt by his reaction, she turned the knob and opened the door for him, stepping away to give him plenty of room.

Keeping his eyes on her, he fled through the door.

She wanted to go after him, but instead, she shut the door, giving him privacy. Whatever she had done must have set off a terrible memory.

Despising herself, she wanted nothing more than to go and comfort him, but she forced herself to take a shower to give him time to recover. As she did, Ginny played back what she had been doing before he had freaked out.

Could it have been the love bites she had been placing on his neck? It was the only thing she did differently. Unless she was circling his neck with her arms, Ginny was careful when she touched him. Gavin preferred to do all the intimate touching, even moving her hands away when she tried to touch his dick. A couple of times, she had kissed his chest and tried to move lower to give the same pleasure he had given her, but Gavin would roll away from her or tug her up higher. Ginny received the silent message—he didn't want oral sex from her. What had been done to him that a little nibble from her could have sent him into a tailspin?

Entering the shower, Ginny saw the towel tied over the nozzle. Leaving the intricate knot alone, she soaped her body before moving under the misty spray. Lifting her face, she let the water wash away any evidence of her telltale tears.

Drying off, she brushed her hair without the benefit of the mirror that was covered before leaving the bathroom, she noticed Gavin had placed her suitcase on the bed. She rummaged through the few belongings and found a pair of faded blue denim shorts and a matching green tank top. Casual and nonchalant were her objectives as she walked out of the bedroom and into the living room.

"Anything in particular you want for lunch?" she asked, opening the freezer.

"No, you choose. Just pick two of the same meal."

"Can do," she chirped, pretending normalcy between them. "How about a pizza?"

"That's fine."

"Righty ho …." Taking the frozen pizza out, she set the temperature on the small oven.

"Stop, Ginny. You don't have to act so fucking cheerful."

She opened the box of pizza and tore the plastic covering off. "Would you rather I act like a gloomy Gus?"

Raising her eyes up to him, she saw Gavin fixated on the television set. "It was no big deal. Just act normal."

She could either let it go and spare him further turmoil, or she could force him to confront the situation. Gavin had been tortured for years into complying with Slate's demands. Did Killyama tell her everything she knew about Gavin's capture? Did the ones responsible for rescuing him know the full sickening details of what he suffered? Coming to the conclusion she wasn't going to fix the damage done to him in three days of having sex with her, if ever, she now understood that they were Gavin's scars to heal, and much as she loved him only he could be the one who gauge when they no longer hurt.

Putting the pizza in the oven, she sat down on the couch with him, broaching the delicate subject despite her misgivings. "You sure you don't want to talk—"

"No," Gavin said harshly, tugging on his ear.

"Oh … okay." Dropping the subject, she started watching the movie Gavin picked.

Five minutes into it, she realized she was freezing. Had Gavin turned the air conditioner down? Three minutes later, when she started shivering, she didn't have to assume he had; she could practically see her breath in the chilly air.

Biting her lip, she wondered if he would get upset if she snuggled up to him. It was a couple's thing to do, but she was unsure if he considered them a couple or just sexual partners. Regardless of what Gavin had gone through, she didn't want him shutting her out anytime she accidently hit a raw nerve.

Confusion swamped her, and Ginny found she didn't like it one bit not knowing if she any rights with him. After all, they were supposed to be married, weren't they? That should give her snuggling privileges. Was she supposed to meekly allow him to call the shots where their relationship was concerned because it made him uncomfortable?

Hell no!

Picking her moment when the hero on the scene was battling a droid, Ginny inched over. Nothing got past Gavin, as he took his eyes off the movie. "How much longer before the pizza is done?"

Ginny drew back. "Ten minutes."

Nodding, he turned back to the television.

A minute later, she got her courage back, inching back toward him.

His eyes shot around again. "What are you doing?"

"I'm cold."

His eyes flickered down to her clothes. "Go put on more clothes."

Hurt almost had her gasping out loud as the knife plunged deeper inside her heart.

"You could raise the temperature of the air conditioner." Biting her lip at the quiver in her voice, Ginny remained seated.

"I'm hot."

"I'm cold." Her bottom lip began trembling. She wasn't going to let Gavin run over her needs, as much as she loved the wild man. He had told her once they were both on the same street, heading in opposite directions. It was time for him to choose which one of them was going to change directions—*and it isn't going to be me*, she told herself—despite every bone in her body wanting to give in to him.

Lifting a heavy arm, Gavin placed it across her shoulders, pulling her toward him.

Burrowing into his heat, Ginny snuggled against him. "Thank-you," she sighed in relief.

"Watch the movie."

Laying her head on his shoulder, she felt him stiffen. Ginny froze, realizing her mouth was too close to his throat. Still, they sat stiffly, watching the movie. Thankfully, Ginny heard the buzzer go off in the kitchen.

"The pizza is done." Ginny started to get up, but Gavin beat her to it.

"Stay still. I'll bring you a slice."

Her attention wasn't on the television, but she let him have his way, pretending an interest she didn't feel as she heard the sounds coming from the kitchen.

"What would you like to drink?"

"I'll take a glass of water."

Gavin carried her water and pizza over, setting them down on the coffee table.

"Do you want me to wait until after you eat?"

"Yes," he said, sitting back down but this time farther away from her.

"Do you have to be so obvious?" she asked pointedly.

"What?" he asked, his pizza poised halfway to his mouth.

"That you don't want me near you."

Gavin lowered his pizza back to the plate. Then, jerking

himself to his feet, he bent down, scooped her into his arms and carried her into the bedroom, using his shoulder to close the door. He dumped her onto the bed.

"Is this what you want?" he snarled at her, throwing himself down on the bed after ripping his jeans off and using a foot to throw them halfway across the room. "Go ahead. Have at it."

Thunderstruck, Ginny slowly rose to a sitting position, then slid off the bed. Bile was rising up her throat; she was afraid she was going to throw up.

"What? Isn't this good enough for you? What in the fuck do you want?"

Ginny fell to her knees, bursting into tears. Unable to look at him, she covered her face with her hands. The sound of Gavin getting off the bed had her dropping her hands to crawl to the bathroom.

"Stop crying."

Ginny found herself sitting on Gavin's lap on the floor, sobbing into his shoulder, unable to stop crying.

"You humiliated both of us. Why did you do that?"

"Stop crying," he slowly crooned, rocking her.

"Loving you should never feel like this," she sobbed. "Why did you do that?"

"I was hurting, and I took it out on you. I'm sorry."

Lowering her hands, she was given a brief glimpse of Gavin's suffering before he managed to erase it from his features. In hindsight, she had a better understanding why Trudy and Sex Piston doubted her staying power with Gavin.

She lovingly stroked down the side of his jaw just as she had the first day at the club. He'd been hurt and had struck out. That was what they had been trying to warn her about. They didn't believe she was strong enough to deserve Gavin. She had to prove them wrong. Prove she was woman enough to deserve the gift of Gavin's love.

"I'm okay. See? I've stopped crying." She gently traced his bottom lip with her fingertip.

"It's not fucking okay ... I hurt you."

"Gavin, being your soul mate doesn't mean we're only going to share in the joy. There's pain too."

Catching her hand, he held it still but didn't move it away. "I'm so fucking sorry."

"I'm the one who's sorry. I shouldn't have pushed you. I knew you were still upset. I should have put on some warmer clothes."

"You don't have anything to be sorry for. I was the one being an ass. Ginny, there are things I don't want to talk about that happened to me, not to you or anyone."

"I shouldn't have pushed ... I was just trying to find out if ...."

"Find out what?" he asked patiently, stroking her back.

"If you consider us a couple? Or sex buddies? Do you even like me as a friend? Couples snuggle; friends don't. I was just trying to find out which we are. I should have waited until you weren't so upset about what happened earlier."

Gavin buried his face in her hair. "You're so fucking naïve. You turn me inside out. I was the biggest dick in the world to you, and you still want to go on a fishing expedition?"

"Yes, please. A woman needs to know if she's allowed to snuggle." Flashing him a humorous smile, she tried to make light of her question while, inside, she was filled with dread, waiting for his answer.

"Woman, I married you. We've gone past the snuggling stage."

"We're no—"

Gavin kissed her, breaking off what she was about to say.

Playfully, Ginny slid her lips out from under his. "We may

be *legally* married," she said with a raised voice, showing Gavin she knew why he cut her off, "but we won't truly be married in the eyes of my church until Pastor Dean gives his blessing. To do that, you have to ask Pastor Dean for permission."

Gavin narrowed his eyes at her. "You're kidding, right?"

"No, I'm serious. Razer and Shade both had to ask his permission."

Gavin burst out into laughter. "Now I know you're joking. Razer maybe—"

He wasn't even giving her the benefit of the doubt.

Despite his words, Ginny shook her head at his misapprehension, trying to wordlessly show him that she was serious.

"—but there is no way, and I mean *no way*, Shade asked for Lucky's blessing and *permission* to marry Lily."

"Lily told me herself." Ginny playfully punched him on shoulder when Gavin burst into another round of laughter at his friend's expense. "What's so funny about Shade being romantic?"

"I wanted proof. I just didn't expect Shade to be the one to give it to me."

Ginny frowned at him at confusion. "What are you talking about?"

Gavin had to wipe a tear of laughter away. "There is a God."

CHAPTER SIXTEEN

G inny placed their lunch containers in the microwave before going to the patio door; she hesitated calling out to Gavin that it was ready. He was staring out at the ocean as if he were a million miles away.

Being alone with Gavin for the last eight days with no one else to keep them company had given her insights into the trauma he continued to suffer through on a daily basis. His air of isolation right now had her aching to go to him, yet she knew he needed this moment outside alone to reaffirm he wasn't locked inside.

She despised herself for letting him come with her. The mental turmoil of being under someone's else control, even though Allerton had yet to show himself, was taking a toll on Gavin. He was increasingly more silent and constantly pacing around the bungalow as if it were a jail cell.

While the lack of freedom was getting to Gavin, Ginny wasn't above using the opportunity to better understand him and to grow closer to the solitary man. She wished she knew what he had been like before his kidnapping. Occasionally, he would make a joke like he had about Shade, and Ginny could see a glimmer of something, or someone, behind his eyes, begging to be let out.

Unable to bear watching him in his isolation any longer, she started forward, then halted at the sound of the phone ringing. It was only the second time it had rung since they arrived.

Taking two steps, she reached for the phone, conscious of Gavin coming through the door.

"I'm afraid to answer it," she admitted.

"I can."

Ginny shook her head. "Hello?"

"Allerton scheduled a meeting for this afternoon at four," Agent Collins informed her.

"We'll be ready."

Hanging up without any pleasantries, she turned to Gavin. "Allerton wants to see us at four."

"Lunch ready?"

"Yes, it's in the microwave. You're not worried?" she asked at his apparent indifference.

Gavin took the containers out, dividing the food between the two plates. "I would be lying if I said no, but we'll deal with whatever happens."

Ginny took a seat at the table to join Gavin, who'd already started eating. "Maybe I should go alone—"

"That's not going to happen." Gavin took another bite of his shrimp scampi before pushing his plate toward her. "Go ahead and eat it. It's good. Best thing we've had so far."

"I'm not hungry."

"Eat. Let me do the worrying."

"That's not going to happen," she mimicked him.

Gavin took another forkful of scampi. "You want to fuck, then?"

Her mouth dropped open. "No."

"It would take your mind off worrying," he suggested. "It's a good way to relax."

Picking up her fork, she stabbed a big fat shrimp. "I take it you've used that relax technique before."

"A time or two." Loading up his fork, he ate, unconcerned about her heated glare. "You sure?"

"Yes, I'm sure. I'm relaxed enough. If you feel the need, have at it on your lonesome. I'll watch."

His interest was piqued. "You'd watch?"

She almost choked on the shrimp at his dirty expression. Ginny had to drink a sip of water before she could get the damn thing down her throat. "I was joking."

"Have you ever watched a man jerk off?"

"No, and I don't want to," she managed to strangle out.

Gavin placed both elbows on the table to give her a lust-filled, come-hither smile. "Don't knock it before you try it."

"I'll pass." Ginny picked up her linen napkin to fan herself.

"The Last Riders and I assumed you didn't know about the rules of the club, but you do. Killyama told you, didn't she?"

Ginny bounced off her chair as if it were on fire with the embarrassing turn in the conversation. "I don't have any idea what you're talking about. You can have the rest of my food. I'm going to take a shower."

"Ginny."

Freezing at the authoritative manner he spoke her name, Ginny regretted letting her smart aleck mouth get her in trouble.

"Yes?" Widening her eyes, she tried to bluff the way Silas had taught her.

Gavin wasn't fooled by her playing stupid. Linking his fingers together, he stared at her. "We were discussing what else Killyama told you."

"I wouldn't call it a discussion," she corrected him. "And for your information, Killyama has never mentioned the rules of the club. Satisfied?"

"Not hardly. Who told you then? T.A. or Sex Piston?"

"No one, okay? Jeez, what got us on this topic anyway?"

"You're lying."

Ginny pulled her shoulders back, affronted. "I am not. I would never lie to you."

"Very well." Gavin dropped his hands and began eating again.

Thinking she was going to get away scot-free, Ginny tried to make her escape again.

"Would you like me to tell you the rules?"

Gritting her teeth, Ginny knew there was no way in hell she was going to be able to listen to Gavin tell her the rules of the club and be able to keep up pretenses. "That's okay. Where is the time going?" she asked inanely. "I better get a move on."

"It's only two o'clock."

"If I'm going to die, I want to look nice."

He didn't appreciate her attempt at humor.

Forestalling him from continuing to talk about the club rules, Ginny began backing out of the room.

"Go ahead. We can talk about this later—"

"Fine with me," she said, not realizing he wasn't done with his sentence.

"—tonight," he finished.

Damn, when Gavin got on a roll, he could beat a dead horse to death. How had she never noticed that before?

"Fine!" she snapped. Allerton was probably going to kill her, so it wouldn't matter anyway.

"I'm not going to let Allerton kill you." Reaching for her plate, he began wolfing down her leftovers.

"I didn't mean to say that out loud."

"Well, you did. My offer to relax you is still open, by the way."

"I'll pass."

Belatedly, a light bulb went off in her head as to why she didn't want to discuss what went on in the club and why she was backing away.

The sexual magnetism emanating from Gavin had her scenting danger. Sexual energy was pouring off him in spades, winding around her like an imaginary rope drawing her back toward him.

Ginny grabbed the doorjamb, feeling ridiculous while, at the same time, wanting to go to back to the table and lick every inch of his body. She'd been attracted to Gavin since she first set eyes on him. The man was undeniably eye candy.

Something had been imperceptibly changing—or *returning?*—so slowly, and it had gone unnoticed until it was practically hitting her in the face. Analyzing the change, Ginny took a few seconds to recognize what it was. Then clarity struck.

His sexuality, which had been traumatized during his captivity, was remerging. Jeez, the man was like dynamite without a freaking fuse, and what would be worse was Gavin figuring it out. He'd be unstoppable where women were concerned … Hell, anyone with two legs and a …

Ginny turned tail and ran like a scalded cat.

She took off her clothes, then turned the shower on before she even took her bra off. Slinging her bra to the floor, Ginny stepped into the shower and snapped the door closed.

Letting the spray dampen her hair, she placed her hands on shower wall, letting the cold water cool her down. The sexual hunger she had just experienced had taken her by surprise. Gavin never had a problem getting a response when he touched her, but him being capable of making her wet just by staring at her was a shock to her system.

She jerked her head to the side at the sound of the shower door opening and closing, and reflexively lifted the washcloth to hide her breasts. "What are you doing?"

"Taking a shower with you. There's no need wasting water."

Keeping the washcloth in place, Ginny freed one hand to attempt to shove him out. "I wanted some privacy."

Grabbing her hand, Gavin moved her so she was standing in front of him. "What's the big deal? We've showered together before."

"The big deal is I wanted to be alone."

"Cool. Just ignore me." Taking the washcloth away from her, he squirted body wash over her breasts.

"Excuse me …" Turning around, she tried to take the washcloth back. "How am I supposed to ignore you when you're doing that and … are poking me with *that*?"

"Ignore it. I am."

"You're just going to ignore it?"

"Yup."

Ginny scowled at the big buffoon as he smoothed the cloth over the body wash, creating a slick foam.

"It's not a big deal." Sliding to her other breast, he used his body to force her backward against the wall.

"It is a big deal." Ginny tried to twist her pelvis to the side. "You're drilling a hole into my stomach."

Gavin lowered his mouth to her neck. "I'd rather drill a hole somewhere else."

Trying to swat his dick away, they ended up tussling in the shower; Ginny lost the battle when Gavin lifted her up, and afraid he would drop her, she wound her thighs around his hips.

"I'm not in the mood."

"Then why are your little nipples cold?'

"The water's cold," she snapped, managing to get the washcloth away from him, then buried his face in it. "You had a spot of gravy on your beard. I took care of it for you," she told him, trying to scrub his face off.

"You can be a vicious little thing when you want to be."

"And you can be a hound dog when you want to be." Glaring at him, she smacked him with the washcloth. "There, I missed another spot!"

Ripping the washcloth away from her, he tossed it over the shower stall. "I'm not a hound dog. They go after any pussy available. I know which one I'm after." He rubbed the head of his dick suggestively between the cleft of her thighs.

"You used to be, didn't you?" she bit out between gritted teeth, fighting the rush of warmth the cool water wasn't helping quell.

"Of course not. I've always been a one-woman man."

Ginny stared at him suspiciously. "Seriously?"

"Would I lie to you?"

Doubts surfaced, but Ginny took his word for it. Why would he lie? She stopped her struggles, thinking she had made a mountain out of a molehill. Maybe her nerves were just getting the better of her and she'd overreacted.

"Did that make your mood better?" He grinned, flexing his hips toward her again.

"I'm getting there."

Sliding his wet hair away from his face, Ginny scanned his innocent-looking face for any sign of deceit. "You're too sexy for your own good."

"Who wants to be good"—slipping the head of his dick easily inside of her opening, he traced her earlobe with his tongue—"when it's more fun to be bad?"

Gavin took control of her senses with each plunge of his cock, smashing through her uncertainty as if using a magic wand. Raspy sighs came from both of them as a passionate haze surrounded them.

She scored her fingernails through Gavin's hair to his shoulders, down his back, wanting to leave her mark on every part of his body. She wanted the experience of them having sex to erase every woman he had touched from his memory. Better yet, she wanted to make him useless to any woman who came within his vicinity.

Giving every ounce of her to him, she clasped her thighs tighter and started bouncing on his dick, making him go faster. Gavin had to place a hand on the shower wall to prevent them from slipping on the slick floor.

His harsh breaths echoed louder as she demanded more of him. Using the showerhead, she lifted herself higher to slam herself down on his thrusting dick, inadvertently hitting the magic spot that sent them down a whirlpool of desire.

Arms shaking, Gavin set her back to her feet. "Damn, woman, you need to relax more often," he teased, removing his hand from her butt cheek to reach down and snag the sodden hand towel from the floor.

Appreciatively watching the supple muscles in his back, Ginny twined her arms around his middle, brushing her mouth over his shoulder as he retied the hand towel back on the showerhead. With her fingertips, she smoothed through the curly hairs at the juncture of his thighs.

Gavin caught her hand, moving it higher up his waist. She didn't try to put it back, knowing very well Gavin had limits, even though she'd given him access to every part of her— body and soul.

"Once this is over, I'll have plenty time to relax."

"You're not going to keep your singing career going?"

"No." Brushing a last kiss over his shoulder blade, she

stepped out of the shower. "I gave my last performance in Nashville."

"That's why you thanked the audience. Why not continue what you're so good at?" he asked, stepping out of the shower and taking the towel she handed him.

"I only sang to draw my stalker out. Since that's no longer an issue, I don't have to anymore," she said matter-of-factly.

"You're too good to stop."

"I never wanted to start."

"You never got over stage fright?"

"I never had stage fright. That was a misapprehension Penny had, which I never corrected."

"Why not?"

"Because I didn't want to sing," she explained. "I want to write."

"You'd rather write songs that could make someone else famous?"

"I never wanted to be famous. I just want people to listen to my words. It doesn't matter who's singing them. The important part to me is if my words invoke feelings they will remember. That's why hit songs have so many covers—the words means something to someone, and they want to put their own spin on it. A good song is never forgotten."

"So, in essence," he said slowly, working it out in his head, "they won't forget you."

"Yes," she answered, pleased he got what she was attempting to explain.

"I remembered you, and you were singing someone else's song."

"You clung to the words of the song. The feelings it invoked were about Taylor." Ginny plugged in the hair dryer. "I was the forgettable part of the equation. I always am. I'm going to write a song that no one will forget about me, even if someone else is singing it," she vowed more to herself than to him.

"Ginny, I didn't forget you … It was just … you were so young … My mind couldn't handle thinking about you without feeling dirty. I didn't want the memory tarnished."

"That's the sweetest thing you've said to me." Giving him a brief kiss, she pushed the button on the hair dryer. "Now, shoo … I have to dry my hair and get dressed."

"In other words, you don't want to talk about it any longer. That's a bad habit of yours—running away when things get too uncomfortable."

Ginny pointed the hair dryer at him. "Hello, pot meet kettle."

Without a leg to stand where that was concerned, Gavin gave up and went to the bedroom.

She *pfft* him as he left. Had she finally been able to get one over him? Not that she disagreed. What could she say? He was right on that particular point. It was far easier to run than realize the inevitable. It was a lesson she had learned at three. She had been, and always would be … expendable.

CHAPTER SEVENTEEN

"Ready?" Reaper looked inquiringly at Ginny when a knock sounded on the bungalow door.

"Yes."

Expecting Ginny to exhibit more nerves, she seemed unfazed by the upcoming encounter.

His hand was on the doorknob when she touched his arm. "Gavin, at any time, if you think this meeting is going shady, pretend you aren't feeling well. Tell them you might have the virus."

"What will you do?"

The nervous woman from all afternoon was gone. Standing before him Ginny held assurance and a quiet confidence that he hoped would carry through the upcoming meeting.

"Come back with you, just like any concerned wife would."

"You have a sneaky side to you that is very concerning to me."

He wasn't taken in by her innocent look. It was the same fucking one Silas had when he fleeced him out of every dollar in his wallet when they played poker, and it was the same one she'd had when his earring was missing.

"Don't be silly. I'm not being sneaky; I'm being prudent. I believe in being prepared." Releasing his arm, she pasted an unconcerned look on her face, which he didn't believe for one flipping second.

"I do, too. Ask me sometime how I was kidnapped. No matter how you prepare, some S.O.B. is out there, better prepared than you. Let's just hope Allerton isn't that S.O.B. today."

He opened the door to find Agent Collins impatiently waiting, about to knock again.

"Allerton is waiting," he said before abruptly heading toward the waiting Moke.

Reaper took her arm protectively as they climbed into the back seat and, before they knew it, the Moke was parked in a shaded area behind the largest building on the island. Agent Collins led them to the side of the building, leaving the driver in the vehicle.

Collins having no problem leading them through three hallways before arriving at the elevator confirmed Reaper's doubts about the agent. Keeping a hand on Ginny's waist as Agent Collins pressed the call button, he gave Collins a measured look when the agent positioned himself to keep them in sight.

"You didn't feel the need to bring any of the other agents with you?" he asked, watching his reaction.

"Unfortunately, one of the men took ill four days ago. In lieu of caution, we determined their isolation be extended."

"You didn't feel the need to extend the caution to yourself?" Reaper asked as they entered the elevator.

Pressing the elevator button, the door closed. "I had a separate bungalow. I let the other two men handle the shifts, watching your bungalow during the day and evening.

I took the night shift. My contact with them was over the phone."

"Which agent became ill?"

"Agent Clark."

"I hope he gets better soon," Ginny spoke up, breaking the stare down that Reaper and Agent Collins had been engaged in.

"I'll extend your well wishes."

The elevator doors opened to reveal a waiting room with a mock waterfall cascading down one wall. A man Gavin's age rose from behind a desk to greet them.

"Agent Collins, Mr. and Mrs. James, I'm Ethan. It's a pleasure meeting you." He motioned them toward two oversized doors. "Mr. Allerton is waiting for your arrival. May I get you a drink?"

"No, Thank-you," Ginny refused politely.

Reaper propelled her forward before she was given the opportunity to give the attractive assistant a smile. Disregarding her glare at his rude behavior, they accompanied Agent Collins through the double doors.

Unlike his secretary, Gabriel Allerton remained seated. "Please, come in and have a seat."

Reaper didn't sit, and instead chose to stand behind Ginny with his hands proprietorially on her shoulders.

As the distinguished man stared at him from over his desk, Reaper didn't flinch from the condescending gaze that assessed his casual appearance before nodding toward Collins.

"Agent Collins, I trust your stay has been enjoyable?"

"Yes, sir. Thank-you. Extremely comfortable."

Gabriel Allerton nodded as if he hadn't expected the agent to say anything differently.

Reaper would kiss both men's bare ass if they hadn't met before.

"Mr. and Mrs. James, I hope the same can be said for you?"

"Yes, Thank-you."

Reaper was proud that Ginny didn't call him sir.

"Perfect. Is everyone in agreement that we can cut right to the business we need to discuss?" Patronizing in his question, Allerton focused on Ginny, not anticipating anyone daring to naysay him.

"Mrs. James, being a personal friend of your mother and father, I was delighted to share in their joy when the FBI contacted them about you being found alive after you purchased an ancestry kit. I'm sure you were devastated to find out the true details of your past."

Reaper kept his eyes trained on Allerton but couldn't help to think, *What the fuck?*

"I was," Ginny agreed.

"May I ask what prompted the search for your ancestral ties?"

"My brother gave it to me as a Christmas gift. My adoptive father never hid that I was adopted. I didn't see the need to search for a family whom I believed deserted me."

"How did you come to be placed with your adopted family in Kentucky?"

"The man who found me had chartered a private yacht. He was the sheriff in Kentucky. He contacted the local authorities, then left me in their care. However, he made calls to check on my welfare. When no one came forward, I was made a ward of the court. A friend of his offered to adopt me, and from there, I ended up in Kentucky when his application was approved."

"Funny, none of your paperwork has been located."

The sarcastic fucker didn't have a funny bone in body.

"I don't find it funny," Ginny said sharply. "As much as I love my adoptive family, I'm looking into legal action that no intensive search was made before I was adopted. I can only assume the social worker was overly burdened and was just relieved to have one less child to keep track of. The DNA was entered into the data bank. In case my body had been recovered, they would have a sample to match. I'm sure it was a surprise when instead of being informed all that was recovered were my bones, they were told I was very much alive."

Reaper found it difficult to keep a straight face at the misdirection of the true facts. Blending crafted lies and the truth, if he hadn't heard the truth from Trudy's lips, hell, he would have believed the lies she was telling.

Unfortunately, Allerton didn't look like he believed anything coming out of her mouth, which could only mean one thing—once the FBI had informed her parents that she was alive and they told Allerton, no rock had been left unturned to uncover her past by him.

"I find it a big coincidence that your sister Trudy was thirty minutes away and both of you were unaware of each other being so close."

"Are you insinuating I'm lying?"

Allerton didn't deny the charge. "Like I said, it's a big coincidence."

"Not really. I was only three. The earliest memory that I can recall is me tumbling down a hill and a rock cutting my forehead. As to my sister, I did meet her several times when I was in my late teens through a woman I worked with. She was introduced to me as T.A. I never knew her given name, and by the time she met me, I was no longer the three-year-old sister she remembered."

The last part, Reaper thought, had such a ring of truth that he even glimpsed a brief expression of uncertainty in Allerton.

"T.A. certainly didn't expect her wedding singer to be the sister she lost at sea," Ginny continued. "Nor did I expect my former boss from the tour company to ask me to do her a personal favor by singing at T.A.'s wedding. I try not think about my sister being so close without my knowledge. It's been deeply hurtful for me, as I'm sure is to T.A., that we spent the time apart unnecessarily. While at the same time, I love my adoptive family and consider them my true family, and I wouldn't take back the time I had with them if the whims of fate hadn't interceded."

"Fate?" Allerton countered snidely. "Excuse me if I don't believe your disappearance had anything to do with the vagaries of fate."

Reaper tightened his hands on Ginny's shoulder at the overt way Allerton was perceptibly disparaging. The condescending fucker was about to have his ass handed to him on a platter if he wasn't careful.

Ginny interrupted his plan to reach across the desk and use the fancy tie to strangle him when she reached up to pat one of his hands, as if saying she had this under control.

Relaxing his hold on her shoulders, Reaper let her storytelling play out. He just hoped like hell that Allerton chilled with the snide comments before the fucker was forced to scream for help from his security, which Reaper was sure were watching from the camera mounted high in the corner of the office.

The outdated camera was a fucking joke. The sophisticated equipment layered throughout their bungalow in was top of the game where surveillance was concerned. The camera in the office was from the Ice Age. Reaper reasoned it was meant for those less tech savvy, to give the assumption Allerton didn't feel the need for more sophisticated equipment on his island. If they bought that, Reaper had some swampland to sell.

"I can certainly understand your skepticism. After the FBI asked me to fly to Sherguevil Island to meet my parents, I was appalled to find out about your accusation that I am a thief, that I had stolen something of importance from the island.

"It isn't an accusation when I have the proof." Allerton's expression became even more condescending.

"I would love to see the proof, as I have no memory of the incident, or what was taken." Ginny dropped her hand from his to splay her hands out in confusion.

Again, Reaper heard the ring of truth in her voice.

"Maybe, if I could see the footage or am told what I've been accused of taking, it would help spark a memory."

"There is no footage. Unfortunately, the incident happened out of camera range. And what was taken is a historical artifact that I am not at liberty to disclose, which was pilfered by *you*."

"I'm unable to deny the allegation, as I do not remember the incident. I wish I could. However, unless something changes that does spark my memory, I'm at a loss as how to make amends. If you want money for it, I can give you my lawyer's phone number, and we can work out a figure that would make you happy."

"Why would you offer to pay for something when you don't believe you took the artifact?" Allerton asked, trying to corner Ginny into admission.

Ginny tilted her head to the side. "Obviously, you have to have some proof. Why else would the FBI have sent a team of men to escort me?" Ginny swung back, placing the ball again in his corner. "I'm a law-abiding citizen. It makes me sick to my stomach that apparently I once was so lacking in morals as to steal. I am a Christian. It goes against my faith to steal. You say I stole a historical artifact; many have religious meanings. If I stole something that does, I would be devasted. Money won't make up for what is stolen, but even if I did steal it, which I truly hope I didn't, the artifact is missed by the person it was taken from, and maybe they can purchase another copy or something else that has the same meaning when we come to an agreeable price.

"The artifact belonged to me, and it was priceless. You don't have enough money to compensate me for the item that you did, in fact, steal."

Reaper had had enough.

"When I was in the Navy, I dealt in securing and retrieving historical artifacts. The fact that you are being vague and refusing to give details about the *supposed* artifact is giving me the impression it could have been stolen, besides the fact you are unable to produce the authentic receipt from your seller. I won't allow Ginny to become a scapegoat."

Allerton didn't like being called a thief any more than Reaper liked Ginny being called one.

"The transaction of the artifact I acquired was legal. I purchased it from a highly respectable auction house. As a matter of fact, the only reason it was so easily stolen was because I was sending it back to the country of origin to facilitate a good will endeavor. The attempt failed and thousands of children are still at risk to this day because the country refuses to accept any aid from any country. I was hoping to use my charity to open the door, which remains firmly closed to any outsiders. Call me an optimist, but if am able to return the artifact, then at long last my charity could be the key to making headway into securing help for people who desperately need food, clean water, and shelter. We would earn their trust as an independent organization by returning the artifact. The only one preventing that success is your wife, Mr. James."

"Then we're in a stalemate, because she doesn't have it to return."

The two men exchanged cold looks. Reaper would be

damned if he was the first to break the stare down, and Allerton appeared the same.

"I have a suggestion." Agent Collins was the one to break the staring contest.

"Then let's hear it." Allerton broke the stare with him to focus on the agent.

In a contest of wills, the wealthy businessman would never give in so easily. Therefore, Reaper wasn't fooled that Agent Collins and Allerton had a prearranged plan.

"I can arrange a lie detector test for Mrs. James to take. If she passes, Mr. Allerton, you will be able to look in other areas for the culprit, and Mrs. James will be able to move on with a clear conscience."

"My wife could have been asked at any time before our arrival on your island for a lie detector test, and she would have happily agreed … after our lawyer assured us of the examiner's credentials. Ginny will not be taking one here without our lawyer present to review the questions being asked. When we return to the States, a test can be arranged once those demands have been met."

"Years have been lost in the search for the artifact. I refuse to waste more valuable time. As owner of Sherguevil Island and where Mrs. James committed the crime, this matter needs to be settled before Mrs. James will be allowed to leave."

"By whose authority?"

"I am the sole authority for this island, which puts Evangeline under my jurisdiction."

"Are you placing me under arrest for a crime you say I committed when I was *three* years old? How does that even make sense?"

Ginny's calmness had him wanting to cheer her on. She was easily holding her own, refusing to let his threats get to her.

"Of course not. I'm merely not approving you to leave until you submit to the lie detector test. If you fail, that means you are withholding knowledge of the crime of stealing the artifact. I have been desperately searching for years, and withholding any information is an obstruction of justice on my island. Mrs. James, I suggest you and your husband deliberate on taking the test and give me an answer by morning. Meanwhile, please accept my invitation to a private dinner party tonight. Your mother will be there. She has been awaiting your arrival."

Reaper wanted to tell him to shove his invitation but let Ginny make the decision.

"My father won't be there?" Ginny asked.

"My dear, I hate to be the one tasked of informing you, but your father was delegated to an emergency response team three days after your arrival."

"You're just now telling me?" Ginny sent Agent Collins a castigating glare.

Allerton drew her gaze back to him. "We didn't anticipate there would be a need to disappoint you. Soleil and I, as well as Jasper, assumed he would be gone only a few days leaving enough time to make it back before you were out of isolation. Regrettably, late last night, Jasper informed us because of the outbreak of Legionnaires from the contaminated water supply, the workers have been ill, thus hampering the efforts to repair the water system.

"I can see your disappointment, which your parents share. Your father promises to fly back as soon as everything is under control, and he's asked me in his absence to provide the emotional support for Soleil. Of course, I gladly agreed.

Ginny deadpanned, "I'm relieved my supposed theft didn't affect your friendship."

"Our friendship has spanned over twenty-five years. I don't believe in holding parents accountable for their children's actions. Your parents have been living on the Sher-guevil Island since your mother's retirement from teaching, which has deepened our ties. Naturally, she is a bundle of nerves at meeting you. It was my suggestion to have a small dinner party to put both of you at ease.

"Soleil is a dear friend of mine, and I've had to watch her grieve your loss and your sister's estrangement for many years. I'm looking forward to witnessing the reunion. So, until tonight, then? Shall we say seven? That should give you ample time to go back to the bungalow and change."

Reaper wanted to call bullshit. Ginny's father, Jasper, wasn't the only water engineer on Allerton's payroll. Even then, there was no reason to make the mother-daughter reunion public. No, either Allerton or Ginny's parents didn't want them to have a private meeting.

"Don't worry. If you didn't include an appropriate change of dress in your luggage, I'll have my personal assistant send over a selection of clothes for you both to wear from my private boutique. Agent Collins, feel free to join us."

"Thank-you. I would love to attend. I'm bored with my own company, and my men can enjoy the night off," Agent Collins accepted, then stood and motioned for Ginny to get up.

Taking Ginny's arm when she rose from the chair, Reaper guided her out of the room, then led her to the elevator to push the button, not waiting for Agent Collins to catch up. Wanting to shove him out the elevator when he managed to make it before the doors closed, Reaper restrained himself. He needed to play nice until he was given no choice, for Ginny's sake. The agent was as dirty as a blackhead pimple. He didn't know if the other agents were, but he wasn't going to pop the pimple until he had no choice. He wanted the poison contained to where he could see it, not spread out where one of the newbies could make a mistake that could get themselves or Ginny killed.

"It was nice of Mr. Allerton to have a party for your mother and you," Collins remarked conversationally as they stepped out of the elevator.

"Very nice."

Reaper gritted his teeth and gave Ginny a searching look to see if she was serious.

"Can you explain to me exactly the role the FBI is supposed to play here?" Reaper asked bluntly the moment they stepped outside. "From where I'm standing, it seems the only reason you're here is to facilitate Allerton throwing Ginny under a fucking bus."

"Gavin, the FBI are only trying to clear up a situation that I could be responsible for. I'm thankful for their help. I want the misunderstanding resolved as much as Mr. Allerton does."

"Mrs. James is correct. The US is determined to assist in having the artifact returned to Mr. Allerton. Your wife is instrumental to the process of accomplishing that objective. The country of origin has a policy of not taking any foreign aid. Any headway Mr. Allerton can accomplish is a foot in the right direction in establishing a trusting relationship with them, which benefits the US by initiating conversations previously denied."

"How is she supposed to help when she can't remember? How much do you remember at that age? Does the FBI know which artifact Allerton claims was stolen?"

"No, unfortunately, we don't. Which is another concern of ours."

"Concern? I didn't see an ounce of concern for Ginny in that office."

"What are you suggesting?" Agent Collins asked stiffly. "I'm getting tired of you insinuating Mrs. James is in some type of danger. Mr. Allerton has been nothing but gracious in this situation. When the FBI contacted Mr. Allerton, he'd already known about Evangeline being alive; her parents told him. While he hasn't been very forthcoming with specific details about the artifact, my superiors understand Mr. Allerton's wariness. He has to take into account the safety of his guests if treasure hunters learn of the value of the lost artifact. We also have to take into consider its disappearance correlated with Mrs. James departure from the island, along with the fact she never returned. When we explained to Evangeline what Mr. Allerton had told us, she agreed to meet with Mr. Allerton to clear up this unfortunate incident. She was given the choice to return to Sherguevil Island or remain on US soil. She chose the former."

"And to convince Ginny to choose Sherguevil Island, the FBI gave The Last Riders a get-out-jail-free card."

"We did," Agent Collins acknowledged with a withering stare, "which directly benefited *you*."

Reaper wanted to ream the agent a new asshole but couldn't because that part was at least the fucking truth. The agent took advantage of the self-flagellation Reaper was experiencing to press on with his agenda. "The easiest way to get Mrs. James homebound is to take the test. With her guilt out of the mix, Mr. Allerton will be forced to reveal more details about the artifact. If the facts Mrs. James has shared are true, I don't see any reason we can't wrap this up in the next couple of days."

Reaper considered the woman he thought he knew. Every day with Ginny, he found out something new. All The Last Riders, including him, thought she was the girl next-door.

Reaper silently laughed, planning to shove that discovery down Shade's and Rider's throats if he ever saw them again. Ginny was no more the girl next-door than he was. She was a shot of tequila when you were expecting a chardonnay. The little worm at the end was a punch to the gut with another secret uncovered.

"What if she doesn't pass?"

Ginny's eyes broke away at his question.

"In the best-case scenario, Mr. Allerton will accept your offer to find him another artifact at a comparable price."

"He said it was priceless," Reaper reminded him.

"Then we'll have to cross that bridge when we come to it. I don't understand your attitude. None of the information Mrs. James has given the FBI would place her life in danger. Mr. Allerton is one of the most well-regarded philanthropists in the world. There isn't a blemish on his record. In fact, his whole life has been, and continues to be, an open book. While yours, on the other hand … well"—the agent was even more reproving—"we'll leave it at that." Assuming they were done talking, Agent Collins resumed walking toward their waiting Moke.

The fucker was stupid enough to turn his back on him after dissing him like he was one of his trainees.

Ginny hastily stepped in front of him, pressing her hands against his chest to hold him back. "Please don't," she begged.

He burned his eyes into her pleading ones. "I wasn't going to fuck him up too badly."

"I don't want him hurt at all."

"I've had about enough with these condescending assholes."

"You get used to it." She blithely placed her arm through his, urging him toward the awaiting vehicle.

"Never in a million years."

"That's because you're one of the condescending assholes."

CHAPTER EIGHTEEN

"I wonder when they'll bring the clothes. I'm bored."

Reaper glowered at Ginny as she wandered around the small living room. "You want to fuck?"

Ginny stopped in her tracks. "No. Besides, it doesn't look like you want to, anyway. Why are you so angry with me?"

"I don't know," he said crossly. "Could be I don't appreciate being referred to as a condescending asshole, or it could be a number of things I can't talk about without being worried another condescending asshole is listening in."

Ginny pointedly stared at the glass jar of broken electronic parts sitting on the low coffee table. "How? You've smashed them all."

He rolled his eyes at her. "Like they didn't use the opportunity with us gone to replace them in new hidey spots."

"We can look if you want to. It would give us something to do. And it could be fun. We can see which one of us can find more."

"Is this a game to you?"

Sitting down next to him, she patted him on his thigh. "Of course not."

Aggrieved, he moved her hand away, nixing her attempt to placate him.

"I don't understand why you're angry with me."

Reaper reached for the small notepad and pen sitting beside the phone. Clicking the end of the pen, he wrote out what he wanted to say.

You deliberately bought the DNA test?

Ginny nodded her answer.

You knew it would flag you?

Again, she nodded.

He wasn't getting the simple answer. Tapping the pad with the pen, he then handed them to her.

I knew Allerton would cover all the bases. I bought the DNA kit that says "other agencies," including law enforcement, are able to use the information.

Reaper took the pen and paper back to scrawl down his next question.

When did you tell Hammer?

Ginny took them back. *After I took the sample and sent it back.*

"You just saved him an ass beating," he said out loud.

"Don't be mad."

Reaper scooted away when she tried to touch him again. Flicking through the television channels, he heard her scribbling on the notepad. When she tried to hand it to him, he ignored her. Ginny was not going to be denied, so she raised the pad so it blocked his sight of the television. Angrily, he snatched it from her hand and threw it across the room.

Giving him a hurt look, she stood up and went to the bedroom, quietly shutting the door behind her.

Tossing the remote down onto the couch, Reaper got up to pick up the notepad.

If you had been warned about being kidnapped, what would you have done? Would you have just let it happen or would you have done something different to prevent it from happening? I would go for the one where it never happened.

It took him a second to understand what she was trying to tell him.

Opening the bedroom door, he saw Ginny lying on her side on the bed. Placing the notepad on the nightstand, Reaper went through the bedroom with the detector. Finding six new devices he carried them into the other room and placed them in the glass jar before coming back to the bedroom to shut the door. Later when he was bored, he'd find the rest of the devices he was sure Allerton had stashed in the living room.

Taking of his shoes to lay down, then curling up against her back, he placed an arm around her waist. "You were warned about something?" Reaper had placed his mouth next to her ear.

"Yes," she whispered back.

"What were you warned about?" Reaper kept his voice whisper-soft.

Ginny buried her face in the pillow instead of answering.

"About you?"

She didn't respond.

"About me?"

Ginny linked her hand with his tightly.

"Anyone else?"

She nodded her head into the pillow.

"The Last Riders," he stated.

"None of you would have survived in prison. The Last Riders have made too many enemies." Ginny rolled over to face him, lifting her hand to his face. "Life wouldn't be worth living without you in the world, whether you're with me or you decided to be with a thousand other women."

"You're the only woman in my life."

"For now. I've been keeping you busy."

His lips curled up into a smile. "Yes, you have. Who gave you the warning?"

"Fynn."

"Is he usually right?"

"Always."

"Does he know, if events are changed, if it's for better or worse?"

Her answer was slower in coming. "Occasionally."

"Did he this time?"

"He wouldn't tell me. Fynn never does. He shares his gift, but to give you the outcome of your chosen path is to interfere with free will. In life, we alone are responsible for our triumphs and our failures."

"What happens if Fynn does?"

"The same thing that happened to one of their ancestors when she healed one of her relatives—the gift was taken away when she needed it most. Their gifts all come with a price; it isn't up to them how much they have to pay back." Ginny continued stroking his cheek as she stared lovingly into his eyes, completely baring her soul for him to see.

"You might not share their gifts, but by you taking the DNA test, it came as a cost that should have been mine to pay."

"There is no price I wouldn't pay for loving you. And I do love you."

"Ginny, I don't even know if I'm capable of loving someone like I did before."

"That's okay. I have enough to share." Teasingly, she removed her hand from his cheek to place it on her chest above her heart. Pretending to pick something up with her thumb and forefinger, she mimicked twining something around her finger and making a squiggly line as if there was imaginary thread, floating toward his chest. Pressing the tip of her finger to his chest, she tapped his chest twice.

"There. A couple more treatments and you'll be as good as new."

"I wish it were that easy."

"I don't believe in wishes; they never come true. Put your faith in someone else."

"I can't. Unlike you, I don't have issues with God. I lost my faith in Him the first year I was held captive."

"I wasn't talking about God. I was talking about me. Trust that my love will stay strong and true. I swear, Gavin, I will be there for you, even when you no longer want me there. Have faith in me. I will be there for you."

Folding her hands on top of each other, she placed her chin on his chest to stare down on him. "Not only are you my soul mate, you're my heart mate now. You'll never be able to escape me," she vowed solemnly. Then, removing her hands, she placed her cheek directly over his heart.

Reaper wanted to move her away, to put space between them. However, lifting his arms with that intention, he found himself hugging her closer. "I'm never going to be the man I used to be." Swirling emotions had him wanting to break free from the upheaval she was creating within him. It was like trying to sludge through quicksand—the more he fought against letting Ginny in, the deeper he sunk.

"That's okay. I love you just as you are." Scooting up his chest, she pressed a delicate kiss on his lips, whispering unintelligible love words to him that, at one time, would have had him running. He had never wanted or needed the lovey-dovey, flowery words that women used to express their emotions, but laying side-by-side with Ginny, he soaked her words up like a dry sponge. Smoothing her hands over his chest and arms, he basked in her attention, wanting more and more ... never wanting the moment to end.

The doorbell ringing from the other room, followed by several knocks couldn't break the spell Ginny had weaved around them. It was only when dusk began to filter through the shaded window that they made a move to leave the sanctuary of their bedroom.

"I'll get the clothes." Languorously stretching, Reaper then snagged Ginny around her waist to give her a quick kiss before releasing her to go into the other room.

Rolling a dress cart back into the room that had been left unattended outside, he found Ginny standing in the same spot he left her. "I thought you would be in the shower."

"I've had three showers today; I'm good." She moved to the dress cart, examining the pieces. "All these gowns are my size. How did he know my exact size?"

Reaper picked the first suit on the cart without interest. "They had our luggage when we arrived." Reaper dressed as Ginny carried one of the gowns into the bathroom.

Taking a few minutes to dress, Reaper then went into the living room to wait for Ginny. Looking in the refrigerator, he saw their meals had been replenished. Figuring now was a good time, he took the tiny bug detector from his pocket. He'd made sure he kept it in his pocket when he left the bungalow earlier for the meeting with Allerton. He had long ago stopped trying to conceal it. If the fucker didn't care that the bugs could be so easily found, Reaper didn't care he could be caught, but that didn't mean he'd leave it out in the open for them to take from him.

He was smashing the three he had found with the bottom of his shoe when Ginny came into the room. The black gown fit her like a glove. The bodice was black silk, heart-shaped, showing the top mounds of her breasts that were covered with sheer lace, forming into a collar around her neck. The silk part of the dress skimmed the tops of her thighs and from there intricate lace fell to her ankles. The black, strappy sandals added at least two inches to her normal height.

"Uh … fuck no. Go change," he ordered, and resumed breaking another electronic bug.

She gaped at him. "Don't be ridiculous. We're already late! There's nothing wrong with this dress."

"It's too short."

"It's comes down to my ankles!"

"You could read a book through that lace."

Ignoring him, she placed a tube of lipstick in the small purse she brought out with her.

"I can see your pussy from over here."

"You cannot!" she yelled, throwing the purse at him.

Dodging, he started to rise from the couch with a growl. With a squeal, she ran back into the bedroom, slamming the door behind her.

Ten minutes later, he was about to heat a meal from the fridge, assuming she had changed her mind about going, when she came back out, dressed in a pink, off-the-shoulder, floral silk dress that draped over her body. The bodice completely covered her chest and breasts, the only skin showing was the one shoulder, and it had a big bow, covering most of the curve of her shoulder.

"Better?" she asked snidely.

"Much." Satisfied, he put the unheated meal back into the refrigerator.

"You're such a jerk." Heatedly glowering at him, she went to pick up the purse that he left on the coffee table.

"I did you a favor." Bravely coming out from behind the kitchen counter, he told her, "No mother wants to see her daughter's coochie."

Ginny trembled as if she was restraining herself. "I was not showing my coochie."

"You weren't seeing it from my viewpoint."

"You were sitting down, and you didn't see anything. You just imagined it. The dress came down to my thighs."

"I didn't imagine shit," he smarted off, enjoying the fire he saw in her eyes. "When we come back, you can try it again, and I'll take a picture on my phone to show you."

"You're not taking a picture of my ... my ..."

"Pussy," he eagerly helped her. "Cunt ... twat."

"Quit being so uncouth!"

Reaper was smart enough to steer clear of her as he made his way to the door and she lifted her purse threateningly.

"Uncouth? What century were you born?" He laughed.

"The one when men knew how to be gentlemen." Giving him a haughty lift of her chin, she smoothed her dress down as if brushing him off. "Obviously, you're much older than me. Much older ...." Giving him a pitiful look, she rushed toward the door. "Here, let me open the door for you. You should conserve your strength ... old man."

The woman had no compunction about swinging below the belt when she wanted to.

"I'm not old!"

"Are, too." Complacent at reaching her goal of rattling him, she opened the door, mockingly waving him forward. "Here you go ... sir."

"I might be older than you chronologically, but I have the cock of a sixteen-year-old. When we come back tonight, I'm going to make you sorry for calling me old man."

Ginny blew out a hiss of hot air, dissing him. "Old man, I've been taking it easy on you. I'm younger; I have more stamina than you," she boasted.

"It's on when we come back."

"Bring it on, ol—"

With a squeal, Ginny side-stepped the palm of his hand, hurrying toward the waiting Moke.

"You can run, but you can't hide," Reaper warned, leisurely following after her.

Giggling lightheartedly, Ginny ran back toward him to

button his jacket for him. "You look very handsome tonight, Mr. James." Grinning, she unabashedly ran her hand over the expensive material.

"We're late, Ginny." He tried to turn her around to get her walking again, but she refused to budge.

"How come you never compliment me? Am I that unattractive?"

An irritated Agent Collins stepped out of the Moke, walking toward them. "Mr. Allerton has called several times. You two can finish this conversation in the vehicle."

Ginny sighed in frustration at the agent hurrying them. "We're coming." Then she gave Reaper a harassed frown.

"Don't blame me; you're the one who kept me in bed all evening."

"Don't blame me when your uncouth ass sleeps on the couch tonight."

Climbing into the Moke, she slapped his hand away when he would have assisted her.

"I see how you are. Is that the thanks I get for taking your mind off seeing your mother and not being able to see your father?"

Ginny nearly tripped over her feet getting inside. "You made us late because you were trying to relax me?" she hissed.

"I thought it would be easier than fucking you, but I didn't want to shower again. I'm becoming a prune."

Both men in the front seat turned around to look at them with their mouths gaping open.

Ginny waited until he was seated in the back seat before turning both barrels on him. "Gavin, remember the good *old* times when you wouldn't talk to me? Channel him back. I miss him."

CHAPTER NINETEEN

Ginny's anger and hurt at Gavin evaporated the moment they entered the lobby of the private resort. The grandeur of the entryway was designed to inspire awe and envy with its masterful strokes of creams, sea foam green, and a touch of gold, making you feel as if you were traveling through a portal that only a few were allowed admission.

As they were led through the lobby, Ginny didn't feel awe-inspired; she felt deeply rooted in sadness. Remembering how she had begged Manny to come inside, too young and innocent to know the beautiful resort was just an illusion meant to hide the ugliness and duplicity ingrained within each building block.

She had no desire to live in this world of luxury. This was the world that Kaden Cross and Dalton Andrews could easily walk among without missing a beat. Ginny had to give them credit for resisting the lure; stronger men and women hadn't.

Going up the curved staircase, Ginny could feel the speculative gazes as their small group was escorted to the right hallway. Unconsciously, her hand went to her side, searching for Gavin's, her exasperation with him put on the back burner as the stressful encounter with her mother loomed closer.

"You've got this." It took a second for Ginny to realize the thought that had popped in her head had actually been Gavin speaking out loud.

Her nerves stretched so tightly as she skimmed over the occupants of the room, not recognizing any of the four female guests as her mother.

Allerton broke away from a tall, charismatic man to greet them.

"Mr. and Mrs. James, Agent Collins, I'm so glad you've joined us. We've been waiting."

Agent Collins gave them an aggrieved look, and then the experienced veteran placed guilt where it belonged. "I'm going to excuse myself to make apologies on their behalf and chase down one of those waiters. Excuse me." Agent Collins left Gavin and Ginny on their own.

Ginny couldn't blame him for cutting and running. She wished she could, too.

Seeking a quick response for their tardy arrival, Gavin cut in with, "Mr. Allerton, please forgive us. Ginny and I are in the honeymoon stage of our marriage. I'm sure you can understand that, when romance beckons, a man wants to keep his wife happy."

Forgetting her issue with God, she prayed the floor would open and swallow her whole.

Allerton looked like he was praying for the same thing for her, except visualizing Gavin being swallowed first. "I'm not married."

"No? That's a shame. You don't know what you're missing," Gavin said blithely, unconcerned that Allerton was staring at them with distaste.

"Yes, well …." Allerton turned a cold shoulder to Gavin.

"Mrs. James, Soleil just stepped out to take a call from Jasper. She should return at any moment."

"That reminds me," Gavin interrupted, making it possible for everyone listening to overhear. "We've not had cell service since we've arrived. Our families will be concerned we haven't called."

"I will have to check into the matter in the morning." Allerton took two glasses of wine from a passing waiter, giving one to Gavin, then one to her, before reaching for another one for himself before dismissing the waiter.

"Come along, my dear," Allerton said brusquely. "I want to introduce you to a few of your parents' friends."

Leaving them to follow him, they made their way to a small group. The two men and one woman smiled politely at their approach. Gavin's firm grip on her hand kept her from approaching too closely.

"Mrs. James, I've been a fan of yours since I heard you sing in Nashville with Kaden Cross."

"Amelia, give me time to introduce you," Allerton scolded the woman. "I should have asked before. Which name do you prefer to be addressed with—Evangeline or Ginny?"

"Ginny," she answered immediately.

"Ginny, this is Amelia Clark and her father, George. Amelia and George, this is Ginny and Gavin James."

"It's nice to meet you," Ginny said as Gavin nodded toward the father and daughter.

Allerton turned to the man standing next to George. "Desmond Beck is also a friend of your parents," he introduced the charismatic man, who she had noticed when they entered the suite.

"I haven't had the opportunity to hear you sing. I hope you won't hold that against me." The mesmerizing man gave Amelia an indulgent look, which had the attractive woman blushing, before turning his charming gaze on Ginny. "I promise, I will rectify the mistake when your next performance is scheduled."

Ginny didn't expect to take a liking to any in the group. However, Desmond was a surprise. He stood out like Gavin, exhibiting the same air of confidence that only certain types of men were able to achieve, regardless of wealth.

Her continued scrutiny of Desmond Beck had Gavin giving her a sharp look; Ginny smiled. Gavin might not be able to express his feelings for her with words, but he was like a dog, possessively watching over his favorite bone when other men paid attention to her.

"My singing days are over. I plan to concentrate on songwriting in the future."

"Oh no, that can't be true," Amelia protested. "Your gift should be shared."

"It will. Just in another way."

Ginny wasn't taken in by the woman's flattery or by Desmond's charm. She had prepared for years for this moment by studying the people whom Allerton called friends or business acquaintances. She wasn't a gentle lamb being led to the slaughter without knowing the butchers who would receive a cut of her demise. What she couldn't find out from media sources or computer searches, Hammer had filled in the gaps. He had prepared her from a young age what she would be up against when she came into contact with the monster.

And George Clark was just that monster. He might seem like the grandfatherly type, having his daughter Amelia later in life, but the tech tycoon was as cutthroat as any of the Predators. Yet, while the Predators were proficient at using guns and blades, Clark's weapon of choice was a computer. He designed computer programs that correlated data from social platforms against internet searches that matched the user to products or social networks. Clark would then sell the data to the highest bidder. His software had been used to win elections, influence stock market prices, and destroy reputations.

His daughter had the same cutthroat attitude, except she'd disguised herself as genial, friendly, and the best BFF you could ever be fortunate to have. On the flip side of the coin, she would sell every secret entrusted to her, steal every dime you had, and take your boyfriend just because she could. She was beautiful, intelligent, and as cold-blooded as they came.

Looking over Amelia's shoulder, Ginny saw an older woman standing outside on the balcony, talking on a cell phone. Tuning out the conversation going on between George and Desmond about golfing the next day, Ginny moved away from Gavin's side to get a look at her mother.

"You don't take after Soleil."

She moved farther to the side of the window away from the small group, knowing Gavin followed at short distance behind her, but she didn't take her gaze off her mother. "No, I don't. T.A. looks more like her."

Leisurely, Desmond broke off conversation with the Clarks to stroll closer to Gavin, eavesdropping into the conversation going on between her and Allerton. Remaining silent, the pair of men made her feel safeguarded. Ginny couldn't explain why she felt the same vibe coming from Desmond as she did from Gavin. She had never met him before today, yet she felt comfortable in his presence.

A movement outside the window had her focusing back on Soleil. Her mother had the same curvy figure, hair color, and facial features as Trudy. The resemblance was startling.

She had deliberately avoided any public pictures of her parents, afraid it would bring back feelings of loss that she wouldn't be able to deal with. Children were born with an innate bond to their mothers, and even though she'd been happy with the Colemans, she'd felt that lack of maternal influence. It was bad enough missing that emotional bond; she never wanted to make it worse by searching for pictures of a mother whom she wouldn't be able to contact.

"Trudy may have Soleil's looks, but not her brains. I think you inherited more than your share in that department."

Every ounce in her being wanted to cut him down to size, which was exactly his goal. Allerton was trying to get under her guard to expose that she was closer to Trudy than she admitted.

"I didn't take you for a man who judges a book by its cover."

Allerton gave her a smile that didn't reach his eyes. "I wouldn't be where I am today if I couldn't spot a winner or a loser."

"I guess that makes Dalton Andrews better at spotting qualities than other men."

Allerton gave a short, humorless laugh. "Touché, Evangeline."

Ginny didn't miss the name hit.

"Which effectively puts me in my place. You dislike me intensely, don't you?"

"I wouldn't call it intensely. Intense involves hatred. I go back and forth between indifference and loathing."

"That's quite a range of emotions from a woman who has only been in my company briefly. It takes time or a specific reason to build those different levels."

"I apologize. I should be thanking you for arranging this party for me to meet my mother."

"I don't need or want an apology, but I would appreciate a reason."

"You don't think me being called a thief is reason enough? You asked me to take a polygraph for something you said I did when I was three. Doesn't it sound as asinine to you as it does to me?" Ginny carefully gauged how much irritation to exhibit in front of the monster. Not enough to seem over-the-top, but she wanted just enough to show indignation, hoping to confuse Allerton, since she had nearly slipped up defending Trudy. "Then you threaten to keep me captive on an island that I never knew existed before I took a DNA test."

"Then I should be the one who should be making the apology. I'm not prone to using my authority on this island unless I'm left with no choice. I find it very distasteful to have to keep you here; still I must do what needs to be done to retrieve the artifact. Surely you can see my point, unless there is another reason you're harboring a grievance toward me?"

Ginny gave an internal sigh. Allerton wasn't buying her story that she didn't remember going on the boat, and he was digging to find out if she'd seen what had happened to Manny and Gyi. The game of deception she was playing held her life and Gavin's in the balance. Since it appeared her convincing wasn't allaying his distrust, it was time to turn it up a notch, or *two*.

"I'm actually more knowledgeable about you than you believe. A friend of mine has made it her life's mission to uncover those who abuse the Earth's natural resources to make a profit. You, and many of your friends, are on her list."

Ginny was thankful that she was able to hide her smirk after seeing Allerton's bewilderment; accusing him of misappropriating charity funds was a direct hit.

"The list," Ginny said gravely, throwing more sand in his face to confuse his thinking. Ginny gave the performance of her life, and she didn't have to sing a single word.

"What list?" he demanded, his voice rising.

"The list that Zoey Mathers gives out as the worst offenders to the environment. Have you ever heard of her?"

Ginny was unaware of everyone stealthily moving closer to overhear their conversation.

"No, I can't say I have."

"I'm surprised. She has over a million followers. You should subscribe. She's amazing. She does podcasts, too, which are very informative. That's how I heard about you."

"Please, go on ..." Allerton's complexion turned an ugly, ruddy color as she provoked his temper. "I'd like to hear more about this woman."

"She's a life coach. I'll give you her name and number if you want to talk to her. She's not accepting new clients but, for you, I'm sure she'd make an exception. Zoey is very accomplished at what she does."

Ginny felt guilty for throwing Zoey under the bus but reasoned that Stump and the Predators would keep her friend safe. Besides, the podcast was open to the public and could be easily searched. Hell, Zoey would be so ecstatic that she mentioned her to Allerton—she might even give her a free session.

"She couldn't have been very effective if she's the one who convinced you to stop performing, especially when your popularity is on the rise."

Ginny nipped Allerton's snide comment in the bud. "Because I want to write, she suggested I should focus more on what I want to accomplish, which isn't singing but song-writing. My voice is nothing compared to other voices that can bring my songs to life. Would you like her number?"

"No ... I'll pass."

"I don't blame you. She wasn't very complimentary to you. Besides, you probably already have her public contact information in the petitions that she has filed against your charity. I signed three of them. I would have signed the last one, but Zoey's website was so overloaded with traffic that I couldn't get on."

"Ready for another drink, Gabriel?" Desmond Beck inserted himself in the conversation by taking Allerton's empty glass and replacing it with a full one.

Regarding her as if she was an alien from another planet, Allerton downed the full glass.

Desmond suavely gave her a half bow. "I didn't think I would live to see the day someone could make Gabriel lose his temper. I hope I'm not on Ms. Mathers' list." Desmond used his charm to defuse the tense situation, giving Allerton time to regroup, which was exactly what Ginny didn't want. She wanted his emotions in an upheaval. Allerton acted like a goldfish, all tiny and innocent on the outside, but Ginny's goal was to poke the hidden monster beneath.

"I can't say for sure. You'll have to check." Ginny shrugged. "But I can save George and Amelia from having to search, as well as"—she gave an imperceptible gesture toward two men who stood to her left—"Mr. Emerson and his partner, Mr. Varela."

"What did we do to make the list?" Aaron Emerson walked closer to the expanding group of irate listeners.

Satisfaction poured through her veins as Desmond's attempt of defusing Allerton's temper was rekindled by her drawing his cronies into the conversation.

"Well, it was something about a mother and child being killed when they were forced to cross a road that you built for your water trucks. There was a well you dug for them in exchange for your company purchasing their water rights—which you use to make bottled water to sell in different countries."

"That was a miscalculation, which was rectified," Aaron defensively explained as he loosened his expensive silk tie.

Ginny's blood boiled at the young mother and child being classified as a "miscalculation."

"How? Did you bring the mother and child back to life?

Did you compensate her other two children and her husband?"

"We built a well closer to their village."

"I'm sure that eased her family's grief." Ginny stared at him disdainfully.

The group of Allerton's cronies sidled closer to Aaron in a show of support, like flies gathering over a pile of shit. The very people who had gathered here to amuse themselves as she was being brought to slaughter were now on the defense.

"It always comes down to money, doesn't it?" Aaron's glass of wine shook with anger. "Will millions of dollars bring them back?

"No price can be placed on a person's life," she answered her own question for him, "but at the very least, it might make you think twice about drilling a well near to where people can use it and don't have to walk for two hours to get clean water, which, by the way, your company promised to do *before* the rights were sold. Instead, you used a loophole, built the wells where you didn't have to use expensive machinery and then you had the gall to convince them you did it all out generosity and concern. But in reality, you didn't make their lives easier, you made their lives hell holes. And those are the lucky ones. Other islands and towns, you convinced them you'd build schools for their children and provide teachers for them. I'm sure those countries and towns thought they hit the jackpot ... until the wells you built were again too far away, and the schools were closed because they were too far for the children to walk to. Saves you money when the schools closed and you didn't have to pay for the teachers and supplies. And what did you do with all of those water rights that the locals couldn't use? We all know the answer to that." Ginny waved her hand toward the cart that a waiter was pushing around with cans of soda and different brands of water. Then she dropped her hand and shrugged. "Or that's what Zoey said in her podcast about you."

"I have built over two hundred schools!"

"Would you like to know how many are still in operation?"

Aaron Emerson was so angry he seemed ready to chew his tongue off. It wasn't a good look.

His partner, Abbott Varela, was in better control. "This Zoey person should be prepared for a letter from our lawyer. As her friend, you may inform her that we don't take negative publicity lightly."

"I would ... if I had cell service."

Ginny glanced toward Gavin at his snort of laughter. She was surprised he hadn't stepped in to shut her up. Instead, she saw him tilt his wine glass at her in a salute, with Desmond chuckling beside him.

"Bravo, Mrs. James." Desmond raised his wine glass toward her, imitating Gavin's salute. "Your adoptive family benefited from our loss. It makes me wonder if you would've had the same outspokenness had you never been lost at sea."

"Naturally, I've questioned the difference of the life I would have had." Ginny looked around the room, taking in the occupants and the opulent surroundings.

"Have you come to any conclusions?" The female voice that came from the glass doorway of the balcony, silenced the room.

Ginny moved around Allerton to get a better view of her mother as she sauntered into the room. Desmond's comments had eased the tense atmosphere she had created, while at the same time allowing Ginny a breather to check the emotions of being so close to her mother once again. The two-fold instinct to grab her mother in a tight hug, while on the other hand keeping a wary distance in place.

"Yes. Basically, the question comes down to nature versus

nurture." Ginny surveyed her mother and the spectators, taking in the glittering dresses, jewelry, and snobby attitudes of the women, as well as the designer suits and arrogant stances of the men How was she supposed to respond? She remembered just the bits and pieces of the mother and father she'd known living in their little bungalow on Clindale. The woman standing in front of her sparked a spurt of fear inside her, yet Ginny couldn't understand why. There was no hint of maternal emotion shining from Soleil, instead Ginny felt as if she was being examined like bug under a microscope. "My father told me early on I had been adopted. When I got in trouble, he would blame himself for not raising me right, while the times I did something especially well, he would say that trait must have come from my biological parents. My adoptive father had several children, and he homeschooled all of us. I have to admit, there were times I felt different from them, that I wasn't as smart or ... as special at doing things the way they could.

"There was this one day, I wasn't able to do something that Leah, my sister, could do easily. I'll never forget my dad's response. He had all of us go outside to the yard to our garden, and he said, 'You see that apple tree? When you pluck an apple, it will always be apple, no matter if you make a pie, candy, peel them, or let them rot. An apple will always be an apple.' Then Freddy pointed to another tree and said, 'You see that tree over yonder in that clay pot?'"

Ginny bit her lip, remembering him standing in that yard as if it were yesterday.

"'That's a Calamondin orange tree,' he said. 'You can use them to make jelly, candy, peel them, or let them rot. An orange will always be an orange. I love them both, or I wouldn't be putting my effort and care into growing them. Don't matter that one's harder to grow, gives as much fruit, or persnickety as heck, and some years, don't give any fruit at all. The only difference between those trees to me is the apple tree is growing in soil, letting the roots spread out, while the orange tree is in a pot, keeping the roots nice and warm. Now, when we pluck those apples and oranges, are we going to be caring about those roots or are we just be going to be thanking God for blessing us with His harvest?'"

Ginny took in her mother's appearance as she walked closer, from her perfectly styled hair, the pearl necklace she wore around her throat, her black cowl-neck satin slip-on dress, which was lovingly clinging to her body, to the high, black satin heels strapped on her feet; the look created a flawless impression of a woman who was as different as day and night from the mother she remembered. In that moment, Ginny felt a deep sense of loss, as if she just found out someone died, because nowhere within the woman staring at her was a mother excited to see the daughter she hadn't laid eyes on in decades.

"Your adoptive father sounds like a remarkable man." Desmond Beck broke the tension in the room after Ginny stopped speaking, and neither Soleil nor she made any further movement toward each other.

"He was." Ginny tore herself out of her grief. She would mourn the loss of her mother when Gavin's and her life didn't depend on her playing a part.

"Hello, Soleil."

"Evangeline." Soleil probed her eyes, as if she was trying to determine if she recognized her own daughter.

Ginny intentionally pretended to misunderstand the calculating look, giving Soleil a compassionate one in return. "I apologize. It has to be hard for you to hear me talking about my family in Kentucky while you were mourning my loss all these years."

"I lost two daughters the day your plane went down."

"How did you lose Trudy?" Pretending confusion, she

glanced toward where Agent Collins stood. "Treepoint is a small town. I would have heard if T.A. died."

Furiously chewing what he was eating, it took a minute for Agent Collins to speak. "She hasn't," he confirmed.

"Trudy refused to come back to Clindale," Soleil started slowly, as if it was painful for her to talk about. "The plane crash was too traumatic for her," she explained.

Ginny nodded. "That's understandable. Fortunately, I don't have any memories of the plane crash."

"For years, I've imagined how frightened you must have been, and I wasn't able to be there for you. I regretted letting my babies go on that trip without me. You don't know how much. Tragedy often brings families together or it can tear them apart. Losing you drove a wedge between Trudy and your father and I. I want us to find a new beginning, one where we can be a family again." Soleil raised her arms as she drew close enough to touch her, but Ginny backed away, refusing the embrace.

"I think, to be on the safe side, we should keep our distance, don't you?"

Soleil dropped her arms to her sides. "You've been in isolation. There's no need to be worried about you giving me the virus."

"I think it would be better for both of us to remain on the safe side, don't you?" Ginny repeated.

Soleil gave her a considering look. She might have looked like Trudy in appearance, but the artificialness of her reactions were as real as a plastic doll—beautiful to look at, but without any warmth or softness.

"If that makes you feel more comfortable, then of course I'll abide to your wishes. I just wanted to feel you in my arms once again. To know you're really here with me."

"I'm really here." Ginny wasn't afraid to touch Soleil; she just didn't want to. Her father was the one who had arranged for her to disappear, to keep her and Trudy safe from Allerton. Trudy and she had always assumed Soleil had known Evangeline didn't die in the plane crash. But did she? It was only a question her father could answer and he wasn't here.

To see the mother she remembered as another carbon copy of the other women in the room was eye-opening to her. Her mother hadn't stayed on the island because she was forced to; it was where she wanted to be—with or without her children. Trudy had figured that out long ago, which was why she didn't like discussing their parents and spared her the pain by not telling her. If Trudy had known of her plan to take the DNA test, she would have forewarned her, spared her the painful discovery of the type of woman their mother really was.

"Mr. Allerton said you were talking to Jasper. When will he be coming?"

"Soon," Soleil prevaricated. "At least a few more days."

Stomach acid boiled in the back of her throat as Soleil curled her arm though Allerton's, as if she needed his emotional support.

"Did he pass on any messages for me? You were on the phone for quite a while," Ginny asked dispassionately.

Soleil removed her arm from Allerton's, dropping the air of fragility. "I only spoke to Jasper for a few minutes …."

Ginny sensed an undercurrent extending from Soleil to Allerton, then traveling around the room to his friends, as if they knew what was about to be said.

"I was talking to Trudy."

CHAPTER TWENTY

S oleil's announcement had Ginny experiencing another spurt of fear. Was she about to be blown out of the water? The wrong word from Soleil could disclose that Trudy knew Evangeline was still alive before being contacted by the FBI. Retaining her composure, Ginny had to quickly think of the best way to respond to the land mine that Soleil could reveal.

Looking at Soleil and Allerton together, Ginny thought about their friendship from another perspective. Far from being a fragile flower, Soleil was a Venus flytrap.

"I hope she is doing well, because of the virus I haven't been able to see her since I found out about our connection."

"Yes. At least, that's what she told me. We really didn't get into the specifics of her health, other than her calling to inform me that Jasper and I are going to be grandparents."

For a woman who had just found out she was about to be a grandmother, Soleil seemed remarkably unmoved. Ginny had no doubt as to why Trudy called their mother. Her sister had to be frantic after finding out she was returning to Clindale. Finding out Trudy had called showed how desperate and concerned Trudy must be at not being to communicate with her. Her mother didn't appear overjoyed by the call or the news.

"Aw … I'm happy for T.A. and Dalton." Ginny didn't experience the same problem, able to funnel the happiness she felt at Trudy's pregnancy while trying to keep herself from being grilled alive if she said the wrong thing. "I'm acquainted with Dalton's daughter. Grace has been concerned about her father since the death of his first wife. I bet she and Ice are ecstatic at Dalton's impending fatherhood."

"Ice?" Circumspect, Soleil looked at Allerton, as if for his approval.

"Grace's husband," Ginny informed Soleil and the onlookers watching the interchange. "Ice is the president of the Predators. Funny enough, Zoey's husband, Stump, belongs to the Predators."

"Who's Zoey?" Soleil asked.

"Don't ask," Allerton told her. "Suffice to say, she a social influencer who won't be able to spread her untruths about me, Abbott, and Emerson once our attorneys are done with her."

"Good luck with that." Ginny poured more salt on the egos of the three men.

"I don't need luck." Imperiously, Aaron gave her his pompous back, moving away.

To Ginny's amusement, she saw him reaching for his phone.

Feeling the censure of the gazes around her, except from Gavin and Desmond Beck, she explained for her mother's benefit, "I'm afraid I upset Mr. Emerson. I was discussing a friend of mine while you were on the phone. He didn't appreciate being a hot topic on one of Zoey's podcasts. I think he's thinking of filing a lawsuit."

"Darling—"

Ginny tried not to flinch when Soleil called her that, then proceeded to speak to her as if she had the mental capacity of a child.

"—Aaron has some very influential friends. Your friend would be wise to steer clear of using him as a topic to further her viewership."

"She doesn't do it to gain more viewers." Ginny furrowed her brow, mimicking confusion, as if the thought hadn't occurred her.

"Then I'm at a loss." Soleil looked up at Allerton as if he could answer her question.

"Zoey isn't afraid of lawsuits," she answered. "In fact, the more the merrier."

"Why not?" Allerton sent out the probing question, taking over the conversation.

"Zoey loves to drag big corporations to court to expose their dishonest business practices. Unlike the businesses, Zoey doesn't have to pay high-price lawyer fees. Her father does the work pro bono."

Allerton was too cultured to roll his eyes at her, but the dismissive way he curled his lip at her evidenced his scorn.

"Free means worthless."

"Then you're the only one in the world who would consider Haden St. Clair's work as worthless."

Shoving his phone back in his dinner jacket, Emerson stalked back toward her. "Zoey's father is Haden St. Clair?"

"Yes. Most people have heard of him. He just won a two-billion-dollar lawsuit from a corporation that tried to take a farmer's land away from him when the crops he planted cross-pollinated with another crop near his land. The corporation lost, and so have the other corporations. But don't let me stop you. You could be the one who breaks St. Clair's winning streak." Giving Emerson fake encouragement and growing bored at antagonizing Allerton and his cronies, Ginny was ready for the small party to be over.

As far as she was concerned, the whole thing had been a bust; definitely unworthy of getting dressed twice. She wondered if it was too soon for Gavin and her to make their excuses and leave.

"Excuse me; my husband was hungry before we left the bungalow." Taking Gavin's hand, she led him toward the small silver trays of food.

"I'm starving. How about you?" Ginny gave Gavin a crystal plate before taking one for herself.

"Better fill your stomach, because if Allerton didn't want to poison us before, he does now."

Ginny gave him a mischievous glance. "You want to reconsider your role as my taste tester?" she teased.

"Where is Greer Porter when I need him?" Gavin ruefully joked, then proceeded to load his plate with the fancy appetizers that Ginny had no palate for and hoped she never would.

Ginny noticed while Gavin was eating, he had looked around the room to see if anyone recognized him. Ginny couldn't understand why he would care if anyone recognized him or not.

Thinking she was imagining his concern, she chose a few things to put on her plate. She wasn't hungry, finally settling on a few grapes, crackers, and a chocolate petit fours. Then she stepped to the side, popping one of the grapes in her mouth as Gavin placed a stack of honey-mint lamb skewers on his plate next to a mound of shrimp tartlets.

Swallowing the grape in her mouth, Ginny picked up the tiny, pretty chocolate cake, putting the whole thing in her mouth. As she bit down, the taste exploded, hitting her gag reflex. She wildly looked around, hoping no one was watching so she could spit it out.

"Just swallow it," Gavin advised humorously. "The longer you hold it in your mouth, the worse you make it."

As badly as she didn't want to take his advice, she was left with no choice, other than making a fool of herself.

"What did I just eat?" she managed to croak out.

"I have no idea." Gavin shrugged, going back to the table and taking one of the petite fours. He bravely put it in his mouth as he came back and waited until he swallowed to tell her what she'd eaten. "Chocolate-covered goat cheese."

"Whoever made that has no taste buds."

"It was pretty good. I'm going to grab a couple more when I finish this plate."

"You thought that was good?" Amazed that Gavin liked the appetizer and wanted more had her reconsidering everything she perceived about his likes and dislikes toward food. Not only that, maybe her taste buds were off. To her, it had tasted hideous.

"You want to try one of the lamb skewers to get the taste out of your mouth?" Gavin offered.

"I'll pass. I've lost my appetite."

"Not very adventuresome where food is concerned, are you?" he teased.

"Not when it comes to chocolate-covered goat cheese," she said stiffly, still tasting the cheese.

Why couldn't she get rid of the aftertaste? She had been raised on goat's milk, none of the goat cheese she'd ate before had that flavor. "Why did it taste like a flower?"

"There was a hint of lavender." Gavin gave her an approving glance.

Ginny made a face at him. "A hint? What I ate was a flat-out assault."

Remaining where she was when Gavin went back to get seconds, Ginny was debating whether she was brave enough to try a slice of cheesecake when she saw Allerton and Soleil making their way toward her.

"Your mother just came up with a brilliant suggestion." Allerton maneuvered himself and Soleil closer, blocking her view of Gavin, just as Desmond Beck initiated a conversation with him at the buffet table. *That certainly screamed setup.*

"I wouldn't call it brilliant."

Ginny nearly gagged as Soleil practically preened under Allerton's regard.

"But I believe it may solve the problem between you and Gabriel. I want all of us to get along. I want you to feel free to come visit your father and me any time, to make this island your second home."

Gavin came up behind Soleil and Allerton, going around them to show he was near.

Soleil gave her a superficial smile, attempting to reach out for her hand. Again, Ginny took a step back, unable to stop herself.

"Sorry, it's become a habit for being cautious. In the States, we're terrified of getting the virus." The thought of letting Soleil touch her made her skin crawl. The only thing worse would be if Allerton made the attempt.

"I would like for us to get along, too," Ginny lied, continuing smoothly. "What was your suggestion?"

"You and I could go alone to Clindale Island and walk around. Maybe that would jog your memory."

"That is brilliant, but I'm sorry, I can't go along with your suggestion."

"Why on earth not?" Soleil wasn't ready to take no for an answer. "We could spend the day together. Those years when we lived on the island were some of the happiest moments of my life."

Ginny had thought so, and sadly she was coming to the realization many of those memories had been centered on the islanders and few were of times she spent with her parents.

Was Soleil putting on an act in front of Allerton like she was? If it was just her life at stake, Ginny might have chanced lowering her guard, but she wouldn't with Gavin's.

"They may have been for me, also, but I'll never know, because I was too young to remember." Ginny gave a frustrated sigh. "I appreciate how difficult this has to be for you. You want to help Mr. Allerton find his artifact, which he believes your daughter stole from him. I truly wish I could be more helpful, but unless he has a magical reset button we can push, we have to accept what was done was done and move on."

"That's easy for you to say." Allerton's palpable resentment left a bad taste in her mouth, worse than the goat cheese. His anger must have been building all those years since discovering the artifact was gone, and then being denied access to the person who'd stolen it. His resentment may have stagnated, but like a fungus, it grew every time he thought of it. Gabriel Allerton was used to getting what he wanted. He was used to having money and erasing anything or anyone standing in his way. Except her. And no amount of money could buy the memories buried in the deepest recesses of her mind.

"I have another idea," Ginny suggested. "Gavin and I could go over to Clindale Island, spend the day exploring on our own." Ginny saw both Soleil and Allerton were going to nix that suggestion, but she hurried on persuasively. "Maybe something *will* come back to me, if I'm not being pressured. If something comes to me, I'll make sure to tell you. You can search us both before and after to make sure we aren't trying to sneak the artifact back. If, after I spend the day there and we can't make any headway, I'll consent to the polygraph test. Either way, you have nothing to lose and everything to gain."

Allerton gave her a considering look. "My men will be stationed around the island with boats."

"However you want to do it is fine. Is that agreeable?"

"Yes. Like you said, I have nothing to lose."

Ginny felt as if a huge weight had just been taken off her chest. Afraid she inadvertently showed her relief, she sought to rectify her mistake by keeping them busy answering her questions.

"Is there someone who lives on the island who can act as our guide and interpreter?" She would have to contain her excitement when she saw Manny's family again ….

"No. The island is completely empty. A hurricane destroyed most of the homes and all of the villagers who had lived there for generations." Pleasure dripped from Allerton's forked tongue at imparting the horrendous information.

Ginny had to concentrate on her mother's hand on Gabriel's arm to keep from falling to the floor in heartbreak. "That's terrible." With a deadpanned voice, Ginny raised her eyes to Allerton's, seeing the pleasure within his. Like the monster he was, he had sensed when his opponent was hurt. "When was the hurricane?"

"Three years ago."

CHAPTER TWENTY-ONE

He had been responsible for the casualties. Ginny felt it in her bones.

Wanting to run screaming from the room, she forced down the hatred and accusations that she wanted to hurl at him. She felt the expectancy from him as he watched her for any telltale signs that could prove she remembered the people on the island.

Ginny plucked one of the chocolate goat cheese petit fours off Gavin's plate, shoving it into her mouth. She didn't have to mask her reaction; it came as soon as the taste hit her tongue.

This time when she gagged, she didn't fight it. Jerking a cocktail napkin from Gavin's other hand, she started retching into it. The onlookers hastily moved away in disgust as Ginny retched louder, deriving a sick pleasure at paying Allerton back for the sadistic way he had told her.

A handful of napkins appeared in front of her face, and Ginny reached out to take them from Desmond Beck with her eyes streaming tears.

"Are you all right?" he asked courteously.

"I think so. Thank-you. God, what was that?" she asked, using a clean napkin to wipe her tears away.

Desmond motioned for a waiter, unperturbed as he whisked the soiled napkins away from her to set them on the empty tray. "Thank-you. Macon, please bring us some wet cloths."

"Yes, sir."

"To answer, Ginny, those delicacies are Allerton's favorite. They're chocolate-covered goat cheese."

"I'm so embarrassed. My family has a herd of goats, and I've learned to make a dozen different things with their milk. Before I leave, I'll have to give your cook my recipe for goat cheese. I could swear I tasted a hint lavender in that one."

Ginny gave the waiter a sweet smile when he held out a silver tray with two steaming wet clothes. Taking one, she daintily wiped her hands, placing it back on the tray when the waiter held it out for Desmond to discard his as well.

"Mr. Allerton, you should try your goat cheese with fig jelly." Ginny let her Kentucky accent come out in full force. "Save the chocolate for strawberries."

Allerton cleared his throat. "You can write the recipe down, and I will see my chef gets it. Going back to what we were discussing before your choking incident." Distastefully, he gave his plate to a passing waiter. "The hurricane occurred three years ago."

Were the people in the room aware of what Allerton had done? Her mother? Her father?

"There were no survivors?"

"None." Allerton took one of the chocolate goat cheese petit fours from a passing waiter, his face showing the enjoyment of the nasty concoction.

She wouldn't be wasting her time to write her recipe. He could fart lavender-scented gas balls out of his uptight butt, and she wouldn't care.

"How fortunate for you that Sherguevil Island didn't incur the same casualties." Ginny couldn't hold back the snapped barb.

"Fortunate, indeed. Sherguevil did incur massive damages. All of the bungalows were destroyed, the resort had extensive damages to the roof, and the first floor flooded. Overall, it wasn't anything that couldn't be repaired. As the owner, I had the power to evacuate the island two days before when the hurricane had been forecasted. I took two boats and offered any of the islanders who wanted to leave Clindale free rooms in one my hotels, but they all refused. Sadly, I didn't have the authority to force an evacuation. I still regret my inability to convince them to heed my warnings."

"We all have our crosses to bear in life." Her hand itched to smack the man who wouldn't experience regret if it bit him on his ass. "Some find it an easy burden to brush off, while others carry the heavy burden for the rest of their lives."

"You believe our decisions have religious connotations?"

"I believe we each have an internal scorecard that is marked with our triumphs and failures. Only we know what those scorecards show. Mine shows the failures and victories I've achieved in regard to how I've lived my life without hurting others."

"Then you would be disappointed in me. I believe others are responsible for their own actions, especially if they refuse aid when it is offered. To that effect, mine would be more of a spreadsheet of the numbers of those I was able to help than those I failed."

Ginny looked around at the agreeing expressions of those who had gravitated closer to them to listen. "You're speaking for them?"

"I believe they feel the same," Allerton disclosed after

searching the faces of those close to him. Soleil was just one of the many nodding her acquiescence.

"Then I find that sad."

The suite went as silent as a tomb at her derogatory comment.

"Why so?" Desmond Beck asked.

"Aren't you all members of the same charity? I would never classify people as numbers on a spreadsheets. Spreadsheets are tools to provide an analytic data. As a charity, I assumed you would think any loss was a failure. I guess that's the difference between a registered charity and a non-profit one."

Desmond gave her a charming smile. "Very true, very true." His agreement with her had dark frowns coming his way from the other guests, which he shut down with an ironic twist of his lips. "Indeed, it is our loss you haven't been here to keep us on the straight and narrow. Gavin, you're a lucky man. I bet Ginny keeps you on your toes."

"I'm the lucky one." Giving Gavin a heartfelt smile, Ginny turned back to find herself under Desmond's perusal.

Feeling uncomfortable, Ginny gave a regretful sigh. "If Gavin and I are going to Clindale early, we should be leaving. Thank-you, Mr. Allerton, for hosting the party, and for the rest of you for attending. Soleil, I hope we have an opportunity to speak together privately in the next few days, to become reacquainted."

Ginny barely gave Gavin enough time to dispose his plate before tugging him toward the door. They weren't quick enough.

"Join me for breakfast in the morning," Soleil invited. "We can eat on the patio here. The resort has a huge breakfast buffet," Soleil went on without giving Ginny time to refuse. "Gabriel, would you join us?"

"Certainly. I usually eat around seven. Is that too early for you? I can push it back."

"Seven, it is," Ginny agreed. "Goodnight."

Ginny was overjoyed at being released from the stifling atmosphere in the suite. She didn't even care that Agent Collins looked downcast by having to accompany them out.

Conscious of Gavin's sidelong glances, Ginny remained silent, not wanting to talk in front of the agent, afraid she would inadvertently let something slip. Ginny was curious, wondering if Allerton used as many listening devices in the rooms of his resort as he placed in their bungalow.

Once seated in the Moke, she despondently stared ahead. Light poles situated along the trail gave enough illumination that the driver didn't have to turn on the headlights.

Getting out of the Moke, she made no move to go inside the bungalow.

She now understood what had bothered her when she first arrived on Sherguevil Island. There were no lights on Clindale. Even at this distance, some type of lights should have been visible.

As if understanding the enormity of feelings going through her, Gavin remained by her side.

"I thought you wanted to have an early night?" Agent Collins sarcastically reminded her.

"I do. I just had a leg cramp. It's better. Good night." Making the jumbled excuse, Ginny practically ran inside, barely waiting for Gavin to get inside before slamming and locking the door.

"Ginny ...."

She laid her forehead on the locked door, raising her hand for him not to speak. She desperately needed to hold in the howl of pain that was ripping her apart.

"Let's go to bed." Gavin took ahold of her outstretched hand, pulling her away from the door.

Letting him lead her through the darkened interior of the living room and into the bedroom, she limply let him undress her before she slipped between the covers. Curling into a ball, she heard Gavin searching around the room for bugs, then the sound of him going into the front room before coming back into the bedroom and shutting the door. Hearing the rustling of his clothes before he slid in next to her and pulled her close, she closed her eyes comforted he was here. She needed the reassurance that no matter how deprived an action an evil person committed, kindness and goodness would triumph in the end. Right now, she felt Allerton was winning all the battles.

Burrowing into his warmth, Ginny didn't feel as if the coldness in her body would ever go away. Resting her head on the same pillow as him, she finally allowed the raw emotions she was feeling escape her.

"He killed them," she whispered achingly. "He killed them all."

"You don't know that for sure."

"I do. I could see it in his eyes." Shaking despite how close Gavin was holding her, she was unable to hold back her tears as she began to silently cry. "I should have been the one who died ... I deserve ...."

Gavin pressed his mouth over hers. "Don't ever say that again. The only one who deserves to die is Allerton, and that's going to come true if he tries to hurt you," he promised her fervently.

"Some monsters are too powerful to kill."

"He can be taken down. He's human."

"I don't think he is ...." Sobbing into his shoulder, she cried for the gentle islanders who had been so kind to her when Manny had taken her there to play. They hadn't had much, but they always shared what they had with her. She'd fallen asleep on the same mats next to their children; they taught her to climb the coconut trees without breaking her neck, how to swim …. The few memories she had from her childhood involved them taking her under their wings and making her one of their own. In the end, it was that kindness that had destroyed them.

Ginny cried harder, feeling as if her soul was being ripped apart. "I hate him so badly."

"I know you do." Rubbing her back, Gavin let her cry until there were only small hiccups coming from her.

"I wanted to go to the island tomorrow to see them, and they won't even be there."

"You don't think it will help you to remember?"

"No."

"Then we won't go."

"We have to. I won't let him win. It'll buy us another day from me having to take the polygraph test."

"Which you've already practically agreed to take."

"He wanted our answer in the morning. I bought us another day."

"One day isn't going to make a difference."

"I have to convince him that I don't remember anything about that day. If I do, maybe he'll leave me alone to go on with my life."

"If that's what you're trying to do, it isn't going to work."

"Why not?"

"A man like Allerton doesn't take chances. I bet he's never gambled a day in his life. That's why he killed the islanders. He wasn't going to take the chance they found what you took."

"Or that I told them I saw him kill Manny's father, Gyi, and I assumed he killed Manny as well. I never saw him again."

"You actually saw him kill Gyi?"

"Yes."

"Then we're fucked."

"Not if I convince him I didn't," she reasoned, "and that I don't remember taking the artifact. He might let us leave, and both of us can go on our merry way."

"There's no way you'll pass a polygraph if he slips any questions about them into the test. The thing I don't get is your mother being friends with the son of bitch. How did you feel about seeing her again?"

"Like finding out Santa Claus doesn't exist."

Gavin's swear word was barely discernable under his breath. "I expected her to shed a tear or two at seeing you again. She was as cool as a cucumber."

"I kinda did, too."

"I'm sorry."

"It's all right." Ginny began to slide out of the bed.

"Where are you going?"

"I need to brush my teeth."

Gavin didn't release the cover to let her slide out. "About that …."

Ginny groaned. "What?" She could tell he was wavering about telling her something. "Just tell me."

"When I was at the buffet, I talked to Desmond."

Ginny frown. "I know. I saw you. So?"

"We might have had a laugh about the goat cheese."

"He knew I ate one before and hated it?"

"Yes …."

This day just went from bad to worse.

"Is there an Easter Bunny?"

CHAPTER TWENTY-TWO

U p at the crack of dawn, then after showering, Ginny went to sit down on the side of the bed next to Gavin. She never grew tired of watching him. While he slept, she could see the man he must have been. If she hadn't cried out all her tears the night before, she would have started crying again now.

Sprawled naked on the bed with the covers twisted off, she was given access to his masculine beauty, unfettered by his normal garb of jeans and a T-shirt. Last night, seeing him dressed in the expensive suit, she wanted to stoke him like a big cat ... until he opened his mouth.

Gavin had a jealous streak a mile long. Had he been jealous with Taylor?

Debating if there anyone she could ask without making her come across as being the jealous one, she ran her fingertips teasingly over his chest and smiled when he reached out to swat her away.

"Time to get up, lazybones." Pressing a sweet kiss on the corner of his mouth, she started to raise up, only to find his hand in her hair, holding her still.

"Don't wake me with that little girl kiss," he said groggily.

"What type of kiss do you want?"

"Like this." He caught her mouth in a passionate kiss that parted her lips and had him thrusting his tongue inside in a soul-melting embrace. Wrapping his arms around her, he used his body to twist her over his until she was laying on the bed beneath him. Lifting his mouth, he then stared down at her before he unknotted the bath towel she had wrapped around herself.

"I don't need to relax." Raising her hand, she drew his hair back behind his ear so she could see his face.

"I do." Gavin rubbed his stiff dick along her waistline.

Ginny parted her thighs, giving him enough space to lay between them, giving in to him immediately.

Placing each of his forearms on the pillow beneath her head, Gavin braced his upper body over hers. "We'll be late," he warned.

"Who cares?" She impishly raised her head off the pillow to kiss the side of his neck.

Gavin pulled his neck away to stare down at her with an expression she had trouble deciphering. "Ginny …?"

"Hmm …?" Wrapping her thighs around his, she raised her eyes to his, surrendering her whole being to him.

"Don't do that."

"Do what?" Confused, she started to slide her legs away, but he caught one leg behind her knee and pulled it back to his hip.

"Love me so much."

She gave him a tender smile. "I'm afraid I can't help that."

"I don't want you hurt."

She wrapped her arms around his shoulders. "Then don't hurt me," she said simply.

Gavin closed his eyes as if he were in terrible pain.

"Hey, wild man." She directed his attention back to her,

not knowing what was going on in his head. "Where'd you go?" Ginny kissed his chin when he opened his eyes.

"I'm here."

"I don't think you are."

"I'm here."

"I don't think you are. I think you went back to that basement. I think a part of you is still locked inside."

"Stop." Gavin tried to pull off her, but she tightened her legs around him, refusing to let go.

"It's okay, wild man. My heart is open whenever you're ready to walk through that door."

"What if I never can?"

"My love doesn't have time limits. It's everlasting."

Ginny could see the toxic train of thoughts that held him.

"Nothing lasts forever."

"My love will."

"You say that now, but what if I piss you off or—"

"Or we get separated?" Ginny finished for him, seeing the fear that her big, tough man would never admit to in a quadrillion years.

"I'll stay true to you forever," she promised, running her hand down his spine and feeling him arch under her touch like a big cat. "My love will," she vowed, giving him the assurance he didn't even know he was asking for. "Forever and a day, my love will be endless."

"People make that promise at least a thousand times a day. I've been promised that before. Promises are meaningless."

"Maybe so, but those promises weren't made by me. I don't forget my promises just because the person isn't there to see me keep track of them." Ginny shifted slightly under him to place her hand over his heart. "Mine is engraved in gold ... right here. You don't even have to lock it inside; it will always be there for you. Only for you. It will never tarnish or go cold, even when we're no longer on this Earth. My love for you isn't fool's gold; it's real and true and will never end."

"You don't know what the future holds. I'm the first man you loved. Time changes a person. Ten years from now, you could be saying the same thing to another man."

"I won't."

"You don't know th—"

"I do. Wild man ... there's only one Gavin James. There was only one key made for my heart."

Gavin crushed her mouth in a kiss that stole her breath at the intensity, as if he was having an inner struggle to believe her.

Returning his kiss, she ferociously battled back, parting her lips to give him what he needed. The mental struggle between them had them passionately wiggling and writhing on the bed as their bodies took over, drowning them in a haze of desire where time stood still and the only sounds in the room were sighs and moans. Ginny held him close when she felt him shuddering over her, surrendering every ounce of her being to him. Giving him a butterfly kiss on the curve of his neck, she wiggled out from under him to tug at him.

"Come on ... up. You've relaxed enough." Seeing what she was doing was useless, she picked up a pillow, whomping him over the head, then hastily running toward the bathroom at his growl.

She was merrily singing "Wrecking Ball" by Miley Cyrus in the shower when Gavin stepped inside. She impishly gave him a sultry look before she stepped out, closing the door behind her.

"Get back in here!"

Pressing her naked breasts against the glass, she seductively teased him. "Nuh-uh … Next time, be quicker. I'm already done."

Gavin moved to press his body on the opposite side. "Come back in here. I have something to give you."

"Like I'm going to fall for that," she taunted, looking back over her shoulder as she reached for the towel to wrap herself.

"You're lucky I used most of my strength fucking you, or I'd come after you."

"Old man, it has nothing to do with strength; you just aren't motivated enough." Ginny giggled, pointing at his limp dick.

"Then come back in here and motivate me some more."

She tsked him with the click of her tongue. "You've been motivated enough for today. I'll give you some more tonight." With a sassy grin, Ginny went into the bedroom to dress.

Putting on a thin pair of blue cotton crop pants and a white linen top, she was putting on her sneakers when Gavin came back in to get dressed. Brushing her hair, she put her hair in a ponytail, then turned to see Gavin putting his shoes on.

"Ready?" he asked as he stood to look at her questioningly.

Finding herself unable to speak, she had to blink back the sudden tears in her eyes.

Gavin walked to her to enclose her in his arms. "We don't have to go."

Shaking her head, she stepped out of his arms. "I'm ready." She gave him a strained smile. "Just in time."

Hearing the knock from the other room, they went to answer the door. Agent Collins was waiting and, without pleasantries, hurried them to the Moke.

The short ride was over too soon for Ginny. She regretted not coming up with a spur-of-the-moment refusal for the meeting with Allerton and her mother for breakfast.

Escorted to the first-floor restaurant, they were led through a private doorway that had a different buffet area than the one in the other room. Bypassing the buffet, they headed toward a balcony doorway then to a large patio that faced the ocean. The area had six tables and each one was occupied by guests. Allerton and a woman sat at the largest table, waiting for them. They were already eating and looked up when Gavin and Ginny took their seats.

"Good morning. I hope you both slept well," Allerton greeted them.

"We did. Thank-you," Ginny answered, placing the linen square on her lap.

"Soleil was hungry. I assured her you wouldn't mind if we didn't wait."

"Not at all." Glancing around the table, she did a double take of the guests, recognizing several she had seen in the media.

A waiter appeared by Allerton's side. "What would you like to drink?"

Both she and Gavin ordered orange juice.

"Would you like the waiter to fix you a selection, or would you prefer to make your own plate?" Allerton asked.

"I'll just take the juice."

"I'll take some eggs, bacon, and toast," Gavin ordered.

"You have a long day ahead of you. I had the kitchen fix you a lunch for when you get hungry on the island."

"Thank-you."

Once their drinks arrived, Ginny didn't touch her drink until Gavin gave her a subtle nod.

It gave Ginny the creeps the way Allerton studied Gavin. She didn't like it, and despite Gavin ignoring the perusal, her protective instincts screamed at a fever pitch.

Underneath the tablecloth, she felt Gavin place a warning hand on her thigh.

"You sure I can't tempt you to try something off the buffet? You didn't eat much last night. Is something wrong with the food?"

"No. I've never been much of a morning person."

Angry as she was with Allerton, Ginny attempted a conversation with her mother.

"Did you sleep well?"

"Yes, thank-you. Would you like a mimosa?" Spreading a dot of orange marmalade on a slice of toast, Soleil then gave the toast to Allerton. "You should try one. The bartender rims the glass with brown sugar."

Was Soleil silently indicting that she and Allerton were in a relationship? Ginny was sickened at the thought.

"No, thank-you. I'll stick with the plain juice."

A barely audible sound came from Gavin, and Ginny turned her head, giving him a questioning glance. He had stopped eating and was looking at Allerton. Her eyes went to him, too, see him staring at Gavin as he ate his toast. The confusing byplay between the two men had Ginny ready to leave the table. Her protective instincts were going off the rail. Whatever Allerton had done, it had upset Gavin, and she wasn't having it.

"Perhaps we should skip breakfast and go ahead to Clindale?" Ginny placed her cloth napkin back on the table, preparing to leave.

"Your husband hasn't finished his breakfast yet. Is there a problem?" Allerton finished his toast and poured himself a cup of tea from a small silver teapot.

"Actually, yes."

"Ginny …." Gavin's voice was so indistinct that she barely heard him.

Turning her head, she looked at him. He was staring

meaningfully and, at first, she didn't get what he was trying to tell her. Then it hit her like a ton of bricks.

Gavin was warning her that Allerton had no intention of them leaving alive. No person as high profile as he was would ever allow his association with the guests on the balcony made public.

"Ah ... then it's the company you're displeased with. Has Soleil or I offended you or *Gavin* in some way?"

Ginny felt like her head was on the guillotine each time she talked to him. Every word had to be examined, and it was grueling. He was counting on her slipping up.

Never in her life had she wanted to be rude to someone, and the idea that the woman who gave birth to her sat there silently across the table, waiting to pull down the release handle of the guillotine at Allerton's order, made her sick.

If Gavin didn't want her confronting Allerton about his strange behavior toward him, then fine, she wouldn't—but it didn't mean she couldn't kick sand in his face.

"How perceptive of you. It is the company," she drawled out, dropping her hand under the table to give Gavin a squeeze of reassurance.

Gavin lowered his fork to the table, his lips twitching at her, waiting for the show to begin.

"Darling ...." Soleil placed her toast back on her plate.

"It's not you"—her mother might be acting like a Stepford wife, but that didn't have her wanting to leave the table—"or Mr. Allerton who has ruined my appetite." That part she plain lied about.

"You seem quite unhappy by my choice of guests. May I ask who?"

Unable to tell him that he was the one who was offending the hell out of her by the creepy, sexual way he watched Gavin, she stared pointedly at the men whose table was catty-corner to theirs.

Having to sit with Allerton was a stomach churner, especially after he basically admitted to killing every soul on Clindale. Yet not even Allerton could hold a candle to the two men she was staring at. Ivan Pavlov and Alek Lukin were eating lobster tails, oysters, caviar, and drinking champagne. The two had imprisoned their own people, forced them into labor camps, and had killed for the tiniest infractions for opposing their dictatorships. They were the exact example of whom Gavin had been warning her about.

"I take it Ivan Pavlov and Alek Lukin were other subjects of your friend's podcasts or do they displease you personally?" Succeeding at having Allerton withdrawing his gaze away from Gavin, Ginny didn't shy away from Allerton's calculating eyes.

"I don't have to watch a podcast or videos. All you have to do is open a paper."

"My dear, you're showing your youth. Their countrymen and women idolize them."

"Not by choice. I wonder, if their countries were open and people were given the choice to stay under their tyranny or have their own say without fear of punishment or death, which they would choose."

"Democracy leads to unrest. Your own country proves that. You should read your own country's papers instead of judging others' form of government."

"We have our faults—sadly, too many—but as far as I know we don't sterilize our women, then force them into labor camps. We certainly don't rape and brutalize those women for sport, and we don't place land mines to keep our population from fleeing our country."

"Do you think, if I shared your idealistic opinion, my charity would have succeeded in helping so many if I let unrealistic optimism color my methods? I find it counterintuitive to change their expectations to agree with mine. No one benefits by standing on moral high ground."

"In case you don't know, it's called basic human rights. You want to talk about benefits? We can go there. Just who benefits? Certainly not the people you said your charity was created to help. *Who* it does help are the businesses and large corporations who take advantage of the loopholes made by *you* by greasing the palms of those countries to make it more *beneficial* for them to use their forced labored, allowing those businesses and large corporations to manufacture products at a fraction of the cost than it would take to make anywhere else," Ginny took the time to take in a deep breath before continuing, "all while pretending to stand on the *moral high ground* with their palms clean."

"Evangeline, perhaps we should change the subject." Her mother motioned for the waiter to order another mimosa.

"Don't worry yourself, Soleil; it's not often that I'm given such stimulating conversation so early in the morning."

It was clear by Allerton's blasé statement that everything she said had been brushed off like water off a duck's back. He was so sure of his status with those in political power that nothing she could say would place a dent in the arrogance of believing he was untouchable.

"I agree." Ginny cast her mother her own assurance, which had Soleil frowning in response. "The feeling is mutual. If not for your friendship with Mr. Allerton, I'm sure he wouldn't have given me the time of day to express my views."

Allerton gave her a supercilious tilt of his head. "I find it amusing you're so vehement in your criticism of my friends yet ignore any lack of moral standards of your own friends."

Ginny finished her juice, refusing to compare her friends to someone like Ivan Pavlov and Alek Lukin, especially Ivan Pavlov.

The thirty-eight-year-old dictator could have been his country's saving grace. At the age of eighteen, he left his country to be educated aboard while his father held the reigns secure. So many countries had pinned their hopes that he would make a change for the better when he succeeded his father. While learning and traveling abroad, the media showcased his enjoyment and interest in touring other countries, even going so far as to show appreciation for various cultures, knowledge that had been kept from him because of the rigid rules his father instituted in his homeland. From all reports, Ivan had been a fun-loving and generous friend to those who had grown close to him during the four years he had spent at university and traveling around the world exploring the globe.

The last year before he was due to return home, he had fallen in love with a beautiful woman, Aanya. She was the daughter of a leader from another neighboring country. Her country was more powerful, larger, and more progressive, with international relationships and ties to some of the largest companies in the world. Although they were more progressive, they controlled their citizens with an iron fist, much the same in that respect.

Aanya was indescribably beautiful, in body as well as in spirit. Her father, Markoff, adored his only daughter, and when Aanya used her power, she convinced her father to ease some the regulations he had imposed on their people. Her humanitarian efforts branched out, seeking to help others worldwide. When Aanya and Ivan Pavlov were sighted together, people from around the globe fell in love with the young couple's burgeoning romance, and when they got engaged, their images were on every TV channel and in every magazine.

When Ivan's father died unexpectedly, he immediately returned to his homeland with Aanya. Their marriage took place a month later, with Ivan letting his country celebrate as they had never done before. Markoff, Aanya's father, and Alek Lukin, her older brother, had also attended. The country, who'd never allowed foreigners inside their gates, welcomed them, as well as many of his high-profiled friends Ivan had made while abroad.

The months afterward showed promising change in the rigid rule his people had lived under during his father's reign. The people praised the changes and grew hopeful for the future, generating a swell of respect for Ivan Pavlov. Those affluent in the country spoke of their suspicions with such drastic changes, but those who had only known deep poverty and mind-numbing work had seen it as a sign their children wouldn't be raised with a hungry belly.

While the country's respect grew for Ivan, they fell in love with Aanya. Unlike other wives of previous leaders, she wasn't closeted in the palace. Every day, she went out to different areas in the country to talk and meet her new countrymen and women. She was photographed playing with their children, talking to the women as they did their chores, and she would listen to the men's concerns, promising to speak with her husband without fear of reprisal for speaking out. Aanya's actions showed a deep commitment to her new homeland, and the people reciprocated by falling in love with her, showing a devotion whenever she was near.

Slowly, insidiously, Aanya's daily walks grew less frequent, and soon the only representation she held from her former life was the pin indicating she was a princess from her country. The people could see the happiness that had always surrounded her disappearing, coincidentally Ivan ordered the media to leave and his friends stopped coming to visit. The media curtain went dark again and, from there, only small leaks of atrocities being committed could be heard from within.

When a month had passed without sight of Aanya, there had been a revolt. From the few accounts that had leaked out, it had been a bloody, brutal battle, only coming to a stop when Aanya made an appearance in front of the massive protestors to stop. Their love for her brought an end to the revolt, but then Aanya once again disappeared back into obscurity within the royal palace. Ivan Pavlov handed down severe punishments for those who had taken part in the revolt, executing and imprisoning his people who violated the rules of his regime.

Ivan Pavlov remained untouched from the sanctions imposed by the UN. Alek Lukin, however, had been gradually taking control of his country as Markoff had grown old and frail. While superpower nations across the globe felt no threat from Ivan, they were wary of Alek Lukin, who was guilty of the same atrocities, yet his nation had been smarter about keeping them hidden from the world's view. Alek revoked many of the changes that Aanya had convinced her father to incorporate, becoming powerful enough not only to rule their own country with an iron fist but he'd gained power to smaller nations across international. Alek was a formidable force that no one wanted to reckon with.

When international pressure rose that Alek was sanctioning Ivan's tyranny, Alek disavowed his relationship with Ivan's behavior and imposed embargos as well. As much he loved his sister, he severed all ties with her to protect his international reputation.

The revolt against Ivan taught him two valuable lessons. While he was their leader, it was Aanya who held their love. And while married to his daughter, Markoff had refused to send troops to help Ivan crush the revolt and until he saw his daughter make an appearance in front of the protestors, showing support of her husband, Markoff only then allowed his son full control.

Alek hadn't allowed Aanya to visit after he had severed ties with Ivan. While Aanya was never allowed the same freedom she had once to leave the palace grounds, she was by his side prominently during the only celebrations Ivan now allowed—his and his father's birthday celebrations. During the ensuing years, Aanya was only visible from the palace balcony, waving to those who lined up in a massive crowd to catch sight of her, and on the rare occasion she rode by his side in a car during a parade to wave gaily to those who chanted out her name. Her friends, charities, and the organizations she had supported missed her involvement as the country she had shown such love and care for degenerated into despair. None of the work she had done changed the lives of those mired in the poverty of her country.

"The people I count as true friends would go to any lengths to protect the people they love." Ginny met her mother's gaze as the woman lifted her mimosa to her lips. "When they give to a charity, it isn't quid pro quo. Their gift is made because their hearts are in the right place and they don't lose sight of whom they are trying to assist."

"You're very protective of your … friends, which is an admirable quality. A quality I also share toward my friends." Allerton placed a comforting hand on Soleil's hand. "Perhaps it would make your mother more comfortable if we just agree to disagree?"

Ginny nodded. "I apologize, Soleil." Making it plain who she was apologizing to, Ginny tried to draw her mother into a conversation. "Have you heard any more news from Jasper as to when he will be coming?"

"I haven't spoken to him," Soleil answered after receiving a nod of permission from Allerton, "this morning."

It wasn't boding well for Gavin and her that the woman made no attempt to hide that she was deferring to Allerton so visibly, making it plain she was just a spectator in this farce.

"When I find out you'll be the first to know."

Had Soleil and her father divorced, and were they waiting until they were together to tell her? Ginny didn't think so. It wasn't like they were in a typical situation where their children would be hurt by a divorce.

Every time Soleil spoke to her, Ginny could feel the distance separating them. Once again she wondered if she had ever had a loving mother and daughter bond, or if it was never there to begin with? Ginny didn't know anymore.

"I need to spend some time with my other guests. Please stay until you're finished." Allerton placed his napkin on the table, preparing to rise. "A driver is waiting outside to take you to the boat that will deliver you to Clindale."

"Are you sure you don't want me to accompany you?" Soleil spoke up when Allerton remained standing at the table as if to prompt her.

"I'm sure," Ginny refused. "Thank-you for the offer. I think it's better if I do this alone with my husband. Gavin?"

"I'm ready."

Agent Collins gave his plate of crab legs a lingering look before rising.

Ginny was glad she and Gavin were getting a reprieve from being under someone's constant surveillance. The emotional toll going to the island was going to be tough enough without having to pretend an objectivity that wasn't there.

The driver drove them in the opposite direction of their bungalow, then went through a forest of imposing palm trees to reach the dock.

As the dock came closer into view, Ginny felt her heart racing at the familiar sight from her childhood. The beauty of the scene of the marina eased some of the tight guilt she had carried within her chest for so long.

Normal-sized boats were docked closer to the island, while the larger yachts were farther out. There were also two mega yachts over eighty meters long. Ginny watched as one person dove off and realized the guests were using the opportunity to go swimming.

As they got out of the Moke, the driver handed Gavin a backpack, explaining it contained lunch, water, and a short-distance radio for him to use when they were ready to return to Sherguevil Island.

Agent Collins remained on the pier as Gavin and she climbed onto the speed boat. The captain started the engine as soon as they sat down on a cream-colored cushioned seat at the rear of the boat. Ginny grabbed Gavin's arm when the boat sped up and the hull came crashing down over the wave; it was a sensation she remembered.

He moved his arm around her shoulders, pulling her closer to him. "Okay?" he probed.

"I think someone just walked over my grave," she told him half-seriously. Her mind puzzled out it must have been the memory of being in a boat with Hammer after she'd been rescued from the plane.

"Don't ever say that."

Ginny firmed her trembling lips, nodding at him.

As the boat sped toward Clindale, they closed in on another mega yacht docked farther out from the marina. "Doesn't it make you want one?" Ginny laughingly yelled out to be heard over the motor.

"No, I'd rather have the other one."

At first, Ginny didn't understand what Gavin was pointing at, her attention more focused on the luxurious multi-level one they were passing. Looking toward where

Gavin pointed, she saw a single level that was anchored just behind the larger one.

Ginny sat motionless, inwardly registering the boat that had been dredged up from her subconscious. As realization struck, so did the reason why it had been strategically placed behind the multi-level yacht.

Whoever owned that boat was on Sherguevil Island. She had possibly been in the same room with the owner without her knowledge, and whoever it was, they were ready for her to know it.

CHAPTER TWENTY-THREE

Reaper gripped Ginny's waist, lifting her off the boat and onto the dilapidated dock. Several boards were either missing or bowing upward, so he prepared himself to catch Ginny if the creaking boards gave way under their feet.

The captain remained on the boat. "I will be returning to Sherguevil. I have other guests waiting for transportation to and from their boats. Radio when you're ready to be picked up."

Taking the radio, they watched the driver leave them standing alone on the dock. Reaper was only mildly surprised they had been left alone on island. It wasn't like he and Ginny could take off swimming for the States; they were stuck there until they radioed for a pick-up.

The decaying condition of the dock had him seriously contemplating whether it had been longer than three years since it had been used.

Looking at the overgrown jungle before them, Reaper cursed that he didn't have a machete. Glancing at Ginny, he saw the mix of emotions she was battling to suppress, knowing it was exactly the response Allerton would want to see *if* he had cameras placed around the beach.

Searching the foliage, he saw an indentation with new growth where the plants weren't as densely packed. "This way. Watch yourself." Reaper stepped forward, parting the throngs of one leafy plant and holding it back until he saw Ginny clear the area before continuing deeper into the recesses of the jungle. She clutched the back of his shirt as they moved through the tangle of vines and brush.

"Fuck. I could kick my ass for not asking for gloves or a machete."

"I don't think you would have gotten a pocketknife from him," Ginny bantered at his back.

"I don't think so either," he agreed. To be honest, his head hadn't been on straight since breakfast. Allerton made a big production of eating his toast, the fucking perv showed every tooth in his mouth, and Reaper knew exactly what the fucker was imagining. Banishing the sexual degradation that Allerton had tried unsuccessfully to inflict upon him to the back of his mind, Reaper knew Allerton's day was fucking coming. And when it did, each of those pearly whites would be smashed and shoved down his throat.

Ginny poked her head around his body. "Go more to the left," she suggested.

Seeing the brush was thinner there, he struck out in that direction, telling her to watch her step on the uneven ground.

Pushing through, he finally managed to drive back one section of vegetation for them to step out and into an immense clearing. They found the island's village. The small homes were crumpled and destroyed as if crushed by a wrecking ball.

Reaper heard Ginny gasp as she stepped around him to get a better look at the destruction.

"Ginny …."

"Just give me a minute. I need to catch my breath." The gamut of emotions crossing her face and heavy breathing wasn't because she overexerted herself.

"They're all dead. I should never have left …." Her face crumpled.

Reaper stepped forward, pulling her to his chest.

"How am I ever going to make this right?"

Lowering his head, he muttered low in his ear, "I know it's hard, but get a grip on yourself. We both know who is responsible for this shit."

Ginny shakily lifted her head, pulling away from him to move around the crumpled huts. Following behind her, Gavin looked around realizing he'd mistakenly assumed there hadn't been many islanders living here. Seeing the sheer number of mangled homes gutted him; he hadn't seen anything this bad since leaving the service. Reaper didn't have to imagine how Ginny was feeling. He knew all too well what evil could do.

"All of this just because I wanted to see a stupid boat." Her voice was so low that it was barely discernable.

Bending down, Reaper picked up a small board. "Ginny, we don't know what precipitated this destruction. It could be unrelated to anything concerning you." Squatting down, Reaper used the board to shift through a stack of planks, then dropped it and dusted his hands off, resting on his knees.

Visualizing where the homes were placed and taking into account the distance they'd walked from the beach, he gauged it to be roughly over a half a mile. Reaper couldn't be certain until he did a computer search of past category-level hurricanes in this area, but with a little work and a hell a lot of luck, they could pinpoint which hurricane could have caused this level of destruction—and when. Allerton plainly stated it was three years ago. If the bastard was lying, it wouldn't be hard to prove, unless Allerton had no intention of letting them return to the States for fear they'd stir up questions.

Reaper stood looking at Ginny, doubting there would be one. Allerton didn't leave witnesses. That was why Gavin believed he was so fixated on Ginny.

"Are you ready to go back to Sherguevil, or do you want to go on?"

With a silent answer, Ginny moved to her left, following a smaller trail that wasn't as overgrown. Reaper noticed Ginny moving faster and faster over the ground as she barreled through the overgrowth. "Slow down."

She let him catch up with her, her footsteps slowing until she came out into another clearing on a different side of the island. Reaper could see the ocean through the palm trees and through tropical foliage around them, there was rubble scattered around the long rectangular area.

"This used to be where we lived. Over there was the school." Ginny went to a pile of rotted lumber. She heaved several of the dank, smelly boards away. "There isn't even a scrap of paper here."

"Careful. I don't want you to get bitten by a bug or a snake. Let me." Reaper started moving more of the boards, finding nothing more than bugs crawling out of their hiding places.

"Every single thing that belonged to the islanders and the school is gone. Everything. Why?"

"It's been picked clean."

Ginny closed her eyes in anguish at his words. Then they flew open. "Gavin ..." Ginny looked around, even though she knew they were alone. "What if they aren't dead?" She grabbed the front of his shirt to bunch it within her fists.

"What if he moved them somewhere else and just told me they're dead? Couldn't that be a possibility?"

Reaper looked around the area. "It's a possibility." It was a possibility. However, though Reaper might have agreed with her out loud, inwardly, the thought was a dismal one. There had been too much care taken to remove every item from this once thriving community.

As they walked alongside the beach, they made their way back to the dock, allowing Reaper time to think. When they returned to the States, he could talk to some of his contacts from the military to see just what the government had on their records. Whatever it was, Reaper didn't have great faith about it being the truth. More than likely, what had happened to the islanders had been swept under the rug. Recognizing some of Allerton's guests who were sitting on the patio this morning, he felt that if they weren't dead, they were either imprisoned in labor camps, or worse, used like him as sex slaves.

He kept the disgusting thought to himself as Ginny took off her shoes as they neared the broken dock and started walking barefoot on the pristine beach. Imitating Ginny, Reaper sat down on the sand to take off his shoes. He broke into a smile when Ginny ran toward the ocean, her feet making footprints in the wet sand, then ran back before the wave could reach her feet. Reaper remembered playing the same game when he was a child living near the ocean.

Twirling around, she gave him a bright smile. "Isn't it beautiful?" Her smile dimming almost as soon as the words came out. Reaper cursed inwardly at the guilt-ridden expression that transformed her face from joy to sadness.

"Yes." He had a lump the size of golf ball in his throat. All it took was one of her fucking smiles to pull him out of the nightmares of his past. If he found out that Allerton had kidnapped these islanders from this paradise, he would rip the fucker's head off with his bare hands. The bastard didn't have the right to take the light out of her smile.

The level of destruction in the village and the buildings on the outskirts had been too carefully gone through to have been a natural disaster. Whoever had done this had one purpose—to find what Ginny had taken, and they had needed the islanders gone to achieve that goal.

The demolition showed the wanton disregard for human life. If there was a God, at least He *may* be capable of some mercy for those who had committed this crime. Reaper, on the other hand, had no intention of showing any to whoever orchestrated this annihilation.

Ginny was standing where the tide was coming in, looking down at her toes as the waves came in, then ebbed back. Taking a step back, Ginny sank down onto the sand to circle her knees with her arms to stare toward Sherguevil Island. His hand unintentionally went to his shirt, over his heart. The primitive emotion that came over him was raw, unadulterated possessiveness.

It was the same feeling he'd had when Shade and Viper had taken the jelly she made. There was no rhyme or reason for the primitive instinct that intensified each day, every fucking time he touched her. He just knew that, when he looked at Ginny, a swell of possessiveness struck him ferociously, demanding him to protect what was his.

Keeping her within his eyesight, Reaper reached to his side to open the backpack and pull out the lunch that had been packed for them. Finding two club sandwiches, chips, and two bottles of sparkling water, he pulled them out and started eating one of the sandwiches as she walked along the beach. Reaper gave her the solitude she needed to adjust to the stark realization of what happened to her childhood home.

"Come eat, Ginny." Tossing the empty paper wrap back into the backpack, he took out a pack of wipes.

Plopping down beside him, she showed him a pale shell she found. It was the size of a thumbnail. "Isn't it pretty?" she winsomely. "Do you think Allerton will let me keep it?"

"I don't see why not. Are you wanting to add it to your bracelet?"

"No." Ginny placed the shell to the side to take the hand wipe that he was holding out for her. "I don't want it damaged."

A ton of bricks raining from the skies couldn't hit him any harder at the difference between Taylor and Ginny. Taylor would never have given the delicate shell a second glance, much less treat it as if it had the value of a precious diamond. How Ginny had witnessed so much of the world's ugliness and was able to remain uncontaminated by the events spoke as to a true testament to Ginny's loving nature.

Taking the bottled water from him, she refused the sandwich. "I'm not hungry. My stomach still hasn't settled from seeing Ivan Pavlov and Alek Lukin chowing down together."

Reaper placed the paper-wrapped sandwich down on his lap to unwrap it and remove all the ingredients. Then he held out the thick slice of French bread. "You haven't eaten since yesterday afternoon, so eat. The bread will help settle your stomach."

Making a face at him, she took the bread, nibbling on it as she stared out at the ocean.

Rolling the inside of the sandwich together, he ate it as he monitored her eating. After taking small nibbles, she took bigger bites, then took the other piece of bread when she finished the first.

"Why didn't you put the charms I gave you on your bracelet?" Reaper refused to admit the ache in his chest was pain from not seeing the charms swinging on her dangling bracelet.

Ginny finished the bit of food in her mouth before answering, "I gave them to Silas to keep them safe. I didn't want to chance anything happening to them."

Her explanation assuaged his unease. "Any other places you want to explore before we go back?" Repacking the backpack with the empty sandwich wraps and empty bottled waters, he zipped it closed.

"Just one." Ginny reluctantly put her shoes back on, as if she didn't want to leave the beach. "I'm hoping I can find my favorite spot on the island."

Reaper followed suit, putting on his shoes before reaching to pull Ginny back to her feet. "Stay close."

"I will," she promised.

"Which way?"

"Back the way we took to get to the village."

It didn't take her two minutes before she was trying to run ahead of him. Taking her hand, he forced her back to his side. He had a new appreciation of how hard it must have been for her parents and T.A. to keep up with her as a child.

Becoming more familiar with the island, it wasn't long before they were back at the main village. Going through the middle, Ginny showed him a small trail that was only a foot wide; it led them right into the middle of a steep jungle.

"Are you sure you want to go this way?" Reaper used the bottom of his T-shirt to wipe his forehead and face.

"I think so." Her excitement was bubbling over as they climbed steadily higher, only her memories guiding her way. "Oh yes, it is. We came this way every morning, Trudy used to carry me until I became too heavy. I vaguely remember it; she loved to talk about some of the things we did when Hammer finally let us talk together again. I guess I remember more than I thought."

By the time he heard the sound of running water, his shirt was clinging to his back.

"You're going to love this," she promised, trying to tug out of the grip he had on her hand like a recalcitrant child. "Come on; you can rest when we get there."

"Why aren't you sweating? It's hot as fuck here."

"I don't know. I guess I don't have the right jeans on." She laughed, tugging on the leg of her thin crop pants. "You should have worn thinner clothing."

"I'm getting ripped to shreds like it is. How come you're not?"

"You're taking the worst of it for me. You want me to go first?"

"No, but it would help if you would slow your roll down."

"Fine. You don't have to be so pissy." She snorted, rolling her eyes at him.

They resumed walking and he continued to clear sections for them to step through. Finally reaching a hidden plateau, Reaper untangled a small grouping of palms, uncovering the amazing beauty of a waterfall. The spectacular height of the narrow waterfall towering above them was another surprise that was hidden from the outside.

Ginny squealed with happiness. "Isn't it wonderful? Let's go swimming!" Ginny was already removing her clothes.

Reaper tried to pull her shirt back down, only to find himself grasping for air when she slipped out of his hands like a fucking eel.

"You're not going swimming naked," Reaper burst out. He didn't trust that Allerton wouldn't send the boat back for them early, and the captain would search for them when they weren't on the beach.

Ginny tossed him her shirt, showing the white swimsuit underneath.

"You could have suggested that I wear mine."

"I thought it was obvious we would go swimming somewhere on the island. Quit being a fuddy-duddy and just leave your underwear on. You can let them dry out before putting your clothes back on," she chirped, toeing out of her shoes.

"Is that what you did when you were a kid?"

"No, we all just swam naked. Most of the children went naked here because of the heat. If we did wear clothes, it was a thin nappy or a pair of shorts."

"Your parents let you run around the island half-naked?"

"Of course not." Ginny scrunched her face at him.

"At least that's one thing I can give your mom credit for," he murmured just to himself.

"I ran around like the ones my age—naked as a jaybird. My mother tried to keep shorts on me, but I would take them off as soon as she put them on," she bragged. Then, going to the large pool, Ginny raised her face to catch the spray of falling water.

Reaper was still taking his jeans off when Ginny jumped into the pool of water, swimming toward the middle. He slowly tried to walk into the pool, only to find it was too deep and he had start swimming to keep his head above the water.

"You swam here when you were three?"

"Mmmhmm ..." Laying on her back, Ginny did back strokes toward him. Then she straightened to tread water next to him. "This is my happy place. Whenever I wanted to run away from Lisa and Dalt, I would come here in my mind and everything would be okay again." Drifting closer to him, she wound her arms around his shoulders as she wrapped her legs around his waist, trusting him to keep them afloat. "Do you have a happy place, Gavin?"

"No."

"Then you do now. I don't mind sharing it with you." She laid her head on his shoulder as they idly drifted around.

"You missed this island, didn't you?"

"So badly ... sometimes I just wanted to scream. I've told you a little lie. I might as well tell you now."

From the whispered, laughing way she made the admission, he could tell the confession wasn't anything to be concerned about.

"What is it?" He placed his hand on her bottom to keep her from drifting away.

"I didn't give you all the parts of my soul. Clindale has a small part and always will." Raising her hand, she used her thumb to press on the nail bed of her pinkie. "So itty bitty that you won't even miss it." Ginny gave a small, heartfelt sigh. "Can we stay here forever? I don't want to leave."

"You would miss your brothers, Willa, and T.A. too badly."

She didn't argue back. "Who would you miss?"

"Viper."

"Aw ... I knew it. You do love your big brother."

"If you tell him, I'll deny it."

"Mums the word."

Suddenly, she raised her head, pretended to zip her mouth shut, and then threw away the key before she wiggled out of his arms to climb out of the basin. Reaper lazily lay back to float when he saw her start climbing the rocks on the side of the waterfall. Loose stones fell down as she climbed higher.

"Ginny ... get your ass back down here!" he bellowed out, frantically swimming to where he could climb out.

He braced his arms, leveraging his body out of the pool, then took off at a run as she went up the rocky incline like quicksilver.

"Wait for me. I'll help you back down!" he yelled, reaching the bottom of the incline, then hesitating when she slipped from his eyesight. "Ginny!"

She came into view at the edge of waterfall.

His heart stopped midbeat as Ginny jumped off the high waterfall, plunging down at a breakneck speed. He watched her fall as if in slow motion as she hit the water in the basin below. He took a halting step forward, his heart still unable to beat in terrorizing fear she was hurt... until her head popped up and her laughter filled the air.

"Evangeline ...," Uncaring his voice sounded as though it went through a cheese grater, he continued, "come here."

"Uh ... no. I don't like the way you're looking at me." Ginny started backstroking farther away from where he was standing.

"How many of your brothers did Freddy have to make watch you to keep you from getting your ass killed?"

"I'm not gonna tell you." Ginny quit swimming long enough to stick her tongue out at him, then went back to swimming. "I don't like your tone of voice," she said haughtily.

Reaper went to the pool, diving into the water to swim under the surface. Ginny swam like a fucking seal to the other side to get away from him.

Doing a sidestroke, Reaper tried to block her escape by getting in front of her, only to feel the strong kick of her foot when she did a fucking flip, turning to go in the other direction. He cursed at finding another little detail that Shade and Rider had neglected to tell him—Ginny was an expert swimmer.

She darted underneath him, and it was only because he had grown up on a beach and had been a diver in the Navy that she wasn't completely able to smoke him.

Going through the motions at pretending to catch Ginny, he gradually saw the glow come back in her expression. Angry as he was at her jumping off the waterfall, he was glad this part of the island hadn't been tarnished by Allerton's actions. Reaper switched tactics, letting her expel her strength by merely lagging behind and letting her wear herself out. When she saw he wasn't following her as closely, she slowed her speed, gauging the distance between them.

Reaper did a fish kick, propelling himself, cutting the distance between them in half. When Ginny looked again, he was almost on her. With a squeal, she tried to flip again, but he beat her, going underwater to come up under her. Grabbing her waist, he propelled her upward, holding her securely so she couldn't slip away from him. Then he opened his mouth to give her blazing hell for jumping off the waterfall, only to go still when, instead of trying to get away, she pressed her body harder against his and dove her tongue into his mouth.

Desire burst into a kaleidoscope of colors, making him forget why he'd been angry. She silkily twined her arms around his neck and brought her thighs around his waist as she hung limply to him, kissing him senseless. The flames of his temper resurfaced in his cock, driving away any plan to punish her for the reckless jump.

His mind jumped backward to their first meeting when he listened to her sing at T.A.'s wedding. This was what he had seen when he stared down into the watery depths of the pool—them embracing in a watery waltz with the glow of the sun playing matchmaker, holding the shadows of their pasts at bay.

The pain of his past and the future he could have converged together, lifting him out of the mire he had been bogged down in.

Possessively holding Ginny, he kicked his feet to float them toward the side of the pool. Using one arm on the bank, he managed to lift both of them out of the water. Laying Ginny down on the ground, he then leaned over her without breaking their kiss.

Pulling the straps of her swimsuit down, he peeled the suit off her body. Then, shifting himself over her, he entered her body in one smooth stroke, easily sliding inside of her warm cavern.

Their bodies clung together damply, moving together as one. Any time he touched Ginny, she gave over herself with her whole heart. It was a heady thing, having that type of devotion centered on him. Despite being with too many women to count, he had never felt this before.

Thrusting harder inside of her, Reaper trembled over her, fighting the urge to fuck even harder until she splintered into a thousand pieces, giving him the submissive surrender he needed from her. Nine years he'd been Slate's sex slave, and in less than a month Ginny gave back what had been stolen from him—control over his body.

Reaper had to admit the sex between them was one-sided. She gave him access to all of her, while he only gave her what he wanted her to have. Mentally, he couldn't handle it when she strayed from the areas of his body that he allowed her to touch. If she tried to initiate another way of having sex, or accidently touched him in the wrong area, it would bring back the memories of being violated. Any move made to suck his dick, ride him, or bite his neck sent him back down the dark path that only held pain and degradation.

Sex with Ginny was as simple as it could get, and that was all he was capable of. He would never be the adventurous, sexual, hedonistic man who had helped create The Last Riders with Rider.

She lay under him, moving in unison with him, not trying to take what he wasn't willing to give, yet each sexual encounter they shared, she was subtly entrenching herself in his heart with her selfless willingness to forego the pleasures he was denying her.

Ginny brought her palm to the curve of his cheek. "Are you still mad?"

"No."

"Good. I don't like it when you're angry with me."

"Don't do that again. You have to be more careful—"

"Trudy said I used to do it four or five times a day."

"You weren't mine then."

"I've always been yours."

Reaper pretended to shake water off his face, not wanting her to see how affected he was by what she said.

"I knew it would be okay. I already know how I'm going to die."

Reaper stopped moving inside of her.

Ginny nodded up at him. "Jody and Fynn told me. They have Freddy's gift. They can read the stars."

"They told you when you're going to die?" His breath came in harsh gasps.

She stared up at him winsomely. "Don't worry; I won't being wearing a halo anytime in the next seventy years." She arched her hips upward toward his.

"You keep moving like that and you won't have a halo waiting for you."

Reaper started moving again in a series of gentle thrusts that had her slipping her hand to the nape of his neck.

"I asked my dad once how angels earned their halos."

"What did he say?"

"That he didn't know. There hadn't been any Colemans worthy of the name as far as he knew." She giggled. "Freddy said He only gave halos to the angels He didn't have to watch over all the time. Colemans kept the good Lord too busy watching over us, so He gave us something else."

"What did He give the Colemans?"

"The Ten Commandments."

His hand shook as he traced the line of her jaw. "I have a

new commandment to add to His list. *Thou shall not jump off anything higher than two inches.*"

"There was nothing to be afraid of," she assured him matter-of-factly. "Silas was there to slow me down. No matter where I am, he always manages to cushion my fall."

He stopped moving his hips. When Ginny jumped off the waterfall as if in slow motion, then hit the basin, he feared Ginny had been hurt. It hadn't been a trick of his mind. Silas had been there catching her.

"The night you and Leah were on the roof, when Silas spanked you, he had to catch you, didn't he?"

"It's beautiful here. I don't want to go back to Sherguevil." She stared at him wistfully, as if memorizing his face.

"Ginny." Refusing to be sidetracked, Reaper used the same tone of voice that he had used to intimidate new recruits under his command when he was in the military.

She made a face up at him. "He cushioned me."

"Caught."

"Cushioned."

His voice grew more intimidating. "How many times has Silas caught you?"

"A few times. It was Leah and my favorite spot."

The woman knew no fear because Silas had always been there to catch her.

When he got back to Treepoint, Hammer wasn't the only one he was going to rip into for enabling Ginny's reckless behavior.

"The first time you went out there, you should have had your ass set on fire."

Ginny gave him her own intimidating stare. "Gavin, I told you I don't believe in corporal punishment."

"Too fucking bad. When it comes to you getting hurt, only what *I* want matters."

"News flash"—Ginny wiggled, trying to shimmy out from

under his dick and almost succeeding in slipping his dick out of his resting place—"what I want matters, too."

Thrusting deeper, he bore his hips down on her, stopping the wiggling movements. Then, changing tactics, his expression went from intimidating to disappointment. Reaper hadn't earned his medals without knowing how to win battles.

"How did you feel when I took off with Slate?"

He knew he had her when her body softened under his.

"I was terrified for you," she admitted.

"That's how I felt when you jumped off the waterfall. You took a risk you didn't need to take." To make his point, he had to expose a part of himself. "You scared the fuck out of me. Please don't jump off anything that high again. Please."

"I'm sorry. I didn't mean to scare you. I won't do it again."

Stroking one of her nipples with the tip of his tongue, Reaper unashamedly used a secret weapon that he'd used more than once on unsuspecting women. Giving Ginny puppy dog eyes to get the capitulation he wanted, he said, "Promise?"

"Aw ... I promise." Ginny stroked his back lovingly. "I didn't mean to scare you."

"Well, you did." He plaintively used his tongue to flip her nipple into the direction of his mouth. Sucking the tender nub, he felt Ginny bucking under him to get him moving. Sliding back and forth in her slick pussy, he drifted his mouth to Ginny's other breast to latch on to her nipple. Opening his mouth wider, he sucked the whole areola into his mouth, swirling his tongue over the delicate flesh, while squeezing her other breast in a tight grip to get the blood rushing to the nipple. He then broke the suction on the breast in his mouth to switch targets. Ginny gave a hiss of air when his mouth hovered over her straining tip.

"No fair."

Reaper barely let his lips touch her nipple without exerting any pressure. "What's wrong?" He grinned, knowing full well what was irritating her.

"You're teasing me." Ginny strained upward, trying to get him to open his mouth.

Reaper flexed his hips upward. "I wouldn't call this teasing."

"My nipple," she gasped.

"What do you want me to do?" He teased her by lifting his lips higher away from her nub.

"Suck it."

Reaper laughed at the uncomfortable demand. Ginny was more like Willa than her own sister, T.A. She was a prude when it came to dirty talk, and he couldn't help but be charmed when she would finally slip and reveal her own desires.

He lowered his mouth to place it over her nipple as he slowly built up the speed of his thrusts.

"Harder," she demanded.

"Which one? You want me to suck your nipple harder or fuck you harder?"

"Both!" She pressed the balls of her feet on his ass harder as she bucked under him.

Pounding inside of her, he tightened his mouth over her breast, giving her the pressure she needed. Feeling her spasming pussy on his cock, he gave in to his own climax, only removing his mouth when he felt her ecstatic thrusting ease into intermittent shudders.

Using his thumb to rub back a strand of her hair clinging to her parted lips, he gave her a kiss before disengaging himself from her body to lift her into his arms. Ginny gave a shrill squeal when he jumped into the cool water. Giving him a dirty look when she came up for air, Reaper did a backstroke away from her, dodging the playful punch she aimed at him.

"Jerk!"

"That wasn't what you thought a second ago when I was fucking your brains out," he taunted.

"Wild man, you're good, but you're not that good," she taunted back.

Reaper turned onto his front in the water and, in one move, did a flip to dive under the water just to come up under her. Taking her by the waist, he lifted her up until she was above him, staring down at him.

"What'd you say?" Giving her a mock threatening look, he dared her to repeat her taunt.

Her lips pressed together in a stubborn line. "Nothin'."

"You sure you have nothing else to say?"

"Pretty sure."

Slowly lowering her back down to the water, he gave her a satisfied smile.

A splash of water aimed directly at his face interrupted his triumph.

Grabbing Ginny's wrist before she could splatter him with more water, they started wrestling in the water, each of them trying to dunk the other. When Ginny slipped behind him to use all her strength to press down on his shoulder with her hands, Reaper turned his head to eye her quizzically.

Out of breath, Ginny laid her head on his shoulder. "Trying to dunk you."

"That was a fail." He snorted sarcastically.

"I wasn't trying hard."

"Seemed like you were." Unable to keep from laughing, Reaper reached behind him, snagging Ginny's hands to float her in front of him. "You're a nut."

"And you take life too seriously," she rebutted. "We can be

serious when we go back to Sherguevil. Sweet man, come out and play with me," she called out coaxingly as if their bodies weren't intertwined to stay afloat.

Reaper felt a sharp stinging pain from inside his chest. He had never felt the strange pain before and was nervous to take a deep breath, wary of the ache hitting him again.

"Aw ... look, Gavin. Isn't that pretty?"

Reaper turned his head to see where Ginny was pointing, only to find himself sinking under the water. Kicking upward, he shook the water out his eyes and saw Ginny swimming away from him, gloating laughter reverberating around the secluded falls. Dunking him should have set off alarm's bells after the game Slate used to torment him with yet hearing Ginny's laugh at her outmaneuvering him only soothed his soul.

The momentary pain in his chest gone, Reaper gave chase after the water nymph, his own laughter filling the air as he pursued her. Reaper had to admire her; it took all of his skill to keep up with her. He had a natural affinity for water as did Ginny.

In olden times, sailors had been warned about sirens and their ability to steal a man's soul with the sound of their voices. Reaper knew his thoughts were fucking ridiculous, blaming Ton who had spoon fed him old legends from Greek mythology of sirens who had healing powers derived from the water to heal the warriors they protected.

Using the rocks near the base of the waterfall, he was able to corral her by the waterfall, rocks, and him. Inwardly congratulating himself that he had her boxed in and would be able to outswim her to the open side, Reaper drifted closer to her.

His win of their game was within reach, until the water nymph spun in the water, her hands going to a large rock, intending to clamber up it.

"No." Reaper's voice sternly rang out to bring the game to an abrupt end. "Come here."

Ginny paused, turning her head to look at him from over her shoulder.

"I don't want you climbing on those rocks. They're too slick."

Ginny turned back to the rocks as if to ignore his warning.

"Come. Here." His voice went deeper, darker. "*Now.*"

Ginny made a face at him, turning in the water to swim toward him. "I wasn't going to get hurt."

Reaper hooked a hand around her neck to pull her closer to him. "So we don't have to keep arguing over this, I'm going to make this rule plain and simple. It doesn't matter what you think, it only matters what I think when it comes to your safety."

"I've already told you I disagree with your high-handedness."

"Are you already breaking your promise to me?"

"Huh? What promise? I promised not to jump off the waterfall—"

"Is it too much for me to ask that anything concerning you getting hurt falls under the one and only rule I'm asking for you to follow—if I'm willing to give you the same say-so in regard to me?"

Her disgruntled expression cleared. "You mean it?"

"Yes. I swear, I won't do anything that will endanger my welfare," he promised, then made an important clarification. "Unless I need to protect you."

"Then I promise the same … with the same condition."

Reaper frowned. "No."

"Then no right back at you."

Reaper gritted his teeth. "If you become so afraid of

something happening to me and you feel the need to step in, then you have to go to Viper first."

"That doesn't seem fair to me."

"I'm a Last Rider; each of the brothers' wives have a replacement brother to turn to. I want Viper to be yours … unless you want one of the other brothers?"

"That wouldn't bother you if I picked someone other than Viper? What if I wanted Shade or Rider?"

His expression was deadpan. "No."

"I don't see Killyama going along with this."

"She did." However, Reaper neglected to tell Ginny about the chaos that erupted within the club when Killyama found out about the brothers having replacements.

Ginny glared at him distrustfully, as if she didn't believe him. "Who did Killyama pick?"

"Rider."

"It seems to me that's another rule, which would make it two."

"No. Just one rule. You won't even need to go to Viper if you just follow the rule of not getting into any situations where you can be hurt."

"Okay. Then if I get a replacement for you, you get one for me. Killyama can be mine."

"Fuck no!"

"I thought you liked Killyama. You've given her roses."

"I meant I'm never going to need a replacement. Nothing is going to happen to you. I won't let it," he said confidently.

"There's something extremely sexy about you right now."

"It's all the tattoos," he teased.

Her eyes flickered over the tattoos scattered over his body and skull. "I can't disagree with that. Are any of them for Taylor?"

A red alert went off in his brain, but he gave her the truth anyway. "No."

"Why?"

"Because good cover-ups are a bitch to find."

"Are any of your tattoos for other women you've been with?"

"No."

"Good."

He rolled his eyes at her satisfaction. "Why?"

"If any woman is going to leave a mark on you, it's gonna be me. You make me want to get a tattoo." Ginny ran a hand lovingly over his shoulder.

"No."

Ginny raised her eyebrows in confusion. "Why not?"

"Getting a tattoo hurts." Reaper gave her the simplest answer, withholding the real truth.

"I can take a lot of pain." She stopped moving her hand to cup the ball of his shoulder. "Getting a tattoo would be child's play," she scoffed.

"Okay …," he scoffed back. "In regard to what?"

"Loving you."

Reaper broke away from her to swim toward the bank to get out and shutting down any opportunity to illuminate her about his own feelings.

"Gavin … come here," she called out in the same voice he had used with her. "*Now.*"

He turned back to face her.

"Come. Here."

She was giving him her ultimatum. If he expected her to obey him when it was important to him, then he had to give as much as he took.

"Fuck," he swore under his breath, swimming back to her.

"Wild man, I didn't say that to hurt you or to get you say something you don't want to. I said it to tell you that I don't need you to take the wheel when I could be hurt." Ginny lifted her hand out the water to show the palm of her hand.

"Fire can be the most destructive force on Earth. It can burn down homes, forests, and civilizations. Nevertheless, we use fire to heat homes, create firebreaks, and build civilizations."

Ginny bore her eyes into his. "You joined the Navy to be a warrior, Gavin. Your service to your country forged a strength in you that was hammered down, then tempered during your kidnapping, over and over again. All this time, you think it destroyed the man you were. It didn't. You're still the same man, except stronger. A steel so powerful that it can no longer be wielded in someone else's hand. A steel so indestructible that it can be used as a sword or a shield against your enemies, or to protect those you love." Ginny raised her hand higher to tap a finger on his brow. "You still believe you returned to The Last Riders as a prodigal son." She dropped her hand to his heart to tap on his chest. "You didn't. You came home a gladiator."

She let her hand fall back to the water. "I can tell you don't believe me, and that's fine. Just know one freakin' thing in that hard head of yours. You … will … never … ever … fight … alone again, and you can take that to the freaking bank."

CHAPTER TWENTY-FOUR

"I knew there was a reason I married you."

"We're not," Ginny fervently denied.

"Are, too."

"Not."

"Are."

Ginny wiggled the fingers of her left hand in his face. "You see a ring here? You don't. There's nothing here. Zip, zilch, nada."

"I have something more important—a legal paper."

"Until Pastor Dean says the words, *I now pronounce you man and wife*, you may be married in what corner of the universe you live in, but in mine, I'm still single and fancy-free."

"You live in the same universe as I do, and we're married."

"I never believed there could be a man more stubborn than Greer Porter, but I was wrong. You beat Greer."

"I take that as a compliment."

"You would," she scoffed.

"People in town just misunderstand him."

"Since when did you two become BFFs?"

"We're not BFFs; we're kindred spirits." Reaper nearly swallowed his own tongue on that whopper.

Ginny went under the water. He didn't get worried until she didn't pop right back up. A few seconds later, he turned in the water to see her getting out, wringing her ponytail out.

"Playtimes over?" He laughed, getting out too.

Ginny shrugged. "You only said that to irritate me. I decided to not let it get to me."

"How magnanimous of you," he quipped, shaking the excess water from his hair.

"Gavin James, you're being a dick, and I know exactly what you're doing."

"What am I doing?" he asked with mock innocence.

"Putting the cart in front of the horse. That way, when we go back to Treepoint, you don't have to decide a future for us. It's all written down on paper if you decide to continue this relationship. Yet, if you decide to break up with me, you can use the same piece of paper to say it wasn't legal. No, thanks. You can ride on your high horse all you want, it's not going to change the facts, which"—Ginny wiggled her fourth finger at him—"plainly states I'm the one who is right."

"Quit wiggling that finger at me. If you want a ring, I'll buy you one when we get home."

"Buy one if you want to ... just don't expect me to wear it."

"You'll wear it." The laughter left his voice.

"Nope, I won't." Ginny raised her chin obstinately in the air.

"You will." His voice became even firmer.

"Won't." Hers became softer.

"Will," he promised.

"I guess we'll see who's right and who's wrong." Reaching for her clothes, she turned her back to him as she got dressed.

"Yes, we will." Turning his back to her, Reaper got dressed, silently vowing to stop at the jewelry store in Treepoint as soon as the plane landed … until he remembered he killed the owners of that store.

"Fuck."

"You say something?" Ginny looked up from putting her shoes on.

"Does Jamestown have an airport?"

Ginny stared at him as if he had a concussion. "I believe anyone flying in and out uses the same one on the outskirts of Treepoint. At least, that's the one that Dalton used when he flew in to see Trudy. Why?"

"No reason. Just curious." With his shoes on, he reached for the backpack, then held out his hand expectantly to help Ginny get to her feet.

"I don't want to go. I have a terrible feeling I'll never come back."

"You'll come back, I promise."

Unhappily, she took his hand as he helped her get to her feet, then they made their way back down to the main village. When he would have kept going, Ginny paused beside one home that had been scattered in different directions; it had been larger than the rest.

Sensing she needed a moment alone, Reaper took a couple of steps ahead while keeping Ginny within his eyesight. From where he stood, he couldn't hear what she said, but when she turned and walked toward him, he saw the resolved posture of her body.

A visceral image of Taylor came to his mind; the differences between the two women were striking.

Taylor's image no longer produced the same feelings they once had. If he was truthful to himself, those feelings had been gone even before his kidnapping. Ginny was younger than Taylor, more playful and outspoken, yet she knew her own mind. Taylor wouldn't even make a decision on which flavor cake she wanted or what color to paint a wall without getting his feedback. There was no depth to Taylor, and he was still trying to figure Ginny out. One minute she was high-spirited, the next she was ruminating, her mind a million miles away. Like now.

He could feel she was holding something back from him. The fierce go-for-broke expression on her face sent fear spiraling through him.

When she would have walked past him, he caught her hand. "Together, Ginny, or not all."

Lifting her grief-stricken eyes from the ground, she came back to earth. "I love you, but he has to pay, one way or another," she vowed.

"I don't have a problem with anything you want to do, as long as we do this together."

Ginny seemed to be grappling with whether to say something. Then her face cleared as if coming to a decision. "Together."

Agent Collins was waiting for them on the dock when they arrived back to Sherguevil Island. Reaper got off the boat, then lifted Ginny to stand next to him. "Allerton is waiting to speak with you. I'll take the backpack."

"Like that's a shocker." Reaper contemptuously handed the backpack over.

The agent gripped the pack by one of the straps. "The sooner we get this over, you'll be allowed to go back to your bungalow."

Reaper walked beside Ginny as they made their way toward the Moke and waited until Ginny was seated before going to the other side. He was getting fed up with this shit.

Wanting to lash out at the agent for being Allerton's errand boy, he restrained himself from sharing his contempt of Collin's disregard to prioritize Ginny's protection instead of giving in to Allerton's orders. It simply conveyed whose side he was on.

Allerton kept them cooling their heels in his waiting room for twenty minutes, which wasn't surprising to Reaper; he had a good guess what the asshole was doing. Ginny was coming to the same conclusion, red staining her cheeks as she continuously rubbed the small seashell she brought back with her between her fingers.

"Quit it," he ordered.

"What?" Her gaze shied away from his.

"You know what. You haven't done anything to be embarrassed about. He's the fucking pervert for watching."

Agent Collins appeared to be chewing his tongue at overhearing his words to Ginny.

Allerton's assistant came out of his office before the agent could unglue his tongue from the roof of his mouth. "Mr. Allerton is ready for you."

Allerton waited until the assistant closed the door, leaving the four of them inside before speaking. "I hope your visit today was productive?"

Instead of answering Allerton's question directly, Ginny looked around the large office. "I expected my mother to be here."

"She wasn't feeling well, so I suggested she remain at her bungalow and have an early night. If she isn't feeling better by tomorrow, I'll make sure she goes to the treatment center to see one of the doctors I keep on staff."

"I could go and check on her after we finish here," Ginny suggested.

"I think it's better to retain your distance from Soleil until one of the doctors gives her a clean bill of health. Your trip to

Clindale?" Tacking on the inquiry, Allerton quelled any further attempts for Ginny to ask about Soleil.

"The only part of the island I vaguely recalled was the waterfall, but I can't be sure if it was that specific one or because it was similar to a few I saw in Hawaii when I toured with Mouth2Mouth. It's a beautiful island, but all islands are spectacular when you see them, so I can't say with certainty that—"

"Mrs. James, whether you remember the waterfall or not has no bearing. I was asking if you recall memories that would help in retrieving the item stolen from me."

Allerton's patience was running thin; his brooding anger was becoming more visible. "Nothing from the village sparked your memory?"

"How? There was nothing left. Sorry, it was a massive failure."

"I wouldn't say it was a failure, just one more step in the process. You said yesterday you would take the polygraph if I let you go to Clindale. I kept my end of the bargain. Anticipating this outcome, I gave Agent Collins a private office to conduct the polygraph in the morning. Will nine o'clock be fine, or would twelve suit you better?"

"Nine."

"Very well. Goodnight."

Reaper remained in place as Ginny and Agent Collins moved away from the desk at Allerton's perfunctory dismissal.

"I'm taking into account the importance of you getting your artifact returned, but whatever plans you and Collins have made for the polygraph better include me being present with the list of questions for me to approve beforehand, or my wife will not be taking the test."

"Of course, Mr. James, you stated the conditions before. My memory isn't the one that's faulty."

"Our driver is waiting, Mr. James," Agent Collins spoke from the doorway, breaking the tug-of-war between him and Allerton.

Reaper turned on his heel to take Ginny's arm.

The agent gave him a sharp glance when the elevator doors closed. "That was extremely rude."

"Fuck you."

The agent was first off the elevator, the heels of his shoes clicking on the polished floor as they walked through the maze of corridors.

He held the door open for them to go outside. "How do you think antagonizing Mr. Allerton will benefit your wife, Mr. James?" Agent Collins kept his tone even as he joined them outside.

Reaper was sick of all the bullshit, stopping midstride to confront the man behind him. "How about you give me the straight-up truth? From where I'm standing, this shitshow is all about throwing Ginny under the bus. What I don't get is why you're aiding and abetting Allerton?"

"I am not aiding Mr. Allerton. I'm facilitating both Mrs. James and Mr. Allerton to reach a mutual conclusion that will allow both of them to move onward with their lives."

"That son of bitch has billions of dollars; he can buy any fucking artifact he wants. I've offered to make restitution, and Allerton's refusal shows he has no intention of moving on. I'm giving you fair notice, after Ginny takes that polygraph, I want a plane waiting to take us back to the States."

"Mr. James, what you want doesn't matter, nor what I want. After the test, if Mrs. James shows no deception, I'm sure Mr. Allerton will allow both of you to return to the States."

"And if she fails?"

"Then we'll cross that bridge when we come with it. Mrs. James says she has no memory of the event. If she's being truthful, I can see no reason for Mr. Allerton to prevent both of you from leaving, if that's what Mrs. James desires."

"Why in the fuck would she want to stay?"

Agent Collins looked inquiringly toward Ginny. "To stay with her mother until her father arrives back to the island. Which would you prefer—to go or to wait for your father?"

Instead of Ginny immediately saying she was ready to get the fuck off the island, she gave him a pleading look for understanding. "I want to do whatever Agent Collins advises."

What the fuck? Was he in a bad episode of *The Twilight Zone?*

Wanting nothing more than to get their asses out of there, Reaper wanted to shake Ginny silly for showing support to the agent. Instead, snapping his mouth closed, he strode rapidly to the Moke, leaving Ginny and Agent Collins to hurry after him.

Already seated in the Moke, he shrugged his arm away when Ginny reached out to touch him. The short drive didn't alleviate his anger. However, despite how furious he was, when he stepped out the Moke, he stopped long enough to help Ginny out, then took her arm to hustle her into the bungalow. Once inside, he refused to release the simmering anger.

Certain the electronic devices he destroyed each time they left the bungalow had been replaced, Reaper went in the bedroom and began sweeping the room. Rather than return to the living room where Ginny was, he sat down on the side of the bed to stare at the devices clenched in his fist.

Why did she want to do what Agent Collins advised? Fucking hell. What was she thinking? The memory of their afternoon together had him going into the other room to place the bugs in the glass jar.

Her eyes followed him across the floor as he went back into the bedroom to sit down on the bed again.

Closing the door she crossed the floor to sit down next to him.

"Ginny …."

Ginny placed a gentle finger on his lips. "Trust me," she whispered.

"I do. I just don't trust those fuckers." He meant his words. He did trust her.

In rehab, after Taylor had left him, he had sworn never to trust another soul, yet here he was, in a position to trust Ginny's ability to navigate the quagmire they were in. He had to hold off from busting her chops about her decision.

Ginny took his hand in hers. "If I can convince Agent Collins to let you leave the island, would you go without me?"

"No."

"Even if I beg?" she pleaded with him.

"Are you?" Reaper raised a brow at her.

"Yes."

"I still wouldn't go."

"I want to leave as badly as you do," she said softly. "I have to do this." She took his hand in hers squeezing it tightly.

"Somehow, I have to make amends. I can't do it if I leave before this is finished. Both Allerton and I have to pay for what happened on Clindale. I was a child and didn't know what I was doing; he did. I have to find out what I took that is so important he's willing to kill anyone to get it back. When I find that out, my questions will be answered and I can stop running."

Reaper removed his hand from hers and began writing, opting not to whisper.

Whatever it was you took is long gone. How will it make a difference if you remember what it was?

Ginny took the pen.

It'll make a difference to me. I won't have to hide anymore. I can return it back to Allerton or the FBI. I can have a life with Trudy, my niece or nephew, and with you, if that's what you want. I can't live closed off from them anymore. I didn't die in that plane crash ... I might have another name, but Evangeline is still here.

I've never lost sight of who I am and how the islanders took me into their hearts and made me one of them. I can't betray them by running away twice. I was too young to take Allerton on before. I'm not a child any longer. At least if I go down, this time, he'll have to answer to everyone who cares about me. Allerton may be powerful enough to kill, make over a hundred native islanders disappear, yet he can't vanquish an army without coming out of hiding. If at the end of the day, all I'm able to accomplish is to expose him enough for everyone to see him for what he is, I'm good with that, especially if it prevents one more person from becoming his next victim.

Ginny took his hand again, and he shook his head at her naïveté. "Military battles that were fought for a cause have been lost and misrepresented since time began."

"That's very true," Ginny agreed. "But how many have come up against an army that is unbeatable?"

"Nymph, I've got a news flash for you. You and me together isn't much of an army."

"It is when one of them is a secret weapon."

Reaper lips curled in amusement. "Who's the secret weapon?"

"Allerton thinks he's taking on a defenseless woman who has only you to protect me. It hasn't dawned on him yet who he's fucking with."

His smile slipped at her seriousness. Was she talking about Agent Collins? "And who would that be?"

"A gladiator who walked through the fires of hell and won."

Reaper closed his eyes, his face twisting in remembered pain. "I didn't win."

"Aw ... sweet man, you did win. The problem is you don't think you deserve the medal."

"There is no medal that will ever make up for what I went through."

"I get that ...." Ginny took his hand in hers. "I wouldn't either, if I were you. That doesn't mean that day won't come."

"I won't be holding my breath."

Rising with his hand still in hers, he tugged her up. "Shower, then we'll find something to eat. I want an early night."

"Me, too."

They slowly walked into the bathroom to shower, both of them refraining from talking, lost in their own thoughts. Rubbing the washcloth over his chest, Reaper knew the evening and night would pass in the blink of an eye. He had a bad feeling about Ginny taking the polygraph. He didn't see any good coming out of it, regardless of the results.

Washing quickly, Reaper stepped out of the shower, not wanting to linger with Ginny as she washed her hair. He got dressed after drying off, then checked each of the doors and windows before going into the kitchen to make himself a cup of coffee.

"I thought you wanted an early night?" Ginny remarked, coming into the room dressed in a nightgown.

"The shower woke me up. You go ahead."

"Is anything wrong?" Ginny gave him a concerned look.

"No." Placing his cup on the counter, he went to place a kiss on her lips. "Go to bed."

Her arms went around his waist as her head fell to his chest. He could feel her trembling in his arms. "I love you, Gavin."

"You've told me that five times today."

"Then one more won't hurt." She shrugged against him. "Gavin … I …." She then mumbled something he couldn't make out.

Reaper cocked his head at her. Several times today he had seen her grappling whether to tell him something. "What?"

"Never mind."

"You sure?"

"Everything's fine. Try to get some sleep." Releasing him, she went into the bedroom.

Checking the door for the third time, he then went to get his coffee. He wouldn't be getting any sleep tonight, other than a couple of catnaps on the sofa.

Wandering around the living room, he felt a familiar heightened awareness he'd experienced when stationed overseas. He had quickly learned to sleep with one eye open, waiting for the sound of an IED to strike at any minute. It was the same eerie feeling surrounding him tonight.

Turning the lights off, he carried his cup to the window and stared out into the darkness. He opened the window a few inches to let the cool ocean breeze flow inside.

"I have a bad feeling tonight, Silas."

Despite feeling ridiculous for talking to a man who wasn't there, he strained to hear if Silas answered him.

"*Same*," the wind answered him.

Reaper uneasily searched the darkness for any sign of movement. Leaning to his right, he saw the two agents on duty talking, one of which was smoking a cigarette. The tip of the cigarette flared each time he took a puff, giving him insight into the identity of one of the guards.

Agent Clark was the only one he had seen smoking during their stay. From the height of the other guard, it had to be Agent Flores.

"Can you hear what they're saying?" he asked Silas.

"*Yes. They're talking about Agent Collins missing their briefing.*"

Holding his cup poised at his lips, Reaper rubbed his thumb along the underside of his jaw. "Whatever is going to happen, his men aren't a part of it."

The gust of wind blew in through the window. "*Agree. Ginny's afraid.*"

"I know. Me, too. I want to get the fuck out of here."

Aware there could be a listening device he hadn't spotted, he kept his voice to a mutter, but at the same time unconcerned if he was being watched. It would look as if he was talking to himself, if they could even make out any of his words.

Another rush of wind slipped under the window. "*Go to sleep. I'll wake you if anyone tries to come in.*"

Nodding, Reaper set his cup on the table. Then laying down on the couch, he placed one of the decorative pillows under his head.

"How many of you had to keep track of Ginny when she was younger?"

"*All of us. It was a never-ending battle to keep her safe.*"

"She keeps me on my toes, and she's a grown woman. I can't imagine trying to keep up with her at four."

The window blew so hard it rattled the shutters as if in laughter. "*You have no idea.*"

"Brother, I'm getting there." Reaper gave an exasperated grunt, rolling to his side. "She won't be happy we're talking about her behind her back."

"*It took all eight of us to keep an eye on her. You don't stand a chance without my help.*"

Tiredly, he laid his head back on the arm cushion. The shutters rattled again.

"*Sleep. I'll keep watch.*"

Lowering his lids, Reaper felt the air in the room go still, the eerie stillness returning. His mind's eye replayed the flying jump that Ginny had taken off the side of the waterfall; it scared him shitless. He could still see the exhilarated joy on her face. It was the same expression he'd seen on his fair share of thrill seekers that he'd encountered—and almost every one of the fuckers ended up in a hospital or the morgue.

Moon was one of the worst. The brother had broken more bones than he hadn't. The worst time was when they'd all gotten shit-faced, and he had the bright idea to jump his bike over a road that was heavily trafficked with speeding semis. The road was flanked with low-lying hills on each side.

The brothers were still in awe that Moon had successfully made the jump. He would have walked away unscathed, too, if his tire hadn't hit a rail tie in the grass. Needless to the say, the brother had ended up staying in Ohio longer than he anticipated.

"Brother, I told you not to make the jump until one of us went to check out the other side of the hill," he'd told Moon while him in the hospital.

Moon had looked up from with a gaping smile, exposing a top tooth missing. "Pfft. Fuck off."

Reaper still remembered laughing at him, with his leg lifted high in a contraction, displaying his gory-looking knee with the metal pins sticking out.

"Going to do it again when I get these pins out," he bragged.

Reaper had shaken his head at him. "You're not that stupid."

"Brother, you know why a cat will always cross a fucking road, even if it knows there's a chance it'll be roadkill?"

"Can't say I do."

Moon had given him a shit-eating grin. "Because there's nothing sweeter than when you make it to the other side."

CHAPTER TWENTY-FIVE

Reaper watched the morning sunrise from the patio door. He had managed to grab a couple of hours sleep during the night before. Looking at the clock on the wall, he quietly went into the bedroom, intending to wake Ginny, only to find her awake. His eyes met hers from across the room.

"What time is it?"

"Seven. What do you want for breakfast?"

"Nothing. I couldn't eat if I had to." Sliding out of bed, Ginny went to the dresser to take out a pair of jeans, then went to the closet to take out a long-sleeved grey top with tiny flowers.

Walking across the room, Reaper took out his own change of clothes, putting them on while Ginny went into the bathroom to dress. He took one of her hair bands to tie his hair back in a ponytail, then braided it before taking another band to loop off the end. With the mirror covered, he wasn't able to see the lopsided braid. Uncaring what the end result might look like, Reaper went back into the front room to make breakfast.

Placing two slices of bread in the toaster, he heated some water before taking out a box of tea. Removing two of the breakfast meals, he heated them in the microwave. By the time Ginny came out the bedroom, he had taken several bites of the meal and was making Ginny a cup of hot tea.

Seeing he set a place for her at the table, she made a face at him. "I told you I'm not hungry."

"At least eat the French toast." Setting the hot tea down in front of her when she sat down, he took the other chair to finish his French toast and sausage.

Staring at him eating from over the cup of tea, her face went pale.

"Take a bite of the toast. It'll settle your stomach."

Giving in, she lifted one of the slices to her mouth. "I need to get back to Treepoint so I can get some real food. All this microwaved food smells artificial."

"That's because it is." Getting up to pour himself more coffee, he was happy to see she had eaten the first slice of toast and was working on the second. "What would you have for breakfast if you were home?"

"Oatmeal with raisins and some of Moses' fresh honey."

He made a face at her.

"You don't like oatmeal?" she asked, picking up her fork to cut a section of French toast he made for her.

"Ate too much of it when I was stationed overseas."

Once she finished her tea, he got up from the table to make her another cup. Satisfied to see she had eaten all of the French toast, he sat down to eat the sausage she hadn't touched.

Afterward, they were washing the dishes when the knock came to the door.

"I guess it's showtime." Her attempt at humor failed miserably; she clutched his arm when he moved to answer the door.

"Gavin … if anything happens, trust Agent Collins." Her eyes pled with his. "I would ask you to stay here, but I know you won't."

"I won't," he agreed.

"Then will you at least promise me to put in the same effort of keeping yourself alive as you would me if anything goes wrong? If anything happens to you, it won't matter to me what Allerton does to me."

"Don't say that."

"It's the truth. I can't go back to living like I did before. I could live with a broken heart if you decide you don't want a relationship with me, but I can't survive in a world where you don't exist. Don't make me."

"We're both getting off this fucking island together, okay?"

Her face fell in disappointment when he wouldn't give her his promise. "Yes."

Reaper went to the window first to see who was at the door, then opened the door to the lone agent standing outside.

Agent Collins gave them a quick once-over, taking in their grim expressions. "Everything is all set. There will be a series of twenty questions. Afterward, you'll be allowed to leave. This evening, you're scheduled to have a private dinner with Mr. Allerton and Soleil where you will discuss the date of your departure from the island and if you want to wait for your father's return. If you're ready, we should go."

With a clenched jaw, Reaper wrapped his arm around Ginny's waist as they went outside to the Moke. He wanted to demand they could leave this afternoon, but it was a futile effort without Allerton's approval.

The agent's behavior and appearance instilled zero confidence in him if shit went down. While his suit was neat and clean, the dress shirt wasn't loose enough to hide the protruding gut around his middle. Reaper guessed it had been several years since the agent had seen any active duty. Reaper almost asked him if he was carrying his service revolver.

As they drove to the resort, he added more mental notes of the surrounding island. The driver pulled up in front of Allerton's place, and the hair of the back of his neck rose in warning as he got out of the Moke and waited for Ginny to follow him. Keeping her on the inside next to the vehicle, they walked to where Agent Collins was waiting at the front.

"Where are the rest of your men?" Reaper asked harshly.

"At their quarters. Mr. James, I don't know what you're expecting, but I can assure you that Mrs. James is not in any danger. I will be the administering the polygraph alone. It will be just the two of us alone in the room."

"Ginny's not fucking leaving my sight!"

"She won't be. You will be in the next room that has two-way glass."

"Let me make myself clearer. Ginny's not going into any room without me," Reaper clarified. "There will be no doors between us."

"I will make your decision clear to Mr. Allerton when we reach his office."

Ginny looked between both men and gave him a concerned look. "I don't want to do this if you don't want me to, Gavin."

Having the ball put in his court didn't lessen the dread he was experiencing. There was no guarantee they would be any safer at their bungalow, or that Allerton would allow them to leave the island once his wishes had been met. They could either put the ball in play or stay put. He wanted the fucking game over. If taking the polygraph gave them the possibility of leaving without a violent confrontation—and Ginny getting hurt—he had to take that chance.

"Let's get it done."

Ginny inhaled a deep breath when Reaper gave her the go-ahead. He couldn't decide if the reaction was caused by relief or fear.

"We're ready," she assured Agent Collins.

The agent gave a curt nod, then gave Ginny an indecipherable look that Reaper couldn't read. Traversing the corridors of the resort took a matter of minutes, and they were soon stepping into the elevator.

Allerton's assistant was waiting for them on the other side of the door when the doors slid open. "Agent Collins, the room is ready for you."

As they filed out of the elevator, Agent Collins approached Allerton's assistant who'd come over to escort them down the hall. "Mr. James wants to talk to Mr. Allerton before the test."

"Have a seat, then, and I'll inform him."

Reaper remained standing as the assistant went behind his desk to buzz Allerton. "Yes, sir." Placing the receiver back down, the assistant gave them a reserved smile. "Agent Collins, Mr. Allerton wishes to speak with you first."

Ginny and he watched as the agent made his way into Allerton's office.

"Do you think he'll give you permission to stay with me during the test?"

"Don't care." Reaper shrugged. "You're staying with me."

Ginny kept her gaze glued to the door of Allerton's office, while Reaper kept his eyes glued on the assistant. About a minute after the agent entered Allerton's office, Reaper saw the assistant look their way as his hand slid under the edge of the desk. Reaper's heart started pumping faster. A frightening scenario of the man drawing a gun on them had him tensing, then relaxing when he heard the rustling of papers. The sign that his instincts were heightened had him reconsidering letting Ginny take the test. He was getting her the hell out of there.

"Mr. Allerton would like you both to join him in his office."

The fucker hadn't lifted the receiver, so how did he know his boss was ready for him?

The answer came to him in a flash. This scenario had been prearranged if Ginny refused to take the polygraph test.

When Ginny rose from her seat, he took her arm. "Can you inform Mr. Allerton that my wife isn't feeling well and I'm taking her back to our bungalow?" Reaper began propelling Ginny toward the elevator. "We'll wait by the Moke for Agent Collins. Thank-you."

Pressing the elevator button, he shuffled Ginny in front of him so she could get on the elevator first.

"Wait! Just give me a minute to let Mr—"

The electronic door slid open, and Reaper didn't spare a second to explain before pushing her inside.

"Oof," Ginny exclaimed, looking over her shoulder as he rushed in and pushed the down arrow. "What's wrong?" she asked as the doors closed.

Inwardly cursing that the elevator wouldn't stop between floors, Reaper kept Ginny at his back, bracing for the doors to open. "Didn't like the vibe I was getting. When the door opens, if anyone is there, press the button to close the door and don't come out until I say it's clear."

She began moving to stand next to the control panel. "But—"

"We'll talk about it when we get to the Moke."

"Okay."

The door opened to an empty hallway. Raising his forearms up to cover each side of his head, he stepped out, glancing quickly to each side. "Clear," he said from over his shoulder.

When Ginny exited the elevator, Reaper took her arm, hurrying her through the hallways. When they turned down the one leading to the front doors, he heard footsteps rushing behind them. Swiveling his head back, he saw four security guards rushing toward them with batons in their hands.

Seeing the batons, Reaper knew instinctively he needed them—or rather Ginny—alive. Slinging the glass door open, he rushed out, propelling them forward so fast that, if any guard was positioned outside, they wouldn't hesitate at trying to take Ginny from him.

"Halt! Mr. James! Mr. Allerton just wants to talk with you as you requested!" one of the guards coming out of the door yelled out to him.

Reaper didn't slow until they neared the Moke and saw their driver was holding his baton out.

"Ginny, stop, and I'll order the guards not to hurt him and take him back to your bungalow." Looking up toward the voice, Reaper saw Allerton standing on the balcony overhead.

"Don't listen to him," Reaper muttered, still moving toward the Moke.

"Ginny!" Allerton barked out.

Both of them looked up to see armed security officers leaning over the balcony with AR-15s, pointing red lasers at Reaper's forehead.

Seeing his reflection in the window below Allerton, Reaper knew he was fighting a losing battle. Ginny wasn't going to take a chance with his life.

"I don't want to kill him, Ginny, but I will."

Ginny pulled her arm away from Reaper. "Where is Agent Collins?" she called out to him.

Allerton made a movement with his hand, and two men

came into view. Collins was pressed against a guard who had his arm around Collins' neck and a gun to his head.

"You really don't want to have these men's death on your conscience, do you?"

"You're going to kill us anyway," Reaper yelled, as the guards who had followed them outside began circling them.

"Killing is what you do, Reaper. Unlike you, I don't have blood on my hands."

Reaper laughed at him. "No, you just pay someone else to carry the kill out for you."

"I'm not going to discuss semantics with you. I don't have all day, Ginny. Make your choice, or I'll make it for you."

Ginny's eyes remained on Reaper's forehead, and Reaper knew her choice before the words were out of her mouth. "Will you let him go?"

"Yes," Allerton answered.

"He's lying, Ginny."

"If you hurt him, I swear to God I won't tell you anything. Do you hear me?" she yelled up to Allerton before lowering her gaze back to him.

"At least you'll have a chance on your own without me. Save yourself."

"Ginny ...."

Before he could stop her, Ginny jerked out of his grasp and was immediately swallowed within the midst of guards.

"Take him back to the bungalow," Allerton ordered his men as they ushered Ginny back inside the building.

"You're a dead man if one hair of hers is hurt."

Allerton gave him a superior smirk as he withdrew from the balcony.

The driver put his baton under the driver's seat. "Mr. James, if you get into the Moke, I'll drive you to your bungalow."

Weighing his options, Reaper glanced toward the

building and saw four of the guards stationed outside the resort. Climbing in the Moke, he got in the front seat beside the driver, giving him a hostile glance when he was about to tell him to get in the back. As they drove toward the bungalow, he wasn't surprised when the driver the turned off the main road; there was line of guards waiting for them.

Bringing the Moke to an abrupt stop, the driver reached for the keys, but with his forearm, Reaper sliced down on the fucker's wrist, nearly breaking it. The guy bailed out of the Moke with a howl of pain and took off running.

Reaper threw himself into the empty driver's seat, realizing he didn't have enough time to escape. Grabbing the keys and sliding them into his pocket, he was suddenly jerked out of the driver's seat.

He was outnumbered by fourteen, so Reaper stood stoically to see what their next move would be. It would be a losing battle to take this many on at once; he had to wait until there were less of them before making his move.

"Move."

Reaper felt a blow on his back when he didn't move.

"Don't make me handcuff you." A guard with a beefy face came near him. "Move."

Seeing the direction they were indicating, Reaper followed the men, who caged him in as they started walking toward the dock. They brought him to a halt beside a speed boat. Three of the guards got on the boat first. "Step over."

Reaper didn't demur. After getting on, one of the guards with the face of a pot roast, shoved him down on a padded metal seat beside the driver.

"Give me your hands."

Reaper knew they were going to cuff him. Wanting the guards to think they were safe, he reached his arms backward, feeling the metal circle his wrists before the guy reached for the radio clipped to his gun belt.

"James is neutralized. Second phase started. On my way back."

Allerton's voice came over the radio. "Stay there until the job is done."

"Yes, sir." Clicking his radio back onto his belt, Beef Face moved to his side.

"You know what to do," he said to the guard in the driver's seat. "Radio in on your way back."

"You're not going?"

"No, Leif and Boom can go with you. That's one more than you need."

Beef Face gave Reaper a wistful glance. "I was hoping like hell you would give me some trouble. That sweet piece won't miss you when I'm done with her."

Reaper lowered his gaze to the shiny deck, containing the comeback he wanted to give.

"Allerton won't be happy you didn't stay," the other man spoke up as Beef Face jumped back onto the dock.

"I'm not wasting my time here," Beef Face spouted his opinion to the other men gathered on the boat. "I was paid for a high-risk mission. Damn." He gave him a disgusted look. "Allerton has more money than brains. I would have done this job for half the pay and the woman. Finish this piece of shit off. Leif, Boom, go with Devlin. Rest of you, come with me."

Reaper watched the eleven men walk back down the dock as the motor started. Marveling at their stupidity, Reaper used his hands to hold onto the metal bars at his back to keep the cuff from cutting his skin. He knew what fate they had devised for him, and he didn't want any blood drawing the sharks to him if he managed to jump from the boat when they took his handcuffs off.

The island was barely out of sight before the motor was cut.

"You should go farther out," one of the guards cautioned the driver.

"Why?" Devlin scoffed, getting off his seat. "It's not like the cocksucker is going to be in any shape to swim back."

Taking his gun out of his holster, Devlin pointed the gun at his temple. "Boom is going to take the cuffs off. If you make one move I don't fucking tell you, I'm going to blow your fucking brains out."

Reaper felt the cuffs loosen around his wrists.

"Stand up."

Slowly, Reaper stood.

"Back up."

Following the order slowly, out of the corner of his eye, he saw Leif reach under a padded bench seat for a roll of duct tape.

"Put your hands behind your back."

With the gun pressed to his temple, Reaper began calculating his chance of survival if he didn't do what was being asked of him. Different scenarios went through his mind in flashes.

Feeling the gun pressed harder against his temple, Reaper put his hands behind his back. He could get out of the tape when the time was right; a bullet to his brain was a game ender.

The tape was wrapped around his wrists several times before he heard it being torn. Dumbasses hadn't even bought a good quality roll to use on him.

"Move to the side," Devlin ordered.

Reaper did as he was told, seeing Boom reach under another bench seat to take out chains with an anchor attached.

About to break the tape on his wrists by a maneuver he'd had been taught in training, Devlin shoved his face in front of him. "I don't want to have to clean up the mess your brains would make, but I will."

Controlling the instinct to fight, Reaper let Leif tape his feet together at the ankles, then let him wind the chain around his neck. One lesson he had learned from the years of being Slate's captive was to save his strength and wait for the right moment to attack. This wasn't it. Any sound of bullets being fired would be heard by the guards on the beach.

"Loop the chain around his waist, too. I don't want him floating to the top."

Reaper lowered his lashes to hide the deadly intent in his eyes. He kept telling himself to wait, and instead he remembered how Ginny looked at him before she took off with Allerton in an effort to save his life. His girl was too trusting.

"Toss him overboard."

"Devlin, shoot him first." Boom hesitated to follow the order.

"You want to spend the afternoon cleaning and have your ass reamed by Allerton? He doesn't want any bullet holes in him when we come back to get his body. He wants it to look like a drowning—which is the reason we aren't using the cuffs, so there are no marks on his body."

Leif didn't take his eyes off him, waiting for him move.

"Damn. That's my worst nightmare. Poor bastard." Boom gave him a pitying glance before he and Leif each hooked an arm under one of his, then gripped his belt as they shuffled him to the edge of the boat.

"Sorry, dude. If I could, I'd put a bullet in you myself to put you out of your misery, but it's Allerton's call, not mine."

"Hurry up. Jesus, the next thing, you'll be praying over him." Devlin gave him a gloating smile. "I want to get back. Guess who gets to go second when Alexei is finished with your little piece? Don't worry; Allerton made arrangements for us to bring her back to you when we're done with her. I have the coordinates on my radar; I'll make sure to drop her next to you. Sayonara, you dumbass bitch. Toss the cocksucker."

Air met his back as he was thrown off the side of the boat before the cool water surrounded him in its soft embrace. Reaper took a deep breath just before the water swallowed him whole, and the anchor did its job sending him plunging downward. His last sight was the three men hanging off the boat witnessing his descent into a watery grave.

Shutting them out of his mind and any emotions, other than survival, Reaper concentrated on getting loose. They had put too much confidence in the duct tape and the chains with the weighted anchor to do the job of killing him instead of doing it with a bullet. Their amateur mistake was going to be the last one they would ever make. They had underestimated his will to survive. Not only that, but they had underestimated his will for Ginny to survive.

People were going to die today, and it wasn't going to be Ginny… and it wasn't going to be him. No, there would be a reckoning today. Before the sun set, they would be begging God for His mercy, and they were going to find out the same fucking thing he had.

Whatever little mercy God had was doled out at the pearly gates, because he'd never seen an ounce of it on Earth. Every single one of those motherfuckers who thought they succeeded in getting rid of him were going to die with only one name on their lips—*his*.

And when the Reaper came for you, it was already too late to run.

CHAPTER TWENTY-SIX

With iron-clad calm, Reaper waited until he reached the ocean floor. Then, opening his eyes, he bent back and dragged his taped hands under his feet before tightening his forearms and using his strength to rip the tape. With his hands free, he then began unwinding the chain from his neck before unhooking his waist. Still holding the chain with the anchor to keep himself from surfacing, he took the key from his pocket to cut the tape at his feet.

Fueled with the need to reach Ginny as fast as possible, Reaper had to put that aside to concentrate on the here and now. Shoving the remains of the tape into his pocket, he released the chain, then swam underwater to glide under the speedboat. Slowly using his feet, he started to swim his way to the water's surface.

Keeping his movements small and efficient, so they wouldn't hear him on the other side of the boat, Reaper raised his head ever so slightly, just enough for let his eyes and ears to breach the water's surface. Hearing them talking on the other side of the boat, he allowed himself to raise his head higher to small breaths to refill his aching lungs.

"How long do we have to wait?"

Recognizing Leif's voice, he stayed still to figure out their positions on the boat. Leif was at the rear starboard.

"Just a couple more," Devlin said from mid-starboard side.

"Shouldn't there be some bubbles coming up?" Boom asked, his voice coming from the same area of the boat as Devlin.

Reaper lowered his head back until only his eyes and ears again were above the water. Then, using the hull as cover, he carefully peeked around the corner. He wanted to confirm Devlin's exact location and if he still had his gun out.

Devlin and Boom were leaning over the side, the gun still in Devlin's hand, though he was holding it carelessly downward as both men peered down into the sea.

"How in the fuck would I know? I've never drowned anyone before." Devlin lowered his face closer to the water.

Noiselessly, Reaper swam underneath the boat and then with a powerful kick, he came back up. Devlin didn't have a chance to react before Reaper jerked the gun out of his hand, pointed it toward Boom and fired, one shot hitting him in his mouth. With his other hand and both feet planted on the side of the boat to give him traction, he sent Devlin flying over the side.

"What the fuck?" Leif yelled from the stern.

In one motion, Reaper pulled himself onto the boat at the same time Leif was trying to get his gun out of the holster. Not wanting to let another gunshot ring out, Reaper threw himself at the stunned man, taking them both down to the deck. Planting one fist with his heavy ring in the fucker's nose, he brought his other fist down, smashing the butt of the gun down on Leif's head. He wanted the motherfucker out for the count but didn't want him dead … yet.

With that target neutralized, he rolled off Leif and raised

the gun to see Devlin heaving himself up to clamber back into the boat. Reaper waited until he was midair before he rolled again, letting the fucker hit the deck.

Raising up into a sitting position before Devlin could lift himself up, Reaper threw himself on Devlin's back, wrapping his free arm around his neck and putting him in a choke hold, holding him down with the weight of his body.

Laying the gun down on the deck next to him, Reaper paced his hand behind Devlin's neck. "You should have kept on swimming," Reaper hissed into his ear. "The name's Reaper. You're a dead motherfucker." With one twisting motion, Reaper broke the fucker's neck.

Releasing the dead body, Reaper snatched his gun and rose from the deck. Walking over to Boom, he checked his pulse, satisfied he was dead. Then Reaper went to Leif, taking the handcuffs from his belt before dragging the unconscious man to the passenger seat and handcuffing him to the metal bars. The only reason Reaper kept him breathing was in case one of the guards from the island radioed in.

Reaper quickly gathered all the weapons, unhooking Devlin's gun belt off his dead body and putting it on. After checking the rounds, he placed the gun in the holster. Efficiently shoving what ammunition he found into his pockets and the guns from the other two men in his waistband, he got in the captain's chair and started the motor. Aiming the boat for Clindale Island, Reaper opened the boat full throttle.

He'd gone no more than a couple of yards before a shining light hit him in the face from the island. Torn at wanting to get back to Ginny, Reaper didn't change direction to Sherguevil, gunning the motor as the boat flew over the ocean. Silas's voice came out of the rushing wind the boat was generating.

"I'm with Ginny."

Silas's reassurance didn't relieve him that he had made the right decision to head for Clindale.

Slowing the speed as he drew near, he pulled the boat into the dock. Cutting the motor, he stayed on the boat, expecting whoever had flashed the light at him to come out in the open. Another flash from had him checking to see if Leif was still incapacitated. Once confirmed, he removed the key, got out of the boat, and followed the flashes.

When he found where a tangled jungle growth had been beaten back, he took one of the guns out as he carefully moved forward until he came to small area that had been recently cleared.

Stopping, Reaper waited for another flash of light to show him which direction to go when he heard a small whistle that he recognized. Looking up, he watched as Shade lithely dropped down from a palm tree where he'd made a tree stand.

Reaper had to press his lips together in a thin line and squint his eyes closed to hold the emotions at bay at seeing the brother standing there. Opening his eyes, Reaper held his hand out to Shade. "Brother, you have no fucking clue how goddamn good you look to me right now."

Shade smacked his hand down in his. "Brother, you have no fucking idea how good you looked to me when I saw your ass coming out of the water after those fuckers threw you in. If it hadn't been for Viper, I would have broken cover to come fish your ass out."

Their hands dropped to their sides as Reaper looked at him questioningly.

"How did he know ...?"

The sound of footsteps coming toward him had Reaper raising the gun again. Shade forestalled him as Viper ran into the small clearing.

"How did ...?" Reaper began, his eyes widening as Lucky,

Knox, Cash, Rider, Train, Moon, Hammer, Jonas, and Jackal all came out, too. Each of the men were dressed in their military gear with their weapons ready.

"How long?" Reaper asked once he was able to control his voice as he started shaking the brothers' hands. Taking Viper's hand last, he pulled him into a bear hug while they smacked each other on the shoulders.

"Shade and Rider left the day after you. Knox and Train over a week ago. Shade sent me a transmission yesterday afternoon; the rest of us got here last night."

The brothers broke apart, and Reaper took a step back to stare at the group of men. "Why didn't you take those fuckers out before they dumped me over the side?"

Shade rested his weapon comfortably on his hip. "I wanted to, but Viper told me no. He said you had it under control. Viper was holding Rider back when I spotted you at the hull."

Rider looked away uncomfortably as Shade recited what had been going on while he'd been underwater.

The fact that Viper commanded all the brothers to hold off, showed more about Viper's confidence in him than words could. He didn't have time to appreciate the fact or ask how they all had managed to slip onto the island. He needed to get to Ginny.

"We can talk on the boat. I have to get to Ginny." Reaper turned back toward the dock. "Any of you got dry clothes to spare—"

"Wait …." Viper stopped him. "Do you know which room they have her in? We've been working on a plan to get you two out, but we need her location."

Reaper closed his eyes as a gust of wind sent a chill through him. "She's in Allerton's office," Reaper told them, taking a pair of blue fatigues from Lucky.

Taking the guns out of the holsters and ammo out his pockets, he tore his clothes off, then started redressing.

"I can get her out. What I'm worried about is getting past the water patrols that Allerton has stationed to keep everyone from entering or leaving." Reaper gave a grunt as he stomped his boot down on the ground to shove his foot farther inside.

"We've been working on a plan. You having the boat makes it a hell of a lot easier," Viper stated as he and Rider lifted a brown tarp that was covering a hole. The men swiftly gathered the weapons and backpacks concealed underneath.

"We'll drop Train, Lucky, and Jonas off at the back of the island, closest to the airport to get a plane ready while we go to the main dock. Allerton's office is closer from there. Unfortunately, it's also close to where he keeps his security headquarters." Viper caught his impatient expression, yet he spared a quick glance to make sure all the men were geared up. "Shade, make the call."

Shade took out a cell phone from the front pocket of his shirt.

"Viper … we need to go."

"We're not going in like a bulldozer, Reaper. We're going in like a well-oiled machine. And to do that we need Shade to make that call."

His sense of urgency multiplied the longer he stood there helpless while Ginny was left alone with Allerton.

Shade watched him dispassionately as he spoke into his cell phone. "Be waiting by the door in ten minutes." Placing the phone back in his pocket, Shade nodded at Viper. "He'll be there."

"Move out," Viper ordered to all the brothers. "Keep to the path where Shade took out the cameras."

The men moved as one, with Viper going first and Jackal

going last. Reaper had only met Shade's brother-in-law a few times when he had accompanied Penni to visit Shade and Lily. While Reaper had never seen him in a fight, he didn't have any concern Jackal was able to hold his own. The man had survived being married to Penni. That in itself earned his respect.

On the boat, Reaper gave Train the keys to unlock the handcuffs on Leif.

"Why'd you cuff him if he was dead?" Train asked, putting the key in the lock.

"My bad. I thought he was still alive." Reaper knelt down next the guard then, without remorse, started removing the uniform from the dead guard. Viper and Rider were already switching out their uniforms from the other two guards, Viper giving Rider the wet one. Reaper gave Leif's to Cash, who seemed close to the same size. The dark color of the uniform hid the blood stains, and the wet state of the one that Rider was wearing.

Viper took the captain's seat to start the motor while the brothers placed the three dead guards on the dock. As soon as Jackal's boots hit the deck, Viper pulled away from Clindale, heading toward the back of Sherguevil Island, which was closer to the airport.

Reaper lay on the deck of the boat with the others while Viper, Rider, and Cash were the only ones visible if any of security guards saw the boat approaching the island.

Staring at the men, his eyes met Shade's. "I expected you on Clindale, I didn't see Rider, Knox or Train."

"Guess your mind must have been on something else. Rider practically fell out of the tree he was hiding in when Ginny took off flying from that waterfall."

"Could have left me a sign they were there." Reaper glared at the brothers surrounding him on the deck.

"We planned to when you were out of range of the cameras, but then you got a busy and we all decided Ginny wouldn't be exactly happy to see us. By the way, you can thank Knox for jamming the transmission of the signal. Allerton wasn't able to make out anything."

Reaper would be able to tell Ginny that when they'd waited outside Allerton's office yesterday, he hadn't been watching footage of them having sex.

Train responded his glare with a raised chin. "She might have earned enough votes to belong to The Last Riders, but my old lady isn't going to be your backup."

The thought of Killyama being his backup had him admitting the truth: he wasn't man enough to handle that hellcat on wheels.

"Get ready to bail." Viper alerted them they were getting closer to the drop-off point.

Adjusting the speed to slow them down, Viper let the boat get as close to the beach as he dared.

"Go."

At Viper's barked order, Train, Lucky, and Jonas bailed out of the boat. Reaper raised his head enough for him to see them slogging through thigh-high water before he lay back down as Viper maneuvered the boat farther away from the beach.

"Get ready. I'm about to pull into the dock. What about the FBI agents who came with Ginny?" Viper asked as he idled the motor to bring it to the dock. "Where are they?"

"They're in the two bungalows next to the one that Ginny and I were given. They're three rookies, and I didn't see them today. The only one I saw was Collins, the agent in charge, and I didn't see him after he went into Allerton's office this morning. Something's not right about him. I can't swear he's dirty, but he didn't fucking do shit to help either. And Ginny kept pestering me to trust him. Something's up with him."

"We'll figure it out. First, we get the rookies, then go to the main resort."

Viper stopped the boat, and Rider and Cash jumped off first.

Waiting for their signal, Reaper put his hands on the deck, preparing to jump up. "Take the brothers, and I'll meet you at the resort. I have to get to Ginny."

Viper got off the boat to stand next to Rider. "There are three guards trying to move the jeep that Reaper stole the key to. Other than that, we're clear. We'll go get the rookies, then Ginny. It's closer. Once we take the three guards out, we have a clear path to the rookies."

The remaining brothers agilely jumped off the boat, swiftly moving toward the Moke. As Reaper landed on the dock, he grabbed the strap of Viper's backpack.

"Here's the key to the Moke. Get the fucking rookies. You'll be right behind me. I have to get to Ginny."

"No, we—"

Viper jerked his hand off the strap while they watched Hammer, Rider, and Shade take the guards out while the others were on the lookout for anyone coming.

Reaper wrenched him back to make him listen. "I'm going to Ginny!" he yelled.

"We are just—"

"Now. We have to go fucking now! One of the guards bragged about what they were going to do to her. I swore I'd never disobey another order from you, but I have to put Ginny first. Viper …"

His brother sent an impatient glare over his shoulder, about to pull away again.

"Ginny doesn't know she's carrying my child."

CHAPTER TWENTY-SEVEN

"Move."

Ginny shrugged her shoulder away from a guard who impatiently shoved her through the doorway of Allerton's office. The alarming sight of Agent Collins sitting in one of the chairs in front of Allerton's desk with his hands cuffed behind his back and his mouth taped closed brought her to a shocking halt.

Glaring at the nameless guard, Ginny went to Agent Collins. The closer she got, the more horrified she became seeing the extent of his injuries. His head fell limply back on his neck, his eyes were swollen shut, and he had a myriad of blue and purple bruises covering his face. The sight of the damage inflicted on the agent had Ginny reaching out to touch him.

"Don't concern yourself, my dear. He's still alive."

"He needs medical attention." Ginny nervously crossed her arms over her chest, adjusting her bracelet so it lay on her wrist and would quit riding up her arm under the sleeve of her shirt.

Ginny glared at Allerton as he came into the office to sit

unconcernedly behind his desk. "Any help for that buffoon will have to wait until after we talk."

Ginny stroked a flower charm to give herself courage as Allerton unveiled the hatred he had been disguising from her. "Provide him medical attention, or I refuse to say anything to you."

Allerton sighed, rising from behind his desk to walk toward her.

Refusing to show fear, Ginny stood her ground as Allerton drew closer. Then, like a striking snake, he back-handed her on the side of her cheek.

"Riz, kill him."

The guard closest to her went to Agent Collins, removing his gun from a holster and preparing to kill the unconscious man right in front of her.

"Wait!" Ginny shouted at Allerton. "We can talk."

Allerton shrugged, calling the guard off. "The next time, I won't stop him. Now that I have your complete attention, I want my questions answered."

Ginny raised her fingertips to her stinging cheek, then pulled them back when she felt the warm wetness of blood. Allerton crossed his arms, his large signet ring openly displayed.

"What did you see when you were on that boat?"

"I've been telling you the truth. I don't remember—"

She wasn't able to finish her sentence before another stinging smack came her way. If her feet hadn't been planted firmly apart, it would have sent her flying.

"Riz, get the machine."

The guard gave her a smirk that made her skin crawl as he left the room.

Agent Collins groaned out, and Ginny attempted to go to him, but Allerton stepped forward, blocking her path. "You want to help him, stop lying to me."

"I'm not lying!"

"You've been lying to me since you've stepped foot on my island. Ah ... you're back, Riz. Set it up."

The guard set a machine on a circular table that near the open balcony door. The three chairs around the table matched the one that Agent Collins was handcuffed to.

As the guard plugged in the machine, Allerton went back to his desk to take out a black box. Ginny saw him stare at his computer screen before opening the box. She no longer felt the painful sting in her cheek seeing Allerton pull out a syringe.

"Have a seat, my dear."

"What's in the syringe?"

"Something to relax you while allowing you to answer my questions ... shall I say ... more truthfully?"

Ginny briefly closed her eyes, shutting out the evil intent of his gaze, then opened them, determined to show him no fear. Recognizing she had reached the end of the road and was out of recourse, Ginny dropped her arms to her sides.

"That won't be necessary. I'll tell you the truth about everything you want to know."

Allerton looked her skeptically but lowered the syringe. "Tell me what you saw on the boat."

"I don't remember anything on the boat, other than climbing up, and that's the God's honest truth. Nothing else. The only thing I do remember about that day was sneaking away from Manny and falling asleep in the space underneath the bunk where he always hid me. I don't remember taking anything from the boat."

"You do remember being on the island?"

"Yes, I remember how pretty it was with all the umbrellas and the different stands that were set up to sell things that I wanted. Maybe if you show me a picture of what you think I stole, it would refresh my memory."

"You can do better than that." Allerton strode forward, removing the cap of the syringe.

Ginny took a step back. "I don't understand why you don't believe me."

When he swung out this time, she was prepared, but it didn't make it hurt any less. Her mouth exploded in pain. Blinking back watery tears, she stared back at him unwaveringly.

"Gavin is going to kill you for that." Using the sleeve of her shirt, Ginny wiped the blood dribbling down her chin.

"Don't put your faith in your husband; you'll be sadly disappointed." Allerton gave her a look of pure disgust. "The only thing your husband has ever been good at is dropping to his knees for an ounce of coke."

"You're not worthy enough to have my husband's name uttered from your mouth." Ginny refused to give him any outward reaction of shock at him being aware of what Gavin had gone through during his kidnapping. "He has honorably served his country, while you have done nothing but your best to lay a foundation to destroy it."

"Save your sanctimonious lecture. Your association with Gavin and The Last Riders shows your serious lack of judgment. I've done more for the United States and other countries than you could ever wish to accomplish in a thousand years."

"At what cost?" Ginny asked, lowering her hand away from her mouth.

"No cost. I didn't have to pay a dime. They paid me."

"There's always a price to pay for taking a life."

Allerton gave a small, mocking laugh. "Maybe for others." He raised his free hand. "My hands are clean. I'm not responsible for the actions of others."

"You don't consider yourself responsible when they are following *your* orders?" Ginny stared at him in pity. "I wonder if you have ever cared about anyone but yourself? People trusted you with their money to make the world a better place, to help others. You have untold wealth to use any way you want. Instead, you use it to garner even more wealth. Just how much money is enough for you? You have enough that you couldn't spend it in five lifetimes. Do you have children to leave it to?"

"I don't have any children," he said stiffly.

"If you did, would it make a difference?"

"For what? You think having children would make me a better person?" Allerton looked at her as if she were three years old. "Or that I work so hard just to leave it to my progeny, as my parents did me? The answer is *no*. As I've said before, you're too naïve. When you die, do you think it will make a difference in the world, other than within the small sphere of Treepoint?" He looked her over disdainfully. "When you die, that fake birth certificate with another name on it will be the only thing left of you to show you were ever born. When I die, I will be remembered for centuries to come."

The man was a deranged lunatic flaunting his power.

"I seriously doubt that. Even if that were to come true, it won't be for the good you pretend to accomplish." Her nails bit into the palm of her hands at his smug smile.

"How will anyone find out? It certainly won't be from you. Your little escape plan has failed, and shortly, you will be reunited with your husband. Neither of you will be in any condition to tarnish my legacy."

Fear for Gavin tried to sideline her, anchoring her thoughts on the man in front of her and not on the man she loved. Gavin was her gladiator; he had survived much worse odds than he encountered today. He would survive, and she would too. Bravely, Ginny squared her shoulders at him, determined to show Allerton she wasn't afraid of his threats.

"Sooner or later, one of your little minions will expose you," Ginny contradicted him.

"Not without exposing their own secrets. The secrets I hold in my care aren't easily explained away."

"Unlike your own?"

"I find myself having to repeat myself. Like I said," his voice condescending, "my hands are clean."

"No ... they ... are ... not." Ginny gave him a withering stare. "I saw you kill Gyi with your own hands."

Slowly, he capped the syringe.

"Finally ... finally!" Satisfaction poured out of Allerton as if he had run a mouse into a corner and was about to beat it to death. "My dear, that was what I waiting for."

Ginny fiddled with her bracelet, as if he was beneath her notice. "What? For me to admit that I saw you kill Gyi, and willingly watched Manny being beaten by your men to what I assume was his death? You should have just asked. I would have told you that first day you sent for me to come to your office." Ginny said carelessly, dropping the secret she had harbored for so long and downplaying the admission to deliberately rile him even further. It was everything she could do to set aside her hatred and disgust of the man to appear unaffected.

Her plan worked.

Angered by her indifference to what he believed to be his victory at getting the admission from her, Allerton reached out, ripped the bracelet from her wrist, and flung it across the room. The metal clinked on the glass table.

"That was very rude."

His veneer of sophistication cracked, exposing the monster within. His hands encircled her throat as he began strangling her, shaking her like a rag doll.

Forcing herself not to panic, she grabbed his wrists, fighting dizziness as she used her nails to rip into his flesh.

At the same time, she brought her knee up … *hard*. Allerton released her with a howl of pain, as he went to his knees.

She would have kneed him in the face, but two guards caught her by the arms and dragged her back. The guard who'd brought the polygraph machine took out a baton from his holster, pulling his arm back, preparing to bring it down on her head.

"Stop," Allerton ordered, using the edge of his desk to help himself to his feet. Holding onto the desk, he slowly limped around it to sit down on his chair. Then, flinging the syringe onto the desk, he opened a side drawer to take out a golden handle.

Ginny frowned at the object, not understanding what it went to.

As Allerton rose from the desk, she watched his eyes go to the computer screen while simultaneously pressing a button on the golden handle. With a click, the handle lengthened into a long cane.

Straightening to his full height, Allerton started to move away from his desk when something must have caught his eye because he turned back to the computer.

"Riz, Desmond is by door six. Go see why he is loitering there."

Ginny wanted to rub her arm when the guard released her, but the second guard secured her other arm. The three additional guards in the room closed in on her.

"You're such a coward. You have to pay other men because you're too much of a wimp to take on one woman by yourself."

Coming out from behind the desk, Allerton slid his hand down from the golden handle to the middle of the cane to twirl it between his fingers. Then, as he drew closer to her, he let the cane slip through his fingers until he held the handle once again. Raising the cane higher in the air, he moved it around and she heard it create a whizzing sound.

"What happened to the islanders on Clindale?" Ginny asked before he could strike her.

An evil smile played on his cruel lips. "I've been waiting for you to ask me that question. What do you think happened to them?"

"I think you killed the strongest ones and sold the weaker ones."

"You're too astute for your own good. Move away from her, Nino."

The guard hastily dropped her arm to move a safe distance away.

Ginny didn't cower or try to run, knowing the guards would be on her in an instant to drag her back. She simply and proudly raised her chin. "Who did you sell them to?"

Swinging the cane in an arch, he then brought it down, hitting her in the thigh. Agonizing pain splintered through her, forcing her to her knees.

"I didn't sell them. I gave them away for free."

"You don't do anything for free." Childhood memories of the generous people who she had considered family gave her the strength to keep antagonizing him.

"I did receive a few perks," he boasted with a mocking laugh at her disgusted expression. "I didn't keep any of them for myself. I haven't kept my wealth intact by being foolish. Being blackmailed or incarcerated holds no appeal for me.

"I have found, while men exercise caution with their businesses, where women are concerned, they tend to lose their judgment. While I'm not above taking advantage of their lapses, I have lived my life above reproach. I have not had to refute claims of any sexual crimes. I keep my sexual activities to those who are willing, and where I can't be accused of coercion. It's not as stimulating or exciting, but then, neither do I have to bow to a woman's demands or deal with an unexpected pregnancy. Too many of my friends have been held hostage to the dictates of their child's mother, both financially and emotionally. I am accountable to no one but myself."

Ginny let her eyes spew the hate she felt. "That's not true. Just because your crimes haven't been discovered, doesn't make you're unaccountable. One day your crimes will catch up with you."

"If that day comes, which it won't," Allerton continued, unperturbed by her threat, "I have several residences where I can live just as comfortably as I do here."

"My death won't go without punishment."

"By whom? The Last Riders?"

The whizzing sound of the cane was the only forewarning she received as Allerton brought it down on her shoulder.

Ginny winced in pain but didn't lower her hate-filled eyes from his.

"Please," he scoffed, "they won't even be a thorn in my side. Your parents?"

The cane whizzed again before striking her other shoulder.

Ginny held Gavin's image to keep strong. He had suffered for years at Slate's abuse; she could bear whatever Allerton dished out to get the answers she needed.

"Jasper?" Allerton gleefully went on, trying to tear her down mentally and physically. "You'll be seeing him when Nino reunites you with Gavin. He was no threat to me. Soleil? She has been loyal only to me, even before your disappearance. Why do you think your parents remained on Clindale after there was no further need of them to do so, and why does she stay on Sherguevil with me now?"

"You tell me." Flippantly Ginny asked the question

wanting the answer more for Trudy than herself. Her sister deserved her own answers.

"Jasper was a brilliant engineer, unfortunately for him, too brilliant. I needed him on my team. No one doubted Jasper's integrity, and it was much easier when several of my patrons needed permits. It took a period of time for him to decide to get on board, but eventually Jasper agreed."

"You blackmailed him, forced him to give the go-ahead for permits," Ginny guessed.

Allerton smug grin became even more pronounced. "You give me too much credit. I wasn't the one who blackmailed him."

"What did Mother use to blackmail him?"

"You'll have to ask her that question. I left that tedious task to her."

"You're lying."

"How does it feel to be lied to?" He said as he swung the cane.

The pain doubled from the two-pronged attack of him using the cane on her while gloating about her mother's betrayal of her father. It hurt deeply, grinding the last visages of her happy childhood memories into the dust, hurting her more gravely than the cane flying at her skin.

Ginny refused to be defeated, not willing to give Allerton anymore satisfaction by deriding her father instead of filling in the gaps of her history.

"You actually think four agents disappearing won't hold any ramifications from the FBI?"

Allerton stopped swinging the cane to point it at Agent Collins. "My dear, I hate to disillusion you, but your little jig with the FBI is up. I never put my eggs in one basket. I knew the real purpose for your return to Sherguevil Island was to get me to incriminate myself. Agent Collins was a double agent, pretending to be on my payroll while in reality he was gathering information to incriminate me. Fortunately, I have multiple sources in the FBI and the CIA; they warned me of the deception. Needless to say, the four agents will disappear without a trace, just like you and Gavin. Those on my payroll will bury the disappearance beneath miles and miles of red tape where it will never be found." Giving a malicious chuckle, he brought the cane down on her shoulder with such force she fell to her side.

"Ginny raised her hand to push her hair from her face to look him in the eye. "Just tell me one thing … What was the artifact you think I stole?"

The cane stopped midswing, as if he was taken by surprise. "You really don't remember?"

"No," she said truthfully.

His chuckle melted into a frown.

"You took it. I saw it with my own eyes."

"How?"

"On videotape. All the interiors of the ships coming into the island are set up with surveillance when visitors dock their boats for screening."

"Why am I not surprised you lied?" Scornfully spat out at him. "You make that a habit, don't you?"

The expected swing of the cane didn't come because of her snide remark. Instead, it gave him the opportunity to gloat. "Sometimes my guests need motivation to come to an agreement with me."

"Agreement? You mean kiss your ass?"

Ginny saw little black dots when he struck out at her.

"That day, with the owner being present, I couldn't get access to the camera. The owner was there and found the artifact missing. He didn't know who had taken it, only that it wasn't where it was supposed to be. He searched for it before he called for my assistance. One of the crew had accidently left a deck door unlatched, which is how you must have gotten inside. By the time we got to the boat, all we had to go on was a vague description of Gyi's son going to different boats at the marina and looking for something or *someone*. We only knew what the owner told us—the artifact was missing. Naturally we assumed it was Manny. Unfortunately back then, I didn't have the state-of-the-art equipment to work with or the feed would have gone to my office. I had to wait until I got access to the equipment on board the owner's boat to see what Manny had stolen. By then, my security had cornered Manny on Gyi's boat. Manny denied being on the board, saying he didn't know what had been taken. Needless to say, he was telling the truth. Unfortunately, I didn't know that at the time, and sadly for Manny and Gyi it was one of the few times in my life I lost control. By the time I was able to retrieve the security tapes, clearly showing you were the one sneaking on the boat, you and Trudy had already been sent to your grandmother's. I was eagerly waiting for your return when the plane went down. Your pretend death was a stroke of genius, by the way. I believed it, but I did cover my bases if you were alive, but *somehow* you managed to keep just out my range. I'd like to know how."

Ginny didn't flinch when Allerton used the tip of the cane to force her shoulder backward so she had to look up at him.

"You admit killing them was a mistake?"

"I've never been a man dwell on my mistakes. Especially" —clicking his tongue at her he walked around her prone body—"because those were your mistakes. You alone are responsible for the events that transpired. I was only trying to appease a guest who was quite angry."

In spite of the excruciating pain of her injuries, Ginny pressed on with her questions, determined to find out the answers since that fateful day had changed the course of her future. "So, the owners of the boats don't even know you're watching them to this day?"

"Depends; it's on a need-to-know basis."

"In other words, you use the tapes to blackmail them to get what you want, when you want?"

"It's a quid pro quo world. I merely take advantage of the fact." He shrugged. "I'll have to re-evaluate that night over again. Don't fear, my dear, you will be reunited with your husband once I'm assured you no longer have any information I need. Then my men will wear away the shine of you being their new toy." As he spoke, he lifted the cane high above his head.

Ginny could see the salacious desire in his face to strike her one more time before he turned her over to his men. She curled tighter into a ball by bringing her thighs up and lowering her arms to cover her belly.

"Have you finally run out of things you want to say to me?"

Holding her head at a proud angle, Ginny refused to utter the pleas of mercy that Allerton was trying to beat out of her. Then a loud sound coming from the office doorway had everyone turning their heads in that direction.

Gavin stood there like a gladiator ready to do battle.

"Ginny might not, but I sure as fuck do."

G inny took one glance at Gavin and the men who came storming into the room with raised military guns and knew reflexively what to do. She was already ducking her head to the floor when shots rang out, shattering the stunned silence of Allerton and his guards.

Peeking through the hair that had fallen over her face, she saw Gavin lunge toward Allerton, jerking the cane out of his hands and beating him with it like a madman.

One of the guards closest to her fell like a tree, his head landing near hers with blank eyes and a hole between them. Ginny didn't have to guess that he was no longer a threat.

"Find the keys to the handcuffs!"

Ginny recognized Viper's voice as she lay still. Moving her gaze away from the dead guard's face, she saw Gavin continue to beat Allerton with the cane. She could tell from his expression that he wasn't going to stop until Allerton was dead.

"Reaper, stop! That's enough!" Hammer yelled, grabbing the cane away from him.

Reaper just started kicking Allerton with his boot.

"Reaper!" Viper shouted out in the sudden silence as the sound of bullets stopped. "The FBI wants him."

"They can have what's left of him." Gavin's voice held no emotions, like the others who were yelling at him to stop, yet the blows he landed on Allerton were vicious.

"Stop him, or we'll never find out what happened on Clindale."

Recognizing Agent Collins' ragged voice had her looking over to see two of the agents supporting Agent Collins as the third helped him rise, then her view was blocked when Shade's stark face appeared before hers, as he reached out to touch her.

"Please, don't," she managed to get the words out through swollen lips.

"Reaper! Stop! We need to get the fuck out of here before reinforcements come. Jesus, just shoot the fucker if it'll make it quicker!" Cash shouted as he, Viper, and Rider tried to get him away from Allerton, while Hammer tried to drag Allerton in another direction, away from Reaper's vicious kicks.

"Good idea." Gavin's struggles stopped as he raised his hand to point a handgun at Allerton.

"Gavin …." Ginny sobbed at the pain of shouting for him. "Gavin, please, I need you."

Gavin's eyes flew in her direction. "Get him to the plane before I change my fucking mind!" he roared, moving toward her.

Hammer lifted Allerton over his shoulder in a fireman's lift, then took off running out of the room, while the three agents supported Collins out as well.

"Let me have her," Gavin demanded.

Shade moved away, and then Gavin was there, kneeling beside her. Ginny looked him over carefully, feeling a tear slide down the edge of her nose. "They didn't hurt you, did they?" she whispered through mostly closed lips, so her jaw wouldn't hurt as much.

"No, nymph. They didn't hurt me," he said gently, reaching out to move her hair away from her face.

"Reaper, we have to go!" Viper was at the desk, looking at the computer screen.

Ginny saw Gavin reach out to lift her. "Don't. I can get up." She attempted to pull herself into a sitting position, but her hand collapsed under her weight at the searing pain in her shoulders and upper back. At her mewling cry, Gavin slowly slid his arms under knees and lower back to gradually lift her into his arms.

"Shade, you go first. Cash, Rider, watch the rear," Viper ordered when Gavin had her in his arms.

Ginny let her head fall to Gavin's chest as they ran down the hallway, expecting them to go to the elevator, but they moved past it as Knox ran out from behind Allerton's assistant to run on the other side of Gavin.

Embarrassed by the pain-filled whimpers she couldn't help coming from her lips, Ginny clutched Gavin's shirt to shove it into her mouth to smother her cries. The vibrations of his movements sent shards of stinging pain through her body.

When he stopped walking, Ginny raised her head from his chest to see what he was doing. Embarrassed that Gavin saw her biting his shirt, she pulled it away from her swollen mouth to take a shuddering breath.

"This is going to hurt like a motherfucker," he warned, not showing an ounce of sympathy for her.

His pitiless regard had her wanting to burst into the tears she was trying to hold back. Would it hurt the big jerk to show a softer side to her just one time, to show that he freakin' cared about her? Soul mates could cry alongside each other, couldn't they?

Gavin could put her down, then. She could just walk. She didn't need his help.

Anger boiled up, displacing the pain she felt ... until she parted her lips to tell him to put her down. She looked in his eyes to show him how serious she was and saw all the emotions his face wasn't expressing. His eyes were mirrors to the pain and torment she was suffering.

Unable to bear his suffering, Ginny looked over his shoulder, taking another shuddering breath as she saw Cash and Rider with their guns pointed with deadly intent toward the stairwell door, waiting for someone to ambush them. When Cash turned his head to see what the holdup was, Ginny read the urgency on his face.

Returning her gaze back to Gavin's, she forced a smile to her lips, ignoring the pain the movement made. "I'm good. It barely hurts."

"Shut up."

About to chastise him for being rude, she decided it wasn't worth the pain it would cause, especially when he went down the first step. Gavin was right; it did hurt like a mother. Her body was already on fire, and as he continued down the steps, it was like adding gasoline to the flames. She was too weak to even lift her head when she heard a metal door being swung open.

As Gavin went through the door, her eyes collided with Desmond Beck's as he held the door open for Gavin.

"This way ... hurry ... I have a Moke waiting," she thought Desmond said but couldn't be sure, her thoughts becoming fuzzy when Gavin started running with her.

The blue sky, palm trees, and beach umbrellas swirled in a dizzy mesh of colors until everything coalesced and she couldn't make anything out. She tightened her grip on Gavin's shirt when he came to a stop and then she could tell from his movements that he was getting inside the Moke.

"I'm … Throw up." Feeling the bile rising in her stomach, she flared her hands out to throw herself away from Gavin.

"No, you're not. You're too tough to throw up."

She desperately gulped lungsful of air, battling the nausea down. "I … hate throwing up."

The rocking motion of the Moke when the other men jumped in made it even worse. She was going to lose it, make a mess all over Gavin and her, and he would never let her live it down.

"Then don't," Gavin told her matter-of-factly.

The welcome rush of air when the Moke began moving dulled the rising tide of nausea welling inside of her.

"I'm dying." All thoughts of being brave in front of Gavin deserted her. She was hurting more than when Allerton had beat her, unaware that she was even talking out loud.

"You're not dying. You're losing the adrenaline rush."

Was the jerk laughing at her?

Disgruntled at the thought, she managed to lift her head. "Are you laughing at me?"

"No."

Ginny laid her head back down. "You better not," she warned.

"Or else?"

"I'll throw up on you."

"You wouldn't. You hate throwing up, remember?"

"I'm becoming comfortable with the thought." She tried to smile at him, then wished she hadn't when he grimaced at her.

"How bad do I look?"

"Nymph, the same as you did the first time I saw you. You look beautiful."

"Aw … that's so sweet. I do feel better. Where are we—"

The Moke came to an abrupt stop, wrenching a startled,

high-pitched scream from her throat. Nothing had ever hurt so badly in her life.

Opening her mouth, Ginny thought she said something but didn't know what or if she'd succeeded in speaking before a thundercloud burst in her head, releasing a flood of darkness that swept her away into oblivion.

A bright light shining in her eye had Ginny trying to turn her head in the other direction.

"Stay still while I finish checking you out."

Thankfully, the light moved away from her eye and she saw Train leaning over her.

"What happened?" Had Train shoved cotton wool in her mouth to keep her from screaming again? Ginny thought dazedly.

"You fainted." Train twisted a narrow, plastic bag in his hand, then laid it gently over her lips. "That should help with the swelling."

"I've never passed out before."

"There's a first time for everything."

As he ran his hand carefully over her body, Ginny felt uncomfortable under his exploratory touch.

She lowered the ice pack from her lips. "Where's Gavin?"

"You're sitting on him," Train answered as he moved his hands down her side, traveling to her back.

"Oh …" Ginny jumped in pain when Train touched where Allerton's cane had struck her.

Gavin gently curled his arms around her waist, holding her still when she would have tried to evade Train touching her again. "Stay still." His stern voice held her in place. "He's making sure you don't have any broken bones."

"Do I?" she asked with interest.

Train's grim profile turned toward her. "Can you move your leg?"

"Do I have to? It'll hurt."

"Gavin won't let me take off until he knows you're stable enough to make the flight home."

"We're going back to Treepoint?"

"That's the plan … if Gavin ever lets me get the plane off the runway."

"Oh … okay." Ginny looked down at her leg, willing it to move.

"Are you sure you're trying?" Gavin asked skeptically, looking over her shoulder.

Bracing herself for the pain, Ginny gingerly lifted her thigh an inch before bringing it back down. "I'm good. We can go."

Train ran both hands over her thigh. When he was done, he gave Gavin a curt nod. "I wished she had stayed out longer. There's no swelling in her hands, and her feet have good blood flow. We good?"

Gavin nodded. "You can take off."

Train immediately headed toward the cockpit.

The plane seemed to be the same size as Kaden Cross's. With Gavin and her sitting in the front row, she could easily observe Train through the partial partition, sliding into the pilot seat. Ginny couldn't help but admire how competent he seemed as he pressed several buttons while putting on a headset.

"Don't forget, Train's Killyama's husband, and you're my wife."

Ginny drew her eyes away from Train at the tinge of jealousy she heard from Gavin. "I know Train is married," she muttered around the ice pack. "And no, we aren't."

"We are. How's your back?"

"Sore, but not as bad as it was."

"When we get closer to Treepoint, we'll radio ahead and have Dr. Price meet us at his office to check you out."

The plane gave a small lurch as it began moving to the top of the runway. The sound of the engine ratcheting higher had her gripping Gavin's arm, knowing she wasn't buckled in her own seat.

"I've got you. Relax," he soothed.

"Shouldn't I be in my own seat?"

"You're fine where you are."

"I am?"

"Yes."

Relaxing as the plane started moving, Ginny looked around, seeing Rider was in the co-pilot seat. Then she moved her eyes to the row of seats next to her, seeing Hammer sitting with an ice pack on his nose. The sight of her friend being hurt had Ginny removing the ice pack she was holding.

"Hammer? Did one of Allerton's men do that to you?"

"No."

"Then what—"

Ginny glared at Gavin when he raised her hand with the ice pack back to her lips.

"Apparently, my use of the brakes on the Moke was too exuberant."

Bristling at Hammer beginning to look like a racoon and the pitiful way he was gazing at her, Ginny made her outrage apparent. "Who hurt my brother?"

Gavin snorted behind her. "He's not your brother."

"He's like my brother," Ginny corrected herself.

"Like doesn't make it so."

"Does, too," she snapped back. "Look at what somebody did …" Ginny moved her accusing gaze to Viper and Cash, who were sitting behind Hammer, and she discovered they weren't looking so hot themselves. "What happened to you guys?"

Cash had a swollen cheek, and Viper, who was wearing a guard's uniform, had his shirt ripped from the collar to his shoulder in three pieces. His lips were suspiciously swollen, as if he had been given a lip enhancer.

Cash turned his head to give the man she was sitting on a heated glare. "Apparently, Reaper wasn't appreciative of us holding him back from going into Allerton's office before you could get the confession out of him."

"You heard?"

"The desk outside his office has a camera monitoring what's going on inside the office. You took a hell of a risk, Ginny."

"A risk I was willing to take. When I found out about him coming after Gavin, I hatched the idea and asked Hammer, but he refused to help me."

"Damn straight, I wasn't going to lead you back to Allerton when I worked my ass off keeping you safe all these years."

Ignoring him, Ginny continued, "That prompted me to take the DNA test. I knew once my DNA was out there, someone in the government would notice."

"Fuck, Ginny," Reaper said.

"Once the FBI contacted me, Hammer's hands were tied, so he set me up with a friend of his in the FBI we could trust."

"It's how Hammer and I managed to set the price of my cooperating with the FBI. Gavin and The Last Riders would be given immunity for any crimes committed, which also included the FBI reneging on their deal with Slate."

Hammer took over. "When I told my friend that Ginny had witnessed Allerton killing Gyi, and Manny's beating, he got on board with the plan to expose him. The FBI and

CIA had been building a case against Allerton and his charity for years and they'd made little headway. They needed concrete evidence to incriminate him. Ginny's word against his wasn't good enough. Ginny's job was to make him lose his cool, hoping he'd unwittingly make an admission or mistake giving them enough evidence to prosecute. In other words, do what Ginny does best, irritate the fuck out of him by taking him out of his comfort zone."

She pushed herself up more on Gavin's lap to situate herself a little better, then took over the story again.

"The FBI wanted one of their agents to pose as Allerton's inside guy."

Looking back at the men staring at her, she continued.

"I made one more condition, if at any time Hammer was in danger, he would be removed immediately to safety." Ginny gave a painful sigh as she pulled herself back off him to make sure she saw him as she spoke. "I wanted to leave with you, but I this was the only way I had to get my life back." Dropping her gaze from the men who were intently listening to her, she was finally able to give Gavin the full truth.

"He didn't deserve to play the world's savior. The only time I almost pulled out, Gavin, was when you refused to let me go to Sherguevil Island without you.

She ran her hand along the length of his arm that lay possessively across her to link her fingers with his, heartened when he clasped hers back.

"Why didn't you?" Gavin asked huskily.

"While I was sure that Hammer was experienced to survive almost anything thrown at him, my decision was easier to make with you going with me rather than Hammer. I'd told myself, if you could survive Slate, you could survive anything."

"Then why in the fuck did you give in to his demand that you go with the guards if you had that much faith in me?"

"Because, as much as I love you, you're not bulletproof. You weren't going to wave and make the bullets bounce off you. Because even as much as I believed you could survive anything, there was still a chance one of those guards could kill you, and it wasn't a chance I was willing to take. I wanted to tell you that Agent Collins was undercover, but they made it a stipulation and even Hammer didn't know about that part of the deal. They believed if Hammer was suspicious, it would make it more believable. The same went for Gavin. When he made no effort to conceal his distrust of Agent Collin's, I continued the charade to keep both of them safe. I thought when Allerton had proof I was telling him the truth, he would let us go or show his true colors. I never imagined he would go off the deep end before I took the polygraph test."

Unable to bear the weight of her head any longer, she laid her head down on Gavin's shoulder.

Ginny heard a series of groans coming from the back of the plane.

"He had no intention of letting you take the polygraph," Agent Collins explained as she watched him approach their seats.

Gavin braced his arm over her legs as the agent sat down in the seat next to Gavin and her.

"When I set the polygraph up the day before and asked for the questions, he put me off by saying his lawyer was still working on them and he would give me them today. When I went into his office, his men were waiting to jump me. I took the payoff from him as part of the setup with the FBI, but someone must have tipped him off that I was double-crossing him.

"He told me he has lots of people in the FBI and the CIA," Ginny said.

"I'm not surprised." The agent shook his head, his expression one of remorse. "The polygraph machine I set up the day before was rigged to make your answers appear truthful, and we'd hidden a listening device within it. It could have been the tip-off, or Allerton could have discovered it, and why he decided to take me and my men out of the picture. Gavin made the better call when he tried to get you out of there. He acted the moment he knew something didn't feel right."

She wanted to look to see who was behind them but wasn't willing to set the pain off again to satisfy her curiosity. "Are your men okay?"

The grave look on Agent Collins' face spoke of the danger the men had been in. "Thanks to Flores, whose bungalow faces this side of the resort, we had devised a signal. Every half an hour, I was to stand in front of the window at the resort for him to see me through binoculars, so when I missed the signal time, he, Garcia, and Clark were prepared. They weren't as easy to take down as I was. Flores told me they were hightailing it to the resort when they came across Gavin and The Last Riders."

"Reaper and I were arguing over all of us going to the FBI's bungalow while he went on ahead by himself." Viper took over explaining what had transpired while she was in Allerton's office. "I went with him while the others went to find the agents, but it was Reaper and I who came across them in their Moke."

"Is that why all of you look beaten up? They mistook you for more guards?" Ginny thought that explained why The Last Riders' odd uniforms were torn and why they looked as if they had gone through a war zone. If the agents mistook them for Allerton security, they were lucky to be alive.

"No. That was all Reaper."

Seeing the heated glares sent pointedly toward Gavin, she snuggled back into him protectively. Just with that slight movement, Ginny had to rapidly blink back the dark spots that heralded she was about to pass out again from the pain. Shoving the ice pack onto her forehead, she was able to gather her equilibrium.

"Stay still."

"I'm going to throw up."

"Rider, see if there are any drinks aboard," Gavin uttered, pulling her back down across his lap. He took the ice pack from her and pressed it more firmly against her forehead.

"I will. I know where they are."

Ginny couldn't place the voice and, at that point, she didn't care, her concentration on keeping her stomach from heaving.

"See if there are any crackers." Shaking out a barf bag that Agent Collins gave him, Gavin placed it under her chin.

"I hate being sick to my stomach," Ginny complained.

"So you've told me."

Taking the bag from him, she debated whacking him with it, she was so miserable.

With his hand free, Gavin began gently rubbing her belly. "I find it amusing that you took Allerton beating the hell out of you without making a sound, yet you're complaining about a sick stomach as if it's the end of the world."

"No woman wants to barf in front of others."

"Believe me; if you do, most of them won't be watching. They'll be joining in. They're a bunch of pansies where puking is concerned."

The thought of making The Last Riders reach for barf bags had her almost laughing. "You're not helping," Ginny berated him through swollen lips that couldn't really smile.

"Perhaps these will."

A Sprite and a package of crackers appeared in front of her. Ginny didn't take the offering after seeing who was holding the items.

"Mr. Beck." She'd seen him holding the door open for them when they left the resort, and while she wasn't afraid of him, she wasn't thrilled to see one of Allerton's close friends either.

Gavin reached out to take the soda and crackers.

Squatting down next to the seat, Desmond made a wry face at her. "I can understand your hesitation. I'm not proud of myself that I was a business associate of a man capable of doing this to you. I do want to make one thing clear, however. I was not involved in the death of your friends or the villagers who lived on Clindale."

"Desmond's the one who gave us the information so we could get onto Clindale. He knew whose palms we had to grease for them to look the other way," Viper offered the information from his seat. "He also helped get us into the resort."

"I wondered how you all managed to get there." Ginny took the opened can of Sprite away from Gavin to take a sip. "How much money are you talking about?"

"That's not important." Opening the crackers, Gavin tried to give her one.

Ginny stared Desmond down to get the answer she asked for.

"Nothing compared to how much it took to pay off Gabriel's assistant; he'd agreed to fake Gabriel's authorization for the plane to take off ... with him on it."

"Allerton is here?" Ginny tensed on Gavin's lap.

"He's handcuffed at the back of the plane," Desmond confirmed, then tried to ease her trepidation. "Jackal and another man—I believe his name is Jonas—are watching him quite diligently. Although, I doubt he has the ability to move in the shape he's in."

Ginny couldn't help the spurt of pity she felt knowing how much pain she was in.

Desmond's keen gaze didn't miss the flashing emotion in her expression. "You feel sorry for Gabriel after what he did to you?"

"That cane hurts," she said simply.

"I feel certain Gabriel was aware of that fact. If not, he definitely knows now." Desmond rose to his feet, intending to go back to his seat.

"Wait—do you know how much money they had to spend?" Ginny asked him before he could move away.

Desmond gave her an appreciative smile. "However much, it was money well spent, don't you agree?"

"I do," Ginny hastened to agree, not wanting any of The Last Riders to think she didn't appreciate their help. "But it doesn't help me figure out how much money I owe them."

"Jesus ...," Viper gave a loud, self-recriminating groan. "You don't owe us any money."

"But I—"

"Ginny, eat the cracker." Gavin removed the Sprite from her hand to give her the cracker. "You can pay Viper back in installments."

Satisfied that Viper would listen to his brother, Ginny took the cracker. "Thank-you for your help, Mr. Beck."

"Anytime." Desmond reached into his suit jacket, then handed her a card. No sooner had Ginny taken the card, it was snatched out of her hand to be replaced with the cracker.

"That was rude." Taking a small nibble of the cracker, she thought her stomach would revolt, but then it settled down enough for her to take another small bite. Her mouth hurt like heck, but the cracker was easing the nausea, so Ginny considered it a trade-off.

Ginny thoughtfully stared down at the cracker in her hand. "Gavin?"

"I haven't gone anywhere."

Ginny ignored his attempt at humor. "Where did they take you after the guards took you away? Allerton said, when his men were done with me, that I would be reunited with you and my father. Did you see him? Was he being held against his will? Was my mother there? Did they want to leave with you?"

The way she was sitting, Ginny wasn't given a good view of Gavin's face, yet she was able to feel his body tense under her.

"Allerton said that he was going to reunite you with me and your father after his men were done with you?"

Blocking the pain out as much as she could, Ginny used her bottom muscles, which were the only ones not hurting, to slightly turn so she could get a better look at him. The strange tenor in his voice was magnified on his face.

"That's what he said."

"Do you think, if I stood and sat you back down on your own, the pain would be too bad?" he asked solicitously.

"You need to go to the restroom?" she inquired innocently.

"No. There's a motherfucker I need to finish off."

CHAPTER TWENTY-NINE

"Don't let him." Agent Collins appeared as if he was the one who was about to vomit at Gavin's threat.

Passing him the barf bag, Ginny dropped the cracker so she had a free hand to press Gavin back down into the seat. "You'll be doing him a favor. What matters most to Allerton is his reputation. If we are able to destroy that, it will hurt more than anything you can do him."

Gavin looked back at her blandly, not swayed by her argument. "You have no idea how painful I can make his death."

"As painful as having him confess to what he did to the islanders? Or watching his bank balance dip to the negative when all the lawsuits come his way from misrepresenting his charity? Or watching everyone turn their backs on him when they discover how evil he is?"

"I can't do all that, but I can come close."

"Coming close doesn't count. I want him to pay publicly for what he has done. I don't want one person on Earth to be able to defend his actions."

"That's a tall order. Allerton has enough money to spin his defense any way he wants."

"How can he spin it when I have him on tape bragging about what he's done?"

"You have it on tape?"

Ginny gave him a cat-who-ate-the-canary grin. "Agent Collin's does." Looking at the man sitting next to Gavin, she had Agent Collins confirm what she was saying. "You said that you would tape any conversations between you and Allerton."

Agent Collins uncomfortably shared a glance with her, then Gavin, as if dreading what he was about to tell her. "The polygraph machine wasn't on, which had one listening device attached when it was in use. His men took the other one I had attached to my badge," he admitted, switching his gaze back to her, as if afraid she was going to freak out at him.

"We have the video from behind the lobby desk," Gavin asserted, "which had no sound. And now we know that the recorder on the polygraph and the one you had weren't working, the only indictment you're going to be able to charge him with is assault, with no audio to back you up." Gavin started to rise again, but Ginny grabbed the arm rest to prevent him.

"That's okay," Ginny assured him. "Mine was on."

"You had a tape recorder?" Gavin quizzed her.

Both men gave her an astounded look.

"I do." Ginny started to raise her arm. "My bracelet ..." As the words came out of her mouth, she remembered Allerton jerking it off her wrist. "We have to go back! Train!" Ginny screeched, about to tear herself out of Gavin's arms, regardless of the amount of pain she caused herself.

Gavin tightened his arms around her waist. "Hell will freeze over before we go back there!"

"I have to get my bracelet …." Her mouth dropped open when she saw what was dangling from Gavin's fingers. Snatching it from him, she inspected the damage. Finding what she was looking for, she gave him a bright smile. "Have I told you today how much I love you?"

"A couple of times."

"Right. Just making sure." Content, she took another sip of her Sprite. "Are there any crackers left?"

"No, you ate both packs."

"Do you think there are any more where Mr. Beck got them from? I'm hungry."

If Gavin and Agent Collins were looking at her like she had a screw loose, Ginny was glad her back was turned away from the rest of the men on the plane.

"I'm on it," Ginny heard Mr. Beck call out.

"Thank-you," she called back, feeling a hand on the back of her head. "What are you doing?"

"Checking you for a concussion. Did Allerton hit you on the head with that cane? You might need to get a CT scan when we get to Treepoint."

"I don't need a CT scan. You're being ridiculous."

"One second you're screaming to go back to Sherguevil Island and the next, you're wanting crackers. You don't think that sounds strange?" Gavin tried to search for bumps on her head again.

"That was before you showed me you had my bracelet. We don't have to go back now."

"Here you go." Desmond Beck moved in front of their seat to give her a handful of pre-packaged crackers.

Ginny smiled her appreciation as she fumbled with the soda can to open a pack of crackers. She almost jumped out of her seat when she felt a stinging sensation on the back of her head.

"Did you just pull my hair?"

"Of course not. My ring must have accidently been caught in it." Gavin gave her an innocent expression that she didn't believe for a second.

"That hurt."

"Did it? I'm sorry."

Ginny let Gavin take the crackers away, giving him a disbelieving glance as she did so.

"Thank-you, Mr. Beck."

"No problem. Glad to help."

Ginny returned Mr. Beck's smile as he started back down the aisle, only to feel the tug on her hair again.

"You did that deliberately," she hissed irritably at Gavin.

"It was an accident." Gavin dropped the crackers on her lap, leaving one in his hand to open for her as he took the can of soda.

"Accident, my ass," she said witheringly, opening the pack of crackers and starting to munch on one to keep from bickering with him where everyone on the plane could hear.

"You were going to tell us why you changed your mind about going back to Sherguevil Island. I assume it has something to do with you getting Allerton's confession?"

"Oh …" Ginny frowned at him, swallowing the last of her cracker. "I forgot what we were talking about when you so rudely pulled my hair."

"Really? I thought you lost that train of the conversation when you were simpering over"—Gavin's voice went sickly sweet—"*Mr. Beck.*"

She narrowed her eyes on him. "So, you admit it wasn't an accident?"

"Ginny …," he said warningly.

"Okay, okay. We don't have to go back because you have my bracelet." She moved her eyes to her lap to where it laid among the crackers and picked it up. Using her fingers, she showed him the flower charm. "It's a tape recorder. Isn't it neat? I bought it online. I recorded every conversation with him including today in his office."

"Why didn't you tell me you had it on you?"

Ginny thought he would be happy instead, but he seemed offended.

Hammer lifted the corner of his ice pack. "Why didn't you tell me either?"

Ginny gave a long, drawn-out sigh. Men could be such dudes sometimes.

"I didn't tell either of you for the same reason I didn't tell Gavin about the tape recorder or how Agent Collins and I were trying to gather proof to convict Allerton—to protect you all."

The relief on Agent Collins' face was profound. Ginny started to smile at him, then decided she didn't want to go bald.

"I'll take that." Agent Collins reached out to take it from her.

Ginny clutched it in her fist before he could. "You can have it after Gavin makes a copy of it for me."

"We can't break the chain of custody."

"We can go to the sheriff's office. Knox can make enough copies to make everyone happy," Gavin suggested.

"I'm okay with that," Ginny acceded.

Agent Collins looked at if his feelings were hurt. "You don't trust me?"

"I trust *you*. I just don't trust that it won't disappear before Allerton goes to court. It shouldn't take long, should it, Gavin?"

"No. Knox will have them on their way before they can finish a cup of coffee."

Ginny looked at him to see the disappointed expression on Gavin's face. "What's wrong?"

"I was looking forward to dropping the fucker off in the middle of the ocean."

"My way is much better, you'll see," she consoled him.

"Let's see if you'll still say that when I tell you what he meant about being reunited with your father and me."

"So tell me."

"I can't."

"Why not?"

"You're still eating."

She lost her appetite at his grim reply. "Never mind, I don't want to know." Ginny stared down at the cracker in her hand as Gavin started to massage the back of her neck. "My father is dead, isn't he?"

"I'm sorry."

"How long?"

"I have no idea."

"Then how can you be sure?"

"That's the part you don't want to know."

Ginny looked toward Agent Collins. "Is he?"

"We've had our suspicions that Jasper was no longer living."

"Then why didn't you or one of the other agents I talked to tell me?"

"We couldn't say without a doubt that he was dead. We were hoping to corroborate that while we were on the island. Anytime I mentioned Jasper's name to Mr. Allerton or Soleil, they would give me the run around about his location."

"Soleil knew then." Ginny picked up the crackers to dump them in the barf bag. The pain in her arm was nothing in comparison to the pain at finding out Jasper was dead. There had been a tiny part of her that yearned for some type of relationship with her parents. When she met Soleil, though, she had known immediately that that wasn't going to happen. Now it seemed it was no longer possible with Jasper either.

Agent Collins looked away from her sympathetically. "I believe she does, yes."

Picking up the bracelet, she gave it back to Gavin. "You can keep it until you make a copy of the tape."

Gavin pocketed it for safekeeping.

"I'm tired, Gavin."

"Then go to sleep. I'll wake you when we're about to land."

Ginny gingerly laid her head on his shoulder as Gavin continued to massage her neck, easing some of the strain. She couldn't understand why she didn't feel more euphoric. With the tape recording on her bracelet, and the tape from the lobby showing what had taken place in the office, everything Allerton had worked to distinguish himself as—a defender of humanity—would be demolished.

Lifting drowsy lids, Ginny saw Agent Collins adjust himself uncomfortably in his seat.

"I'm too old for this shit," he grumbled, adjusting his tie. "When I get to the office, I'm retiring."

She instantly woke up. "You can't!"

Realizing she heard him, Agent Collins turned in her direction. "My retirement was in the works when I was asked to take this case. My body has had it. Not only that, but I failed to protect you and the men under my command. I'm more than ready to step down. I don't have the heart for it anymore. Do you think, if I had the opportunity, I wouldn't have done the same thing with that cane as Gavin did?"

"You wouldn't have," Ginny disputed with surety.

"Probably not," he said wearily. "I would have shot him."

Ginny didn't argue with him. She could kind of see him doing that.

"See the case through, and if you still feel the same way,

then retire. Hammer told me you were chosen for this case because you have integrity. Allerton will be counting on his money and prestige to buy himself out of reaping the justice he deserves. You have to be the firewall that prevents it from happening. If not you, then who else do you think will be able to say no to the money he can throw at them? I didn't risk my life and Gavin's just to see him walk away. Please … wait." Ginny gave him an encouraging grin. "I'll even spring for your retirement party if you do. I have a friend of mine I'll introduce you to. You two would be perfect together," she coaxed.

"I'm too old. I've missed my chance. No woman would want an old fart like me."

"Aw … that's not true," she insisted. "You're not old. I would date you"—Ginny ignored Gavin going rigid under her—"if I didn't love Gavin so much." Giving the agent a sweet smile to show she meant it, she felt another hair parting from her scalp.

"Stop that! It hurts," she hissed up at Gavin.

"Purely an accident. Besides, there is no way that hurt you."

"How do you know? You're not the one who's getting his hair plucked out one hair at a time. Pure my butt, it does hurt …," she add plaintively. "I'm tender-headed."

"No, you're not." Dissing her with a hiss of air, Ginny saw red.

"How would you know? It's not your head that's getting snatched bald—"

Gavin leaned his head forward so he could look her dead in the eyes with an expression she recognized instantly. It was the one that said he could tear her apart in seconds when they were having sex, when he would roughly grab her hair to tilt her head back and she would melt into the flames of his ….

Ginny cleared her throat. "Never mind." She snapped her mouth shut as she caught Agent Collins' amused gaze.

"You don't want to finish what you were saying?" Gavin prompted.

There was no way she was going to let him one-up her. She had her dignity to uphold.

Leaning her head back on Gavin's shoulder as if she was going back to sleep, she painfully raised an arm over the top of her hair.

"Mr. Beck ... would you mind bringing me another soda?"

CHAPTER THIRTY

Smothering a yawn, Ginny sat in Viper's SUV as she waited with Gavin for Viper to come out of the sheriff's office. As soon as they'd landed, Knox had been waiting for them at the airport to transport Allerton to his holding cell. Viper and the federal agents followed Knox straight to the sheriff's office to have copies of the recorder made. The others on board had taken off in Shade's and Cash's vehicles.

"I still say we should stop by Dr. Price's office and have him check you out."

"No, I just want to go home." Ginny put an end to that suggestion. "I'm sore. I'll be fine in a couple of days."

"Don't you think we have something to discuss?"

"Like what?"

"About where we're going to be staying."

Her heart plunged. She had assumed he would be staying with her at Silas's house. Was this it? The great send-off? Was Taylor still at the club? Was that why he wanted to get rid of her?

"Ginny ... are you listening to me?"

She quit fiddling with her bracelet that Gavin had hooked

back around her wrist after he removed the flower tape recorder.

"I'm listening. I ... assumed that you would be staying with me at Silas's. Are you not wanting to? Are you still angry because I smiled at Mr. Beck? I'm sorry. I was teasing you for being jealous."

"I was not jealous." Interrupting her flurry of questions, Gavin waved back at Greer as he came out of the sheriff's office.

"You were—" Ginny broke off when there was a tapping on the window, she pressed the electronic button to roll the window down.

"What's up?" Greer said.

"Not much. Waiting for Viper so he can drive me home," Ginny told him.

"Viper said that fucker whining in the jail cell beat the hell out of you. You okay?"

"Yes, other than being sore. I'll be fine in a couple of days."

"Then you're doing better than the twat waffle in the cell. He's crying for a doctor."

Greer's gaze went to Gavin. "Boy, I'm disappointed in you. If that fucker had taken a cane to my wife, I'd have blown his hand clean off."

Ginny didn't doubt he would have. Greer was blood-thirsty as hell when came to defending women. Truth to tell, all the Porter men were. The other men in town would cross the road rather than take a chance on getting on their bad side.

"He's not my husband," Ginny quickly corrected his misunderstanding.

"I would have, but Ginny stopped me."

Her hackles came back at Gavin agreeing with Greer's violent dismemberment of Allerton.

"Take a piece of my advice. When it comes to shootin' someone, what the wife don't know don't hurt her none."

Ginny moved her finger back to electronic button. The last thing Gavin needed was to take any of Greer's marital advice.

"Hey!" Greer shouted.

Ginny reluctantly took her finger of the button.

"You damn near cut my arm off."

"Sorry." She really wasn't sorry, and from Greer's keen gaze, he was aware of the fact.

"It's a sorry day when you save that fucker's arm who beat the fuck out of you, while you try to cut mine off with a window."

"I didn't mean to."

"Like I believe that crock. And here I only came over to give you my congratulations on getting hitched."

"Thank-you. I appreciate your well wishes."

Ginny raised her voice to be heard over Gavin's. "Gavin and I aren't hitched!"

Greer stared at Gavin pityingly. "Boy, you gotta show her who's boss. She running over your ass now, it won't be long before she's taking over your checking account. Won't let you drink a beer in front of the youngins—"

Greer poked his head up over the roof of the car as another car pulled in next to Viper's.

Ginny saw Greer's wife getting out the car as she said something to her sister-in-law, who was behind the steering wheel. From the open window, Ginny could hear the squabble of childish voices coming from the back seat before Holly closed the door to walk around Viper's car.

"Hey, Ginny," Holly greeted her.

"Hey, Holly," Ginny responded. "Sounds like you and Sutton have your hands full with the kids."

"They're tired of being cooped up, and so are we. Sutton

and I are getting them some takeout and letting them go hiking toward Big Eddy's Creek."

"Sounds like fun."

Holly laughed. "We're hoping they'll come back and crash for the rest of evening. Sutton and I need a girls' night."

Greer snorted rudely. "How about a hubby night? You promised me for the last week that you would switch out with Sutton and Jessie. What's a man gotta do to get some lovin'?"

Holly wiggled the back of her finger to Greer, indicting she wanted to talk to him privately.

Mulishly, Greer stomped over to her. "What?"

"I need forty dollars for the takeout."

"Where you eatin'? Kings?" Greer sulkily took out his wallet. "There's a twenty; take 'em to 7-Eleven. Their Big Gulps are on sale. Buy two for them heathens to share. It'll cost you a couple of dollars. Take what's left and go to White Castle; you can get a ton of those little burgers to feed all of you. Forget the fries; they're too expensive." Greer started to put his wallet back in his pants.

Holly determinedly remained standing in front of him with her hand out. "I like fries, and so do your children, Sutton, and your nephews."

"Woman, you're killin' me!" Greer opened his wallet, giving her the money she requested.

Holly still didn't move her hand away. "You can also hand over the check you stole from the back of our checkbook this morning."

"Woman, I told you I'ma buyin' that new rifle that just came back in stock at Beacon's."

"And I told you *no*."

"It's my money!" Greer caterwauled.

"*Our* money. And if you want it that badly, you can ask Santa to bring it to you for Christmas. Give it back."

"Too late. I already bought it."

"No, you didn't. I called and checked before I left the house."

Greer puffed his chest out like a rooster. "You better not have told Dan why you called! A man's got pride—"

Holly said something to Greer that she couldn't hear, so Ginny leaned her head out the window, straining to hear. Whatever she said, it had Greer opening his wallet to give the check back and the extra twenty.

"See? That wasn't so hard, was it?" Holly said in a normal voice before giving Greer a peck on the check.

"Bye, Ginny!" Holly waved at her as she went back to Sutton's car.

"Bye!" Ginny called back, watching as Greer swaggered back to lean against the car.

"I didn't want that gun anyway." Trying to salvage his ego, he tried to explain why he hadn't taken his own marital advice but failed to regain his rooster status. "Dan's got another sweet one coming in next month."

Unable to prevent herself from smiling, she immediately brought her hand to her lips at the pain. The movement intensified the discomfort she was downplaying.

Greer reached through the open window to rest his hand on her shoulder as he directed his gaze on Gavin. "Friday still good for you? I could use a night out from the ball and chain."

"Yes, I'm right there with you," Gavin commiserated.

"What do you mean by that?" Ginny snapped.

"No need to get on your high horse." Greer laid his hand more firmly on her shoulder, as if afraid she needed to be held back from attacking Gavin. "Ain't gonna be no hoochie mamas there." Dipping his head farther into the window, Greer asked wistfully, "Are there?"

"No, just Silas."

"Uh ... Greer? You really shouldn't be so close." Ginny began to feel uncomfortable with Greer standing so close to her. The heat coming from his hand on her shoulder was creating tingling through her body.

"Why? The whole town has been vaccinated."

Ginny looked at him questioningly. "The whole town? When I left PharmFYOU, they were trying to get the vaccine approved for the study."

"They got approval. Arin sent enough doses for the whole town. I reckon it didn't hurt none that Jewell and Arin are like sisters, and her man is a Last Rider."

"Still, the study would have to have a certain number of placebos for the study to be accurate."

"Do they?" Greer wiggled his eyebrows at her. "Reckon she'll have to throw out the town's results. Nice to have people in high places, ain't it?"

"*The whole town?*" she repeated.

Ginny found it surprising the town's mayor and the health professionals in Treepoint were able to convince the whole town's population to take it. Many had the wait-and-see mentality that had been bred into them from waiting to see how something tasted until some sucker tried it first, or seeing if a neighbor could pull them out of a ditch before they put their snow chains on.

"You can thank me for that. Since Knox left me in charge while he was out of town, I spread the news around that if any of my *deputies* wrote them a ticket, they could bring the ticket to me, and if they showed me their vaccination cards, I would tear up the ticket."

"Is that legal?"

"Of course, I was the sheriff. I could do anything I wanted."

"But ... how in the world was everyone else convinced to take it?" Ginny was stunned. She would have bet that a large section of the town's population wouldn't be convinced to take the vaccine. How many tickets had been written?

Greer removed his hand and straightened from the car to pull his pants up. "That was all my doing, too," he bragged.

Ginny narrowed her gaze on Greer. "What else did you do?"

Greer squinted down at her, unfazed. "It might have gotten around town that everyone who took the vaccine would be given a free ticket to the concert you're going to have when the state lets us start having them again."

"The whole town took the vaccine just to come hear me sing?" Misty tears came to her eyes. For the townspeople to be willing to take the vaccine showed how happy they were that she had found a measure of success. However, she was only to experience the joy for a second before Greer brought her back to earth.

Frowning at her as if she misheard him, he clarified what he meant. "I wouldn't go that far. Some people in town ... you know how they be needin' some more convincing."

Ginny furrowed her brow. "How'd you do that?"

"When I was having lunch, I might have told a few of the men that I was in the trials and my dick grew three inches."

"You didn't?" Ginny gasped.

"Why not? It's not like I had to show them a before and after picture."

"That's false advertising." *Besides, what knuckleheads would believe that?*

Greer shrugged. "How's it false advertising? PharmFYOU wasn't saying it; I was."

Resting her elbow on the door ledge, Ginny started rubbing her forehead. He was giving her a headache trying to keep up with his train of thought.

"The men in town believed you?"

"Sure did." Greer snickered. "You should have seen the line outside the health department."

"Okay. I can see men being stupid enough to believe that nonsense." She couldn't, but men's psyches had never been her strong point. "But you said the whole town: How'd you convince the women?"

Greer blew out a sarcastic raspberry. "They were the ones making sure their men stayed in those long lines."

"Still …" She couldn't believe those were the two reasons that got the town inoculated.

Seeing her doubts, Greer looked over both his shoulders to make sure no one was listening then said, "I might—I ain't saying I did or didn't—but I might have threw in a couple of greens of Tate's Tennessee Gold."

That Ginny believed. "Isn't that illegal for a *sheriff* to do?"

Greer didn't argue that point. "Who's gonna tell? Tate's weed is harder to get than the vaccine. We only have a small supply. The wives don't want us growing it no more. A man has to have their hobbies, you know?" He squinted at her like she should be agreeing with him.

"I can see their point. It's hard to raise children when their father is in prison."

"We'd have to be caught first."

Dismissing her concern, Greer gave a nod to Viper as he walked toward the SUV. "Is that whiny baby still crying for a doctor?"

"Yes. Where's Dr. Price at? I thought you were supposed to give him a ride from the Fieldman's when he couldn't get his car started?"

"On my way." Greer didn't rush away at getting caught lingering with them instead of doing the job that Knox had sent him on.

"We headed for the club?" Viper asked once he was seated in the back seat.

"Gavin is taking me to Silas's home. I'm staying there."

"We're staying at the club," Gavin contradicted her as if it were a done deal. "My wife is staying with me."

Embarrassed at Gavin making the claim in front of Greer and Viper had her voice raising. "We're not married!"

Gavin shifted in his seat to give her a steely look. "Viper, are Ginny and I married?"

"Yes."

Gavin gave her a smart aleck bob of his head as if to say "I told you so" at Viper's answer.

"We. Are. Not. Married!"

Gavin just arched his brows, refusing to argue with her.

"We aren't!"

"Ah … Reaper, you want a piece of advice from me?" Greer poked his head back through the window.

"No! We don't!" Pressing the button to roll the window up, Greer barely managed to get his head out before being decapitated. Unfortunately, it wasn't enough to keep him from yelling his advice out.

"Damn, boy, if my wife said she weren't married to me, I know what I would do."

Ginny shot Gavin a killing look when he pressed the electronic button on his door to roll her window back down.

"What would you do?" Gavin asked with interest.

"Run."

CHAPTER THIRTY-ONE

"Will you two quit laughing?" Ginny said stiffly, which made them laugh even harder. "I don't know what you two find so amusing."

"Yeah, you wouldn't."

Ginny turned in her seat to see Viper practically curling in laughter in the back seat he was laughing so hard.

"I bet Winter wouldn't find it amusing either," Ginny warned him.

Viper howled louder, agreeing with her. "She wouldn't."

Ginny loftily stared out the window as they pulled out of the sheriff's office rather than strangle the two buffoons.

"Hardy har har. Holly is a saint to be married to that man." Ginny thought back to the way Greer had looked when they left. "Did either of you notice Greer wasn't looking so hot?" When he stepped away from the car, Greer had seemed ready to drop. Feeling bad for the unkind thoughts about the He-Man attitude that generally came out of Greer's mouth, Ginny regretted not asking if he was feeling okay. "Should I call him and check on him?"

"Use my phone." Gavin motioned toward the charging

station on the console. "In my contacts is Dr. Price; ask him to check Greer out before worrying about Allerton."

Ginny looked askance at him before taking the phone. "You want me to use your phone?"

Gavin took his eyes away from the road to give her a frown at the question. "Yes. Why? You afraid of my germs?"

"No. I just thought men hated women using their phones?"

"There's nothing on there that you can't see."

"Viper, do you let Winter see your phone?" Ginny looked at Viper in the rearview mirror, interested in another man's take on their conversation.

"Fuck no. Not anymore."

Ginny decided to ask Winter about Viper's reaction the next time she saw her. She would have asked Viper, but she didn't want to come across as nosy in front of both men.

Disconnecting the cell phone from the charging cable, Ginny felt an inexplicable rush of pleasure at doing something some couples refused to share. She knew it was silly, but it felt as if Gavin was sharing another part of his life with her.

Making the call, she felt better once she had spoken to Dr. Price.

Disconnecting the call when she finished, she put it back on the charging station.

As they were driving past Mick's bar, Ginny was tempted to ask him to pull over for a burger, then decided against it. Her mouth was still too sore, and she realized she hadn't put the ice pack back on her lips and jaw, moving her finger up to explore her face.

Confused at the absence of pain, she lowered the sun visor to look in the mirror. She was still staring at her face in bewilderment when the SUV stopped.

Flipping the visor up, she saw they were at The Last Riders' clubhouse and factory.

"You dropping Viper off before taking me home?" Holding her anger back until her suspicion was confirmed, Ginny gave him the opportunity to answer before she reached for his phone to call Silas to come get her.

"Viper, you go ahead. Ginny and I will be up in a few."

Waiting until Viper closed the door behind him after getting out, Gavin turned the motor off, studying her face as he unbuckled his seat belt before turning in his seat to face her. "You're looking better." Reaching out, he brushed a fingertip across her bottom lip. "Ginny, for now, it makes more sense to stay here."

She didn't let his softness sway her. "How does it make more sense?"

"Allerton may be in the FBI's custody, but he has enough money to take you out in the blink of an eye. No one will be able to get near you at the clubhouse. We both know you won't stay in Silas's house. You'll be running all over the property, putting not only yourself at risk, but your brothers."

"No one comes on our property without the dogs or one of my brothers knowing."

"Silas's house has a road right in front of it with another property that someone could get access to without your knowledge. A sharpshooter could take you out while Silas is out of the house, or they could take him out also."

Ginny swallowed hard at the thought of one of her brothers being caught in the crossfire. She started fiddling with the ice pack on her lap, unable to come up with another reason not to stay at the club.

"Ginny, am I taking it too much for granted? Do you not want to live with me?"

"I do."

"You just want it on your terms, then."

"That's not true. I want us both to be happy." Ginny licked her dry lips, still shocked at how much of the swelling had gone down. "I thought you liked living at Silas's house and working with my brothers."

"I do, and I will be again when we build our home where you want to. I'm too old to be waiting for Silas to go to bed for you to sneak down to my room, and yours is too small. And take into account whether you would be comfortable having sex with your brother in the house. Would you?"

"No," she admitted.

"Why don't you want to stay at the clubhouse?"

Her stomach did a flip at the gentle way he spoke to her.

"I know why Willa and Viper made it a rule for me not to go upstairs when I worked at the club and why I had to be out of the clubhouse by five on Fridays."

"Killyama told you?"

"Gavin, if you get Killyama in trouble, I'll never forgive you. She's like a sister to me."

"Ginny, it wouldn't take a rocket scientist to figure out what goes on upstairs. It's a motorcycle club, hell, not an apartment building."

"I would die if I were to see one of the men naked." She hastily qualified, "I wouldn't be thrilled to see any of the women naked either."

"I'll make sure that they'll behave themselves as long as we live here," he promised.

"Won't that make them mad at you?"

"They can deal. It'll only be temporary."

"How long are we talking about?"

Gavin shrugged. "However long it takes us to build our house. With your brothers and The Last Riders working on it, shouldn't take longer than three or fourth months. If the weather stays good and it doesn't rain much, two or three."

"Is Taylor still here?"

"I don't know. I haven't asked. If she is, I'll tell her to leave."

"You don't have to."

"Why not?"

"I don't want to be with you if your mind is still on her."

"Taylor is the last thing on my mind. I'm more concerned about making you happy right now."

"You are?"

"I am."

Her heat melted. It was the nicest thing he had ever said to her.

She lifted her hand from her lap, about to unbuckle her seat belt. "It's going to be embarrassing for me to tell Silas I'm going to be staying with you at the clubhouse."

Gavin looked as if she struck him. "You're embarrassed to tell him you're going to be living with me?"

From his expression, Gavin had taken what she had said the wrong way.

"My brothers might not act like Greer, but they're just as old-fashioned. Freddy would turn over in his grave if he knew I was thinking about living with you."

"Are we talking about the same man who fathered half the town with how many women?"

"But that's beside the point. I'm his daughter; a different rule applies to me. Besides that, he was searching for his soul mate. I found mine; he never did. Freddy would consider it a sin if I lived with you."

Gavin's expression went from hurt to incredulous. "Are you serious?"

Hurt that he didn't see the difference, Ginny bit her lip and stared back down at her lap. "Yes. I know it's old-fashioned. My brothers will think the same way."

"Would they? Or are we discussing your feelings?" His

voice had turned gentle again, making it hard for her to concentrate when her stomach started flipping again.

"My brothers, of course." Lying to herself as well as Gavin, she raised her eyes to see him staring at her as if he didn't believe her before his expression went impassive, hiding his own thoughts from her.

"Then they'll be ecstatic after I inform them of our marriage. All you have to say when they ask why we're not living with them is that it's a wife's place to live with her husband."

"This is the last time I'm telling you we are not married." Ginny folded her arms over her chest stubbornly, turning to face forward. "I don't care how you managed to fake a marriage license or a certificate, we are not married."

"Legally, we are."

"By you attained the certificate *illegally.*"

"How we got there may be illegal, but that doesn't mean it isn't legal."

Ginny rubbed her forehead. "Gavin, I'm not asking you to marry me, or even become engaged, before you're ready. Hiding behind an illegal doc—"

"We're married, and that's what I'm telling you. If I were hiding from having a commitment to you, then I would be denying we are married. We're married, and that's that."

Ginny gaped at his reasoning and his attitude. "I don't know what century you're living in, but you need to come back to the one I'm living in."

"We're living in the same century," Gavin said unabashedly. "You ready to go in? I'm starved."

Her mouth dropped opened farther when he just got out the car, then came across the front to open the door for her.

"I'm not go—"

Before she could stop him, Gavin unbuckled her seat belt and lifted her out the car, using his hip to slam the door shut.

Ginny started to struggle to get away from him.

"Careful, you'll hurt yourself," Gavin warned her.

Waiting for the rush of pain to hit her, Ginny realized she felt almost normal, other than being a little sore. What happened to the pain?

Ginny stopped struggling against Gavin, letting him carry her up the long flight of steps, afraid her anger at his idiotic reasoning had her overexerting herself and the pain would come back when her anger dimmed.

Reaching the top of the steps, Nickel moved to open the door for them. "Glad to see you back, brother. You, too, Ginny." He grinned, turning the door handle.

Ginny returned his smile. "Thank-you, Nickel. It's go—"

Ginny wasn't given the opportunity to finish what she was saying as Gavin rudely carried her through the door, then used his foot to slam the door on Nickel's face. At least she managed to give Nickel an apologetic moue of her lips over Gavin's shoulder at his ill-mannered behavior before the door was shut.

Turning her head face forward, intending to give him a lecture that he would never forget, she was struck speechless at seeing a naked backside going up and down on a woman underneath him on the stairwell.

Before squishing her eyes closed, Ginny noticed the clothes that were scattered around the steps and a shirt hanging from the handrail before it clicked in her mind what she was witnessing.

Swinging her head back around, Ginny buried her face in Gavin's shirt. Then she cringed in embarrassment when Gavin started moving and she could tell he was climbing the steps.

"Move your ass, Moon," Gavin grunted as he shifted her into a more comfortable position in his arms.

Ginny plastered her face tighter against Gavin at the

sounds of scrambled movements before they thankfully started moving again.

She wanted to wail at Gavin for giving her a name to the naked ass she had seen. Now it would be engraved in her memory what his ass looked like every time she saw him. Ginny didn't lift her face until she heard the sound of a door being closed. Opening her eyes, she was prepared for the first words to come out for him to take her Silas's house.

"Well"—Gavin shrugged as he gently set her down on her feet—"I proved you wrong about one thing you said."

Frowning, she forgot what she was going to say. "About what?"

"You didn't die."

CHAPTER THIRTY-TWO

"Please tell me I didn't see Moon's ass," Ginny begged.

Reaper turned to lock the door, fighting the overpowering urge to break into laughter. Ginny looked as if she'd been hit by a lightning bolt. The thunderstruck expression on her face after witnessing Moon and Jade fucking on the steps was hilarious, but that it happened right after he promised her he would make the brothers behave doomed the likelihood of him being able to convince her to stay—especially if he gave into his mirth the way he was dying to.

Making sure the door was securely locked so he'd have a fighting chance of catching her if she tried to escape, he told her, "Okay, then I won't."

He moved next to her and began slowly raising her top so he could see the damage Allerton had inflicted on her.

"Gavin, I'm not in the mood to have sex right now."

He stopped, her top rolled under her breasts, and gaped down at her. "You're kidding, right?"

The last thing on his mind was sex. She was a hot mess, with her hair disheveled, hanging loosely around a face covered in bruises, highlighted by lips that were puffy and split. Ginny looked like the feminine version of Edward Scissorhands.

Perplexed at what he was doing, she frowned at him. "Then why are you taking my top off?"

"I want to make sure we don't need to take you to the doctor."

"I look that bad?"

"Let's see how much damage we're dealing with."

"I don't feel as sore." Ginny experimentally raised her arms in the air, acquiescing for him to continue removing her clothes.

Making sure he kept his body blocking the mirror above the dresser, Reaper slowly rolled her shirt over her breasts, then helped her slip each arm out. Casting the top aside, Reaper had a full view of the bruises marring her body.

"Can you turn around? I want to see your back."

Gradually turning, Ginny exposed her back and shoulders. Bruises covered her skin. However, expecting them to be black and purple he was relieved to see they were already turning a muted brown and yellow. Either Ginny was an extremely fast healer, or Greer's touchy-feely behavior saved her a couple of weeks of recuperating.

"Greer healed me, didn't he?" Ginny prodded him when he remained silent and unhooked her bra. Going to the bed, she sat down to remove her shoes.

"I was so aggravated with his craziness that I didn't realize what he was doing until after we left." Lifting up off the bed, she started pulling her jeans down, grimacing when she bent down to get them over her knees.

"Greer makes a habit of irritating everyone." Reaper knelt down and helped peel her jeans off. Then, lifting Ginny back in his arms, he carried her into his bathroom.

Setting her down, he filled the tub with warm water, then grabbed Epson salt, towels, and washcloths from the closet.

"He does it to make people keep their distance from him, or that they won't notice what he's doing."

Generously pouring the salt into the tub, Reaper shot a quick text to Nickel before removing his own clothing. He swirled his hand in the water to check the temperature before lifting Ginny back into his arms and depositing her into the tub.

Ginny gave a moan of pleasure, luxuriating in the warmth.

Stepping into the tub behind her, he sat down and grabbed the washcloth he had hung over the side. "If Greer's only pretending to be an asshole, he's got it down pat." Reaper gave his own sigh, relaxing back in the tub. "He isn't the only one good at pretending."

Reaper watched the line of Ginny's spine go straight. "Do you mean me?"

His lips twitched as he gently wet the two cloths in the water, then laid them over her shoulders. "You could have given me an inkling that Agent Collins wasn't as shady as he was pretending to be, or that your plan was to incriminate Allerton and it was never about helping him find the artifact to get him off your back."

"I wanted to. A couple of times, I almost did."

"Why didn't you?"

"I'm sorry, but you kind of suck at pretending," she said apologetically. "You don't hide when you dislike someone, and in front of Allerton you made it plain that you disliked and distrusted Agent Collins."

"In other words, I helped the plan by being kept in the dark?"

"Yes. Are you mad at me?"

"No. You did what you felt you had to do to stop Allerton, regardless of your feelings for me. You trusted me that I could handle my own shit, while you took care of what you needed to."

"I thought you would be angry with me."

"Nymph." Reaper took one of the cloths, dipping it into the warm water before replacing it back over her shoulder, then did the same to the other one. "How am I supposed to be mad at you when you're covered in bruises?" Reaper leaned forward to place a feather-light kiss over one particularly yellow bruise. "I've been in your position when I was in the service; most of us in the club have been. You share what you can when you're on a mission. You went in, determined to beat Allerton. You did. Don't apologize for that, not to me or anyone else."

"I love you, Gavin."

Reaper squeezed his eyes shut, throwing himself in front of the steel door in his heart where the last part of Gavin's soul lay entombed, barricaded inside.

"You want me to wash your hair?" he asked thickly.

"Yes, please."

Wetting her hair with the sprayer, Reaper lathered her hair with shampoo. Massaging her scalp as he worked the shampoo through her hair, he saw goosebumps rising along her skin. Leaning forward, he pointing the nozzle down to gently spray the warm water over her before he resumed washing her hair.

Finishing washing them both up, he got out of the tub and grabbed the towels from the towel warmer. Helping Ginny to her feet, he wrapped the towel around her before lifting her up and out of the tub. Ginny stood quietly and let him dry her off.

Sweeping her back into his arms, he carried her to the chair in his bedroom.

"Gavin, I'm not helpless. I can walk."

"I like taking care of you." Picking up his brush, he started brushing the tangles out of her hair.

"I'm going to need some clothes if we're staying here. After my hair is dry, we can drive to Silas's house and get them."

"Silas is packing your things. He and Moses are going to drop them off in the morning along with Suki."

Ginny looked at him from over her shoulder. "When was that decided?"

"When we were waiting for Viper," he told her unapologetically.

"What's wrong with me going there?"

"Safer for your brothers if we make it plain where we'll be living." Reaper hid his anxiety that she wouldn't want to stay if he gave Ginny the opportunity. "We were just saving you the trouble. I didn't know if you wanted him or any of your other brothers to see you in the condition you're in."

"Aw … that was sweet of you. Thank you." Ginny looked toward the mirror, which was across the room, but she wasn't able to see her reflection. "I look that bad?"

"Not now."

"What about Trudy? I want to see her and explain—"

"She and Dalton are coming in the morning for breakfast. I told her you needed to rest tonight. I'll be right back. I'm going to get my blow dryer."

Striding into the bathroom, he took the blow dryer out from under the sink and when he came back into the bedroom, he found Ginny standing in front of the mirror.

"Thank you for thinking about my brothers and them seeing me this way. I'll ask Jewell if I can borrow some makeup before they come over tomorrow."

"They're going to be glad you're home."

Taking her hand, he led her back to the chair, then

plugged the dryer in and began blowing her hair out. He had just finished when there was a knock at the door.

"Give me a minute," Reaper yelled out.

Going to his dresser, he took out a clean T-shirt and a pair of shorts. He gave Ginny the oversized T-shirt as she was about to go hide in the bathroom. "Don't bother. Just stay where you are."

Pulling the shorts on, Reaper went to the side of the door first, then opened it.

"Here you go." Nickel held out a large paper bag and two plastic cups with straws.

"Thanks."

"Anytime. Later."

Reaper closed the door with his shoulder.

"Do you want to eat on the bed or the couch?"

Ginny sniffed the air appreciatively. "The couch is fine."

Setting the food and drinks on the table in front of the couch, he sat down next to Ginny and started unpacking the bag.

"The food smells amazing. How did you know I was craving burgers?"

Unwrapping one of the burgers, he placed it and an order of fries front of her. "Either I'm psychic or it was how you practically climbed over me when we passed the bar," he teased, setting his own food out. "You see that?" He waved a hand over his food.

Ginny looked up, about to eat a fry. "What?"

"These big boys burgers aren't the size of a postage stamps, and we have the same amount of fries."

Ginny rolled her eyes at him. "You're exaggerating."

"Maybe about the burgers, but not the fries." Reaper picked up his monster burger, using two hands, giving a moan of satisfaction before he bit down.

He was almost done before he realized Ginny was silently

eating her food without her normal banter. As he took a sip of his soda, he watched her; she seemed to be ruminating as she picked at her food. Now familiar with the way her mind worked, Reaper knew it spelled trouble.

"Something wrong with the food?"

"No. I'm just tired, I guess." She shrugged.

Reaper started on his second burger, not buying her tired excuse for a second. Something was bothering her, but she wasn't ready to tell him what it was.

"Then go to sleep," he encouraged. "I'll take care of the cleanup when I'm done. I need to do some work on the computer, then I'll come to bed."

When she got up off the couch, he grabbed her hand before she could move away. "Are you sure you're okay? No pain anywhere?"

"No, I'm fine." Pressing a kiss to his forehead, she slipped her hand from his to climb in bed.

Reaper didn't want to press her, assuming she needed some time to process what Allerton had done to her. After he finished eating and disposed the trash, he looked at the bed, seeing she was pretending to be asleep.

Turning on the light beside his desk, he flicked off the overhead light. He settled down at the computer and went to work tracking the history of hurricanes near Sherguevil and Clindale area over the past twenty years.

Two hours later, his aching eyes had him calling it quits for the night. Before getting ready for bed, he sent several texts to the brothers, then sent a mass text to everyone in the club.

He put his hands on his thighs, about to rise, when he looked over at Ginny as she lay sleeping. Laying on her side, facing his direction, she had kicked the covers off, and he could see a bruise on her thigh.

This morning, when he told Viper that Ginny was pregnant, his brother had known that, if the heavens had suddenly rained down fireballs, nothing was going to keep him from getting to Ginny first.

Viper had been running alongside of him, ordering the others to find the FBI agents, when they saw a Moke speeding toward them. Every man raised his weapon at the vehicle as it pulled up alongside of them.

"Don't fire," Reaper commanded as Agent Clark jumped out of the Moke.

"Allerton's security just tried to take us out in my bungalow. I have them contained. Agent Collins hasn't checked in this morning. We're going to the resort."

"Allerton has Collins and Ginny."

Viper and Reaper followed Agent Clark back into the Moke.

"Go!" Reaper yelled loud enough for Cash to take off in the first Moke.

The two vehicles sped away, leaving Stud, Calder, and Knox behind on foot, heading in another direction.

"Where are they going?" Agent Clark shouted.

"To the security building. They're going to stop Allerton's additional security at the resort and the airfield," Viper told him.

Reaper saw Cash stop his Moke at the side door of the resort.

"Park next to him," Reaper told Agent Garcia, who was driving.

Springing out of the vehicle with his gun at the ready, Reaper ran toward the side door where the other brothers were nearly mowing down Hammer when Desmond Beck opened the door.

Reaper pointed his gun at Beck, prepared to take him out.

Viper tilted his gun down. "It's cool. Desmond helped us get on Clindale."

"Ginny's in Gabriel's office with Agent Collins. I've managed to take care of the two guards inside. Gabriel will send more and will want to lock the building down. He does that, we won't be able to get off the island," Desmond informed them.

Reaper jumped over the downed guards and ran through the

interconnected hallways with Beck, Viper, and the rest of the brothers following. Stabbing the button of the elevator repeatedly, he decided to head for the exit door just a few feet away.

Desmond grabbed his arm. "You open the door, it'll set off an alarm. The button for the stairwell is in Gabriel's office. It's a security feature to keep anyone from getting on or off his floor."

"Fuck." Reaper returned to the elevator, eyeing Beck suspiciously. "He doesn't have the same safeguard for the elevator?"

"Ethan, his assistant, supervises anyone getting access. Gabriel doesn't want to be bothered by deliveries. Ethan has a master switch behind his desk. Unless he presses it, the doors won't open."

Reaper coldly focused on the steel doors, wanting to pry them open. He would allow the extra minute for Ethan to send the elevator down instead of running up the stairwell, and if what Beck said was true, Allerton had opened the elevator door when he and Ginny escaped this morning.

Fuck this ....

The doors sliding open had Reaper rushing inside. Viper and the rest of the men crowded in after him. Shade and Rider remained outside.

"Ethan will send the elevator back," Desmond promised.

Reaper pushed the button.

"Beck, if this is a setup, you're going to be the first motherfucker I take out," Viper warned. "How'd you manage to get Allerton's assistant to agree to help?"

"Not from the generosity of his heart." Desmond stared at Viper cuttingly. "King and Shade gave me carte blanche to spend what I needed to spend. What you paid Abbott Varela's ship captain to let you stow away and get you to Clindale is chump change to what you're paying Ethan. Without him, we won't be getting off this island."

The metal doors opening had Viper and Desmond going out first.

"Clear." On Viper's signal they rushed out.

Reaper started toward Allerton's office. "Reaper, hold."

Viper and Desmond had gone behind Ethan's desk to stand next to the assistant, who'd handed Viper one of his earbuds.

Reaper joined Viper and they all watched a bank of computer screens. On one of the screens they saw what Allerton was doing to Ginny. Enraged, Reaper moved away from the desk. The mother-fucker was dead.

"Wait—we can't go in there yet." Agent Garcia blocked him.

"Why in the hell not?" Reaper was prepared to throw the agent over the desk if he didn't move.

"Listen to her. Ginny's getting a confession out of him."

With the furious pounding rushing through his head, Reaper could barely hear the low voices coming from earbuds.

"Listen," Agent Garcia urged.

"This may help." Ethan reached under the flap of his suit. At the movement, he had eight guns pointed at him. "I was only going to raise the volume." He pointed to the white plastic cord that extended upward to the collar of his shirt. "They don't know I'm listening in."

Reaper nodded, so Ethan could turn the volume up, and they all heard Allerton and Ginny.

"Depends on a need-to-know basis."

"In other words, when you use the tapes to blackmail them to get what you want?"

Reaper and the others watched the computer screen as Ginny's voice sounded through the headset.

"Can you make a copy of this tape?"

"When you're ready, all you have to do is press this button." Ethan showed them the button on the computer. "It isn't equipped with sound."

"Then fuck it." Reaper again tried to move toward Allerton's office.

"Wait—the polygraph machine is in there," Garcia said. "It's on the table. It has a recording feature; the conversation is being taped.

That's why Ginny is asking Allerton questions to incriminate himself."

"Ginny knows she's being recorded?" Reaper didn't take his eyes off the computer. Allerton stood over Ginny with a cane in his hand.

"Yes," Hammer interjected. "The idea was to make him so frustrated that he would slip up, which the bastard is doing. Give Ginny a few ...."

Shade and Rider stepped off the elevator and walked toward the desk as the men continued to listen and watch an infuriated Allerton talk to Ginny while holding a cane poised above her head.

She was on her knees, proudly refusing to cower, even as he swung that fucking cane again. His nymph was battling a demon, with only the power of her voice. Despite being tortured, she was leading the demon to his own destruction.

Every man listening and watching had the same expression. Ginny had earned a purple heart in their eyes.

When Allerton raised the cane higher above his head, Reaper knew how much force he was going to exert, and it was about to come down on his nymph.

He fucking snapped.

Shoving the agent out of his way, he went for the door. Viper and Hammer tried to stop him.

"Wait—she's trying to find out about Clindale," Hammer gasped out when Reaper's fist struck out, hitting his cheekbone. Hammer fell backward and landed in the computer chair, which slammed back into a small table with a coffee maker, sending it crashing against the wall.

Trying to peel Viper off him, Reaper continued to move down the hallway. Rider went to his other side and found himself dragged along in Reaper's wake.

"Let me fucking go ... I'm going to kill that motherfucker."

"Just a min—" Cash huffed, while grabbing him around the waist.

Reaper used his strength to throw the three men off. Viper was easier to rip off, because his brother didn't want to hurt him; Rider was harder. Reaper knocked him off by barreling into the plotted plant, forcing the plant and Rider to go face-first into the wall. With his arms free, he reached behind him to pull Cash over his shoulder, and he sent him flying into the door. Unconcerned with the brother's welfare, Reaper picked him up and tossed him into the agent, whose face went pale when he saw Cash flying toward him.

"Shade?" Reaper's tone of voice stated exactly what he wanted from the brother as he grabbed the doorknob.

"Ready," Shade coldly directed him. "Now open the fucking door."

CHAPTER THIRTY-THREE

Rising from the chair, Reaper placed it under the doorknob. He turned off the desk light, then went to the other side of the bed and slid in slowly, so as not to disturb her. She was sleeping on his side of the bed. When she had crawled in, he hadn't had the inclination to tell her to sleep on the other side. He was too happy she was there, in his bed, in his room, *with him.*

Scooting over in small movements, Reaper curled against her backside. Pressing his hand on the pillow, he was able scoot his arm under, so her head lay on him, as he curled his other hand over her hip, which was one of the few places on her body that wasn't bruised.

Reaper fell asleep listening to the sound of Ginny's breathing, his chest rising and falling in accord with hers. Dreams filtered through his unconscious state, taking him to another place and time, where their souls met for the first time, where they pledged their love for eternity and a day. Visceral images so real that when he woke in the morning, he sat up in bed in a cold sweat.

Shoving his hair out of his face, he looked over and

noticed the bed empty. Falling back to the pillow, he stared up at the ceiling. The dream he'd been experiencing was already dissipating with the bright light of day. He had always been a light sleeper. How did she manage to slip out of his bed without him noticing?

Hearing the sounds from the floor below, Reaper figured most of the house was already up and moving around. Climbing out of bed, he went into the bathroom to take a quick shower before dressing in jeans and a T-shirt that had a small skull on the pocket; he hadn't worn the shirt in years. Viper had packed most of his favorite ones, which were still on the island, along with Ginny's suitcase.

Opening the top drawer, he took out a pair of socks, and as he started to close the drawer, he grabbed a black knit hat. Putting his socks and boots on, Reaper went to the mirror to brush out the long portion of his hair, then slid the cap on.

Feeling properly presentable, he went downstairs and found the main room empty, but from the smell coming from the kitchen, he gauged everyone was eating breakfast. Going through the swinging door, Reaper glowered at the others in front of him in the long line. Nickel and Moon, who were in front and closest to him, moved aside.

Rider looked over his shoulder but remained in his spot. "You're not cutting in front of me. You can wait your turn."

Reaper cut his eyes over him, not giving a fuck about the food.

His wife placed a sheet filled with biscuits on the kitchen island, then picked up the empty one; he saw red.

"Ginny, what in the fuck are you doing?" Reaper roared, seeing the two men who were behind the counter with her.

Ginny jumped at hearing her name yelled and dropped the pan, sending it crashing to the floor.

Reaper narrowed his eyes at the asshole who bent over,

picked up the pan, then carried it to the sink for her. "What in the fuck are you doing here?"

Puck came from around the counter to hold out his hand. The brother was the sergeant-at-arms of the Ohio chapter of The Last Riders. "Yo, brah. Glad to see you made it home."

Reaper didn't take his hand.

Puck wore his hair like his Viking ancestors, which he bragged about being a descendent of every single fucking time his ass was drunk. Both sides of his head were shaved, with the top part of his light blond hair pulled back into a tight ponytail. Being the same height as Reaper, Puck met his gaze directly.

"What are you doing here?"

Puck frowned at his unwelcoming scowl. "Viper sent for me to stay here when the brothers left to have your back."

Reaper looked over Puck's shoulder to see Jesus standing beside Ginny, talking as they dished out food for The Last Riders.

Viper had actually sent for the Ohio's enforcer and sergeant-at-arms to watch over their wives? Was his brother out of his fucking mind? He had been smart to take Moon, but he'd left the two biggest dicks to watch over their flock of doves.

The brothers had earned their nicknames from their expertise at luring the most unattainable women to their beds. Reaper conveniently forgot his own expertise in the same field, but at least his nickname had been earned in the military. Jesus had the ability to talk any woman into giving it up to him, and Puck was able to sneak past any boyfriend or husband to score.

"Where's Viper?"

Puck's frown became more pronounced. "Haven't seen him this morning. What time does he usually eat breakfast?"

Looking at his watch, Reaper took out his cell phone, sending a text to Viper.

Get your ass to the club. I'm in the kitchen.

Reaper pocketed is cell phone, rudely shoving past Puck to go behind the counter. "What in the fuck are you doing?" he asked Ginny a third time.

Ginny continued spooning gigantic portions of eggs onto Moon's outstretched plate. "What does it look like I'm doing? Are you feeling all right this morning? Do you need to go back to sleep and get up on the right side?"

"No. What I *need* is for you to stop doing what you're doing, I didn't have you stay here to turn you back into their housekeeper and cook again." Glaring at Moon, who was standing with his plate, Reaper turned his wrath on him. "What in the fuck you wanting?"

Moon gave Ginny an innocent expression, which Reaper wasn't buying for a hot second, considering the laughter in his eyes. "A biscuit."

"Fuck off!" he snarled.

Ginny gave the fucker two biscuits. "Is that enough?"

"Yes, ma'am."

"You better not," Reaper warned her.

"Do what?" Confused, Ginny looked at him.

"Smile at that asshole."

"Gavin, would you like me to make you a plate? Maybe that would put you in a better mood."

"I wouldn't be in a bad mood if you weren't doing what you're not supposed to be doing."

"I came down for breakfast, and Jesus had burnt the eggs. I offered to help." Ginny continued spooning eggs, giving a heaping spoonful to Jewell. "Moving around is helping me work the kinks out of my body."

"So would a warm bath and me giving you a massage,"

Reaper told her, glaring at Rider, who was already coming back for seconds.

"I offered to give her one." Puck grinned, coming back behind the counter, carrying dirty dishes. "It's the least I could do with her offering to help out."

As every bone in Reaper's body went taut and he took a threatening step forward, the dishes in Puck's hands shook.

"Reaper!" Viper called from the doorway. "You wanted to talk to me?"

Reaper pointed two fingers at his eyes, then turned his hand and pointed them at Puck in a show of "I'm watching you," before walking around the counter to meet Viper. "We need to talk."

Viper tilted his head to the side, then toward the front of the kitchen before bobbing his head back. "We can talk as I eat. I'm starving, and I haven't eaten Ginny's cooking since she quit."

Reaper stayed where he was, blocking Viper's path to the food.

"Move."

Reaper gritted his teeth at the order. Stepping to the side, he made himself a cup of coffee and found an empty table in the room off the kitchen. His gaze passed over Shade and Rider before he spotted the jar of jelly sitting prominently on their table.

A plate full of food slapping the table heralded the arrival of Viper as he pulled out a chair. "What's up?" Viper pulled his biscuit apart to layer it with butter.

"I want you to explain to me"—Reaper scooted farther up his seat to ground out his complaint—"what in the fuck you were thinking bringing Jesus and Puck here."

Viper raised his brows at him. "I was thinking that, since I was taking my enforcer and sergeant-at-arms with me, as well as most of the other brothers, Razer would need some help if shit went down while we were away."

"You had any fucking brothers from Ohio you could have chosen; you didn't have to pick Puck and Jesus."

Viper frowned at him. "What wrong with Puck and Jesus? Puck has proven his loyalty over and over. You're the one who convinced him to join The Last Riders when he got out of the service."

Reaper scowled at the reminder.

"And what the fuck with Jesus? I can name half a dozen instances you've needed his help within the last six months." Viper shoved the biscuit in his mouth, saving Reaper from doing it for him, Reaper thought angrily.

Reaper scooted farther on his seat until his ass was barely on the chair. "They're both satyromaniacs; that's what the fuck is wrong with them."

"What in the fuck is a satyromaniac?" Viper asked, pausing his hand holding a forkful of scrambled eggs.

Reaper waved his hand at him as if he should know the answer. "You know what a nymphomaniac is, don't you?"

Viper gave him a shit-eating grin. "I hope so."

Reaper gave him a dirty look at his attempt of humor. When he wasn't so angry, Reaper reminded himself to tell his brother his sense of humor sucked.

"A satyromaniac is the male equivalent," Reaper informed him.

"No shit? Damn, you learn something new every day."

"This isn't funny. You left Winter and the other wives to be watched over by *them*."

"I also left Razer." Viper shrugged. "Besides, I trust my wife."

"My wife has too much of a trusting nature. Those men think every woman wants to fuck them, and there's a bet going with Moon to see who can catch the most. I want them gone. Moon can stay," he ended magnanimously.

"Are we talking about Ginny?"

"Who else would I be talking about?"

"Technically, you aren't—"

Reaper leaned his upper body over the table. "Ginny is my wife, and she's going to stay that way. She's innocent, impressionable, and too sweet for her own good. Puck and Jesus, if they have the opportunity—"

"Which I'm sure they won't." Viper picked up his coffee cup and started to get up.

"Where are you going?"

"Get another biscuit and refill my coffee. Is that okay with you?"

"Ginny only gave you one biscuit. She gave Rider two."

"So?"

"Never mind." Reaper tugged his hat farther down his forehead, fiddling with it because he was becoming increasingly irritated with Viper.

He was about to go search for Viper when his brother returned, followed by Ginny holding a plate of food. Relieved that she was planning to sit with him—and therefore out of Puck's and Jesus' reach—he started to relax.

Ginny placed the food down in front of him as Viper sat back down with another plate filled with biscuits and a fucking jar of Ginny's jelly.

"I thought you might be hungry."

Reaper frowned when she started to turn away. "Where are you going? T.A. and Dalton are joining us for breakfast."

"Dalton called. He's letting Trudy sleep in. He said she hasn't slept much while I've been gone. He invited me to their house this afternoon. I told him yes. Do you mind taking me around twelve?"

"No, I don't mind. Have a seat," he urged, trying to keep her away from Puck and Jesus, "while I finish breakfast."

"I can't. I'm just waiting for the last pan of biscuits to come out of the oven, then I'm going to take a shower and meet Silas."

"Have you eaten?"

Ginny gave him her bright smile. "First thing I did this morning. I ate a big bowl of oatmeal. Silas is bringing me a jar of honey when he comes. You need anything before I go?"

Reaper gave her a pleading look. "You could get me the jelly on the table over there." He nodded at the table Rider and Shade were sitting at.

"Of course." Ginny turned to see where he was nodding. Giving him a suspicious glance, she nevertheless went to get the jelly for him.

"Jesus. Do you have to make it so obvious?" Viper snorted, buttering his biscuit.

"Shut the fuck up," Reaper snarled at him, then pasted a saccharine smile on as Ginny brought the jelly to him. "Thank you."

"You're welcome."

When Ginny went to move away, Reaper caught her hand. "You haven't given me my morning kiss," he reminded her.

Ginny blushed bright red. Darting a quick glance at Viper, she then bent and gave him a light kiss on his lips. "My biscuits will burn."

Reaper watched her with a calculating gaze as she made her escape.

Viper reached out, taking the jelly away from him to unscrew the lid and smear a healthy dollop on his biscuit. "I think the only one who Ginny needs protecting from is you," Viper said.

"With all of us home"—Reaper took the jelly back—"you

can send Puck and Jesus back to Ohio. I'll even gas their bikes for them."

"Sorry, they won't be leaving anytime soon."

"Why not?"

"Did you forget that mass text you sent out last night?"

"What in the fuck does that have …? *Fuck*."

"You told all The Last Riders that, in their free time, they can volunteer to help you build your and Ginny's new house, and that you would pay them time and a half. Puck and Jesus checked with me last night, asking if they could stay and work with you instead of going back to Ohio. They said they needed the extra cash, so I gave them the go-ahead."

"I didn't know they were here when I sent the text."

"Doesn't matter. You're going to need their help. The brothers here are tired of building. I don't care how much you offer them. Killyama drove them nuts nitpicking them to death. And may I remind you that Train and Rider both asked for an extra hand from you when Train's was being built and Rider wanted help when Jo remodeled her house?"

"Fuck," Reaper groused.

"That's the way it goes sometimes. Payback is a bitch."

Reaper looked down at his plate, irritated that Puck or Jesus wouldn't be leaving anytime soon. He frowned, then raised his head, remembering the plate of biscuits that Viper had carried to the table. All those fucking biscuits hadn't been just for him. The plate was now empty with Viper placing the last biscuit in his mouth.

"You ate my biscuits."

"Yes, I did. Sometimes payback isn't a bitch; it's the brother who you dragged out of bed when Winter was—"

Reaper raised his hand, stopping him.

"—sound asleep," Viper continued, undeterred.

Forking a bite of eggs in his mouth, he intended to go upstairs with Ginny and remind her who she belonged to.

And to reinforce that thought, when Ginny was with T.A., he would take the opportunity to go shopping.

Thinking of T.A., he wanted to ask Ginny if Sex Piston would be there—she had threatened ... Then a thought dawned on him so urgently that he rose to his feet, horror stricken.

"Text Train and tell him to keep Killyama home!"

Viper immediately reached for his phone, his face equally as horror stricken.

His ass wasn't off his chair when he heard a loud crash and then a loud scream filled the air, which had the hair on his arms standing on his arms.

"Who in the fuck hit my bitch!"

CHAPTER THIRTY-FOUR

Setting the sheet of biscuits on the counter, Ginny grabbed the empty bowl to refill with more eggs when the back door opened. Excited at seeing Killyama coming through the door with Train, Ginny started toward her to say hello when Killyama spotted her.

Ginny took another step forward, then started backing up seeing the expression on Killyama's face, deciding it would be better to talk to the furious woman when she wasn't so angry.

Turning, she was unaware of Puck walking over, carrying an empty platter. She was trying to miss bumping into him when a loud scream reverberated off the walls.

Puck jerked at the sound, dropping the platter to reach behind his back. Seeing the metal when the back of his shirt came up had Ginny dropping the bowl to grab his arm before he could pull the gun out.

"*Who in the fuck hit my bitch!*" Killyama screamed .

"Don't shoot her!" Ginny shrieked, trying to be heard over Killyama.

Seeing his wife was about to get shot, Train grabbed

Killyama around the waist and, in one motion, turned around, protectively placing himself in front of his wife in case a bullet went off.

Puck jerked his arm away. "Woman!" he roared. "Don't you know better than to reach for a man's gun when he's rea—"

Ginny opened her mouth to apologize when Gavin tore her away from Puck and began strangling him.

"Don't you ever raise your fucking voice to my wife!"

"Gavin! Stop it! You're hurting him." Ginny hit at Gavin's back when he didn't release Puck. "Let him go!"

"Reaper, let go!" Viper roared from the other side of the counter.

Gavin slowly released Puck, who fell back, gasping for air.

"Are you okay?" Ginny frantically tried to move around Gavin to see if Puck had been hurt.

"He's fine. I barely touched him."

Ginny placed her hands on her hips. "Tell him you're sorry."

Attempting to see for herself that Puck was all right, Reaper pulled her away, but not before she saw Puck give Gavin a one-handed "fuck you" behind his back, while his other hand was on the mark Gavin left on his neck.

"He's sorry," Ginny told him.

"No, I'm not."

"Move. I don't need you taking a bullet for me," Killyama yelled at her husband, moving around him. "Bitch, I want the name, and I want the fucking name *now*!"

"Name?" Her mind was still on Gavin and Puck. She motioned to Gavin. "You know Gavin. Oh, you mean Puck. You haven't been introduced to him yet?" she asked in confusion.

Killyama lunged toward her, and Gavin blocked her protectively.

Shocked at her reaction, Ginny stepped back, deciding once again it might be safer to talk to Killyama later when she wasn't so emotional.

"Little bitch, you take one step for that door, I'll call Sex Piston."

Ginny felt the blood drain from her face. "Is she as mad at me as you are?"

"What I'm feeling is going to be *nothing* compared to how Sex Piston is going to react when she sees you!"

Ginny poked her head around Gavin's arm to look at her friend. "I had to do it, Killy. You would have done the same for Train," she pleaded for her friend's understanding. "We got him. Allerton's in jail."

"Who. Is. The. Son. Of. A. Bitch. Who. Hit. You!"

"Oh …" That was what she was so upset about? "Allerton." Ginny relaxed when Gavin became the focus of her fury.

"You didn't kill the son of a bitch?" Killyama ranted at him.

"I tried." Gavin folded his arms over his chest, not budging from standing in front of her. "Ginny wouldn't let me."

Ginny gave Gavin a dirty look for throwing her under the bus.

"If you calm down, I'll explain to you why I couldn't let Gavin kill him."

"Bitch, all I can say is it better be good."

Going down the hallway, Ginny gave Gavin the cold shoulder. Entering the bedroom, she went into the bathroom to change into the outfit that Killyama brought over for her to wear until Silas came over with her clothes. She had also loaned her some makeup to cover the bruises on her face.

Shutting the bathroom door, Ginny removed her clothes, then stepped into the shower. Pointing the showerhead down so she wouldn't get her hair wet, she was lathering the washcloth with bodywash when Gavin stepped into the shower, shutting the door.

"Go away. I'm still mad at you."

Gavin took the washcloth from her to soap her back. "What for?"

"For strangling Puck and telling Killy I wouldn't let you kill Allerton."

"Puck shouldn't have yelled at you, and you *should* have let me kill Allerton."

"Puck was angry only because he was afraid I'd get accidentally shot when I wouldn't let him grab his gun to shoot Killyama." Ginny pulled her hair to the side so it wouldn't get wet. "And we can't let anything happen to Allerton until I find out what happened on Clindale."

"Puck wouldn't have shot Killyama. He was right; you shouldn't have touched him when he was going for his gun. My issue with him was him raising his voice at you. It was also a lesson for everyone in the club not to do the same. I'm pretty sure you're going to get on their nerves before we can get our house built. And lastly"—Gavin moved closer to her, sliding the cloth around her hip to the front of her waist, the movement pressing her back against his chest. There wasn't a time that his touch, however innocent or sensual, failed to bring back the excitement she had felt the first time she stroked his jaw—"when I'm done with Allerton, he's going to pray for death."

Ginny turned in his arms to circle his neck. "Wild man, relax and let the FBI finish the job." She ran her hand over his tattooed shoulders, luxuriating in the feel of Gavin's skin under her palm. "We're safe and sound at home." She could feel the coiled tension in the muscles that rippled under his flesh as if he was holding himself back.

"You haven't told me you love me today." Gavin jutted his jaw out like a three-year-old ready to have a hissy fit.

Ginny feathered a kiss over his heart. "I love you."

He tucked a loose strand of hair behind her ear. "I don't want you cooking and cleaning while you're staying here."

Her lips trembled over his skin at his arrogance. "I will help out whenever I see the need. I thought that was the rule, and everyone has to help out if they live here?"

Her head was tilted back as Gavin wound her ponytail around his fist.

"You don't."

"Why not?"

"Because I said you don't."

"I'll go insane without anything to do."

"Then use the opportunity to write songs."

"Then that's what I'll do," she agreed, tracing his nipple with her tongue.

Gavin stared down at her suspiciously.

"You looked very handsome this morning. I think it's the first time I've seen you in anything other than black. The grey"—Ginny ran her hand down his slick arm—"shows off your tattoos."

"Puck has a lot of tattoos."

Ginny rubbed her breasts on his chest as she started to lick his other nipple. "Does he? I didn't notice."

The washcloth hit the shower tiles as Gavin grabbed her waist to lift her up so her nipple was within reach of his mouth. "Tell me to suck your nipple."

If she wasn't wet enough in the shower with the water

spraying down on her, his demand had her insides clenching in want. "Suck my nipple."

She felt her nipple sucked into Gavin's mouth, and goose-bumps spread across her body when his tongue played with the tight bud.

"Gavin, I'm only guessing …," she managed to get out between the rapid beating of her heart, "that I'm higher than two inches off the ground."

His sensual mouth curled over her nipple. "I'm making an exception. I'll catch you if you fall."

She couldn't help but stare at his masculine beauty. Gavin was so beautiful that it sometimes hurt to freaking look at him. There was no way on God's green earth that she would be able to hold onto him. He was a twenty on a scale of one to ten, and she was a solid five. This glorious man was meant for greater happiness than she would ever be able to give him, no matter how hard she tried.

Last night, when he had taken such care of her by drawing her a bath, wrapping her gently in the towel, and blow-drying her hair, his efficient movements signaled he'd done it before. Many, many times. Gavin knew a woman's body like the back of his hand.

Switching breasts, Gavin caressed her nipple before drawing it inside his mouth. "Tell me you want me to fuck you," he demanded.

Ginny felt as if the water had gone ice-cold.

Slightly withdrawing her breast from his mouth, she gave him a grin she didn't mean. "Silas will be here in ten minutes. I don't want to keep him waiting." Wiggling herself down his body, she picked up the washcloth to finish washing herself. "You're going to have to take a rain check." Giving a slight laugh, she wrung out the cloth, then hung it over the metal bar to the side of the shower. Opening the door, she reached for the towel she had laid out and started to dry herself off.

"Ginny ... what's bothering you?"

Ginny put more effort into the smile she gave him. "Nothing." Wrapping the towel around her, she dried her face before tucking it between her breasts.

"You're lying."

"I'm not." Ginny sighed, realizing she was going to have to give him a partial truth. "There are just some things that are difficult to discuss with you because we haven't been together long, and to tell you the truth, I find it embarrassing to talk about."

"Like what?"

"Like us not using protection. I'm not on birth control, and we've never used condoms. I haven't had the opportunity to take care of it with me leaving the day after our first time together, and I couldn't bring myself to ask to see one of Allerton's doctors or ask for condoms."

"Ginny, I—"

"Don't worry," Ginny hurried on. "I got my period this morning, so we're all good. I also made an appointment with Dr. Price tomorrow morning, so after that, we'll be set to go once I'm off my period."

Seeing his poleaxed expression, she lowered her head to tuck the towel tighter around her. Damn, why was Gavin looking so shell-shocked? Was the possibility of her not being pregnant that big of a relief to him?

"Was that what you were worried about last night?"

"Yes." Ginny gave a nod of her head. "Do you mind? I'd like to get dressed."

Gavin went to the bathroom closet to take out a towel, then wrapped it around his hips.

Holding his stare, Ginny smiled at him. "I won't be long."

Striding closer to her, he gave her an inflexible stare. "There's something I should tell you."

Ginny looked at him questioningly.

"But fair is fair. I'm going to be as honest with you as you were with me just now."

Walking past her, he left the room, closing the door behind him and leaving what he wanted to say unsaid.

Damn ... he was such big jerk.

She pressed her hand to her stomach. She had known it was too early to tell if she was pregnant, but Ginny had imagined seeing their baby in Gavin's arms. This morning when she went to the bathroom, she cried. Then she'd called Dr. Price's office before she left the bathroom to go downstairs to keep herself from dwelling about the loss of a child who had never existed. She bet he was doing summersaults in the bedroom, out of her sight. She should have been the one doing summersaults, Ginny thought crankily. He was the one who was a big jerk.

CHAPTER THIRTY-FIVE

Ginny jumped off the third step from the bottom of the stairs outside the clubhouse and into Moses' waiting arms.

"I missed you!" Ginny exclaimed cheerfully, turning to Silas when Moses set her back on her feet. Her good mood vanished once she got a good look at her brother.

"You look terrible!" Ginny gasped.

Silas gently lifted her chin to look at her accusingly. "Doesn't seem as bad as I expected. Either Greer healed you more that he should have, or you're getting better at putting makeup on."

Ginny hugged her big brother to her. "A little of both," she confessed tearfully. "Is that what's wrong with you, it's because of me?"

Silas hugged her back, lacking the strength he usually held her with. "I'll be as good as new in a few days. Just do me a favor and keep out of trouble for a couple of weeks. Give me time to get my strength back before you do more skydiving off waterfalls."

"I'm sorry. I knew what I was doing. You shouldn't have wasted your strength."

"Old habits die hard. I'll always be there to catch you."

Tears brimmed her eyes. "You need someone in your life to look after so you'll quit worrying over us."

"Doesn't matter who enters my life; I'll never stop watching over my family."

Ginny laughed, releasing him. "I'll remind you of that when she comes."

A faraway look entered his eyes. "It won't be this year, maybe next."

Ginny wanted to tell Silas whoever his soul mate was, she worth waiting for, but she didn't have to tell him. He already knew. The waiting was torture, and Silas had been waiting longer than she had. When you were lonely and just wanted someone to cuddle with, each year seemed like an eternity.

Moving to the side, Ginny realized she had been so focused on Moses and Silas that she hadn't noticed Suki had made a beeline for Gavin. The excited dog was jumping up and down waiting to throw herself into Gavin's arms. Bending down, Gavin rubbed her fur, smiling at the dog's exuberant behavior.

Moses went to his truck, reached over, and then placed a heavy bag down by the front wheel. "I brought you a bag of dog food to tide you over until you can get to the store."

"Give me five, and I'll get you a check," Gavin said, straightening.

"Don't worry about it. We're just happy Ginny's home." Taking a bundled cord out his pocket, he gave it to Gavin. "It's Suki's leash and collar. I brought her over several times while you were gone to get her familiar with the surroundings and to show her the boundaries. She'll stay in the backyard if you let her outside alone. Suki won't go past Razer and Shade's house, nor will she go past the front or the sides."

"Thanks, Moses."

"We brought Ginny's suitcases. I'll get them for you."

Gavin reached out to shake Silas's hand as Moses went back to his truck.

"You look like you need a solid week of recuperation."

Silas returned his handshake. "I plan to take more than a week." Her brother gave Gavin a wry smile. "She's a handful. Be careful, or she'll wear you out before your time."

Ginny patted Suki's head as she pushed herself between the dog and Gavin. "She's just excited with Gavin being back," she said, excusing the high-spirited dog.

Both men looked at her soberly. Silas was the one who broke the news to her.

"Ginny, we weren't talking about the dog. We were talking about you."

"I still don't think it was funny," Ginny said huffily while bopping her head to the song that she was listening to on the radio as they drove to Trudy and Dalton's house.

"I didn't laugh."

"You might not have, but I could tell you wanted to." She gave him another bop of her head.

"But I didn't. *Didn't* is the key word here." Putting on the blinker, Gavin turned down the tree-lined street.

"I don't understand why you and Silas think I'm some sort of Calamity Jane. I live a very boring life."

Parking in the driveway, Gavin waited until he put the car in Park, waiting for her to quit dramatically singing I see "I See Red" by Everybody Loves an Outlaw.

"You know that's funny as fuck you saying that, right?" Taking the key out of the ignition, Gavin rested his arm along the back of the seat. "There's nothing boring about you. You couldn't sit still if your life depended on it; you've had several people stalking you—"

"Slate wasn't my fault, may I remind you?" Ginny bopped her head at him.

Gavin turned the radio off. "Aggravated one man so bad that he nearly beat you to death."

"That's an exaggeration. Allerton didn't even break a bone."

"Greer and Silas look like they are both at death's door. Ginny, you're more than a handful. You're a booby trap, ready to cause an explosion anytime you're near."

"How hurtful."

"You don't act like your feelings are hurt."

"They are … deep down."

Gavin gave her a sarcastic snort.

"Okay, not really," she admitted. "Because I know none of it is my fault."

"Then whose fault is it?"

"Men."

"Men?"

"Men," Ginny repeated. "Do you know, statistically speaking, men are responsible for everything wrong in world? I'm serious." Ginny raised her voice to make sure he heard her when he pretended to clean his ears out with his finger. "Men are the ones who commit 98 percent of rapes, 87 percent of robberies, 83 percent of arsons, and almost 80 percent of crimes against their partners and children. If it weren't for men, women around the world could sleep with their windows open."

Gavin just stared at her.

"You don't have anything to say about that?" She bopped her head self-righteously. "Huh? I'm right, aren't I?"

"How'd you know those statistics off the top of your head?"

"The more you know the more empowered you are."

"You're a nut. I want to see the results of your DNA test. Somewhere you have a blood connection to Greer."

Taking off his sunglasses, he hung them on the visor. As he did, the long-sleeved shirt accented the muscular abs underneath. With the grey knit he wore on his head, his long hair falling down to his shoulders, Gavin was the epitome of a woman's wet fantasy, not that she ever had one, but he would be the star if she did.

He gave her a dark look as she closed the car door. "I was coming to open the door for you."

Ginny reached out to touch his cheek. "Are you running a fever?"

Taking her hand, Gavin began striding to the door.

"What's the hurry?" Ginny asked with interest, waving to Trudy's neighbor, who was nosily watching them as she got her mail.

"After I talk to Dalton, I'm going to run out to the store. Will you be all right if I leave you for about an hour?"

"Yes," she said patiently. "You're acting ridiculous."

"The last time I left you alone in Treepoint for an hour, I had to take a helicopter to find you, and I ended up on an island."

Ginny stabbed the doorbell. "Okay, you might have a small point," she admitted, holding out her pinky. "If I promise to stay out of trouble for the next month, will you promise to quit acting as if I'm Calamity Jane?"

"Hell, I'd quit if you'd just give me a break for two days. A month would be a dream."

"The James men's sense of humor sucks, just so you know."

The door opening saved Ginny from the sarcastic response that Gavin was sure to make. Dalton opened the door wider when he saw them outside.

"Hello, Dalton, may I see Trudy?"

The movie star and producer flicked his eyes over both of them, then stepped aside. Ginny entered nervously, aware Dalton wouldn't be happy with her for upsetting Trudy when she was carrying his child.

"T.A.'s in the living room. It's been everything I could do to keep her here after she woke. She wanted to see you last night, but when Reaper texted, he said you were exhausted from your trip." Dalton's eyes were on her face as he talked, making her anxious that he could see the bruises under the makeup she put on.

"I feel much better today." Walking forward, Ginny made a left to see Trudy standing there, waiting to be noticed.

"Ginny ...."

Ginny ran into her sister's arm, and both of them burst into tears trying to talk at the same time.

"I'm so sorry. I wanted to tell you, but I was afraid you would have talked me out of going to Sherguevil," Ginny blurted out.

"Don't you ever scare me like that again! If you scare me like that again, I'm going to lock you in my spare bedroom." Trudy fussed at her like a mother hen, giving her a small shake, then enfolding her back in her arms to start crying louder.

"Trudy, stop. You're going to give the baby hiccups."

Trudy stopped crying. "Is that true?" she asked, riveted at the thought, moving her hand to her baby bump.

"I don't know, but it got you to stop crying, didn't it?"

Trudy made a face at her. "I had another few minutes in me. I've been trying to talk Dalton into ordering Chinese for us for lunch. He won't let me have it," she complained as her husband wound an arm around Trudy's waist.

"Chinese makes her blood pressure too high," Dalton revealed. "I've made us some avocado, grilled chicken wraps."

Trudy mouthed, "*Help me.*"

Ginny burst out laughing. "That sounds amazing to me."

"Good, then you can have mine."

As Dalton, Trudy, and she were about to go into the living room, Gavin interrupted them. "I have a few things I need to take care of."

Ginny wanted to sink to the floor when Gavin gave Dalton a steely-eyed look.

"I'm going to leave Ginny in your care." The way Gavin looked at Dalton left no doubt who he was talking to. "Turn the alarm on once I leave and don't let them go outside. Allerton will do everything possible to get out of the charges brought against him. Anything happens to Ginny, it's his get-out-of-jail-free card until the FBI can gather more evidence."

"What about the beating he gave Agent Collins, or him ordering his men to kill you?" Ginny disputed, not wanting to frighten Trudy when she'd just settled down.

"He can say his men acted on their own," Gavin hypothesized. "I don't want any chances taken with your safety."

"I'll keep the alarm engaged," Dalton assured him. "Go take care of what you need to. I have no plans to go out today."

Ginny wiggled her pinky at Gavin when he hesitated leaving just to give her a threatening glare, reminding her of the promise she had made to him.

"Take your time," she encouraged, waving him off.

Ginny grinned when Dalton and Trudy looked confused at the byplay. Exasperated at Gavin's behavior, she explained, "For some crazy reason, Gavin thinks I have a knack for getting into trouble."

Trudy lifted her eyes to the ceiling. "I wonder why he thinks that?"

"I know, right?" Ginny shrugged lightly. "Gavin can be so uptight sometimes. I think it comes from him being in the military." Ginny gave her a polite version of what she really thought, since she didn't want Trudy to find out Gavin was a big jerk.

Ginny cleared her expression when she felt Dalton studying her a little too closely, afraid he read her thoughts.

"You two go sit down. I'll get lunch ready, then come get you," Dalton told them as he went to the alarm box by the door.

Arm in arm, they went to the living room. Smiling at her sister, Ginny ran her hand over Trudy's baby bump.

"You're lucky I'm too far along to kick your ass."

"Do you really think I would have been able to stay away when you went in labor? Or not being here to babysit? We've missed out on so much, Trudy. I couldn't take losing another minute."

"Something is better than nothing. You could have been killed, Ginny! What if Reaper is right, and Allerton does try to kill you?"

"No one is getting by Gavin," Ginny reassured her.

Trudy reached out to touch her cheek. "Someone already did."

Ginny pressed her hand over Trudy's. "He was busy saving his own life. We don't have to be afraid of Allerton anymore."

"That isn't exactly what Reaper was saying."

"He's just being overprotective."

"Are you really sure?"

"I'm positive."

Trudy searched her face. "What happened while you were there?"

Lowering their hands, Ginny kept Trudy's hand in hers as they sank down onto the couch.

"First things first, what's wrong with your blood pressure?"

"Nothing, my readings are slightly higher than normal. I'm watching it carefully." Trudy made a comical face, but it didn't eliminate Ginny's concern.

"Unfortunately, so are Dalton and Dr. Price. I don't want to talk about me anymore. I want to know why you didn't tell me what you were going to do?" Trudy pressed. "Don't say you were afraid I'd talk you out of doing it. Once you make up your mind, you never go back."

"I would have for you." Ginny brought her hand to Trudy's bump again. "It would have broken me if I couldn't get you to see it was the right thing to do—and I knew you wouldn't. My safety has been your highest priority since I was three. It was time to unlock the chain that bound us together with all the lies we've had to tell to deceive everyone. You wouldn't even tell Dalton that I was your sister, even when he found out your sister hadn't died in the plane crash. You don't have to lie to him anymore, and I don't have to hide who I am either."

"Sex Piston is furious with you."

Sex Piston wasn't the only one. Trudy was just as angry, but she was containing herself.

"I had a small preview from Killyama this morning. I'm dreading seeing her again."

"She's on her way."

"Darn." Ginny wondered how long Gavin would be gone. She wanted to escape before Sex Piston arrived.

"Nuh-uh, you're not going to get out of it that easy. Besides"—Trudy gently touched the bruises on her face—"she might take it easy on you since you're already covered in bruises."

Ginny snorted. "I'm not going to hold out hope for that."

"I wouldn't either." Trudy gave her a smile that didn't reach her eyes. "I want to know how you got those bruises."

Ginny started from the beginning, telling Trudy about the

DNA test and the agreement with the FBI. Trudy didn't interrupt as she talked, even when Dalton came into the living room to tell them lunch was ready. They moved into the dining room where Dalton joined them, and she continued to recount what had taken place.

"I was terrified when I called Soleil, but I just couldn't take it any longer without knowing you were safe. I just did basic pleasantries with her. I didn't tell her anything of substance. I used the excuse to tell her about the baby. The only reaction from her was how nice and keep me updated." Trudy sat back in the dining room chair taking a deep breath before continuing. "I've only called her twice after the plane crash; once when Granny died and the other was when Dalton and I were on our honeymoon. I don't know what I was expecting by telling her and I'd gotten married, though I guess I'd hoped there would be some sort of motherly response. I never heard from Jasper, which I guess isn't a surprise, considering he was never home when we lived there," she said on a sigh. "You know, I've had that number since our last Christmas with Granny, but since never hearing from them I couldn't bring myself to maintain a relationship they clearly never wanted."

Ginny recognized the emotional turmoil Trudy was feeling. Trudy's reaction was compounded by her pregnancy and wanting a maternal bond as this new phase of her life began. Trudy was thirteen years old when they left Clindale, so her memories of their mother were greater and the cut deeper by Soleil's disregard of them.

"She was nothing like what I remember her being. There was no connection between us emotionally or physically. When I was around her, I could see she didn't want me there and wanted me gone."

"Do you think it was because Soleil was afraid you would tell Allerton that Dad was the one who planned our escape?"

Trudy was as puzzled as she was by their mother's behavior.

"I've always assumed Soleil was aware that Dad organized my disappearance. What if she doesn't know it was him?"

"When they came in for our grandmother's funeral," Trudy added, "she was just as cold and standoffish as you are describing, and Allerton wasn't there."

"How did Jasper act?" Ginny delicately probed. She needed to let her sister know that the FBI and Gavin believed Allerton had their father killed. Taking into account Dalton's concern for Trudy's blood pressure, she decided to wait until after the baby was born to share that information. They didn't have definite proof, so there was no need to upset Trudy until they found out the truth.

"Sad," Trudy said, and then her eyes widened. "Angry, now that I think about it. Looking back, I assumed his anger was directed toward me. I've never understood why they cut off all ties with me after the plane crash, especially since Dad made the arrangements to save us. During Granny's funeral, I assumed they were angry with me. What if it wasn't that? What if they were angry at each other?" T.A. pressed her fingertips to her forehead, as if she had a headache. "What if she still doesn't know Dad was the mastermind behind our escape and she'd blamed me for your death? That could certainly be why she'd be angry with me, and maybe Jasper was acting in order to keep protecting the secret?"

Seeing Dalton's body tensing, Ginny abruptly switched the conversation to a happier topic. "Are you going to keep me in suspense, or do I have to ask Dalton?" Ginny teased.

Trudy dropped her hand back to the table. "About what?"

"You told Gavin I would be the first one to find out if you're having a boy or a girl?"

Smiling, Trudy got up from the table to take her hand. "You coming?" she asked Dalton.

Dalton rose and gave her a kiss. "You two go ahead. I'll do the dishes and load the dishwasher."

Ginny wanted to reach out and hug Dalton for being so kind to her sister. In the past, Trudy's boyfriends wouldn't spring for a box of popcorn, much less make her lunch or do the dishes for her.

"You've got a winner this time," Ginny told her sister.

"Not only did I get a winner, but I hit the jackpot," Trudy gushed, starting to get teary-eyed as they climbed the steps.

Trudy wiped them away. "Ignore them. My hormones are all over the place. I can cry at the drop of a hat, then threaten to burn the house down if Dalton doesn't go out to get me my favorite ice cream or order me a pizza. I quit asking for the pizza when he wouldn't order me one and had come up with a better idea."

"What did he do?"

Trudy went to open a door next to the master suite, which was wide open. "Dalton fucking made me a pizza with vegetarian cheese and cauliflower crust instead."

"He didn't!" Ginny giggled. "What did you do?"

"I ate it. I couldn't hurt his feeling. Last time I asked for pizza, though."

They were laughing when Trudy opened the door and let her go in first.

Misty-eyed, Ginny turned back to her sister. "You're having a boy."

Trudy walked farther into the room to open the closet and show her the tiny outfits. Ginny was admiring the crib when the sound of a horn blared from outside. Both women went to the window to see Sex Piston and Killyama getting out of the car and Fat Louise getting out from the driver's side. Ginny could hear Sex Piston and Killy's loud yells at Fat Louise for sounding the horn.

Her sweet friend was giving her a head start so she could hide.

Ginny didn't use the opportunity, seeing what Sex Piston was carrying. She put her hands on her hips as she gave Trudy a censoring stare. "You asked Sex Piston to bring you a pizza?"

"Mind ya business, bitch." Trudy gave her an unrepentant stare back. Clearly, pizza deprivation had made her sister a tad cranky. "Dalton's going to be so busy protecting you from Sex Piston that he won't even notice I'm eating a slice … or two."

CHAPTER THIRTY-SIX

Reaper parallel parked in front of the jewelry store. He worried he would have to make the thirty-minute drive to Jamestown, but when he texted Knox to ask if the West's jewelry store was still open, Knox had texted back that it was.

The store was quiet without a single customer. A woman came out of the glass office, seeing him at the ring display case. "May I help you?"

Gavin recognized her; she was the same salesperson who had waited on him the last time he'd been in the store. As she drew closer, her polite veneer changed to one of eagerness when she recognized him. "Mr. James, what can I do you for you today?"

"I want to buy a wedding ring set for my wife."

"Congratulations!" Charline gushed. "Have you decided on the cut and style?" She hovered her hand over a tray of diamond rings in the glass case.

"I'm not particular about either. It's the stone that's most important to me. I want a black diamond."

The saleswoman removed her hand from the case,

moving to another long glass case. Taking out a velvet-lined tray, she placed it on the counter.

Reaper stared down at the beautiful rings. However, none of them struck him as being the one he wanted for Ginny.

"Will any of these do?" she asked politely.

"No. I don't see any that would suit her." Damn, he wanted to get the ring today.

Swearing to himself, he kept staring at the rings for a long minute, coming to the conclusion he would have to drive to Jamestown to find the one he wanted.

"Sorry to take your time. Thanks for your—"

"We could look on the computer to see the other rings we have available. If you find one you're interested in, we can have it expressed shipped, and it could be here by tomorrow afternoon. The ring would have to be paid for first, so the timing will depend on your credit score. Shall I bring the computer over and show you the different options?"

"Yes, thank you."

As he clicked through the pages of rings, Reaper still didn't see anything close to what he was searching for.

"Find anything?" the saleswoman asked helpfully.

Giving Charline the tablet back, Reaper shook his head. "Not even close. Thank you, anyway."

Seeing a hefty commission about to walk out the door, the saleswoman made another suggestion. "The new owner lives in Lexington. Ms. Cassidy just returned from a buying trip from London. I could ask her if she has a black diamond that hasn't been entered into our website yet, or if she's seen anything she could procure on your behalf. Would you like me to call?"

"Yes."

Stepping to the side of the counter, Reaper texted Dalton that he was taking longer than expected. When Dalton's text came back that they were still eating lunch, he relaxed. He didn't like leaving Ginny alone. The only reason Reaper left Ginny with T.A. and Dalton was that the alarm was set, and the security was monitored by The Last Riders. Viper had installed the system when Winter's aunt had lived there and Winter was often visiting.

Seeing the saleswoman talking on the phone, Reaper texted Shade.

Who's working in the security room?

Shade texted back before he put his phone back in his pocket.

Nickel.

Reaper, shot off another text.

Ginny's at T.A.'s house. I want either you or Rider working security until I get there.

Will do. On my way.

"Mr. James," the saleswoman signaled him.

Reaper pocketed his phone as he moved back to the counter.

"Ms. Cassidy has one black diamond wedding set that hasn't been entered into our database. She's sending me a picture. Give me a moment, and I'll get my personal phone."

The woman went to her office, coming back with her phone. Setting it on the counter, she had already clicked the text, showing the ring.

His breath hitched in his chest. That was Ginny's ring.

"Ms. Cassidy procured it in London on her buying trip. She had intended to offer it a client of hers who collects unique jewelry. The diamond is ten carats, set in titanium. The smaller diamonds surrounding the larger stone are one carat. The stones in the enhancers are—"

"I'll take it. Have her send it."

The saleswoman's phone wobbled in her hand when she picked it up. "There *could* be a slight problem with the sale."

"What's the problem?"

"This ring only comes in one size. As the band is titanium, it cannot be cut down to size."

Reaper pulled a ring off his pinky and handed it to the saleswoman. "What size is this ring?"

Reaching to the side, she picked up a metal sizer. The beaming smile she gave him as she handed the ring back eased his worry. "Size seven. The ring will fit. I'll just go to my office and get an application for credit—"

"I don't need credit." Reaper took out his wallet and pulled out his bank card. "I can pay cash. Make sure you add the expedited shipping so it will be here tomorrow."

The woman looked like she was going to cry with happiness as she took the debit card from him. "Yes, sir. I'll inform Ms. Cassidy that the purchase has been made and have her ship it out immediately."

As he waited, Reaper checked in with Shade to make sure everything was cool with Ginny. He had just received the thumbs-up when the saleswoman returned to the counter. Signing the receipt, he put his card back into his wallet.

"Thank you. If you give me your number, I'll call you when the ring arrives."

"I'll be in town tomorrow. I'll just stop in," he said, refusing to give his number.

"Very well. I'll look forward to seeing you then." Smilingly, she came out from behind the counter to walk him to the door. "Thank you. Your wife is going to be ecstatic with your choice."

Reaper rudely went out the door, ignoring her spiel, trying to hurry back to Ginny when three black Escalades sped past on the street. The dark tint made it impossible to see inside, but that wasn't what drew his attention—it was how fast they were traveling on the main street of the tiny town.

"Wow," the saleswoman said. "I'm surprised Greer hasn't caught them."

Striding out to the sidewalk, Reaper noted their direction. When he saw the brake lights flashing as they turned the corner, Reaper was already moving to Viper's SUV.

"Fuck me." Since he'd been in the store, there were new cars parked in front and back, so close to his vehicle that there was no way to get out unless he used Viper's car as a battering ram.

Not wanting to lose precious minutes—if his bumpers became hung up on the other cars—he took off at a run. Taking out his phone, he called Knox. "Get to Dalton's house," Reaper ordered.

"I can't. I'm ten minutes away. My deputy is missing—"

"Call Shade," Reaper cut him off. "Tell him to send everyone to Dalton's house. Now!"

Kicking his feet faster, Reaper shoved his phone in his pocket. Running across the street, he dodged around Mick as he was putting a sign in the diner's window. Straining his body to move faster, Reaper reached to his back, taking out his gun.

"Fuck," he swore when an older woman came out onto the sidewalk with two leashed yapping dogs. Unless he slowed, he was going to mow the old woman down.

Spotting him, the woman froze like a deer caught in headlights.

Veering to the left, Reaper strained to give a burst of speed to jump over the two dogs, nearly busting a nut when one of the dogs rose up on its hind legs to snap at him. Landing on the concrete, Reaper sprinted forward, coming to the end of the street. Veering left, he took off at a mad dash toward Dalton and T.A.'s house.

Reaper was running so fast that he didn't think he could run any faster—until he heard a series of pops fill the air.

"Shit." Crossing the street, he put himself on the same side as Dalton's house. Jumping over a low hedge, he ran across one lawn, then had to take another leap over another hedge before he was at the house next-door to Dalton's.

Taking cover behind a tree, Reaper fired off a shot at a man standing behind the passenger door of one of the Escalades parked behind Sex Piston's car.

Sex Piston, Killyama, and Fat Louise were hunkered down in front of Sex Piston's car in front of the garage. Killyama had a gun and was returning fire at the two Escalades that had parked catty-corner, providing a shield to the men who were shooting at the women.

Satisfied the fucker who he shot was down for the count, Reaper took out his phone to call Dalton.

Hearing the click of the phone being answered, Reaper didn't time to listen to the greeting. "Open your garage enough to let the women slide under. I'll provide cover."

Seeing an opportunity to take out another fucker who had raised his head over the engine block, Reaper made the shot as the garage door started raising high enough for the women to slip through.

"Go!" Reaper yelled.

Fat Louise went first, with Sex Piston going under after her.

Reaper had to contain himself from shouting at Sex Piston when she crawled back out to reach for the pizza box that was laying on the driveway before slipping back under the garage door.

Killyama made no move to follow the other two women.

He was ready to lose his shit. The only thing calming his impeding tirade was seeing Drake and King take positions behind the house across the street.

"Killyama, go!" Reaper shot again, taking down one of the shooters from the second Escalade.

"You go!" she yelled back. "I'm not—"

Reaper jerked his head back behind the tree when he saw a gun pointed in his direction from behind the Escalade in the driveway.

"Get your ass in the garage, or I'm coming over there and throwing your ass in there!" he roared.

King and Drake provided a volley of bullets, giving Killyama time to escape, which she refused to take.

Sticking his head out long enough to get a visual, he saw one of the men break cover to get away from where King was firing. Reaper nabbed him as soon as he came out from behind the vehicle.

Looking back at the house, he saw Dalton slide under the garage door with a gun in his hand. From his angry expression, he was telling Killyama the same thing he had.

Finally, Killyama angrily slid under the garage door as Dalton and his eyes met. Then Reaper heard the garage door going down.

Dalton lifted four fingers, then pointed to his side, indicting the number of men he couldn't see. He lifted his hand two more times, indicating to Gavin there was a total of twelve men.

The roar of motorcycles and sirens coming down the street had the men scattering into neighboring yards. Raising his hand so Viper would sight him behind the tree two houses away, Reaper went back to firing as one of the gunmen tried to make a dash for the tree across the street. Reaper neatly shot him in the back of his head.

Viper, Cash, and Shade formed a sideways line with their bikes with the other Last Riders following suit behind them, preventing the Escalades from leaving—unless they plowed down fifteen bikes. Reaper could hear Viper issuing commands from where he stood behind the tree.

"Nuts to Bolts behind the Dodge," Viper ordered.

The Last Riders left their bikes to sprint toward a Dodge minivan. In groups of three, the men crouched together, with Cash and Viper standing on opposite sides near the taillights.

"Train, go!" Viper sent off a volley of bullets.

Train and two of the men on his line took off running toward Dalton's house. The three men who crouched behind Train's line moved forward, as did the men behind them, all in unison. When Train's foot hit the doorstep, the door opened, giving them entry into the house.

Reaper steadied his hand, firing as he ran to Sex Piston's car to hunker down next to Dalton. He no longer had to keep his focus on the house with Train, Moon, and Rider inside with the women.

"Puck, get ready!" Viper yelled right before Knox drove the sheriff's Bronco onto the sidewalk on the other side of the Dodge.

"Puck, go." Viper sent another volley of bullets to cover Puck, Jesus, and Razer. Staying behind the Bronco, they were able to fire at the remaining gunmen using the Escalade as cover.

Reaper saw two of the perps taking off toward Dalton's neighbor. Both of them started firing at will.

"Fuck." Swearing, Reaper saw the two men run inside the house where earlier he'd seen a woman getting her mail.

"Cover me," Reaper told Dalton as he rose from the front of the car, taking off toward the side yard. Keeping low, Reaper went to the window at the side of the house. He raised his head slightly and saw the woman and a man standing in the dining room. Lowering his head, he made his way to the back door, finding it locked. "Why can't just one fucking time something be fucking easy?"

Gauging the door, Reaper took a step back just as he saw Dalton come around the corner.

Using his booted foot, Reaper kicked at the weakest part

of the door, and it flew open. When it did, Reaper launch himself inside, taking in the room at a glance. Aiming his gun at the perp, who came running into the room, he hit him in the abdomen just before Reaper landed on his stomach. At the same time, the perp fell to the floor, spilling blood onto the tiles.

He was still getting his knees under him when the second perp came running in. Reaper managed to hit him in the throat.

He was getting to his feet when Dalton came through the broken door.

"I could have saved myself the trouble," Dalton said, lowering his gun at seeing the prone bodies on the ground.

"How many live here?" Reaper asked, moving toward an open doorway.

"An older couple, man and woman."

Entering the room that he had seen from the outside, Reaper didn't see the older couple.

Dalton followed him, both men searching for the couple to make sure they were all right. Rounding the corner, Reaper entered a hallway. Gunshots outside had him wanting to hurry so he could help the brothers.

Seeing a partially opened door down the hallway, Reaper went to the side of the door, using the wall to protect his body; he turned his head slightly to peer inside the room. "You're safe! I'm here with your neighbor, Dalton," Reaper called out.

Hearing his voice, they turned from the window to him, the curtains fluttering, revealing the man was holding a gun.

Reaper held up two fingers behind his back to keep Dalton from moving closer. He had only a moment to process that the elderly couple weren't frightened, and they hadn't only just been looking outside—the man had been firing a gun.

Reaper moved his finger to the trigger. "Damn. I have to give it to the fucker. Allerton is good. He's been having you watch T.A. since she moved in, hasn't he?" he yelled out to the couple.

The woman gave a quick glance to her partner, her face growing pinched, as if cautioning him to remain silent.

Staring at them closer, Reaper realized they were much younger than he originally assumed. He'd taken a wild guess that they were Allerton's people, and when neither of them said anything, he figured they knew who he was, proving him right.

"I thought you were fucking nosy. Damn good fucking job. You're how those fuckers outside knew Ginny was here."

The man glanced wildly at the woman. When he saw him waver his weapon, Reaper figured out what he was silently telling her.

"Ah … you're out of bullets? That's what you trying to tell her?" Reaper gave him a grim smile. "Then I suggest you place the weapon down and take off. Bank the money you earned today. At least you'll live to see another day."

Reaper was cutting it close with his own ammo. He was just better at hiding it than the man inside the bedroom. The problem was that he couldn't tell if the woman had a gun or not with the way she stood partially behind the curtain.

"Put your weapons down," Reaper ordered.

"You first. I have bullets; you're the one out of bullets." The fucker finally grew a set of balls, even though, Reaper knew he was lying.

"I have a couple left; one for each of you." With his head cocked around the door jam, Reaper nodded at the man while Dalton remained behind him out of sight. "Put it down and step away. Take my advice. It's the only chance you have."

A gust of wind had the curtain billowing out, exposing

the weapon in the woman's hand; she had it pointed directly at him.

Reaper froze. His mind went back to the lifeless eyes that he still saw in his nightmares. Then his mind flashed back to the day Rider's wife had denoted the bomb when they'd been overseas. Rider hadn't been able to extinguish his wife's life with her carrying his unborn child.

The split-second he hesitated would have cost him his life … if Dalton hadn't jerked the door wide open and, in one smooth move, he shot the woman in the heart, then sent her partner to hell with her. A gush of blood coming the man's chest showed Dalton had placed his bullet in the same spot as the woman's.

Dalton gave him a hard pat on his shoulder to shake him out of the daze he'd fallen into. "They were shit for neighbors. I'm going to cut down that tree in the backyard before this house gets sold again. I'm fucking sick of having to skim the leaves from my pool."

"I couldn't kill her … You saved my life."

"Brother, you just fucking saved my wife, my child, her sister, and her best friends, who are sisters to her and me. I wouldn't have gone down without a fight, but I didn't have enough firepower to take them all down. And just so you fucking know, if I had been here first, I'd be dead now. I would've assumed they were protecting themselves from the gunmen outside. You're the one who figured out they were Allerton's, providing him information on Trudy."

When another burst of gunfire sounded from outside, Reaper strode across the room to pick up the woman's weapon, checking it for ammo.

Dalton raked his eyes over his face. "You good?"

"Yeah, I am." Reaper gave him a nod before striding down the hallway to make his way back through the house and out the back door.

Edging to the corner of the building, Reaper looked toward the front yard, no longer hearing any gunfire.

Viper and Knox had the men lined up on Dalton's yard, on their knees with their hands on their heads. The rest of the brothers were guarding them as Knox patted them down one at time then zip-tied their hands.

"We're good to go," Reaper told Dalton.

Viper pressed two fingers to his lip to give a shrill whistle before he walked over to them as they approached. "We were starting to get worried. Where did you disappear to?"

"Dalton's neighbors. They were the ones responsible for this shit show," Reaper explained.

"Fuck. How many inside?"

"Four. Two in the kitchen, two in the bedroom."

"They need an ambulance?"

"No, you can call the coroner."

"He's already on his way. Three dead across the street, four dead behind the Escalades."

Knox came over as Viper talked. "None of them are admitting to being Allerton's hired hitmen." Running a hand over his bald head, Knox seemed as if he were angry enough to bite a bullet.

"How's your deputy?"

"In ICU. He's only been on the force for a year. Usually, Greer was the one working the speed trap."

"Greer wasn't working today?" Reaper was glad it wasn't Greer in ICU. Then he thought better of it, realizing Greer kept enough green on him when he was on duty to take down a tank.

"I fired him the day I got back to town," Knox answered, as if he had swallowed a bullet.

"He posted two deputies on both ends of the bridge. He was keeping track of anyone coming into town and making them isolate in the hotel for a week. I had over twenty people threatening to sue the town. But, if I left the security posts on the bridge like Greer set up, these assholes wouldn't have made it into town."

"The town would have been bankrupt, too." Viper tried to make Knox feel better about his decision.

"That wasn't the main reason I fired him. He was fired because he hooked a trailer to his truck and drove around town, knocking on doors and asking people if they'd enrolled in the study. And if they told him they weren't, he asked if they wanted to buy the pig on the trailer."

Reaper felt better when Dalton and Viper appeared as confused as he was.

"Where'd Greer get the pig?" Viper broke down and asked.

"From his nephew, Logan. Holly bought it for Logan's birthday two years ago. It was supposed to be a miniature pig."

Reaper pressed his lips together to keep from laughing. "I take it that it wasn't."

"The thing's as big as a horse and fatter."

"I'm confused," Dalton interjected. "Why would people want to buy the pig if they didn't get vaccinated? What does one have to do with the other?"

Reaper had to turn his head away, unable to see it was a sore point with Knox.

"He didn't want to sell the whole pig, just the heart."

He wasn't the only one who was having trouble holding back his laughter.

"Go ahead and laugh. The dispatcher was threatening to quit if she got any more calls concerning Greer."

"Sorry, brother," Reaper managed to get out. "I can't say anything. I owe him a favor."

"You know the worst part?"

"It gets worse?"

Knox nodded at Viper's question. "Look at the Escalade over there."

The three men looked to where Knox was pointing, seeing Greer going through one of the Escalades. None of the men had to ask why Knox was looking so green at the gills when Greer got out of the vehicle, wearing his deputy uniform.

"I rehired the son of bitch."

CHAPTER THIRTY-SEVEN

"You're going to make yourself sick," Ginny told her sister, taking another slice for herself.

"Three pieces won't hurt me." Content, Trudy rubbed her belly with one hand while taking another bite of her pizza. "They were small."

Sex Piston moved the pizza box toward her, taking a slice for herself and leaving the last piece for Fat Louise. Killyama came back from the kitchen, took the slice away, and put it back in the box.

Using the pizza cutter she found after Trudy's vague directions about which drawer it was in, Killyama cut it into two, giving the smaller piece to Fat Louise.

Trudy moved the empty chair next to her to put her feet up. "Did you buy the pot stickers I wanted?"

"Yes." Sex Piston nudged her chair to the side to put her feet next to Trudy's. "They're in the back seat. You want Killyama to go get them for you?"

Trudy cocked her head to the side, as if listening. "You hear any more gunshots?"

Ginny shook her head. "Not in the last five minutes."

"Killy …." Trudy looked pitifully at her friend.

"Bitch, you want those pot stickers, go get them yourself. Train is by the door. I'm not going near him until he calms his ass down."

"You should have come in when the garage door opened," Ginny chimed in, risking Killyama's displeasure when Trudy pouted at the set down.

"If she wants them so bad, you go get them. T.A. isn't the only one knocked up."

Ginny jumped out her chair to hug Killyama. "Congratulations. I'm going to have a gigantic baby shower for both of you! I'll go get the pot stickers."

Killyama caught her by the end of her shirt. "Sit your ass down. Train!"

Ginny sat down and pretended she didn't know anyone at the table, avoiding looking at Train as Killyama ordered him to get the pot stickers out of the car.

Train stood over his wife, giving her a glare that had Ginny wanting to sneak out of the room. Unfazed, Killyama gave him one of her own. The stand-off broke when they heard two shots from outside.

"It can wait," Killyama backed down.

Train returned to the other room.

"Bitch, you took your life in your hands with that one," Sex Piston said, stretching her neck to make sure Train was out of earshot.

"He'll get over it." Her friend didn't sound as confident as she usually did.

Ginny didn't blame her. She had received her own share of the shaming stare from Gavin.

"You could give him those new leather gloves you bought him for his birthday," Ginny suggested.

"Won't work. He's got his mad on. Only thing going to get me out of the doghouse is …"

Ginny's interest piqued when Killy and the other women at the table shared the same knowledgeable wry smile.

"To be nice."

Her mouth drooped in disappointment.

Trudy picked up on her thwarted expectations. "What did you think Killy was going to say?"

"I don't know." Ginny shrugged as she closed the empty box. "Something good."

All the women stared at her in confusion.

Ginny propped her chin on her hand. "You know ..." Ginny lowered her voice, embarrassed, not wanting any of the men in the house to hear. "Like a special way to give a"— Ginny's voice dipped lower— "a blowjob, or something like that."

"Is there a special way to give a blowjob?" Killyama looked at Sex Piston as if she was the authority on the matter.

Fat Louise and Trudy seemed equally interested.

Sex Piston leaned forward as if she was about to reveal her own personal secret. Instead, she snatched the bag of Skittles laying in the middle of the table.

"The real question is: If you're so interested, why don't you ask your men? They know what they like better than I would. Each man is different; some like to be played and teased, others just want you to open your mouth and say *ahh*. Those are the fuckers you want to watch out for."

"Why are those the ones we need to watch out for?" Ginny asked as she started gathering the candy wrappers from the candy they'd been gorging on from Trudy's hidden stash.

"Those fuckers are the ones who just lay on their backs and stick their tongues out and say *ride me*."

Peeling the Skittles bag open, Ginny dismally thought

neither sounded bad to her. Gavin was as adventuresome in bed as Mr. Rogers.

Raising her head, Ginny found herself under the scrutiny of the women at the table.

"What?" *Had she missed something?*

"Bitch, did you just compare Reaper to Mr. Rogers?" Sex Piston looked at the other women to make sure she wasn't the only one who heard the comparison.

"No ..." Ginny swiftly tried to backtrack her unintentional slipup she was sure she had only said in her head.

"Maybe ... I can't be sure," Fat Louise tried to give her a break.

"I am." Killyama gave her a considering look. "Whatcha doing wrong?"

Ginny brought her hand to her chest. "*Me?* Why's it my fault?"

"Girl, maybe you aren't giving him ... encouragement for him to get his freak on."

From Killyama's and the other women's expressions, they were thinking the same.

Killyama snapped her fingers as if a brilliant idea had come to her. "You need Crazy Bitch. She's bringing another pizza when she closes the shop. That bitch has been with so many men she'll be able to tell you how to get Reaper's motor running."

Fat Louise raised a wondering eyebrow. "If Crazy Bitch was so good, how come she got dumped so much before Calder?"

"Didn't mean she couldn't get their motors running," Trudy said, taking up for the woman who was going to sneak her another pizza.

"Gavin doesn't have a problem with his motor." Ginny didn't want them thinking there was something wrong with Gavin's machine.

"Ah ... then it's lack of pressure." Fat Louise sympathetically gave her the last of her M&M's. "There's a pill for that. Dalton has some. Get T.A. to sneak you some."

Trudy put her feet back down onto the floor. "Those are vitamins!"

The women stared at her unbelievingly.

"I believe you." Loyal to a fault, Ginny reassured her sister.

"You would," Sex Piston rejoined. "Reaper's got the same problem. Not being able to satisfy your man must run in the family."

"Count yourself lucky. If I wasn't knocked up, I would kick your ass. I satisfy Dalton so much that he has to drink a gallon of juice to keep up with me."

Sex Piston folded her arms over her chest. "I rest my case."

"Remember who brought you the pizza ...," Ginny reminded her sister when Trudy started to get up. "And you really shouldn't be committing acts of aggression when you're pregnant."

None of the women seemed to agree with her. Instead, they discussed when and where to have Trudy's baby shower.

"We can have it at the church," Ginny suggested.

"Fuck nah, that won't be any fun," Sex Piston put in her two cents.

Trudy made her feelings known. "Same reason I don't want to have it here. Dalton will throw out anything good to eat."

Killyama hit the table, laughing. "Be careful he don't throw you out."

Trudy gave her a killing glare.

Ginny gave her the last few M&M's, thinking that was what she was mad at.

"Next time, don't mention sex in front of these bitches."

"Sorry," Ginny apologized, pulling the candy back, but Trudy snatched it before she could.

"I haven't heard any shots in a while. You think it's cool for Fat Louise to go out and get the pot stickers?" Tilting the candy in her hand, Trudy and the rest of the women focused on Fat Louise.

"I'll go get the pot stickers." Feeling sorry for Fat Louise, Ginny went to where Train was standing at the door and gave him a smile.

"Is it okay to go out?"

"The pot stickers?"

"There are two pregnant women in there," Ginny pleaded. "Don't ask me to go back in there without them."

"Who else is pregnant? Killyama didn't mention Fat Louise or Sex Piston expecting." Train gave her a smile, and Ginny immediately understood why Killyama had fallen in love with him. "You're pregnant?"

"No." Confused as to why Train didn't say his wife's name, she said it for him. "Killy is."

Train's face drained of color. "It's clear, wait here and I'll take you." Instead of opening the door, he hurried to the dining room.

Confused at his strange behavior, Ginny assumed she'd misheard him and went outside without waiting for him, not wanting to keep Trudy waiting. Ginny walked to Sex Piston's car, seeing Viper, Dalton, and Knox talking at the side of the house. There were two coroner vans parked in the middle of the streets, and two men were placing a sheet on a body, and another two men were wheeling another sheet-covered body.

Opening the back door with her attention on the sheet-covered bodies being wheeled to the coroner's van, Ginny started to reach inside Sex Piston's back seat, only to find her hand caught and twisted behind her back as the man hiding in the back seat climbed out and jerked her to him as he raised his gun to her head.

Shocked at finding herself in the precarious situation, Ginny didn't emit a sound, terrified the man holding her would start shooting at the four men within a few feet of them.

"Give me the fucking keys."

The whisper in her ear had Ginny centering her focus on him.

"I don't have them."

A rush of wind had the tendrils of her hair stirring. She stared at Gavin as he pivoted on his heel, sighting her beside the car.

Viper, Dalton, and Knox turned at Gavin's sudden movement, registering what was going on and edged to different sides of the car, coming toward her.

"Don't fucking move, or I'll blow her fucking brains out!" the gunman behind her shouted, seeing what they were trying to do.

"Dude, let her go, and you can get in the car and leave. None of us will stop you." Gavin raised his hands in the air as he squatted, placing his guns on the grass. "You can drive out of here, or you can be carried out on a stretcher if you hurt her."

"Make them drop their guns and let the others go, and I'll think about it."

Ginny felt the gunman gaining confidence as he pressed the gun harder to her temple. "Careful," Ginny warned. "You don't want to hurt your only way out of here."

"Bitch, shut the fuck up."

Ginny cringed when the gunman pressed his cheek against hers.

"Hurry the fuck up. I don't have all fucking day. Make them—"

A sudden explosion had Ginny screaming, thinking the gunman had shot her since the sound was so close to her.

Falling backward with her arm still twisted behind her back, her eyes wildly went to Gavin, wanting to see him one more time before she died. The excruciating pain in her arm had her releasing another scream as she found herself laying on top of the gunman who had pulled her down with him.

"I've got you, Ginny. Stop screaming."

Ginny felt herself being lifted into Gavin's arms before he placed her on the hood of the car. She took shuddering breaths, moving her chest away from Gavin's.

Sitting on the car, Ginny reached for her arm, nearly blacking out from the pain. "My arm ..."

"Train!" Gavin bellowed.

"Move, Reaper. Let me see her."

Gavin moved to the side as he gently placed his hands under hers as she cupped her arm.

Greer slid in to take Gavin's spot, reaching out to touch her.

"No. Don't touch me!" Ginny turned more toward Gavin, blocking Greer from touching her. His haggard features had her shaking her head at him. "I'm okay. It doesn't hurt."

"Then why were you yelling your head off?" Greer pointed out.

"Because I thought I was dead. What happened?" Ginny looked at the group of men who had gathered around her.

"I shot the motherfucker," Greer said complacently. "I was sitting in the Escalade behind him. Blew the windshield out of my new vehicle. Guess I'll be taking one of the others."

"I'm confiscating those vehicles for the sheriff's office." Knox's face went bloodred as he disputed Greer's claim.

"Bullshit. I give it two days before they're parked in front of The Last Riders." Leaning against the car, Greer placed his hand on the hood, then gradually started inching toward her as he talked. "You can have two, but one is mine for me doing my civic duty." Greer snorted.

"Stop it, Greer," Ginny demanded, seeing what he was trying to do and scooting away from him. "Gavin can drive me to the hospital." Ginny reached out to place a fingertip onto his cheek. "You can't help yourself, can you? That's why you've been so fanatical about getting everyone in town vaccinated, because you didn't trust yourself not to break and then heal them if any one of them got sick." Ginny's lips trembled when Greer let his guard slip and she was given a rare insight of the man within. "How many have you already healed?"

Greer turned his head away to tug his loose britches up. "I ain't—"

"Greer, don't lie," Ginny said softly. "You're skin and bones, and your hair is getting greyer every time I see you."

"Holly ain't the best cook in the county—"

"I'm not buyin' it." Ginny shook her head at him. "Thank you for trying. You took my pain yesterday. Let Train and Dr. Price fix me today. Give yourself a break. The rate I'm going, I'll probably need you tomorrow."

"Let me see her," Train said from behind Greer.

Greer didn't immediately step away. "You sure?"

"I'm sure." Ginny leaned forward to place a light kiss on Greer's cheek. "Holly's a lucky woman."

Greer gave a shit-eating grin. "I tell her that all the time. Going to invite you to dinner so you can tell her yourself. She don't believe me when I tell her."

Ginny gave Greer a misty smile. "I think she does, Greer. I really thinks she does."

CHAPTER THIRTY-EIGHT

Train set his medic bag on the hood when Greer moved away. "Sorry, brother." Train carefully began examining her arm. "I got distracted, and she slipped out of the house."

"What was so damn important that you came outside?" Gavin grumbled by her side.

Sheer willpower kept Ginny from flinching away when Train slowly tried to straighten her arm. "I was getting Trudy her pot stickers—"

At a curse behind Train, Ginny poked her head around him to see Dalton.

"I mean, I was getting them for Sex Piston."

"Where are they?" Dalton exploded.

Ginny jumped. Trudy had never mentioned Dalton had anger issues. "In the back seat."

Gavin sent him a scorching glare. "Don't yell at her."

Dalton lowered his voice to a reasonable tone. "I meant the girls."

"In the dining room."

Dalton stalked off.

"Don't forget to take the pot stickers," she reminded him.

Both Train and Gavin placed themselves in front of Ginny.

Ginny rolled her eyes at them, stretching her neck so she could look between the two men to make sure Dalton retrieved the pot stickers.

The slam of the car door answered the question for her.

"Dalton," Ginny called out when she saw him heading toward the house with the large carton of Chinese takeout. "At least let her have a couple before you throw them out."

"Be quiet," Gavin hissed.

Ginny was about to take exception to Gavin's rudeness when Viper and Knox placed themselves beside Train and Gavin. From their fierce expressions aimed at Dalton, Ginny had to think twice about saying anything more to her brother-in-law.

The slam of the front door had the men around her relaxing.

"I'm going to call Zoey and get her to call Dalton. Trudy didn't tell me Dalton had such a bad temper."

Gavin gave her a narrowed-eyed stare that had her scooting away from him.

"Train, what distracted you that Ginny was able to slip out?"

"She told me that Killy is pregnant."

Ginny hastily ducked her head, trying to divert Gavin's attention. "How's my arm?"

"Seems to be a strain." Train opened his bag and took out a box. Pulling out a sling, he put it on her. "You need an X-ray to make sure."

"Congratulations, brother." Viper and Knox both slapped Train when he was done adjusting the sling.

"Thanks." Train grinned. "I was giving Killy hell for not being the first one in the garage when the shots went off. Sorry, brother, I fucked up."

While Gavin didn't give Train good wishes on the pregnancy, he did say, "Not your fault. I should have given you and the others the heads-up that Ginny has a tendency to get her ass in trouble."

Ginny gaped at him. "You're blaming this on *me*?"

"You wouldn't have been hurt if you stayed inside the house. I told you to stay in there before I left the house. You promised me you would stay out of trouble for a month. I asked for two days and got less than two hours." He turned to the other man. "She good to go, Train?"

"Yes."

Gavin lifted her into his arms as Train took his bag and went back into the house.

Walking by Greer, Gavin stopped. "Forget the Escalade. Go to the car dealership and pick out any vehicle you want."

"Can't do that. I was just doing my duty, wasn't I, Knox?" Greer shoved his hands in his back pockets as he rocked back and forth on the heels of his boots.

Knox remained silent.

"Wasn't I?" Greer yelled out as if Knox was ten feet away instead of a couple inches.

Knox stomped over to Greer. "Ginny's damn lucky you didn't kill her. The gun could have gone off when you shot him."

"No, it couldn't have. He was out of bullets." Greer smirked.

"How in the fuck do you know that? He had his back to you; you couldn't see his gun, much less know how many bullets he had left."

"I just knew." Greer shrugged.

Knox was so angry that his eyes nearly bulged out of his eyes. "*You just knew?*"

"Yeah."

Knox walked over to the dead gunman, picked up the gun, opened the chamber, and then clicked it closed. "You can have your job back. And take your pick of the Escalades. I'll write it off as overtime." Knox sounded like he wanted to have a good cry.

Ginny buried her face in Gavin's shoulder to keep from laughing as Gavin moved to carry her toward the sheriff's Bronco.

Ginny raised her head when she realized Gavin wanted to leave. "I need to go in to say good-bye to everyone."

"I'll text Dalton when we get to the hospital. You're not going into that house for a while."

"Why not?"

"It's not safe."

"I don't see why not."

"Then look around."

"They were here to kill me?"

Dalton's lawn had a line of men handcuffed and on their knees. She had counted four bodies being loaded into the coroner vans, as a white sheet was placed on the one on the ground.

"Yes."

"Dalton's never going to let me visit Trudy again, is he?"

"Not in this lifetime."

"Gavin, I can walk." Ginny stopped Gavin when he would have lifted her from Knox's vehicle.

Remaining close, he watched every move she made as she

got out and they walked toward the hospital entrance. "I'll register you in. Go ahead and have a seat."

"I left my purse at Trudy's. You need my insurance information."

"I'll have one of the brothers bring it over. Go sit."

Mumbling to herself about arrogant men, she found two empty seats in the waiting room. There were only a couple of people waiting to be seen.

Gavin carried the clipboard over to her, and Ginny answered the questions as Gavin filled out the paperwork. They were finishing when Knox came in, carrying her purse and another clipboard. Taking a seat next to Gavin, Knox handed Ginny her purse. "I need to get a statement about what happened."

Reaching into her purse for her insurance card, she handed it to Gavin. Jolting down the information, he then carried the clipboard back to the desk before returning.

Gavin wrote out a statement for her, describing what had taken place, when her name was called. As she stood, Gavin started to as well. "Stay and finish your statement. They're not going to let you in the X-ray room," she told him.

"I'll find you when I'm done," he agreed.

"No one is allowed back with the patients," the nurse interjected. "I'll keep you appraised of your wife's status."

Ginny gave Gavin a dirty look for telling the nurse that they were married, before she followed the nurse through a side door.

Escorted into a small curtained-off room with a hospital bed, the nurse nodded toward a hospital gown that was laying on the bedside table. "Go ahead and change into the gown. The doctor will be with you shortly."

"Thank you."

Ginny one-handedly managed to remove her clothes, and

just as she sat on the bed the doctor came through the curtain.

"Mrs. James. I'm Dr. Griffin."

"Ms. Bellamy," Ginny corrected the female doctor coming to her side.

The doctor looked down at her clipboard in confusion. "Excuse me. I must have the wrong room. Let me check—"

"You have the right room but wrong last name," Ginny verified. "My boyfriend filled out my paperwork. I'm afraid he put the cart before the horse. I'm sorry for the confusion."

The attractive doctor maintained her professional behavior, yet Ginny could see curiosity glinting in her eyes. Placing the clipboard on the bedside table, the doctor began examining her arm. "Your chart shows your arm was hurt. How did the injury occur?"

"My arm was twisted behind my back when he fell, and I landed on top of him with my arm under me," Ginny explained.

"Was the one who hurt you the same one who listed your name wrong?" The doctor's tone grew serious. "I can put you in touch with a someone who can help if you're in danger from your partner."

"Gavin would never hurt me. If anything, he's overprotective. If you can recommend someone to help me with that problem, that would be useful."

The doctor's professionalism broke as she laughed.

Ginny had taken an immediate liking to the doctor. She had the same gentle, caring attitude that Willa had. She placed her at Winter's age, yet the woman didn't look like either woman. The doctor was barely over five feet, Ginny guessed, with her brown hair pulled back. The most prominent feature on her face were the large glasses she wore.

"Then who hurt your arm?"

"A car thief." Ginny left out the intent behind the crime. "He was trying to steal a friend's car."

"This happened in Treepoint?"

"A few miles from here."

"First one I've heard about here since I've been here. Nothing goes on here other than the deputy who's made it his life's mission to catch every speeder in town, and one of the nurses told me there is a motorcycle club, but I haven't seen anyone I would consider a biker in the two weeks I've been here. My brother used to ride a motorcycle. I'll have to ask if he still does."

"Oh … they're around." Ginny hid her amusement. "You'll probably run into one of them sooner or later."

The doctor picked up her clipboard. "We'll have to get an X-ray of your arm. I'll come back when I receive the results. Is there any chance you are pregnant?"

"No. I thought it may be possible, but I got my period this morning."

"I'll order a pregnancy test, just to be certain, before you go to X-ray. Many women experience a light period during the early stages of their pregnancies."

"Okay."

"I'll send the nurse in with the test."

"Thanks."

"It was nice meeting you, Ginny. We'll have you on your way soon. Have you made a report to the sheriff's office about your injury and attempted car theft?"

"My boyfriend is making the report to the sheriff in the waiting room."

"Good. I hope the carjacker didn't get away?"

"No, he didn't. The deputy you were talking about took care of him."

"That's good to know. Greer caught him?"

"Yes."

"He's given me three tickets. I'm sad to say I underestimated his ability. I thought he was just being a pain to fill his
quota."

Ginny couldn't let the doctor leave without giving her the
full truth. Treepoint was a small town. It was only a matter of
time before someone told the doctor about him.

"Greer doesn't have quotas to fill. He just enjoys being a
jerk."

CHAPTER THIRTY-NINE

Ginny studied the hand-drawn map in her good hand as she walked along the stakes and strings that Gavin had used to mark where their house would be built. Shamelessly playing the sympathy card a day after having a gun pointed at her head and having her arm sprained, she took full advantage of the men trying to please her.

"Well? Is this how you want it?" Gavin asked.

Ginny lowered the map, biting her lip in indecision. "I'm thinking. Are you happy with the layout?"

"I've been happy with the last three of your plans. That didn't stop you from changing your mind."

"There're too many plans to choose from." She pulled out her phone. "How do you think this one would look?"

Silas, Isaac, and Matthew all groaned when she showed them the next plan she was considering.

Stepping over one of the strings, Gavin gave her brothers a quelling look before taking the phone and studying the plans. "You said you wanted a one story. This plan has two."

Ginny settled her sling more comfortably on her shoulder. "This would give us a larger master bedroom."

"You can have a larger master bedroom with the plan we've already staked out. We won't need four bedrooms, anyway. Three spare bedrooms are more than enough. You have enough family living nearby, and any extra guests can stay with them or at the club."

Ginny took her phone back from Gavin and walked around the area that had been marked off as the four men watched her.

"You could half the size of the laundry room," Silas suggested. "It would be the size of the one in my house, and it would be next to the master bedroom, which would be convenient when you have children."

"I've always wanted a big laundry room, with a folding table that can be used as a craft table," she said wistfully.

"Then I agree with Gavin. Three spare bedrooms should be enough … depending on how many children you're planning on having."

"Two," Gavin said firmly.

Ginny looked at her phone again. She really didn't want a two-story home.

"Ginny … how many children are you wanting to have?"

"Depends on the man I marry. The man I might marry could be so old that he might want two. On the other hand, I might marry a younger man who wants to give me as many as I want," Ginny said unconcernedly, ignoring Gavin's heated expression.

"I want a house that can grow with however many I'm blessed with."

"I can tell you one fucking thing. You won't be blessed with a younger husband," Gavin snarled.

"Then it's a good thing whomever I marry isn't your decision," she said sagely.

"The hell it isn't, since I'm the one you're married to."

"Silas, did you give me away at my wedding?"

Her brother gave Gavin a sympathetic grimace. "No."

Ginny glared at her brothers, daring them to lie. "Isaac, Matthew, were you at my wedding?"

"No," they mumbled.

Ginny scrolled down the list of plans. "I want to keep the big trees, but if we get rid of this big oak"—Ginny placed her hand on the oak tree—"would it give me enough room for another bedroom?"

"Yes," Silas answered, placing a staying hand on Gavin's shoulder when he would have reached for her as she breezed past him to walk toward where the laundry room had been staked off.

Placing her phone in her pocket, she twirled. "I love it! I can hardly wait until it's built!" She stopped twirling. "How long do you think it will take to build?"

"Two to four months, depending on the weather." His eyes latched on to what she was doing with her sling. "Is your arm hurting?"

"No. I wouldn't even know it was sprained if I didn't accidentally try to do something with it. The sling is what is bothering me. The material on my shoulder is cutting into me."

"Let me adjust it and see if it helps." Gavin solicitously began adjusting the length so it sat easier on her shoulder. "When we get back to the club, I'll find something to pad it with."

"Thank you." Ginny put her good arm through Gavin's, then leaned against him and gave him an appreciative smile.

"That twirl make you dizzy?"

"Nope, just appreciating I have a big, strong man to lean on."

Matthew made gagging noises. "I'm out. I have work to do." He stepped over the string to stand next to her. "I'm glad you weren't hurt worse than a sprained arm yesterday."

Ruffling her hair, he smoothed it back down before dropping his hand. "How long did the doctor say until it's healed?"

"Three to eight weeks. The doctor said it was just a mild strain, so she estimated about three to four, but not to pick up anything heavy for over eight weeks."

Matthew closed one eye, pinning her with a suspicious look. "You sure?"

"I am." Ginny straightened off Gavin. "Why?"

"When we were kids and went to bring in firewood, you would only bring in one or two logs, leaving us to haul the majority."

"One of the few perks of having so many strong brothers is getting them to do the heavy lifting."

Matthew gave her a side hug, making sure not to jar her arm. "When I was younger, you told me it was to take out the trash."

Isaac moved closer. "She told me it was to cut bugs."

"All valid reasons." Ginny grinned.

Isaac gave her a half hug before letting her go. "Let us know when you want to get started, and we'll order the lumber and have it ready to go."

"I can handle all of that," Gavin said. "After I leave here, I'm going to order what we'll need. I'll text Silas when the materials will be delivered. I'll also order a metal shed where we can store the lumber and tools."

"What kind of shed?" Matthew's interest piqued. Ginny could tell that Silas and Isaac were just as interested.

"Fairly good size. Why?"

"You need any help picking one out, I can go with you," Matthew offered.

"Me, too," Isaac chimed in.

Ginny rolled her eyes at her brothers' eagerness.

"You've stepped into it now," Ginny warned Gavin. "Sheds are porn candy to my brothers."

Silas shook his head at her. "She's exaggerating." He nudged her out of the way to place himself between Gavin and her. Placing a companionly arm around Gavin, he began edging him away from her as Isaac and Matthew flanked his other sides. "What size are you thinking about getting? Plastic, wood, or metal?"

"Does it matter?"

Ginny knew Gavin was done for at his inquiry.

"For sure." Matthew nodded authoritatively. "The size is important, too. You don't want it too small, or you'll have to buy another one. Size is important."

Yes, it was. Ginny had to concur with that one.

Restless, she moved away, trying to keep her impatient gaze away from Gavin. Was it her imagination, or was he getting better-looking every day? Today, he was wearing worn-out grey jeans that snugly accentuated his body, and the long-sleeved black thermal was as soft as butter. She should know, since she'd been using every opportunity to rub against it since they dressed this morning.

Ginny went around the staked-out area again, imagining the home for years she'd longed for. A home centered with her brothers around her, with a man she loved more than life itself. She wanted to pinch herself she was so happy. With the happiness came fear it could be taken away just as easily. Each time in her life that she had found happiness, it had been callously ripped away. Her hand unconsciously went to her belly, fear rising that she'd be faced with losing her family again, and this time the loss would be unrecoverable.

Ginny turned when she heard footsteps coming, placing her hand in her jacket as she turned to see Gavin.

"Your brothers want to go with me to the store. What time is your appointment with Dr. Price? Should we get the sheds tomorrow?"

"No, you can go today. Trudy has an appointment with

him before mine. Dalton and she are going to pick me up at the club in an hour."

"I planned to take you."

"There's no need for you to take me. Dalton has to wait in the car. No one other than patients are allowed in the office. Afterward, we're going to the diner. I want to introduce Trudy to Marty."

"You're wanting one of his burgers."

Ginny laughed. "I want several of his burgers."

"Keep your phone on you," he ordered.

"Yes, sir," she smarted off.

"Damn, that sounds good."

She raised her chin in the air, moving toward her excited brothers, who weren't hiding their impatience to leave.

"Dream on." Taking his arm, she pretended she needed his help to step off a branch.

"What?" he pretended innocence.

Ginny snorted. She was much better at pretending.

"I'm in a great mood today." Stroking her cheek on his shirt, she raised her eyes to his, wanting to gauge his mood.

"I can see that. Any particular reason?"

"Mmhmm. I love you, I love you, I love you."

"Are you trying to talk me into a bigger shed, like your brothers are?"

As always, Gavin showed no hint of emotion toward her. The only time he exhibited any visual reactions to her was when he was aggravated, especially when she denied the legality of their marriage. Each time she did it upped the level of his irritation and his doubling down that they were legally married.

"Of course," she teased. "Bigger is always better."

Gavin winced. "Is the shed gonna cost me as much as the house?"

"Could be … Silas has his eye on the Tuft Tahoe, and Matthew has his on a kit the size of a manor."

"How about Isaac?"

"He wants the Hansen. It has a garage."

"They make a shed with a garage?"

"Oh yes. Isaac even has the color picked out. Red."

"How much does Isaac's cost?"

"Around twenty thousand. I would go for Silas's. The one he wants is four."

"Thousand?"

Ginny laughed. "Yes, thousand."

"Which one do you want?"

"The one I already bought. Just don't tell my brothers. It'll ruin their day."

Gavin stopped in his tracks. "I was going to pay for it."

"You can pay for the inside when we get the outside done. The lumber and the shed, I've already taken care of. I've been saving for this house since I was a little girl. I didn't know how much lumber to order, so if it goes beyond what I arranged for, let me know and I'll transfer more money."

"I'll take care of it if the price exceeds what you paid."

"Perhaps I should go." Ginny stubbornly raised her chin again at him. "I can reschedule my appointment. Of course, we won't be having anymore sex until I see Dr. Price."

"I can take care of it, and you can pay me back if it exceeds what you prepaid."

"I'm good with that. We should be going. Trudy and Dalton will be at the club in twenty minutes."

"We'll meet you at the lumber store. We're going to take Silas's truck," Isaac shouted out as they went ahead of them.

"Seriously, I can take care of it."

"Seriously, so can I."

Ginny waved at her brothers as Silas backed his truck out of the driveway.

Going to the side door of Viper's SUV, she reached out to open the door, but Gavin beat her. Getting inside, she buckled her seat belt as he got in the driver's seat. Expecting him to back up, she looked over to him to find him staring at her.

"I like babies."

Her insides melted like a chocolate bar and marshmallows on a s'more.

"You do?"

"I'm not getting any younger, as you pointed out."

With her good hand, she caressed his arm. "I was teasing you."

He nodded, staring ahead out of the windshield. "There really isn't a need to worry about birth control if we're ready to have a baby."

"I'm not ready, Gavin."

Gavin nodded again, still not looking at her. "When do you think you'll be ready? A year or two."

"When I'm married *for real*," she emphasized, removing her hand. "We need to go. I don't want to be late. Ginny didn't see that happening any time in the near future, unless he was willing to ask Pastor Dean to marry her. All of the women who went to their church received his permission before the vows were spoken.

The Pastor would determine the man's commitment to the woman, and unless the male was able to prove he would be dedicated, faithful, and ready to be both, Pastor Dean withheld his permission. It allowed the man time to make sure marriage was what he really wanted. Ginny had faith in Pastor Dean and knew he was holding this power to help the couple from making an egregious mistake. If Gavin received Pastor's Dean permission, she would trust he really wanted to marry her.

The ride back to the club was chilly.

Turning the radio on, Ginny tried to rock out to her favorite song. Gavin turned it off. "I was listening to that," she protested.

"The radio is off limits until you admit we're already married."

"You're joking?"

"No. No more music."

She was still gaping at him when they pulled into the club parking lot.

"You're such a jerk." Unbuckling her seat belt, she started to reach for the door handle.

"Maybe so, but you love me, anyway."

The big jerk knew she would cut her tongue out before she would deny her feelings for him.

"Yes, I do." Leaning across the console, Ginny pressed a kiss to the corner of his lips. "I'll call you when I get back to the club. Do you want me to bring you a bag of burgers?"

"No. Your brothers and I will grab something while we're out."

"Okay."

"I'll get the door." Gavin gave her a hard look when she would have reached for the door handle.

Waiting for him to open the door, she gave him another kiss once she was outside.

"Toodle-oo," she wisecracked to Gavin. She waved to Dalton and Trudy as they pulled into the parking lot, giving a low whistle when she got a better look at the gorgeous car.

"I like." Ginny admired the sleek car appreciably. "What kind of car is that?" she asked Gavin.

"A Bugatti."

"How much you want to bet Dalton doesn't let Trudy drive that bad boy?"

"I bet he does," Gavin contradicted her.

"You think so?"

"Oh yeah. No car, regardless of how expensive it is, compares to what they have in their possession."

Ginny started to get angry. "Do you mean, because she's pregnant with his baby?"

"No."

"Then what does she have?"

"His balls."

CHAPTER FORTY

Sitting on the bed, Ginny listened to the news on the television as she painted her toenails. Satisfied with the color, she began painting the other foot. Lifting her gaze, she saw Gavin and Suki coming into the bedroom.

"How did the doctor appointment go?"

"Fine." Continuing polishing her toenails, Ginny noticed Gavin limping. Suki didn't seem to be in any better shape, plopping down on the huge, pink dog bed that Gavin had bought for her. "You get everything bought?"

Sitting down on the bed, Gavin removed his boots.

"A heads-up that you bought the shed Isaac wanted, as well, would have been nice."

"Was he happy?"

Gavin laid back on his elbow to watch what she was doing.

"Happy doesn't come close. Ecstatic was more like it. So were Silas and Matthew when theirs were brought out to the loading dock."

"How did you like the one I picked out for us?"

"I learned something new today."

"You did?" Ginny's lips curled in a smile as she placed the nail brush in the bottle and twisted it closed.

"Yes, I learned they sell kits where you can make sheds that have two-car garages out of bricks."

"Go figure." Shoving a pillow behind her, Ginny met Gavin's eyes. "Are you angry? My brothers will build it."

"We had to rent a big truck for everything you bought, load the trucks, then drive to Silas's. We just finished unloading it. I'll drive the truck back in morning." Yawning, Gavin straightened from the bed.

"You're not angry?"

"No, I've had more exercise today than I've had in a month. You want to take a shower with me?"

"No." She wiggled her toes at him. "They're still wet."

Ginny pulled out a decorating magazine as Gavin took his shower. She was looking at a kitchen layout when breaking news flashed across the screen.

She was still watching it when Gavin came back in the room, drying his hair with a towel. He must have heard the newscast from the bathroom because he was already focused on the television.

When the reporter cut to another story, Gavin flicked the television off.

"It took longer to hit the news than I expected." Slinging the towel around his neck, he moved his boots out of the way.

"The report said that he's going in front of a judge in the morning for a bond hearing." Ginny closed the magazine. The glow she had been feeling faded as the dark fear she had lived with most of her life returned with a vengeance. "They're going to let him go," she said numbly.

Gavin pulled on a pair of pajama bottoms, then hung his damp towel in the bathroom before laying down on the bed beside her. "I talked to Agent Collins this morning. Allerton won't get out. He's too much of a flight risk. There were three vehicles filled with men who were trying to take you yesterday, and you didn't bat an eyelash. Why are you so worried tonight?"

Her eyes flew to his. "I've lost every home I've lived in. I'm jinxed."

"I see, you're worried because you bought the lumber for the house."

"Yes. Leah and I planned what our houses would look like when we were playing in the playhouse Silas built for us. We would take turns playing mommy. Leah was never able to live out her dream, and I'm terrified Allerton won't let me either."

"You're not jinxed."

"I am."

"Nymph, you're not jinxed. In fact, you're the exact opposite."

Her heart lightened. "I am?"

"For real." He laughed, turning the light off. "I have proof." Pulling her into his arms, he rested his chin on top of her head. "You dodged a bullet yesterday and today. Two bullets, two days in a row; that's pure luck."

Ginny frowned at him in the darkness. "I didn't dodge a bullet today."

"You did when you didn't go to the lumberyard with me. I backed up my truck to the loading dock, Silas backed his up, and then four sheds started coming out, then the lumber came out, then the bricks—"

Ginny gurgled in laughter. "You wouldn't have shot me."

"No, but damn, woman, a shed made out of bricks?"

Rubbing her hand over his smooth chest, she placed feathery kisses on the crook of his neck. "I wanted you to have a sturdy place to park your bike."

Swinging the door open, Ginny sauntered into the kitchen. "Good morning," she greeted the two lone men sitting at the kitchen table as she went to the stove to heat a pot of water.

"You're up early this morning," Puck said as he made coffee.

"I had an early night. How are you this morning?"

"Be doing better next week when it's someone else's turn to do kitchen detail," Puck complained with a yawn.

"Could be worse. Wait until it's your turn to do laundry and everyone has put their wet towels in the laundry baskets."

Jesus made a face at him. "I could have lived without knowing that."

"The Ohio chapter doesn't have chore duties?"

"Yes, but so far, I've managed to escape that one." Opening the refrigerator, Jesus took out a large plastic bag of bacon, while Puck started making another pot of coffee.

"Don't forget to make one decaf," Ginny reminded him as she went to the cabinet to open a lower door.

"I will."

"Would you mind taking out the crockpot for me and put it on the middle island? I'm in the mood for oatmeal. You could grab the baking sheets down there, too."

Jesus set the bacon down to get the crockpot for her. "Where do you want the baking sheets?"

"Where the crockpot is, is fine. Thank you."

Separating the stacked baking pans, she nodded toward the bacon. "I've already turned the oven on, just lay the bacon out and put it in the oven."

Going back to the cabinet, she took out the oatmeal and honey that Silas brought over, measuring the oats into the boiling water. She then efficiently organized the two men until the smell of food filled the kitchen.

Pouring the oatmeal in the crockpot to keep it warm, Puck kept glancing at the swinging door. "Reaper catches you helping us, he'll send us packing back to Ohio."

"Don't worry; Gavin's sound asleep." Ginny went back and forth between the freezer and the counter to lay out four boxes of spinach egg cups and six boxes of frozen waffles. "Jesus, you can put the egg cups in the oven when the bacon comes out and put the waffles in the toaster oven. Everything should be ready before everyone comes in to eat."

The men rushed around the kitchen, hurrying to cook the food, while sending wary glances toward the door.

Heating a smaller pan of water, Ginny went to the cabinet and did the same routine as earlier with her good hand. She took out several tumblers for The Last Riders who worked the early morning shift. Setting them out, she then took out the small basket she had bought to keep the matching lids with the tumblers. Frowning, she found one without a lid. Searching through the drawers and cabinets, she still couldn't find the missing lid. Going to the pantry, she took out a metal bin where measuring cups were stored, rooting through the cups where she finally found the missing lid. Placing it next to the matching tumbler, she was satisfied the men would manage the rest by themselves.

Ginny used the hot water to make herself a cup of tea and made herself a bowl of oatmeal after she generously swirled honey in it and fresh fruit before adding a scoop of almonds.

Taking her bowl and her tea, she sat at the table to enjoy her breakfast.

Jesus and Puck joined her, each having a bowl of the oatmeal that she made, their guard finally relaxing.

"Thanks for your help, Ginny."

"Yeah, thanks. Now all we have to do is get past two more meals today and tonight, and we're home free."

"For lunch, one of you could run to the grocery store. They sell rotisserie chickens in the deli section. Buy six different flavors. They also sell a gigantic tub of mashed potatoes, macaroni, and coleslaw. Sneak in the back door and set the food out in bowls and platters. Serve them that for lunch. Put the containers in the dumpsters; no one will know you didn't make it. It's Friday, so order ten pizzas, six orders of bread sticks, and ten orders of hot wings, different flavors. There you go, you're welcome."

The men's laughter was abruptly cut off when the kitchen door was pushed open.

Ginny made a face at them when they visibly relaxed seeing it was Moon.

Refraining from speaking to Moon, who was a grump in the morning, Ginny carried her dirty dishes to the sink to rinse them out and placed them in the dishwasher. Filling one of the tumblers with decaf coffee, Ginny then went to the kitchen door.

"Just so you know, whoever has the job of watching me today, I'll be needing a ride in about thirty minutes to go to church. I would appreciate it if you don't wake Gavin. He has a long day ahead of him, so I don't want him disturbed."

In Gavin's bedroom, she gathered a long-sleeved, heather grey maxi dress and her bra and panties before going into the bathroom to shower. She had washed her hair last night before Gavin had come home, so her shower this morning didn't take long. Drying off, she dressed, then snuck out of the bathroom to find a pair of thick stockings and pair of flat boots. Placing her sling back on, Ginny brushed her hair, deciding to leave it long.

Grabbing her purse, she went to the bed, seeing Gavin

was still asleep. Brushing a kiss over his forehead, she went to the other side of the bed where Suki had taken her spot.

"Keep an eye on him for me, girl," she whispered, giving the dog a loving pat.

Leaving the bedroom, she made her way downstairs where Moon was waiting for her by the door.

"Sorry," she apologized. "Once you drop me off, you can come back and catch a few hours of sleep. Pastor Dean will be at the church, and I'll be staying there until after lunch."

"I'm cool. I shouldn't have pulled an all-nighter. Once the coffee kicks in, I'll wake up."

Carrying her own tumbler, she looked at him questioningly. "I hope you didn't fill yours from the left pot on top; it's decaf."

"Fuck. I'll be right back."

"You should mention to Puck to mark the decaf," she called after him.

"Already planned to," he groused, pushing the door open.

"You hurt his feelings, I won't be happy. Puck and Jesus worked hard to get breakfast ready."

Ginny debated following Moon into the kitchen to double-check that Moon wasn't being mean to the nice men. Obviously, Jesus had been nicknamed for being deeply religious and having a caring manner. Ginny especially didn't want Puck's feelings hurt because he made the coffee just for her.

When Moon came back in a worse temper than he left, Ginny blocked the door when he would have opened it.

"Were you mean to him?"

"No. I was extremely polite."

"Good."

"Can we go now?"

"Of course." Ginny moved away from the door. "You

should really start drinking tea. It'll put you in a better frame of mind," she advised.

"So would eight hours of sleep," he said, going down the steps beside her.

"Yes, it would. Early to bed, early to rise will make Moon nicer in the morning," she chirped, taking the last step.

"Which car are we taking?" Ginny asked when Moon looked at her.

"I was about to ask you the same question."

"I don't have a car, and Gavin has been using Viper's."

"I'll be right back. Gavin has the key to the car the club uses."

Ginny stopped him. "Don't wake him; he's tired."

"We can take my bike."

"I've never ridden on a bike. Can I do it wearing a dress?"

"Yes, just tuck it around you," Moon explained as he got on his bike.

Placing her arms around his waist, Ginny experimentally bounced on the seat. "This is cool. I'm excited."

"Yeah, me, too. Yippee."

Ginny heard the sarcasm in his voice and didn't care. Holding on tighter when Moon started the motorcycle, Ginny felt the thrill of excitement from doing something new. However, the elation was gone before they made it to the first curve. Moon drove like he was giving a ride to a ninety-year-old, who would fall off if he went too fast.

Parking in the church lot, Ginny climbed off.

"How was your first ride?"

Ginny shrugged, taking her coffee tumbler from Moon. "I'm sure the next time I ride on one will be better. It was kinda boring. I don't get why Sex Piston and Crazy Bitch like riding on them. Maybe the Predators do it differently. I'll have to ask. Anyway, thanks for the ride."

Heedless of the glowering stare following her as she

walked to the door of the church, she went inside. Ginny hoped Moon would be in a much better mood when she came out. He was a sour puss first thing in the morning. No wonder he didn't have a girlfriend.

Making her way into the kitchen, she found Willa hard at work.

"Good morning," she said softly so as not to startle her friend.

Seeing her, Willa turned the mixer off. "Good morning." Willa caught her in a big hug that made Ginny feel safe and protected.

"I missed you," Ginny said when they broke apart.

"I'm so glad you're home."

"Me, too." Her face went serious. "Trudy told me you gave money to Viper to help them get on Clindale. However much did you give, I'm going to make sure to pay you back. Trudy didn't know how much—"

"You don't owe me any money."

"I'm going to pay you back." She refused to take no for answer.

"You don't understand. You don't owe me any money. Reaper paid me back what I'd given to Viper, and Lucky told me Reaper paid Viper back the money he spent."

"How much did you give Viper?"

"The money didn't matter to me. It still doesn't. I just wanted you back safely."

Ginny gave Willa an imposing stare. "How much?"

The amount Willa confessed had Ginny going to the stool behind the counter to sit down.

"I would never be able to pay that back in three lifetimes."

"Do you know how much Gavin repaid Viper? Two hundred thousand more than I gave."

"I'm going to be sick." Ginny placed her head on her knees.

Ginny heard Willa rush around the kitchen. "Here drink this." Willa placed a glass of orange juice in her hand.

Sipping the cold juice slowly, she felt her stomach settle. "I'll never be able to pay him back." She hated owing people money.

"I don't think he wants the money back. He did it for you."

Drinking the rest of the juice, she then took the glass to the sink. "I have an appointment with Pastor Dean this morning. Is he in his office?" she asked thickly.

Willa looked at her in concern. "Yes, he's expecting you."

Placing her hand on the counter to steady herself, she went around the counter.

"Ginny, are you okay?"

"I don't know anymore. That's why I'm here to talk to Pastor Dean."

Walking from the kitchen, Ginny went back to the front of the church to knock on the pastor's office door. Hearing his voice from the other side, she went in.

"Good morning, Ginny." Her pastor stood up and stepped around his desk and took her hand. "Other than the sling, you're looking much better than the last time I saw you."

"Thank you for leaving your church to come to the island to help Gavin and me."

"You're very welcome. Have a seat." Pastor Dean motioned for her to take the chair in front of his desk. Then he leaned back on his desk, crossing his arms over his chest, and stared at her appraisingly. "What did you want to discuss with me this morning?"

Looking around his office, Ginny remembered the many times she sat at his desk as he helped her finish schoolwork. Sitting down, Ginny adjusted her sling rather than meet his eyes.

"I'm here to ask for your help."

"My help? Is there something you haven't told Reaper? Has Allerton—"

"No," she interrupted him. "I need you to help me get my faith back."

Pastor Dean's fierce expression cleared. "Why do you feel like you've lost faith?"

"Because of Gavin."

"You lost faith because of Reaper? Has he done something to—"

"No." Ginny corrected the misconception. "It wasn't what he did, but what was done to him that made me lose my faith."

Nodding, Pastor Dean looked down at his shoes. "I see. Go on."

"I'm so angry at God, that He left Gavin in that hellhole for so many years." Ginny used her fingers to rub her forehead. "I keep imagining him screaming in pain, pleading for God's help." Her hand fell limply to her side. "Sometimes, I feel like he's still screaming for help."

Ginny blinked back tears. "I don't know what to do to make the screaming stop. Whatever they did affected him sexually." Blushing, Ginny forced herself to go on. "He doesn't discuss things with me, and I don't ask, because I think it will take the small piece of faith I have left. Have you ever had a crisis of faith?"

"I did ... right before Willa and I married," he admitted.

"How did you get your faith back?"

"My crisis was different. I didn't lose faith in God; I lost faith in myself that I could serve God the way I believed He deserved to be served."

Ginny remembered when he stepped away from the church.

"Willa helped you find your way back to the church," she stated.

"Yes, she did."

"I'm glad. The church wasn't the same without you."

"I missed the church just as badly. It's hard to turn your back on your beliefs, which is what you're going through. Our beliefs offer hope and comfort that God will be by our sides, regardless of the situation we find ourselves facing."

"He wasn't with Gavin," Ginny argued.

"He was. God was protecting Reaper until it was time to return him to us. We're not supposed to understand the reasons different events in our lives play out. God provides the plan, and as believers, we're expected to do our part by providing the faith to take the steps that fulfill the journeys He sets for us to take, in order to end up where we are meant to be. Some journeys are easier than others. Ginny, your journey has been difficult, yet you never lost your faith. Reaper's pain and suffering shouldn't be the reason you lose faith with as much as you love him. When you love someone you can't take on their pain or suffering; otherwise, we become as lost as they are."

"What are we supposed to do?"

"Be God's messenger. Hold him close when he needs to be held, love him when he needs to be loved, and offer him hope when he has lost his."

"How can I stop the screaming in my head? Am I just imagining it?"

Pastor Dean slipped his hands into his pocket. "You're hearing his screams. The brothers and I see the pain in his eyes. The abuse Reaper went through was horrific. Perhaps what we're hearing and seeing is an echo of the man he once was. I truly don't know." Pastor Dean rubbed his eyes as if he found it just as unbearable as she did to know the amount of pain Gavin was in.

"What do we do?"

"Keep doing what you're doing. He's making headway,

slowly, but each of the brothers have seen it. I thought I'd never see him smile again, and I saw him do it several times on the flight back from Sherguevil Island. You can have faith in God, Ginny. He placed you in Gavin's path. Taylor would have never been able to deal with the horrors that Reaper is dealing with. She always had to be first with him. What he needs now is someone who can give that to him."

"Gavin doesn't want what I can give him. He doesn't believe he has the heart capable of loving another woman, and ..." Embarrassed, Ginny looked away from her pastor. "He doesn't like me touching him."

"Have you and Reaper been intimate?"

"Yes." Ginny wanted to sink through the floor, but she forced herself to be truthful and open. "He touches me, but he doesn't like me to touch him. I asked Trudy and Sex Piston if I was doing it wrong, and they seemed to think something is wrong with his *motor*."

At the strangled sound of his voice, Ginny looked to see Pastor Dean returning to his desk, sitting, his face expressionless, making her feel better.

"I see." Pastor Dean began searching through his folders. "Perhaps there is someone else you can talk with who can give some advice that I won't be able to."

"Perhaps I could talk with Willa.."

"God no!" One of the folders the pastor was holding fell out of his hand and to the floor. "One of the women at the club could make a few suggestions."

"I can't do that. I'm worried one of them will tell me they've been with Gavin, and I won't be able to get it out of my head. I really would prefer an objective opinion."

"Reaper hasn't been with any women at the club since his kidnapping," her pastor said, standing up holding the folder. "So, anything she could tell you would have been in the past."

Ginny thought about it, then decided against it. "No, none of them will be able to help me."

"Why not?"

"I'm pretty sure they would have fixed his motor if Reaper was interested. Since he still has the problem ..." Ginny shrugged. "Is there anyone else you could suggest?"

A thought came to her mind just as Pastor Dean shook his head.

Ginny gave Pastor Dean a bright smile. "I believe I know the right person. Thank you, Pastor Dean. Our talk has been a big help."

Moving around the chair, she heard Pastor Dean scratch the floor as he pushed the chair back.

"Uh ... Ginny, who's the woman whose advice you're going to ask? Perhaps I can talk to Willa ...," he hastily offered.

"That won't be necessary. I think that's where I've been wrong. The problem is one that a woman can't fix. I need a man's point of view. Thank you again, Pastor Dean. I'll see myself out."

Ginny turned when she heard him give a grunt of pain, seeing Pastor Dean holding his leg.

"What happened?"

"I accidentally hit the corner of the chair. Listen, Ginny —"

A knock behind her had Ginny hurrying to answer the door.

"Lucky, could you help me load a wedding cake into the van?"

Ginny's interest was piqued at the mention of someone in town getting married. "Who's getting married?"

"Dr. Griffin. She's new to town," Willa cheerfully told her. "Have you met her?"

Ginny was instantly thrilled for the woman.

"I'll be with you in a minute, Willa." Breaking into the conversation, Lucky tried to keep her from being sidetracked.

"She's the one who examined my arm. Who's she marrying?"

"He's from out of town. I haven't met him yet."

"Two new people are moving to Treepoint? Wow. Drake will have to change the sign as you come into town."

Willa and Ginny broke into laughter about the sign indicating the town name and the population number that would go up instead of down.

"Ladies ... Ginny, we really need to finish our conversation." Lucky attempted once again to get her back on track.

Seeing he was becoming frustrated with Willa and not wanting to hold Willa up, she decided it was better to leave.

"That's okay, Pastor Dean. I'll let you know what I find out." Giving Willa a brief one-sided hug, Ginny left the married couple, knowing she made the right decision when she heard them arguing as she left.

Who knew Pastor Dean could be so anal about his meetings with his parishioners being interrupted? Next time she needed his advice, she would make sure Willa didn't have a big order to get out. Men could be such jerks sometimes.

The new doctor was lucky her fiancé was from out of town. That meant he didn't have the same affliction that most of the men in this town had—jerk-itis.

CHAPTER FORTY-ONE

Pushing the swinging door to the kitchen open with the flat of his hand, Reaper stared at the room full of people in frustration when he didn't see who he was looking for.

"Where's Ginny? And why didn't someone answer my texts?" he asked in frustration.

"Because we're eating." Viper set his cup down on the table. "I was getting ready to text you back."

"When? After you ate that pound of waffles?" Reaper snarled, going to the back door to let Suki out. Leaving the dog to do her business, he then went to the coffee machine. Grabbing a cup, he chose a nearly full pot.

"That's ..."

Reaper turned a death glare at Puck, who was doing dishes. "What?"

"Nothing," Puck mumbled, putting a glass in the dishwasher.

Reaper poured his coffee, giving Jesus his own death glare when he appeared to be debating saying something. "You need a haircut," he snapped at the brother.

Jesus brought his hand protectively to the back of his hair. "Yours is longer."

Reaper's glare intensified. "I don't work around food."

"I won't be either after today." Jesus moved to stand next to Jewell, as if the woman could protect him.

When Jewell gave him her own death glare, Reaper went to take a seat at the table. "Where's Ginny?"

"You have no problem texting everyone else; have you tried texting her?" Viper asked.

"She hasn't answered," Reaper admitted, taking a sip of his coffee. Scalding his tongue, he forced himself swallow the hot liquid rather than add to Viper's amusement.

"She's at the church."

"How in the fuck did she get to the church? Why wasn't I woken up? Someone better be—"

"Chill. Reaper, it's too early in the morning. What's with you?" Pouring syrup over his waffles, Viper then closed the lid with a *snap*.

Reaper knew he was acting like a fucking dick. Ginny had turned his mind to mush from the moment she touched him. Why wasn't his mind clearing the more time he spent with her? When was the monotony going to kick in? He just wanted one turmoil-free day. Was that too much to ask for?

Reaper could see he wouldn't be getting any answers until he calmed down.

"Who drove Ginny to the church?"

"Moon," Viper finally gave the information he wanted. "He'll tail her and bring her back when she's done. What's your plan for the day?"

"Putting sheds together."

"Sheds?"

"Don't ask." Getting up, reassured that Ginny was being watched by Moon and Lucky, Reaper went to the door to let Suki inside before making himself a plate.

Loading his plate down with waffles, he was passing the crockpot when he curiously lifted the lid to see what was inside. Oatmeal. He fucking hated the goo.

Going to the cabinet, he took a bowl at the same time as Shade took one. Hurrying back to the counter, Reaper took the remaining oatmeal before considerately turning the crockpot off.

"You couldn't have saved me a spoonful?"

"You snooze, you lose."

Ignoring the dark look Shade gave him, Reaper went back to the table.

Pouring the syrup over the waffles, he started eating as Shade sat down with Viper and him.

"You going to be back before the party starts tonight, to make sure Ginny is out of the way?" Viper asked.

"I plan to be back at four. I'm going out later tonight with Silas and Greer. I'll make sure she knows to stay in my room while I'm gone. Tell the brothers while I'm gone to keep the noise down until I get back."

"How long you going to be gone?"

"A few hours. I'm not asking them not to party, just to keep the noise down so Ginny won't have to listen."

"How're you going to keep her from hearing what's going on when you come back?" Shade questioned, dropping his eyes to the uneaten oatmeal.

"She'll be more concerned with what's going on in our room rather than the rest of the club," he bragged, pulling the oatmeal toward him and starting to eat the goo. Expecting to gag under Shade's scrutiny, Reaper was pleasantly surprised at the taste.

Finishing the bowl, he looked at his cell phone and saw that Ginny still hadn't texted him back. Sending her another, he told her that he was heading to Silas's.

Taking his dishes to the sink, he grabbed one of the

tumblers sitting out, then went back to the table, pouring the hot coffee into it. "I'm going to Silas's. If anything comes up, you can text or reach me there. Any of the brothers want to earn any extra cash this afternoon, we could use help building the sheds."

Shade gave him a quizzical look. "How many are you building?"

"Four."

"Four?"

"Four," Reaper repeated, aware of the brothers in the kitchen listening in. "Any of them have experience laying bricks, I'll pay extra."

The humorous expressions had him instantly regretting asking, but dammit, he didn't want a crooked shed.

"They make brick sheds?"

Tuning out the snickers from the brothers, Reaper answered Viper. "Yes." Then he gave Viper a condescending-asshole look, like *how didn't you know*. "It's the size of a two-door garage."

"Hm … And why did you want it to be brick?"

"Ginny bought it for me. She wanted a sturdy garage for my bike."

The jealous looks the brothers gave him made up for being the source of their prior amusement. Well, except for Shade, who wasn't buying what he was selling.

"Jesus has the most construction experience; ask him." Viper nodded his head back.

Reaper dragged his eyes to where Jesus was standing behind the counter with a shit-eating grin on his face. "I worked as brick layer for three summers when I was in high school and worked as one for two years when I worked for my dad's construction company."

Did he really care if the walls weren't straight? Damn, the garage doors might be off track if they weren't.

"I have to finish with kitchen duty today. I wasn't planning on going to work for you until Monday, but I wouldn't mind giving up my weekend. I do charge extra for brick laying."

"Just let me know how much you want, and I'll make a check out to you."

Jesus didn't let him off so easily. "I'm not cutting my hair."

"Brah, I was joking. I didn't expect you to cut your hair." Calling Suki to him, Reaper got the hell out the kitchen.

Frustrated, he was angrier at himself than he was at Jesus. He didn't know why in the hell Jesus' hair bothered him. He just knew it did. He was absolutely losing it.

Ginny wasn't making him lose his ever-loving mind. He was already there.

Going through the living room and out the front door, Reaper went down the steps to Viper's car. Opening the back door to let Suki inside, Reaper shut the door before getting in the front seat. He needed to take a day to buy a car. He had basically taken over Viper's, and while his brother hadn't said anything, Reaper didn't want to keep imposing.

He had never owned a car, even when he was in high school. He'd used Ton's or Viper's when he'd gone out on dates, if he hadn't wanted to ride his bike. He needed a vehicle for Ginny and Suki.

Arriving at the Colemans' property, he found the brothers hard at work. They had started on Silas's shed, where they would store the lumber and equipment until the house was built.

"How's it going?" Carrying his tumbler, Reaper walked up to the busy men.

"Pretty good." Silas wiped a band of sweat away from his forehead with the sleeve of his shirt. "We've got two of the side walls built. Matt and Isaac are starting on the garage doors."

"Lucky for me, there are so many of you." Taking a drink of his coffee, he nearly spit it back out.

Silas saw the face he made. "Something wrong?"

"Decaf."

Silas grimaced in sympathy. "I'd offer you some, but we made the last in the can this morning. I have to buy more when I go to the store tomorrow."

"I'll make do." Reaper set the tumbler aside.

Checking to see where Suki was, he saw her sleeping on the porch.

Taking his phone out, he looked to see if Ginny had called. No messages. Irritated that she hadn't answered, he almost called, then decided against it. She was probably just catching up with Willa and hadn't seen his messages. Still, the woman could have at least texted him that she loved him. She could have told him when he was sleeping, and he hadn't heard her. He would have to ask her when he caught up with her.

Pitching in with Silas and Matt, they worked steadily for the rest of the morning. Breaking for lunch, they went inside Silas's house to make sandwiches and grab drinks, then returned back outside. They finished Silas's shed and spent a good hour filling it with the lumber and equipment. Locking it when they were done, they walked over to Matthew's house and began putting his shed together.

Clicking the last wall in place, the men all stood back to admire their handiwork.

Glancing at his phone, Reaper saw that it was four.

"I'm going to have to head out. We can do your shed tomorrow, Isaac. One of the brothers from the club will be coming to help with the brickwork. By Monday, we should be able to get started on the house."

"Sounds good," Silas said. "What time do you want Greer and me to pick you up?"

"Six good?"

"Yes, that gives me enough time to eat and shower."

Saying good-bye to Ginny's brothers, Reaper called for Suki, who had been playing with the goats that were eating the cleared-out brush and weed from where they built his shed.

Driving back to the club, he felt the physical toll of the work he'd done last night and today catching up with him. Stiffly getting out the SUV, he let Suki run up the front steps before him, wishing he chosen the back steps instead. If Puck, Nickel, and Jesus weren't standing on the front porch, smoking cigarettes, he would have cut across the yard to do just that.

Nickel hurried to open the door before he was on the porch. "Looking rough, brother. Tough day?"

"Fuck off," Reaper said, going inside.

Bypassing the stairs, he went through the living room, heading to kitchen to get a drink before attempting the steps. He was surprised to see Ginny and Killyama behind the bar, placing bottles of liquor into a blue grocery bag. The brothers were standing on the other side, watching what the two women were doing with tortured expressions on their faces.

Reaper was tempted to go back outside. He would rather be out there than stuck playing referee between Viper and the two women. But when Viper sent him a glare to stop the women—as Ginny picked out a tequila bottle—he walked over to stand with the brothers. He may be curious as to what the women wanted with all that alcohol, but he already knew it was going to be a losing battle to prevent Killyama from taking what she wanted. The clever woman was smart enough to know that without Ginny with her, Viper would never have let her take them. Viper was outgunned.

"Ginny, what are you doing?"

Ginny held the tequila bottle closer to her chest. "You're back! I was just getting ready to text you!"

Reaper shoved his hands in his pockets. "You've had all day to answer my texts, and you're now ready to respond to them?"

Ginny frowned. "You texted me? I must have missed it. The girls have a sleepover once a month at Sex Piston's house." Giving him an excited grin, she placed the bottle of liquor in the grocery bag. "This is the first one I've been able to go to."

"Didn't you learn a lesson yesterday? It isn't safe—"

Raising her hand, Ginny lifted a finger one by one while calling out names. "Stud, Calder, Dalton, Train, and Cade will be there. The guys stay upstairs when the girls stay for the night. Stud was going to invite you, but I told him that you were going out tonight with Silas and Greer. He said you're welcome next month."

When Ginny bent down to gather more supplies, Reaper was about to go around the corner to see what she was doing when cans of sodas began appearing. When the ginger ales began forming their own row Reaper had to press Viper back down on the stool.

Seeing that he wasn't stopping Ginny and Killyama from the pilfering, the brothers turned their gazes to Train, who was playing pool with Razer. "Killy, Viper stocked the bar for the party tonight," Train yelled over.

"Thanks, Viper." Killyama popped one of the ginger ales to take a drink, eyeballing her husband who had quickly turned back to his pool game. "Sex Piston, Crazy Bitch, and T.A. thank you, too."

Ginny popped back up. "You forgot to include me."

"Bitch, you've got a tongue; thank himself yourself."

Ginny started placing the sodas in the bag with the bottles. "Thanks, Viper. We really appreciate you letting us take party supplies. I was going to go to the store, but time got away from me. When I go, I'll rebuy what we're taking."

"When are you going to the store?" Jewell asked, leaning over the bar to see what Ginny had placed in the bag.

Ginny zipped the bag closed. "Tomorrow. I need to restock my brothers' groceries, so I'll just throw in what I'm borrowing from you guys. I'll keep the empty bottles, so I remember which liquors to replace."

"Why do you need so much alcohol? Two of the women are pregnant," Reaper questioned, studying Ginny closely.

"Just Trudy." Killyama pulled another bottle of alcohol from the rack on the wall, placing it proprietary in the crook of her arm. "Mine was a false alarm. I didn't expect Ginny to go blabbing it to Train before I could take a test."

Ginny made a comical face at her. "Admit it; you used it as an excuse not to get the pot stickers."

A buzzing had Ginny taking her phone from an outside pocket of the grocery bag. Reading the message, she then placed the phone back. "Trudy is here. Gavin, do you mind taking this bag down to the car for us?"

Internally groaning, Reaper used the strap to pick the bag up and nearly dropped it when he lifted it.

"You need me to do it?"

Reaper searched for the brother who made the muttered offer. They all suddenly seemed interested in playing cards as he walked the girls to the door.

Seeing they were heading out, Train gave his pool stick to Rider.

Letting the women go ahead of him, Reaper motioned for Train to go next, and when he reached his side, Reaper shoved an elbow into his stomach and handed the bag to Train.

He almost fell down twice. His legs felt like jelly. Promising himself to return back to his regular workout routine, he took another painful step, annoyed he'd had to take such a long break during his time on the Island.

At the car, his fingers tightened on Ginny's elbow to prevent her from getting into the Lincoln Navigator. Reaper wanted to flip off the fucker behind the wheel. "How many expensive cars does Dalton have?"

Missing the snide edge to his voice, Ginny said, "I don't know. You want me to ask?"

Reaper turned her until her back was to the group inside Dalton's car. "Why didn't you tell me last night that you're staying the night with the girls?"

"I didn't know it was tonight until Killyama called me this afternoon. I didn't think it was a big deal with you going out. Do you not want me to go?"

"I want you to go. I was just curious why you didn't mention it to me last night. I don't want you to miss the first sleepover with the girls." Reaper found it hard to convince her when he was finding it hard to convince himself he was cool with her going. "Did you take everything you need? You want to ask Trudy? I could send Train back up to the club to get what she wants."

"No, we're good. I took one more bottle than we usually drink when we spend the night together." Going up onto her tiptoes, she tried to kiss him, but Reaper pulled his head back slightly.

"I thought you haven't been to their sleepovers before?"

"Oh … not at Sex Piston's. We've had sleepovers when we could sneak off to Lexington after scrounging enough money together."

Lowering his mouth, Reaper gave her a hard kiss. "Keep your phone on you."

"I will," she promised. "You have a good time with Silas and Greer."

Reaper watched her get in the Lincoln, forcing himself

not to remind her that she was forgetting something. He stood there until the vehicle was out of sight, thinking she would've remembered and was expecting her to roll the window down and yell out to him.

Going to the side of the house, he went up the back path to the club. There was no way he would be able to make it up the front steps. It would be a miracle if he made it up the stairs to take a shower.

Coming from the kitchen and into the main room, Reaper found the party had already started. Jewell was behind the bar, pouring drinks for the brothers. Jesus and Puck had come inside and were tongue-fucking two of the female members on one of the long couches. As he turned the corner, Reaper saw Knox and Diamond coming into the room, with Bliss and Drake following behind them.

"Come, Suki." Reaper gave them curt nods as he went up the stairs, using the handrail to pull himself upward.

Today was the first day she hadn't told him she loved him. Glumly, he thought about driving to Stud's house after Silas and Greer brought him back from their boys' night out. It would give her another opportunity to remember what she'd forgotten to do.

Wasn't telling him she loved him as important to her as it had been? Was she getting bored with him? Closing his bedroom door, he walked toward his dresser for clean clothes, and seeing the mirror perched above, the tight feeling in his chest eased.

I love you.
I love you.
I love you.
I love you.
I love you.
I love you.

She had written it out six times on his mirror with eyeliner.

Finding a sweatshirt and jeans, he went into the bathroom, his reflection in the mirror distorted by the sentences written across the glass.

She had written it six times.

CHAPTER FORTY-TWO

"You can have this one." Prying the old folding chair open, Greer placed the chair down on the ground. Opening two others, Greer plopped down on the best of the three rickety chairs and sprawled his legs out.

Reaper felt as if the old chair was going to break at any moment as he tried to find a comfortable spot on the worn-out plastic. He caught the ice-cold bottle of beer Greer tossed him from the small cooler that Silas brought.

"Next week, I'll bring the chairs."

"Suit yourself. You have some fancy ones in that factory of yours? Bring three, and I'll keep them in my trunk for us." Greer reached in his pocket, coming out with a joint and a lighter. "Ain't you got that fire lit yet, cuz?"

Twisting the bottle open, he and Greer watched as Silas got the fire started.

Taking a beer from Greer, Silas sat down on the chair catty corner to Greer's.

"God, it's good to get away from them heathens," Greer groused, sucking in a hit of the joint.

Reaper took a hit, and when he started to pass it back to

Greer, Silas held out his hand. Taking a hit, Silas propped his feet up on the cooler.

"Thank God that smell finally went away," he said, taking another hit before passing it back to him. Reaper took another hit before giving it back to Greer.

"Which one is this one?" Enjoying the cold beer sliding down his throat, Reaper rested his beer bottle on his abs.

"Dustin grew this one. He named it Hollar Wowie."

"Kentucky Gold is better, but this is a close second." Reaper took the joint back from him. "Why haven't you brought us a blunt you've grown?"

"Boy, you can live without Kentucky Gold and Hollar Wowie, but once you taste Mountain Flame, you'd think you've died and gone to heaven. I keep those to sell to people who are celebrating special occasions."

"Like what?" Reaper passed the joint to Silas.

"Watching your youngest kid going to his first day of school, getting divorced, catching your woman cheating, killing the motherfucker she cheated on you with. Shit like that."

Greer's offbeat humor had him laughing as he took another drink of his beer. "Your wife doesn't mind you going out?"

"Nah. Friday nights are the girls' nights. Tate and Dustin watch the kids at my house, while the womenfolk go to Jesse's house to sit around and watch those pussy movies and drink wine."

"They go to your house with all the kids?" Reaper took another hit off the joint, then passed it back to Greer.

"Yep."

"Pretty convenient, it's the same night you wanted a boys' night out with Silas and me."

"Ain't it?" Greer snickered.

Reaper looked over at Silas. "Every muscle in my body

aches from building those sheds and moving that lumber. Aren't you sore?"

"Nah, I'm good. You need to work out more."

"I thought I was in good shape, but damn, you're making me feel my age."

Greer gave a sarcastic snort. "Tell him the fucking truth."

"Shut up, Greer."

"The boy has a brain. I reckon sooner or later, he's going to figure it out." Greer shrugged. Then he started laughing at Reaper's confusion. "Ain't quick on the uptake, are you?"

Stretching his legs out, Silas rested his head back on the chair. "Lot of stars out tonight."

"Yep." Greer opened himself another beer. "Bet a bunch of those stars wish they could switch places with us. Aren't you glad Silas didn't let you take a nosedive?"

Staring at the lit end of the joint, Reaper took a hit before handing it over to Greer. Letting his hand drop down to his side, he rubbed Suki's fur. "Yes."

"You could sound happier about it," Greer groused.

"You don't know what it's like living with nightmares."

Silas and Greer gave low laughs.

"Boy, you think you're the only one with nightmares?"

Greer and Silas shared a bleak glance.

Silas stood up to get himself another beer. "Don't answer, Reaper. The wrong answer will have Greer ripping that misconception away. Suffice to say, you aren't."

"Damn right. You put up with that fucker rotting away for what? Nine years? I put up with the meanest son of bitch in the state of Kentucky for seventeen. The only good thing he taught us was how to shoot. His idea of being a good father was to teach us boys to be tough enough to take any hit and to turn women into doormats. You say or do the wrong thing to piss him off ... kapow!" Greer flashed his fist out.

Silas twisted the cap of his beer off. "When Greer says his

dad was mean, he isn't exaggerating. Everyone in town was terrified of him."

"Shit. I hated that son of a bitch. Still do." The tiny flame of the joint was visible between Greer's fingers as he turned his head to spit on the ground. "One night, he gave Tate and me a beating bad enough it left Tate unconscious. He didn't give a rat's ass. Locked us in the barn without any heat in the dead of winter. It was no never mind that Tate was sick with the flu. Had to listen to my ma trying to dig us out while Pa was passed out, high as a fucking kite, for Lord knows how long before he caught her and dragged her back in the house to lock her and my baby sister in the bedroom so she wouldn't let us out. Yeah … those were some good fucking times." Greer's voice was filled with sarcasm as he extinguished the tip of the joint with his fingers.

Squatting down by the fire, Silas stared in the crackling flames. "What we say while we're on this mountain, around this fire, is forgotten when we walk away. Deal?" Silas turned to stare at them gravely. "Neither of you have to share your own personal shit—that's your prerogative—but it stays only between us."

"Got my word." Greer shrugged. "Probably won't remember it no way."

"You have mine." Reaper had no intention of sharing. He would keep anything said to himself.

Silas threw some more wood on the fire. "You have my word, too, so I'll be expecting you keeping yours."

Rising to go back to his chair, Silas stared moodily into the twinkling sky. "Freddy didn't always have custody of me. I lived with my mom until I was seven. Freddy would come and get me on the weekends and had to have me back by Sunday morning before church. She wanted my stepdad and me there to make sure we appeared to be one happy family in front of that sanctimonious hypocrite preacher we used to have in town before Pastor Dean."

"Saul Cornett." Reaper placed his empty bottle on the ground, patting Suki as he listened.

"Saul was a sadistic bastard. He used to get his kicks by spanking kids in front of the congregation. Makes me sick to my stomach to this day remembering the joy on his face when he would beat those kids. The parents would tell him what they'd done bad during the week, and Saul would beat the demon that had caused them to act that way. My mother and stepfather never told on me, not because they didn't believe in the stupidity he was preaching. No, they didn't tell because they didn't trust Saul wouldn't leave a mark on me. They knew if Freddy ever saw that a hand had been laid on me, they would be minus one preacher. Instead, they had their own way of handling my discipline.

"Every Sunday night after dinner, my mother would go to her bedroom and turn the television on high. She'd let my stepfather punish me. My stepfather would take me into my bedroom, read off the list my mother made of my "sins." After he read the list, he would make me take my clothes off, then spend the rest of the night raping me."

Reaper heard Suki give a low whine.

"He and my mother told me that if I ever told anyone, especially Freddy, my stepfather would sneak into my dad's house and kill him and me."

"Did you father find out?" Reaper asked gruffly.

Silas turned his face from the sky to look at him. "Has Ginny told you what Freddy's gift was?"

"Some. Greer, toss me another beer." Reaper was careful with what he said, not wanting to get Ginny in trouble with the little she had told.

Greer took two beers out, handing him one, then took his

plastic baggie out. "I'll be taking another myself. I'm lighting a second one of these bad boys up, too."

Studying Greer closely, Reaper could tell from his reaction that he had been unaware of Silas's abuse.

Silas waited until Greer had the joint lit.

"Each member of my family has separate and distinct gifts, except Freddy and Fynn. Freddy could read the skies like you and I read books. He knew when things were going to happen and when to intervene within reason. If he interfered in someone's life, it put the book out of whack. Chapter ten would happen in chapter six, or events were skipped ahead to chapter fifteen. That wasn't even the worst. Freddy said some events wouldn't appear at all. They were deleted. Only one member is born in a generation with Freddy's gift, and usually toward the end of the previous generation's lifetime. When Fynn's gifts became apparent, Freddy knew it was a matter of time before he passed on."

Reaper stared down at Suki as he continued stroking her fur. Gavin understood why Silas was describing Freddy's gifts. "Freddy knew you were being abused."

"One Friday he came to pick me up. When we got to the house, as I was getting out of the car, he asked if I wanted to go for walk before dinner. We walked to where Moses' house is now; there's a big rock not too far from there. He said, 'let's rest before we head back.' So I sat down on the rock with Dad, thinking we were taking a break before heading back to the house. As we sat there, he looked down at my shoes and asked why I wasn't wearing the new tennis shoes he bought me."

Reaper heard Greer begin to cough. "You okay, Greer?"

"Yeah," he rasped out, handing him the joint.

Silas waited until Greer stopped coughing before continuing his story. "I told him that the whole class had been making fun of the way Greer's shoes smelled. Freddy asked me if I was one of the kids making fun of him. I told him I was. Then I told him how Greer followed me into the bathroom and stole my shoes when I was taking a shit."

Reaper took another hit of the joint. He wasn't stupid; he knew the men were trying to steer the conversation into him sharing what had happened to him. He had no intention of giving in to the sneaky maneuver. Still, his interest was caught as Silas's story unfolded.

"You swapped shoes with Silas?"

"I was pissed." Greer glared at his cousin. "He was always on my fuckin' back."

"We were both dicks." Silas gave a crooked smile. "I grew up. I'm still waiting for Greer to. Looking back, most of it was acting out because our home lives were shit. I hadn't told my mom about my shoes, because it would give my mother another excuse to punish me.

"I expected my dad to tell me that he would get me another pair. Instead, he told me it wouldn't hurt for me to walk in Greer's shoes for a while. I started crying because I knew my mother would see Greer's old shoes before we went to church. Freddy started crying, too. 'Son, no matter how hungry you get when you miss dinner or miss lunch, you're never going to feel true hunger until you experience it yourself. You have a girl in your classroom whose father was laid off from the mines and hasn't had anything to eat in two days. No matter how sorry you feel for her, you don't understand the hunger pains that eventually go away because your body has given up hope of being fed. When I look at Greer's shoes, I see his parents don't have enough money to buy him a new pair. I also see parents refusing to take a handout. The sole is worn down on them. It's a chilly day. Are your feet cold?' he'd asked me.

"I admitted they were freezing and my socks were wet. Then my father asked, 'So, you understand how Greer felt when he was wearing them?' When I nodded my head, Freddie added, 'Wearing those shoes, you now understand how he felt, but most importantly, you feel a small portion of what Greer's life is like. As a father, I want to say let's go to the store and get you a new pair, but that isn't what Greer's father would do, is it?'"

Silas took a hit of the joint and stretched his long legs before continuing. "When I said, 'No,' he said, 'Then, since you're walking in his shoes, you should fix the problem, shouldn't you?' Damn I wanted out of those shoes so bad. My toes were freezing off, my ass was freezing off on that rock, and Dad was still crying."

Reaper saw the sheen of tears on Silas's cheeks in the firelight.

"By then, it was getting dark, and I told him I was cold and wanted to go back to the house. He said he was waiting for the stars to come out. It took me for my ass to go numb before I figured out what he was doing. Dad told me he could read the stars to see what was going on in people's lives. That's when something clicked, and I scrunched up my legs to sit better on the rock. Dad could read the stars, like he had me looking at Greer's shoes to find the details of Greer's life. He wasn't buying me a new pair of shoes, because he wanted me to solve my own problems.

"I told him about my stepfather and my mom and what she was allowing. When I told him, he quit crying. He didn't get angry at Mom or her husband; he just sat there and listened without making a noise, even when I told him that my stepfather would kill us because I told.

"Freddy said he was going to call the sheriff, and I wouldn't be going back to my mom's house to live. Then he got off the rock, took out his pocketknife, and said, 'Come here, Son.' I got off the rock, and Freddy pointed at it. 'This rock doesn't have any feelings. No matter how hard you beat it with your fists, it won't break or chip,' Freddy went to the rock and used his knife to scratch the surface to make a mark. 'Is the rock different now?' he asked, and I told him it was, because he gouged it.

"He said, 'This rock has sat here untouched for years with storms passing overhead, yet I made a mark when a tornado hasn't. The mark will always be there because of what I did. If we use our gifts the wrong way, we could hurt someone without meaning to, where you can't hurt the rock. No matter how angry and mad at someone we can be for pain they've caused someone we love, we can't interfere.'"

Silas weaved his fingers together around his beer bottle as he talked. "I asked him what I was supposed to do. Freddy handed me the knife and told me to make a mark, and then walk away, leaving all the pain and anger in the rock. That the rock would hold the pain and rage, and that I wouldn't have to carry that burden any longer. So I scratched a line on the rock, then gave Freddy his knife back. After that we went home; Freddy carried me all the way."

Greer took a hit. "Freddy was a good man. Didn't weigh hundred ten pounds soaking wet."

Reaper stroked Suki's head. "How long did you have to wear those shoes?"

"Until Monday, when I asked Greer if I could have the shoes the teacher had given him, which was why the kids had made fun of him. Greer had hidden them in the coat closet and then stole mine when I was in the bathroom. He gave them to me, but never gave mine back. Greer and I never fought after that."

"Yep, we came to an agreement that benefited both of us."

"Which was?" Reaper asked curiously.

"I'd leave him alone to take his dumps, and he'd give me a new pair of shoes each year." Greer waved his boot tips. "Thanks, cuz, these may be my favorite pair." Standing, Greer squashed the bud out to put it back into the plastic baggie. Reaching into his pocket, Greer then took out a pocketknife and went to stand next to the large rock. He looked down at it as he took something out of his pocket. Reaper heard a scraping sound and saw a flame and knew Greer was holding a lighter in order to see the rock.

Rising, Reaper went to the rock to see what Greer was staring at. What he saw had his knees shaking.

"Can I see the lighter?" Reaper held his hand out to Greer.

The flame went out and the lighter was placed in his hand.

"Careful, it's hot," Greer warned.

Flicking the lighter, Reaper went to his haunches to see the straight lines marked on the rock. There were so many that he had to shuffle his feet on the ground to keep looking. When he couldn't bear to count any longer, Reaper moved his thumb away from the light, shutting off the flame.

Letting the lighter fall to the ground, Reaper buried his face in his hands, fighting the years of bottled-up emotions spilling out. Dropping to the ground, he felt Suki land on his lap as Silas and Greer knelt by his side, enfolding him in their arms.

The rock hadn't broken after nine and half years' worth of lines scratched on its surface. The rock hadn't broken, regardless of how many times a knife had been used on it to release the pain and rage the person was feeling. The rock hadn't ... but that night, he did.

CHAPTER FORTY-THREE

Reaper shut the truck door, giving a final wave to Silas and Greer as they drove off.

Going up the steps, he reached the front porch where Moon was pulling guard duty. In the early morning sun, Moon looked like death warmed over.

"Lucky was looking for you last night. Said he'd catch up with you today."

Why hadn't the brother called or texted? Mentally shrugging, he figured it must not have been important. Noticing the grey pallor of Moon's skin, Reaper thought the brother must have played hard last night. "Had fun at the party?"

Moon tugged his skull cap over his ears. "Had better, had worse."

Reaper went into the house, knowing where the brother was coming from. The parties, as much fun as they were, didn't fill the void from the emptiness. He had felt the same void before meeting Taylor. Being with her had temporarily filled it, but that void had been opening again before his kidnapping.

Walking through the door, he found the main room

empty. Deciding to get breakfast before going upstairs to shower, he pushed the kitchen door open and stared, dumb-founded, at the huge half-eaten wedding cake sitting on the kitchen counter.

He blinked to make sure it was really there and not the effects of the joint and the two beers he'd had last night. When he opened his eyes and saw it still sitting there, he turned his head to see Puck and Nickel sitting at the table, eating slices of the cake.

"It must have been a real party last night" was all Reaper could think to say.

"Help yourself," Nickel offered. "There're some fancy appetizers in the fridge, too, that no one knows how to pronounce."

"I'll pass."

Going behind the counter, he made himself a bowl of cereal and poured himself a glass of orange juice. "It must have been a hell of party last night. Who got married?"

"No one, which is why we have the cake," Nickel explained as Reaper took a chair at the table.

Eating his cereal, he thought about asking more questions, then decided he didn't care enough. He was looking at his phone to make sure he hadn't missed a phone call when Jewell and Jesus came into the kitchen.

When neither of them asked any questions about the cake but began pulling trays of food out of the refrigerator, Reaper knew they were aware of where the food and cake had come from.

Jesus sat down across from him at the table. "Lucky was looking for you last night."

"I heard." He would call Lucky when he went upstairs to take a shower.

He was finishing his juice when Lucky and Willa came through the back door, saving him the trouble of making the call. Nickel and Puck left the table to go the counter and started loading the dishwasher from the mountain of dishes that had been left there from the party.

Lucky and Willa took their seats at the table.

"Heard you were looking for me last night. What's up?"

Lucky shook his head. "We can talk later."

"What's wrong with now? I need a shower and want to grab a nap. Was it important?"

"Not to me, brother, but to you, probably."

Reaper frowned at the curious way Lucky was responding.

"Finish your breakfast, and we can go to my room."

"Good idea."

His curiosity rose when Reaper saw the amusement on his face.

Willa must have been in the dark, because she looked just as confused as he was. Finding no clue from her husband, Willa gave up, wiping a dot of frosting from the corner of his mouth.

Giving Lucky her napkin, Willa glanced toward him. "Where's Ginny this morning?"

"She went to a slumber party at Sex Piston's. They must not be up yet, because she hasn't texted me."

"Darn, I wanted to see what she thought of the picture I took of her yesterday. She didn't text me back last night, and I'm getting ready to leave."

"What picture? May I see?"

"Sure." Willa took out her phone. "I'll text it to you."

Picking his phone up off the table, he saw Lucky lean his head to his side to glance at the picture Willa was sending.

"Wait—"

Lucky snapped his mouth shut when Willa must have pressed Send.

When Lucky's gaze jerked to his to see his reaction to the

picture, Reaper didn't need a fortune teller to tell him he wasn't going to appreciate whatever image Willa had captured.

Ginny was riding a motorcycle in front of the church. She was riding on a fucking motorcycle that wasn't his! She had ridden on motorcycle for the first fucking time, and it *wasn't his fucking motorcycle!*

Fury hit him with the magnitude of a hundred bulls stampeding through his head. Everyone in the kitchen froze at the bellow of rage coming from his chest as he rose from the table, sending his chair skittering to the side. Then he angrily threw his phone at the wall with enough force that his high school coach would've shed tears of joy.

"Fuck …," Lucky moaned. "Reaper, don't overreact. He was just giving Ginny a ride to the church and back. She had a meeting with me."

"Whose fucking bike was she riding?" Reaper shouted. He had been so furious that he'd forgotten to look at whose bike it was before he busted his phone to smithereens.

"Let's go to your room." Lucky stood, coming around the table as Razer and Beth came up the basement steps. From their disheveled appearance, he had woken them up when he his phone hit the wall.

"Who's …?" Reaper glared at Jesus, who was frozen in place. "Were *you* the one to give Ginny a ride yesterday?"

Jesus' face went ashen. "No, brother. I didn't leave the club all day. I swear, brah."

Clenching his teeth, he glared at Puck. "Was it *you*?"

Puck stepped behind Jewell. "No, I was here with Jesus. I left to go to the store … but I *swear* I took Cash's truck and Ginny didn't go with me.

Lucky put his hand up in the air when Reaper started toward Nickel. "Reaper, let's go talk. There is no need for this jealousy—"

"I am not jealous. I'm angry!" Reaper shouted. "I want to know which motherfucker put my property on his bike without my permission. Lucky, if one of the squids gave her a ride and you knew, brother, you won't be giving a service tomorrow. You'll being attending a fucking funeral!"

Lucky took a step forward. "Don't threaten me. You know damn good and well she wouldn't be given a squid for protection, must less let her leave with her at his back. I didn't know how she got there."

"Did you see who she left with?"

"No, I had gone out to the back of the church to pull the van to the back door."

Curtly, Reaper let Lucky off the hook. "Willa, can I see that picture again?"

Willa waited until she was standing behind Lucky to answer. "I accidentally deleted it."

Lucky looked over his shoulder at his wife. "Go on to the house. Tell Jade we won't be needing her for babysitting this morning."

Waiting until she was out the door, Lucky gave him a brusque nod toward the kitchen door.

Reaper irately stalked into the living room, set on dealing with Lucky, showering, and then going to Shade for a new phone.

The men kept their silence as they went up the stairs to his room. Lucky went into the room, then turned when Reaper closed the door after them. "I tried to catch up with you yesterday. There're some—"

"I want you to tell Ginny to marry me," Reaper said as he folded his arms over his chest.

Lucky's mouth went slack jawed. "Pardon me?"

"Ginny said she won't get married without your permission. I want you to tell her to marry me, preferably this morning, if she comes back. Tonight, if she doesn't."

"No." Lucky folded his arms against his chest, mimicking his stance.

"Give her the permission. She won't marry me if you don't."

"Then I don't know what to tell you. I guess you won't be getting married anytime soon."

"She's pregnant and won't even tell me she is until you give her permission to marry me!"

"Ginny hasn't told you she's pregnant?"

"No."

"Then how do you know she is?"

"I don't know …." Reaper raked his hand through his hair, beginning to pace around the room. "When you give her permission, she'll tell me. Ginny has convoluted beliefs of living together and marriage. You can't tell me Lily would have married Shade without your permission. Did you have to ask yourself to marry Willa?"

"Maybe her beliefs aren't the ones convoluted."

"You're seriously telling me no?"

"I'm seriously telling you no," Lucky said decisively. "Before you place the blame on my shoulders for Ginny not willing to marry you without my approval, or why she hasn't told you she's pregnant, you should consider there could be another reason."

"Like what?" Reaper stopped pacing in front of him.

"Could it possibly be that the root of your problem isn't with Ginny's religious views but what's going on in the bedroom?"

"Huh?" Reaper stared at Lucky, thinking he misheard the brother.

"The sexual problems Ginny and you are having," Lucky clarified.

Reaper was confused at the direction their conversation

had turned. "We don't have any sexual problems. I'm the father of her child. It wasn't an immaculate conception."

"I didn't think it was." Lucky relaxed his stance, his voice becoming more understanding. "Ginny wanted to talk to me yesterday for two reason; one I could help her with. She is angry at God on your behalf."

"Join the club," Reaper said sarcastically.

"Reaper, Ginny's faith is very important to her."

"Were you able to help her?"

"I believe so."

"What was the other problem? The one you couldn't help her with?"

Lucky dropped his gaze to his shoes. "Ginny believes her inexperience is the reason she can't get your ... motor running."

"Huh?"

"Your dick."

"I know what the fuck you were referring to. My dick is working fine. I don't understand."

"She says you don't let her touch you, which is why she thinks she's doing it wrong."

"What in the fuck did you tell her?"

"I suggested she ask some of the women here."

"You didn't."

"Would you have me give her the advice she was searching for?"

"No. Which woman was she going to talk to?"

"None of them. Ginny was afraid they would say they had been with you and she didn't want that picture in her head."

"So, who in the fuck did she ask? Willa?"

"She was going to, but I nixed that idea. By the way, you owe me for that one, brother. Miss Adventuresome isn't Willa's strong suit."

Reaper looked heavenward. *You just had to screw me over again, didn't You?* he blamed the man upstairs.

"Sex Piston had a slumber party last night. Don't fucking lie to me that she didn't tell them I have a problem getting a hard-on."

"I'll take that bet for a hundred."

"You don't think she did?"

"No. I think it was one of the brothers."

"*What?*"

Lucky's gave him a sympathetic nod. "From my understanding, that was the plan. She wanted a male's perspective."

Reaper reached behind his back for his gun, handing it to Lucky.

"Why are you giving me your gun?"

"Who was the one who gave Ginny sex advice?"

"I don't know. She took off before she told me. I tried to give you a heads-up, but I couldn't find you."

"You didn't think my woman going to one of the brothers to talk about our sex life was worth a phone call?" Reaper shouted in frustration.

"I felt it would be better if I told you in person. You been kinda off the wall lately where Ginny's concerned."

"I wonder why! She's as looney as Daffy Duck on crack." Reaper raked his hand through his hair in irritation, then dropped his hand when he saw Lucky watching him humorously. "You think I'm joking?" Reaper raised his hand. "See this? She's making me lose my hair!"

Getting no sympathy, Reaper resumed pacing again.

"What I want to fucking know is how Shade and Rider fucking screwed up their intel on her. I should have been warned! She doesn't have a lick of common sense, and brother, if she isn't ADHD, I'll kiss your fucking ass. If she talks to someone twice, somehow, miraculously, they're family. She smiles at every man, regardless of age, as if they hung the fucking moon. Do you know how many fucking kids she wants?" Shouting his rants about Ginny, he paced back and forth across the room.

Giving a low cough, Lucky covered his mouth. "No. How many?"

Reaper moved to the end of the room. "You sick?"

Lucky lowered his hand. "No, I'm good."

Reaper eyed Lucky suspiciously. "You think this is funny?" he roared. "She wants a gazillion kids. Brother, I'm old. I'm getting older the more time I'm around her. The way I'm going, I'll be bald in two months."

"I don't see the problem. Just shave the other half off," Lucky suggested.

Reaper gave him a pained glance. "I can't. Ginny runs her hands through my hair. I like it."

"I offer premarital sessions for parishioners. I can make an appointment."

"Fuck you. You think I'm going to take marital advice from you? No, thanks. I can't fit in those leather pants, and I am for fucking sure not pretending to be a fucking pirate."

"Really? You really want to go there?"

Reaper wanted to smashed his booted foot on Lucky's cocksure grin.

"My wife isn't the one running around, finding out how to satisfy me. Willa is a deeply religious person, who also has the misconception that she isn't as physically appealing as other women. Playacting gives her the opportunity to be naughty without feeling like she's sinning. Plus, I seem to remember a few times you didn't mind playing a few games when you fucked your way from one state to the next when you came out of the service."

"That was before ..."

"Reaper, there was no one who enjoyed sex more than you. Well, except for Rider and Moon ... and ..." Lucky started over. "Do you know why you used to be the number one go-to when the brothers had sex?"

Reaper turned his back on Lucky, unable to take the sincerity that was coming from him.

"You have an intangible sex appeal that drives women crazy. They would get wet by something as simple as you taking your shirt off. The brothers would be one step behind in the game before you even hit the bed."

"I don't want to talk about this."

"Reaper, you can't bury the sexuality that is so much a part of you, no matter how hard you try. Your sexuality doesn't define you, but it is a part of the whole. That sexuality was used against you as a weapon, and when you feel betrayed, you stick a nail in the coffin and say you're done. Normally, I'd agree with you. I can't know how I would react if I had to endure the same vicious acts you did."

"I don't want to talk about this with you."

"Why not? We fucked women together dozens of times all over the Ohio club, but we can't stand here and talk about sex? Be fucking real. I'm going to be real with you, because I love you, brother, but you need to get your head out of your ass. You being raped by men didn't change your sexuality, you giving men blow jobs or whatever else didn't either, nor does it make you a whore when you had to perform for the women who bought you. They may have used and treated you a million different ways sexually, but they never *ever* owned your sexuality. That can't be bought or stolen; it's held within where no one can touch it, regardless of how hard they tried to tear it away from you."

"Then why do I feel so fucking dirty?" Reaper yelled.

Lucky moved from behind his back to hold out his hand. "I think I may know something that could work. Will you trust me, brother?"

Reaper stared at the hand held out to him. How could he

not trust Lucky? Lucky had risked his life to go to Sherguevil for him and Ginny.

Placing his hand in Lucky's, the brother led him into his bathroom where Lucky released his hand. "Take off your clothes, Reaper."

He wanted out of the closed-off room. However, concentrating on the blue towel hanging on the rack, Reaper removed his clothes as Lucky started the shower.

"Get in the shower," Lucky instructed.

Out of the corner of his eyes, he saw Lucky removing his clothes. Reaper froze as Lucky sat on the side of the tub to remove his shoes, then stood up to remove his pants.

Lucky paused when Reaper didn't go fully in the shower.

He trusted Lucky ... He trusted Lucky ... Reaper told himself, repeating the refrain to get his heart rate back in control. He stepped in the shower, shivering under the warm water when Lucky stepped inside, completely naked.

Staying to his side, Lucky cupped his hand under the spray. "This may not be a river, but this water is drawn from one. Matthew 3:11: *I baptize you with water for repentance*." Lucky raised his hands filled with water over his hand. The water slid over his head and body to the drain underneath his feet.

"I don't believe in God."

"He believes in you, Gavin." Lucky placed his hand on Reaper's shoulder. "God never lost faith in you. His arms remain open to you anytime you're ready to walk into them. This water is a symbol of your purification. Let your sins, and the sins committed against you, go down the drain, never to touch your soul again."

Lucky turned the water off, leaving him alone in the shower.

Moved despite his lack of faith, Reaper kept his eyes averted from Lucky as he left the shower.

Grabbing the towel from the rack, he started drying off. "Since I'm all clean, you going to tell Ginny to marry me now?" he said, attempting to lighten the unexpected and intense feelings of Lucky's words. When he stepped into the shower, he'd felt as if he shed an outer layer of filth that no matter how often he'd previously washed he could never get clean. Drying off he didn't feel brand-new but didn't feel nearly as contaminated.

"No."

Reaper went into the bedroom to dress, still not understanding this hold Lucky had over Ginny. Then thinking about Ginny, his mind went to which of the brothers Ginny would have asked for advice.

Sitting on the bed, Reaper was putting on his boots when Lucky came out of his en suite.

"Any idea who Ginny would have talked to yesterday?"

Lucky was as perplexed as he was. "None. She spent the most time with Rider and Shade when they were trying to find her stalker."

Going to the dresser, Reaper picked up his gun where Lucky had placed it. As he put the gun at the notch of his back, he realized he must have forgotten Suki.

Blocking the door from Lucky leaving, he ignored the brothers and the women who scattered when he opened his door. He let Suki inside before slamming the door for those who were still brave enough to remain on the same floor.

Lucky arched a brow at him for not letting him leave.

Reaching for his gun, he handed it back to Lucky.

"Shoot me."

CHAPTER FORTY-FOUR

"I am not wearing this." Ginny started to slide the zipper down that held the pieces of her top together with the use of her uninjured hand.

"You're wearing it." Trudy swatted her hand away to rezip the black top. "Why didn't you just ask for some help?"

"Sorry, I'm used to doing things on my own." Ginny turned to face the mirror more fully, then wished she hadn't. "I can't wear this tonight. There are going to be too many people coming to The Last Riders' tonight, and that doesn't include how many are already there."

"That's the plan." Killyama unceremoniously shoved her down onto the bed.

Ginny had to hold onto the side to keep herself from toppling over when the woman shoved a stiletto onto each of her resisting feet, while Trudy carefully slid the sling back on her sprained arm.

"Ouch!" Ginny muttered when Killyama pinched her calf to keep her from wiggling.

"Bitch, that didn't hurt." Killyama helped her to stand, as

Trudy finished adjusting the sling comfortably around her shoulder.

The five women circled her to critique her appearance.

"Not bad. Something's missing," Sex Piston mumbled, staring at her fixedly. "I know." Snapping her fingers, she went to her dresser, coming back with her teasing comb.

When Sex Piston was done, she gave another once-over, and Ginny saw her reflection in the floor-length dressing mirror. "I look like a floozy. I'm going to hell." Ginny whined at the women who had turned to admire their own reflections.

"So?" Crazy Bitch turned to get a better view of her ass in the snug red miniskirt. "We're all going to be there with you. What's the big deal?"

Ginny moved in front of Crazy Bitch to see if tugging the black skirt down lower would cover more of her womanly parts. Pulling it higher when it exposed more of her pouch, she narrowed her eyes on Killyama. "Change outfits with me."

"Bitch these pants are too long for you."

Damn. Killyama was right.

"I'll switch with you," Crazy Bitch offered.

"No, thanks." The woman was wearing a red lace top with a red bra underneath, paired with a red skirt that was even shorter than hers.

"We all ready?" Sex Piston asked, throwing different colored lipsticks into her purse. "The boys are waiting."

"Do Stud, Calder, Cade, and Dalton know The Last Riders haven't invited us over tonight?" Ginny refused to budge from her spot on the carpet as the women waited by the door.

Sex Piston shrugged unapologetically. "It's on a need-to-know basis. When they need to know, I'll tell them."

Ginny looked at Killyama. "At least tell me Train knows you're having a party at their clubhouse."

"Okay, he knows."

Suspicious, Ginny stared Killyama down. It didn't work. The woman opened the door, ushering the women out. "Move it. Diamond isn't going to order the burgers and fries until we're ten minutes from Treepoint. I've been craving those burgers all day."

Ginny followed them out into the living room where the men were waiting. The appreciative catcalls the men made for their wives had them prancing around to show off their clothes.

Killyama stopped in front of Train. "You like?"

"I like." He grinned at her. "Where're we going?"

"Mick is going to make us some burgers."

Ginny frowned at Killyama sidestepping the question. Then she decided to speak up. She wasn't going to let the men be bamboozled into letting the wolves enter a lion's den. "We're—"

"Gotta go." Killyama shoved Train toward the door, while the other women manhandled their men.

Trudy linked their arms together, maneuvering her outside.

"Dalton will be furious with you going to The Last Riders' club without him."

"Then he should have come with us."

Trudy opened Cade's back door for her before going around to the other side.

Ginny resumed the conversation when Trudy was in the car. "You sent him to the store so we wouldn't have to wait in the car for him."

"Don't worry; he'll get over it. You can get away with a lot of crap when you're pregnant."

"Really?"

"Yes. The bad part is when this little bundle of joy pops out of me, the get-out-of-jail pass expires."

"What are you going to do then?" Ginny laughed.

"Have another one, of course."

The drive back to Treepoint was uneventful and over much too soon.

Driving through main street, Ginny's nerves were making her feel nauseous. There was no freaking way she would be able to let the men see her in this outfit. Gavin acted like a priest when she wore clothes that he considered remotely suggestive. The clothes she was wearing now blew past suggestive; they were an outright feast for the male of the species.

There was still a chance she could escape Gavin's wrath with a little luck. She had formulated the plan on the drive. She would lag behind the girls as they went into the club, then duck upstairs and change clothes. If Gavin was in the room, it wouldn't matter, because none of men had seen her dressed in the woo-woo outfit. Ginny conveniently forgot that Gavin would consider Train, Cade, Stud, and Calder men.

Fat Louise's husband parked beside Stud's van. Sex Piston, Crazy Bitch, and Killyama were out of Stud's van before she and Trudy.

"Took you long enough." Sex Piston took out her comb to make last minute adjustments to her hair. "Don't look like a scaredy cat. Reaper isn't going to eat you. Wait—that's the whole point. If he doesn't, I've wasted my whole Saturday."

The women burst into laughter.

"Move 'em out, girls. Diamond is on her way with the burgers." Crazy Bitch, Calder, Fat Louise, and Cade walked to the steps of the club.

Train came from the other side of the van. "Where are they going?" he asked Killyama. "You said we were picking up Reaper. Why didn't he just meet us at the diner?"

"Change of plans." Killyama took Train's hand and began walking toward the club as she explained, "Diamond wanted to join us, but Knox refuses to step foot in the diner with Marty there. She placed an order and is bringing it here with Knox. That way, we can all still hang out together."

"Damn, she's good," Ginny whispered to Trudy so Train couldn't hear.

"She's my idol," Trudy whispered back.

As they neared the top of the steps, Ginny released Trudy's arm to let her go inside first.

"Hi, Nickel, do you happen to know if Gavin is in his room?"

Nickel gave her an unblinking stare. "I wouldn't know. I'm out here."

"Oh ... yes. I meant, do you know if Gavin is in the club or out?"

"He's inside unless he went out the back door."

"Okay. Thank you."

When she turned from talking to Nickel, Trudy was waiting inside the doorway. She had waited for her. *Darn it.*

Time to switch to plan two.

Inside the club, Ginny put her foot on the bottom step.

"I need to run to the restroom."

Trudy pulled her back down the steps. "Hold it."

"Trudy—"

"Evangeline," Trudy mocked. "Why is it you're the bravest person I know until it involves Reaper and sex? Then you wimp out."

"I don't want to pressure him."

Trudy made a face at her. "Save me."

"Ditto."

Left with no choice, Ginny was ushered into the main room with Trudy hanging onto her arm like a leech. Moon was playing pool with Jewell. Cade and Train joined them while Calder and Stud took the other table.

Viper and Shade were coming in from the kitchen. They took one look at who was in the room and left.

"That was rude." Ginny sent Trudy an apologetic glance.

The insult was like water off a duck's back. "Who cares?"

Trudy dragged her to the bar. "Have a seat. I'm going to play bartender."

Ginny slid onto a stool. "Barkeep, I'll take a ginger ale."

Trudy looked cute as a button, maneuvering her baby bump behind the bar to get her a bottle of soda. "I'll take one of these, too."

Ginny was unscrewing the lid when Crazy Bitch badgered Moon to turn the music on. His eyes lit up when Diamond and Knox walked in the front door carrying bags of food.

Everyone in the main room gravitated toward the kitchen to eat.

"Who got married?"

Puck went around the counter to slide the cake to the side.

"Willa made it for someone's wedding yesterday. The groom backed out, so she brought it here for everyone to share."

"Willa told me she was making a wedding cake for the doctor who checked me out at the hospital. I feel bad for her."

"I don't." Crazy Bitch went searching through the cabinets to find a plate, then went rummaging to find the silverware. "The bitch is better off without the low-down motherfucker."

Cutting a humongous slice of cake, she then took her two burgers and order of fries and carried it out of the kitchen and into the main room.

Ginny had to smother her laughter when Puck stared after her, awestruck.

"She's married." Ginny felt bad dashing his hopes.

"Happily?"

"Yes."

"Fuck."

Ginny placed a couple of burgers on his plate. "I have a friend I can hook you up with," she consoled him.

Puck cut himself an extra-large helping of cake. "No, thanks. I'm going to need some time to get over her."

Ginny was getting Crazy Bitch to set out several trays of appetizers from the refrigerator when Beth, Razer, Lily, and Shade came in from the back door.

Hungry, Ginny ate a couple of burgers. She had tried to sneak out a couple of times, but one of the women would catch her each time. Doomed to fail, Ginny began loosening up when it was apparent Gavin wasn't in the house. Either that or he was asleep, which was a win-win in her eyes. She would stay thirty more minutes, then go upstairs, even if she had to climb up there from the tree outside the bedroom window with one hand.

Once everyone was done eating, they went back into the main room, where other members came in and out.

A few of the couples were dancing. Ginny watched them jealously. She loved to dance, and the one and only time she had danced with Gavin, he had accused her of rigging the tape deck.

"Come dance with me." Trudy took her hand, pulling her off the stool.

Ginny loved her sister. Trudy knew her too well.

"I love this song." Ginny moved to the music. "I wish I could sing a song like that."

"What do you mean?"

"A song that, no matter how many people sing it, they will never achieve the same perfection. The song was meant for the original artist."

"Like Katy Perry and 'Fireworks'?"

Ginny wholeheartedly agreed. "Yes, also like 'Girl on Fire' by Alicia Keys."

"You'll do it."

"No, I'm meant to write those songs for other singers."

Trudy frowned at her as they danced. "Why don't you think you can?"

"Because I'm not going to sing anymore. My singer career is over."

"Why?"

"I'm not going to risk what I have with Gavin. To be popular, you have to do concerts and be willing to make sacrifices. I'm not willing to do that. I want to be here for Gavin and our children."

"There's still time. Just put off having kids for a while."

Dancing as they talked, Ginny noticed that Jewell was dancing with Jesus, and Puck was dancing with Jade. Space was running out, forcing couples dance closer together. Killyama and Train joined the throng behind them, crowding Jesus and Jewell even more.

"We'll see," Ginny said noncommittedly.

"Mayday, Mayday." Killyama leaned her head between Trudy and her, alerting them.

Ginny gave a silent groan. She meant to go upstairs fifteen minutes ago, but she'd been enjoying dancing with Trudy.

Dalton and Gavin came in the door to the main room,

searching the crowd with their eyes. Ginny was tempted to duck down and crawl out of the room.

"Why is Gavin with Dalton?"

"I might have texted Gavin that he could pick you up at my house." Trudy continued dancing, unperturbed that her husband was glowering at her.

"Oh God. He's going to kill me. I'm dead."

"You've always been so melodramatic. We won't let him kill you. We got your back," Trudy promised.

"That's right, bitch!" Killyama clenched her hand in a fist. "Bitches stick together."

Dalton went to the end of the crowd and crooked his finger to her.

"Aw … isn't that cute." Sex Piston had danced herself and Stud nearer to them. "He thinks you're a puppy."

Ginny didn't spare a glance for Dalton, her concentration on Gavin. His cold features stared at her, then went behind her. Whatever he saw had his lips tightening into a thin line.

Ginny turned her head to see Jewel and Jesus dancing. Gavin's eyes went down her body before raising them to hers. Breaking the contact, Gavin then turned and went up the steps two at a time.

"I'm so dead." Ginny made a move to go after Gavin.

"Hell no," Sex Piston warned. "Make 'em come get you. Stud came after me."

Ginny was tempted to ignore Sex Piston, but truth be told, she was kind of afraid to go upstairs until he cooled down. There were couches in the back room off the kitchen and in the basement; she could sleep there.

"I need some water." Ginny slid between the twisting bodies, heading toward the bar.

"Me, too." Trudy hastily followed after her when Dalton gave up trying to get her to come to him and was coming after her with a thundercloud expression.

Ginny got her and Trudy waters as Trudy grabbed a bottle of whiskey and poured some in a glass. Giving Trudy the bottle of water, Ginny stood to the side, interested to see how her sister talked herself out of trouble. She might need a few pointers for when she was brave enough to go upstairs.

Sex Piston, Crazy Bitch, Killyama, and Fat Louise ditched their husbands on the dance floor to make their way to the bar. Ginny teared up at watching the sisterhood in action.

"Babe"—Trudy gave Dalton the glass of whiskey—"I'm *so* sorry. Diamond called and wanted us to stop by to show off the new shoes that Knox bought her, and I lost time. I was just about to call you to come get me. Train told me he would take me home an hour ago, but he and Stud started playing pool."

Dalton emptied his glass before lowering it to the counter. "I'm just glad you're okay. I was worried."

"Aw …." Trudy reached over the counter, pulling Dalton over the bar top to kiss him.

Ginny shifted her gaze, embarrassed at the way she was kissing Dalton. She had never kissed Gavin that way. Her shoulders slumped. It was her inability on top of the trauma that Gavin had experienced. She was a dud in the bedroom.

Pulling away from Dalton's kiss, Trudy wiped the smear of lipstick on his bottom lip. "Why don't you go play a couple of games with Stud and Train? I'll just stay here and chat with the girls, if that's all right with you?" Trudy reached in the bar fridge and gave Dalton a beer to take with him.

Dalton took the beer, twisting off the cap. "One game and then we're leaving."

"Of course. Go have fun. I'll be waiting right here."

Dalton gave her promising kiss before striding off.

"I wish I could handle Gavin that easily," Ginny said dolefully.

Trudy rubbed her belly. "Thanks, kid."

Ginny closed her bottled water, setting it on the bar morosely. Dalton had immediately gone to Trudy. Gavin hadn't. Feeling deflated, she decided to go upstairs.

"I'm going to call it a night."

Sensing her hurt, Trudy took her hand to prevent her from leaving. "Don't leave. Dance with me one more—Holy shit ..." Trudy broke off, her eyes going wide. "Is that Reaper?"

Killyama, Sex Piston, Crazy Bitch, and Fat Louise turned in unison at Trudy's expression.

Ginny lifted her eyes, and her breath caught in her throat.

The man standing on the small landing at the top of the stairs had to be Gavin. He looked just like him. What made it difficult to tell was the clothes the man was wearing.

"Mother fucking hell ... Come to mama." Sex Piston gaped at Gavin, then turned to look at her. "You lucky bitch."

Was it physically possible to swallow one's own tongue when confronted with pure man candy?

Her eyes were glued to Gavin as she took in tight, cream-colored shirt that had been left casually unbuttoned, exposing his neck tattoos and the top of his chest. Gazing down his body, the slim-fit brown pants drew attention to the muscles of his legs. He'd swapped the normal boots he wore to a soft leather dress boot.

"Where's Train?" Killyama put one foot on the bottom rung of the stool so she could raise herself higher to find her husband.

"What you wanting Train for?" Sex Piston asked, her eyes just as glued to Gavin as hers were.

"Because I'm a fucking married woman, and I plan to stay that way." Killyama waved to her husband again.

Ginny frowned. "What about being my backup?"

"You have four other bitches here to take your back; you don't need me."

"What do you need?" Train asked, coming up to Killyama.

"We're leaving."

"What's the hurry? Dalton and I have a game going. I'll lose a hundred bucks …" Train turned his head to see what the women were staring at as Diamond stopped dancing with Knox to stand next to Sex Piston.

"Is that Reaper?"

"Fuck no, that's what you call God's gift to women," Sex Piston said in awe.

"God bless America," Diamond reverently muttered.

Train took out his wallet, pulling out a one-hundred-dollar bill. Giving it to Knox, Train grabbed Killyama's hand and hustled her out of the room.

Fat Louise waved her hand in front of her face. "I'm burning up in here."

"He can come and light my fire." Crazy Bitch picked up the bottle of water to take a drink.

"That's mine," Ginny protested.

"The Last Riders share. You with Gavin, that means you're a Last Rider. Bitch, you need to learn to share with your friends!" Crazy Bitch's eyes went down Gavin's body like hers had. "Jesus … please share. I'll share Calder—"

"Who you giving me to?" Calder went behind the bar, hearing the tail end of Crazy Bitch's offer. Following the women's line of vision, he started to take a drink of his beer when he carefully set it back down. "We're leaving."

"Hell no, we aren't. Bitch, why didn't you tell us he's packing? A woman needs a snack someti—"

Ginny's eyes widened when Calder lifted Crazy Bitch over his shoulder and headed out the door. Calder did stop to say a few words to Gavin before carrying his wife out.

What was he waiting for? Was he wanting her to go to

him? She needed more water but was afraid one of the women in the room would make a move on him if she dared to look away.

The music switched to another song. Recognizing "I See Red" by Everybody Loves an Outlaw, Ginny felt the sexy vibe of the song to the marrow of her bones.

Gavin motioned to where everyone was dancing, indicting he wanted her to meet him there. When Gavin took the final step off the stair landing, Ginny felt her womanly parts clench in aching need. She hadn't had this reaction when he had worn the dinner suit on Sherguevil Island. This was different. This was like what she had felt when he had been sitting at the table and she had rushed away ... on steroids.

Gavin was excluding a powerfully sexy quality that drew women like an erotic scent enveloping them into a fantasy-land where all you wanted to do was lick him like a snow cone to cool the heat.

Walking to a spot four inches away, Gavin motioned for her again.

Sex Piston shifted so she was no longer looking at him. "Bitch, go," she hissed. "Or in the next two minutes, I'm going to give Stud a reason to divorce me."

Moving from behind the counter, Ginny felt her feet crossing the floor, stopping two inches from him, afraid to go any farther. Her top felt as tight as a corset, and it had a stranglehold on her heart.

Belatedly remembering the advice, she licked her bottom lip and took the step needed for their bodies to meet. Sliding her arms around the lower part of his waist, she hooked her hands over his belt and held on for dear life. She wanted to ask if he was mad at her, but she took the advice she had been given; the less talking, the better.

Someone in the room turned the overhead light off,

leaving the room bathed in soft lamplight.

The song ended and the playlist replayed the first song that she and Trudy had danced to. "Girl on Fire." Sweet Jesus, this was the last song she needed to listen to with the sensual way Gavin was holding her.

Song after song played, each one ratcheting up the sensual tension between them.

"Did you have fun at Sex Piston's slumber party?" The sensual quality in his whispery-soft voice had chills going up her back.

Ginny managed to get out a strangled, "Yes."

"Did you enjoy me running around Treepoint trying to meet up with you?"

This was so not good. The hair on her arms stood up.

"I didn't know Trudy texted you to meet me."

Gavin curled his hands around the back of her neck. "You would have known if you had answered my texts or calls."

"I forgot my phone in my bag and I rode in Sex Piston's van."

Ginny stopped speaking. He didn't want to hear excuses of why she hadn't kept her phone with her.

"I screwed up," she admitted.

"Shh ... don't be afraid." When his hand went to her ass to jerk her hips to his, it pressed her breasts tighter against his chest. "I would never hurt you, Ginny, ever."

Ginny couldn't relax. The slow, sensual way he talked to her was scaring the bejesus out of her.

"I would never hurt you," Gavin repeated. "But I am going to punish you. So, are you ready to go upstairs?"

Ginny felt his hand slide along her arm until he linked his fingers through hers. Then he pulled arm behind her back until they were dancing with her arm twisted behind her back. There was no pain, as her injured arm was still cocooned in her sling. With both of her arms out of commission, however, it gave her a helpless feeling, as Gavin danced with her, controlling their movements.

"No." Ginny pretended the strangled word that came out of her mouth was articulated perfectly. It would have worked, too, if Gavin had made a modicum of effort to hide the knowing gleam in his eyes. The jerk didn't.

They listened to Sam Smith sing "Fire On Fire." The sensual words and voice were heightened by the hedonistic way Gavin watched every move her body made with his.

"Delaying the inevitable won't make it any easier." Gavin lowered his head to lick her bottom lip.

"Maybe not, but it's making me feel better."

"Why? Because we're surrounded by all these people?" Gavin's lips curled in a smile that went right to her crotch. "With one snap of my fingers, I could have those you think will protect you cleared out. No one would lift a hand to stop me from laying you on the pool table and unzipping that tiny skirt to find out how wet you are."

Ginny's breathing escalated.

Keeping her hand twisted behind her back, he used his other hand to stroke a fingertip across the tops of her exposed breasts. Goosebumps appeared beneath his touch.

"Do you believe me?"

"Yes."

"I was hoping you would give me a different answer. Was wearing this sexy little bit of nothing the bravest thing you planned to do tonight, Nymph?"

Ginny averted her gaze and saw Fat Louise dancing with Cade. She looked at her for help. All she got back was a thumbs-up as the woman stared at Gavin with limpid pools of desire, as if he were cotton candy on a stick. The saddest part was that Ginny agreed—he was like cotton candy; once you touched him, you wanted more.

"I didn't have a plan," she denied. Liar. Liar. Her pants were on fire. Lord, forgive her. Her body whole body was, and there wasn't a fire extinguisher in the whole room. Her ride or die friends had either left or were ogling Gavin, as fixated on his every movement as she was.

Gavin slid a hand up her chest to her neck to curl around the back of her neck. "How did you get to the church this morning?"

Why did she feel as if she was about to walk over a bed of scorching coals?

"Moon gave me a ride."

"How was your first ride?"

She didn't like the way he was asking his questions. They seemed casual, but he was staring at her like a wolf anticipating jumping on his prey.

"Don't tell Moon—I wouldn't want to hurt his feelings—but it was boring. I could have walked there faster and had more fun."

"You just saved Moon's life."

Ginny frowned. "You're joking."

"Do I look like I'm joking?"

No, he definitely did not look like he was joking.

"Have you ever seen any of the other wives riding on the back of the brothers' bikes to whom they aren't married?"

"No, but I—"

"Doesn't matter if they are married or not. It's *who* the women belong to, ring or not. You belong to me; your ass doesn't belong on any brother's bike. Only mine."

"I needed a ride, and I didn't want to disturb you. I asked for whoever was watching me to take me. He did. How we got there is irrelevant."

"It's relevant to me. Your first time on a bike belonged to

me, just like the first time you fucked belonged to me. You know something else? For the rest of your life, all your firsts belong to me."

"Riding a motorcycle for the first time isn't like having sex for the first time."

"That's because you haven't ridden with me."

How could discussing something as simple as a motorcycle ride leave her crotch melting?

Gavin wasn't like cotton candy; he was cotton candy. The naughty images he invoked were sticking in places that had her pelvis unconsciously rubbing across his as the music dipped lower.

"Are you done playing this game, or can we go upstairs and fuck?"

Indecision about what to do next had her wanting to stay exactly where she was. Unconsciously, she bit her lip, thinking about the advice she had been given. Could she actually do it?

"I'm ready."

Gavin dropped his arm from her neck to hook around her waist. Each step felt as if she were being led to the guillotine. As they slowly climbed the steps, Gavin dropped his hand to the curve of her ass. Suki ran in front them and down the hallway, patiently waiting for them.

Opening the door, Ginny let Suki run in first before going inside. Moving farther into the room, Ginny then turned to face the door, seeing Gavin shutting it. Staring into her eyes, he locked the door.

Unconsciously, Ginny took a step back. She couldn't do this.

Feeling overwhelmed by the overt sexual intent he was displaying toward her was hard for a woman like her to take. Men didn't normally look at her like they wanted to rip her clothes off and have their way with her.

Damn, Sex Piston was good. Too good. She had no idea what to do with the man who was stalking toward her like a lion entering his den. She could only do what she'd been advised.

The thought bubble broke when Gavin reached out to grab her by the throat, backstepping her to the bed. Ginny's eyes frantically went around the room. Alighting on Suki, she debated calling for the dog that had sprawled out onto the dog bed, closing her eyes.

Reading her mind, he gave a satisfied smile. "Don't. I'll call Moses, and I'll give her back."

Ginny didn't call for Suki. Gavin wasn't hurting her. While he was holding her neck, it wasn't tight and she could easily break free.

"Feel like playing a game?"

She really didn't.

Why ask for advice if you're not going to take it? she railed at herself.

Because Gavin is scaring the bejesus out of me, the saner part of her brain yelled back.

"What kind of game?"

"You have to do everything I say when it's my turn." Gavin hooked a finger over the zipper of her top. Ginny felt her heart race when he stroked his knuckle over the skin between her breasts. "Everything."

"What do I do when it's my turn?"

"The same. I'll do everything you say."

"What do I win?"

"The winner gets to set the punishment."

"What if I really don't want to do something you tell me to do?"

"Then say … nutcracker. The person who says it first loses. Any more questions?"

"No."

"So"—Gavin slid her zipper down a centimeter—"are you ready to play with me?"

"Sure." Ginny swallowed hard. "Why not?"

Gavin's lips curled into the smile that made her both frightened and excited. She was really beginning to dread that smile.

"Who gets to go first?"

"First time player always gets to go first." Gavin removed his hand from her clothes and her neck. Giving her a mocking bow, he swept his arm in front of him. "What would you like me to do?"

Ginny licked her lips. Taking a glance at the clock, she committed the time to memory. She had a feeling, during this game, seconds could be a matter of winning and losing.

She would start with something easy. "Take your shirt off."

Gavin brought his hand behind his back to grab the material and pull his shirt off.

"Take your shoes and socks off."

Gavin went to the bottom of the bed to sit, removing his shoes and socks. Then he stood.

Ginny moved to stand in front of him. "Kiss me."

Obediently, Gavin kissed her.

Wrapping her good arm around his neck, Ginny began to relax. This wasn't so bad. She could really get into this game. Pulling her mouth teasingly away to nibble on his earlobe, she then moved to his chest to lick each of his nipples. She was having a field day having Gavin at her command. How had she never heard of this game before?

Slowly, Ginny unbuckled his leather belt, her mouth going dry in excitement, anticipating touching his cock.

"Time."

Blinking, Ginny looked at the clock. Realizing she had

gotten carried away when kissing him, she removed her hand away from his pants to step back.

Expecting him to command her to remove her clothes, she was surprised when he told her to carry the desk chair to the middle of the room. Following his instructions, she waited for his next command.

Gavin sat down on the chair. "Go sit on the bed, facing me."

Ginny sat on the bed.

"Pull you skirt up without standing up."

Her blood began rushing through her veins like white water rapids. With one arm in the sling, Ginny had to take turns twisting her skirt to raise it, exposing the black panties underneath. The task accomplished, Ginny looked at Gavin, whose legs were sprawled out in front of him.

"Take off your panties."

Ginny gave an internal groan. Using the same tiring method, Ginny removed her panties. She had just slid her panties off when Gavin called time.

Ginny knew she was in trouble when realization struck; he had timed the two tasks to the second.

Ginny lost precious seconds trying to decide what she wanted him to do next.

"Sit straight."

Immediately, Gavin straightened in his chair.

Raising from the bed, she brazenly strolled toward him, as she had been advised. Leaning forward, she gave him her next order. "Unzip my top."

Gavin slowly unzipped her top.

"Take it off."

Gavin pulled the leather top off.

"Take my bra off."

Gavin leaned forward to wrap his arms around her sides to unhook her bra.

Was she going to be brave and make him do what she wanted? Yes, she was.

"Lick my nipples."

Gavin began licking her nipples.

Be bold, Ginny.

"Bite my nipples ... gently," Ginny hastened to add. Pain had never been her strong suit.

She brought her hand to his shoulder, steadying himself. Her knees felt as if they were about to crumble.

Be bold, flashed through her mind again.

Moving forward, Ginny straddled Gavin. She barely managed to keep her eyes from rolling back in her head at the exquisite sensations as his cloth-covered cock nestled under her crotch. Winding her arm around his neck, she wanted to tell him to kiss her but was afraid she would lose track of time again.

"My turn."

Ginny's eyes flew to the clock. Damn. She was going to have to do better with time management.

"Stand up."

Ginny made a face at him. She was happy where she was.

Gavin stood, walking to the bed, then climbed onto it, laying down sideways on the bed. "Get on the bed, Ginny."

Ginny lay down sideways like he had done.

Folding his arms under his head, he gave his next order. "Sit on my face."

Ginny hesitated, wary of following his order. Gavin had never let her on top, regardless of what they were doing.

"I'm adding two minutes to my time ... three ...."

Ginny moved before she lost any more time.

Slowly, she lowered her crotch to his face, nervously watching his reaction until his tongue ran amok. This time, she wasn't able to prevent her eyes from rolling backward.

Ginny couldn't have cared less about time as she felt

desire skyrocket from her clit, mind-numbing ecstasy beckoning.

"Your turn."

Blinking owlishly, on the edge of an orgasm, her throbbing pussy had her mind unable to form a thought.

Gavin turned his head to kiss the inside of her thigh. "May I make a suggestion? You could say *make me come*."

"Yes," she nearly screeched in happiness at the suggestion. "Make me come."

Bracing her good arm on the mattress, Ginny spent the next twenty-seven minutes enjoying what Gavin could do with his mouth. She was in a middle of the most intense orgasm she'd had when the unimaginable joy was cut short at the dreaded word.

"Time."

Wanting to cry, Ginny moved off his face.

"Stand on the floor by bed," he directed. "Place your hand on the bed."

Doing as he instructed, Ginny put her hand on the bed.

"Move it forward until I tell you to stop."

Inching her hand forward, she stopped when he told her to. Ginny blushed at the position of her being hunched over the bed with her ass up in the air.

"Use your forearm to hold yourself up. I don't want you uncomfortable."

Letting her wrist go slack, Ginny balanced on her good forearm.

"Comfortable?"

"Yes."

He smoothed his hand over the leather of her skirt before he twisted the skirt upward to her waist. "Don't move."

Walking around the bed to the opposite side, his eyes met hers. His hand went to the heavy end of his belt and he jerked the already loosened belt from his pants.

Ginny couldn't take her eyes off Gavin as he laid the belt in front of her face on the bed, then began removing his pants to fold them before laying them on top of his hamper.

Sauntering back to where she was, Gavin leaned over her back without placing his weight on her, despite their skin touching. Ginny could feel his hard cock nestle between the crack of her ass.

"I am not a jealous man, Nymph," he whispered in her ear. "But I am a possessive one. I'm not PBS; I don't give other men free shows of what belongs to me. You knew if I didn't let you wear that black dress on Sherguevil Island, I wouldn't want you wearing what you are tonight, didn't you?"

"Yes."

"I don't care whose bright idea it was to wear it, only that you did. Big mistake, Ginny. Big." Gavin moved his mouth to the curve of her throat, sucking the flesh.

Ginny's pussy clenched, renewing the fire within that hadn't been put out.

Gavin wrapped his arm around her waist, then moved it up her chest between her breasts to her shoulder taking her weight off her arm.

The longer he sucked on her neck, the hotter she got.

"Gavin ...," she moaned.

Ginny felt his cock move between her thighs to slide in her damp pussy. Driving his cock in with strong thrusts, Ginny gasped at the force he was using. If he hadn't braced her, she would have fallen onto the bed.

Pushing back against him, they developed a rhythm that had her pushing her butt back at him as he slammed forward. Gavin started a wildfire that had another orgasm rolling through her.

"Time."

"No!"

"All you have to do is tell me what you want."

"Don't stop!"

Her feverous desire stroked higher, building into a conflagration that had her abandoning the idea that there wasn't a chance in hell of winning this game. When Gavin played, he played to win.

"Time." Gavin placed her facedown on the bed, sliding his arm out from underneath her.

Ginny then heard the shower start and him calling her name. He was already in the shower with the water coursing over his body.

"Remove your sling and come inside."

Setting the sling on the sink, Ginny stepped inside the shower.

He washed her meticulously, then moved her under the spray to remove the silky bubbles.

Gavin leaned on the side of shower wall, facing her. "Suck my dick."

Ginny didn't move. Gavin never let her touch his cock.

Opening the shower door, she started to get out.

"Are you quitting the game?"

Ginny turned back to him. "You don't want me to touch you."

"I don't ask for what I don't want. Suck my dick. I have fifteen minutes left. If you don't make me come in that time, when it's my turn again, I'm going to fuck you in your ass."

Ginny went down to her knees.

"I've never done this before." She observed every detail of Gavin's reaction as she softly grasped his cock as if it were a fragile glass that would shatter if handled too roughly.

"Cover the head with your mouth."

Obeying him, Ginny watched him, waiting for him to jerk away or be told to stop.

Gavin burrowed his hand through her hair, pulling her mouth off his cock. "When you have a sucker in your mouth, do you think when you suck it or do you just do it?"

She moved her mouth back to his dick. Relaxing when Gavin didn't jerk his hips away from her, Ginny moved closer to him. As she sucked on his cock, Gavin twisted her hair around, pulling her closer to him. Watching Gavin as she sucked on him was a picture of erotic beauty. The turgid length of his cock, the bulging veins, the taste, it all had been an unknown mystery to her. When his hand went to the other wall to brace himself, he revealed he was close to his orgasm.

"You have two minutes left."

Removing her mouth from the head of his cock, she licked her way from the top, delicately flicking her tongue before covering the head again.

"Take your mouth off." The expression on his face was one she was familiar with; Gavin was getting ready to come.

Refusing to remove her mouth, Ginny led him down the same path of bliss that he had taken her down. The incredible elation it gave her to pleasure Gavin this gave her a sense of intimacy that she hadn't felt before. The water showering down on her disguised the drops of tears that managed to escape through her tightly closed lids. The trust Gavin was giving her was the prize she had worked so hard to attain. When he finished, she lovingly placed gentle kisses on his each of his hips trailing her lips over the tattoos, marking his sleek body.

With a croak in his voice, he reminded her they were still playing. "Stand up. It's your turn."

"Dry me and my hair."

Ginny watched Gavin's facial expressions as he blow-dried her hair.

"Sex Piston may be a bitch from hell, but she did an excellent job of hiding your hair color." Gavin placed a damp swathe of her hair on his palm to apply the hot air. "You look more like T.A. with this hair color." Gavin's eyes met hers in the mirror. The sandy brown hair had streaks of lighter blond within the depths that shone in the lamplight. "Especially with the different eye color. Must have been pain hiding your light under the bushel."

She had been dreading his reaction to her removing her colored contacts before she came back to the clubhouse. Her blue-green eyes staring back at her from the mirror were darker than Trudy's. She would never be a raving beauty like Taylor, but she no longer felt as if the woman in mirror was a distorted vision of herself.

"Hammer was the one who noticed we looked more alike as we grew older. My hair didn't grow lighter until I was four or five, while Trudy's was always light. I won't miss having to keep up with maintenance, the contacts were a definite pain. Are you surprised? I can get Sex Piston to color it back, but I'd really prefer not to have to wear the contacts."

"Ginny, I have stopped being surprised by anything you do. Leave it, I don't give a fuck about your hair or eye color. Anything else, you haven't told me? That you're an alien from Mars, had breast reduction, that your teeth are veneers. Kind of would like to know who the real you is or is everything completely fake as shit?"

"Nothing about me that is important is fake." Ginny met his stoic gaze with a golf-sized lump in her throat, afraid that she had lost the ground she gained in the shower with him.

"Which is why you're still in my bed and not at the Coleman's. Like I said, I don't give a fuck about your hair or your eye color."

Breathing easier at his matter-of-fact acceptance of her appearance, Ginny made an observation of her own. She had noticed a different air of confidence when he came downstairs, as if there was a weight lifted off his shoulders.

Wondering about the changes, as she luxuriated in the care Gavin was giving her.

At the end of the thirty minutes, he laid the blow dryer down on the dresser.

"Put on something warm. We're going out." Gavin gave his order as he dressed himself.

Wearing a pair of corduroy pants and a bulky grey sweater, she put on a thick pair of socks and tugged on a pair of boots. Taking a jacket out of his closet, he held it out for her to slide into. Adjusting the sling, Gavin then took out another jacket for himself before taking her hand and leading her to the door. Suki started to stir.

"Stay."

Leaving the dog in the bedroom, they went down the steps. The living room was still full, and Ginny kept her eyes averted when she saw what many of them were doing.

He slid his arm over her shoulders as they stepped off the porch to go down the steps. Reaching his bike, he took a helmet off Viper's bike that she had seen Winter wear.

"Put it on."

She started to argue with him that Moon hadn't made her, then figured that might not be a wise decision.

Gavin swung his leg over the seat. "Get on."

As he started the bike with one kick, Ginny grabbed Gavin around the waist and held on tight.

They hadn't passed the Porters' land before it kicked in why Gavin had been so angry with her about her riding with Moon. You didn't share this magic with just anyone. This wasn't like riding in a car. On a motorcycle, it was you, the high-powered beast you were straddling, and the road. Like a blind person reading a book, you had to feel the road, your body reacting, and the rush of adrenaline you felt at the challenge.

Ginny laid her head on Gavin's back. She could never

ride behind anyone else ever again, any more than she would ever be able to be with another man. Gavin might not love her, but he didn't want her experiencing this with anyone else. She had given up being hopeful about many things in life, but Gavin loving her wasn't one.

CHAPTER FORTY-FIVE

"Where are we going?" Ginny practically bounced in her seat as Gavin shut the door of the Escalade he'd bought at the police auction.

The excitement at doing something was exhilarating. For the last two months, they had been confined to the clubhouse, unless she went to Silas's house for brief spurts of time or went with Trudy and Dalton to the doctor appointments.

Gavin took her protection seriously, and she had been planning to put her foot down tonight when he unexpectedly told her to get changed into something warm.

"Are we going to the movies?" she prodded him once he was behind the wheel.

"No. Just wait. You'll see."

Putting on her seat belt, Ginny was surprised when they didn't turn toward town as he drove out of the parking lot. Her excitement ebbed a little bit when she realized they were heading toward Silas's house. She thought maybe he was taking her out to a restaurant or the movies—like a real date.

When they pulled into the driveway, she saw the lights were on inside. "Are we having dinner with Silas?"

"No." Getting out the Escalade, Gavin came around to open the door for her.

About to head toward the house, she was surprised when he took her hand and turned toward their house. She was just there yesterday. The outer structure and the roof were now finished, and tomorrow the electricians were coming, so she couldn't understand what he wanted to show her.

When he continued walking past their house and went the small knob of the hill, past a copse of trees, she saw flickering firelights. A lump settled in her throat as they grew nearer and she saw what Gavin had done.

"I thought we could have a picnic and watch the stars for a while."

Staring down, she saw the thick sleeping bags spread alongside each other, and Gavin had placed four lanterns around them. There was also a cooler to the side, a dozen or so pillows, and a thick blanket on one end.

Sinking down onto the sleeping bag, Ginny let him unpack the cooler.

"You did this before coming to the club?"

"Yes."

The romantic atmosphere Gavin had created tugged at her heart. She had been searching for the perfect moment to share something with him, and he had done it for her. She couldn't think of a better spot to tell him that he was going to be a father.

Unpacking the cooler, he set out sandwiches and chips. The simple meal reminded her of when they had traveled to Treepoint after she had taken off from Nashville.

"This is where Leah and I sat when we watched the stars," she reminisced.

"Silas told me."

As they ate, Ginny planned it out in her head how she was going to tell Gavin she was pregnant. She had been thinking about it since the moment she found out, but she put it off because she was paranoid about it being so early in her pregnancy. Then, as one month turned into two and so on, Ginny couldn't explain why she held back.

Spending so much time with Gavin for the last two months had only strengthened the love she felt for him, and despite how he never spoke his feelings for her, she knew he cared for her. She no longer heard the silent screams in her head at the level of intensity she felt before speaking with Pastor Dean, but they were still there, as if someone was caged inside of her and wanted to escape.

Clearing away what was left of their meal, they lay down on the sleeping bags with the blanket over them to watch the night sky. Cuddled next to him, Ginny felt Gavin take her hand under the blanket. Feeling something slide onto her finger, she pulled her hand out from underneath the blanket.

A beautiful ring and wedding band.

"Marry me, Ginny."

Raising up on one elbow, Ginny stared down at the man who she would give her last breath of air to if he needed it.

"Normally, you wait until there is a ceremony before you wear the wedding band."

"Normally, men aren't asked to get the pastor's permission, either. Marry me, Ginny. I'll get Diamond to undo the paperwork that were married and then we can go to the courthouse and get married properly."

Ginny raised up into a sitting position to look down at him. "Did you even bother to ask for Pastor Dean's permission?" She turned her head to the side when Gavin remained silent.

"If you love me, it shouldn't matter whether he does or not."

Blowing out an angry huff of air, Ginny stared up at starry sky until she could reply in a calm voice. Then she turned her face back to him. "It's important to me."

Gavin sat up in frustration. "Why?"

"Razer or Shade didn't ask Beth or Lily why. They just did it. Can't you do the same for me?"

"Did they make it mandatory for them before they were married?"

"I don't know."

"Then why are you? Just because they did?"

"No, because it's important to me." Ginny placed her hand over her heart. "Do you know that every couple that Pastor Dean has married is still married?"

"No."

"It's not a rule to ask for his permission because of our faith, but it makes the women feel special that the men are willing to walk that extra mile for them. Pastor Dean had Harley Evan's learn ten Bible verses before he gave Janine permission. Harley can't read. Anytime anyone tried to help, he refused. Three months later, Harley recited the ten Bible verses, plus showed the pastor he'd gotten his GED. I'm sure Shade or Rider weren't excited to ask for Pastor Dean's permission, but they did it anyway, because unless he gives his permission, he won't perform the ceremony. I don't want to get married at the courthouse. Even if it's just the three of us, I want him to read the words that I'm willing to pledge my life to you."

Gavin rested his long arms across his knees. "Then I guess we're at an impasse."

"I guess so." Ginny started to slide the ring off her finger.

Gavin caught the movement. "It's a good thing then that we're already married."

Taking one of the pillows, Ginny bopped him with it.

Plopping back down on the sleeping bag, he reached out

to curl an arm around her shoulders to tug her down next to him.

"You're such a nimrod."

"Shh … the stars may hear you."

"They already know," she smarted off. Then, raising to her elbow, Ginny opened her mouth to tell him she was pregnant, and he better get a move on when she stopped. Closing her eyes, she could hear a male voice screaming in her head.

"Planning a ceremony isn't as much fun as you expect. To this day, I can't stand cake because Taylor had to try five different bakers before she chose."

Ginny tilted her head to the side. Was he seriously mentioning Taylor's name after proposing to her?

Being so close to Gavin, the screams' intensity became unbearable. They were back to the level that she had heard months ago. The hurt she felt at hearing Taylor's name dissipated. Gavin was in agonizing pain.

Ginny laid her hand on his cheek, turning his face toward hers. "I love you. No woman on earth will love a man more than I do you."

His face grew serious at her words.

"You can't pretend he doesn't exist because you're afraid to get hurt again."

Gavin jackknifed back into a sitting position. "I don't know what in the fuck you're talking about," he snapped.

"The part of you who you've locked away; let him out, Reaper."

"You've lost your mind." He angrily shrugged away from her touch when she reached out to him again.

"No, I haven't. You know I haven't. You want to pretend you're Reaper, but Gavin is still a part of you. Until you acknowledge him, you both will never heal."

"Drop it. I'm done talking about this."

"We need to talk about this." She tried to soothe him while still holding her stance. Someone had to answer the pleas of the man she heard screaming. If Reaper wouldn't fight for Gavin she would.

"You want to talk about something? I think we have something more serious to talk about than a figment of your imagination."

"I'm willing to talk about anything. Are you?"

Reaper blew past the part where he was willing to talk about him, focusing his attention on her. "When are you planning to tell me you're pregnant?"

"What makes you think I'm pregnant?"

"I know you are."

"Really? How sure are you?" She narrowed her eyes on him, raising her chin just as stubbornly as his was. "As sure am I about you having a part of you locked away?"

The light cast from the lantern flickered across his face.

"There isn't," he snarled.

"Then I'm not pregnant." Laying back down, Ginny shoved another pillow under her head.

"That's not how being pregnant works."

Ginny gave him a determined stare. "I don't need you to 'mansplain' anything to me, thank you very much. It's my body, and if I say I'm not pregnant, I'm not pregnant."

"Woman …"

Seeing the telltale sign that she was getting to Reaper when he raked a hand through his hair, she gave him a smug grin. "I'll admit to being pregnant when you're ready to tell me you've got a part of yourself locked away. And …" she drawled out, "while you're at it, get Pastor Dean's permission for us to get married. If my father was still alive, he would have already put a load of buckshot in your britches for messing with his baby girl."

Ginny stared up at the sky trying not to burst into

laughter at his poleaxed expression. She knew she was being ridiculous in her demands, but she didn't care. She was fighting for her man, and she would use any weapon available to her, even if it was the child they had created.

She was a great believer in learning from observation. If Trudy could use being pregnant to get what she wanted out of Dalton, Ginny wasn't above using the same method.

"It doesn't work that way." Reaper snorted in frustration. "We'll see who lasts."

"Yes, we will."

"Aren't you going to take a shower with me?" Looking up from the magazine that she was reading as she lay on the bed, Ginny nearly changed her mind. Naked, Gavin was a work of art. Damn.

"No, I took a shower before we went out. I'm good." Her lips pressed together to keep from smiling at his irritation when he went into the shower alone.

Big jerk.

She got up to undress, sliding on a nightgown, then went to the dresser and opened the top drawer that held his shirts. Taking out a leather jewelry case, she placed the rings that he had given her inside before closing the drawer.

Returning to the bed, she slid under the covers, curling her hand over her small bump.

"Don't worry, sweet one; we got this."

CHAPTER FORTY-SIX

S watting a glittery balloon out of the way, Reaper closed the door after working a back-breaking shift at the factory. Being greeted by a floating baby foot balloon wasn't totally unexpected, as Ginny had been telling him nonstop about all the decorations she purchased for T.A.'s baby shower tonight. Still, it was kind of sad to see the club house room decked out in baby blue with swirly ribbons hanging down from the ceiling.

"I could cry," Nickel moaned, coming into the room with the rest of the brothers.

"The brothers in Ohio would have cardiac arrest," Jesus groaned in aggrievement.

Puck stepped in rainbow-colored shit. "Better not let Wizard hear about this. He'll never let Viper live it down."

Suki gave a low whine, sensing the pain from the brothers who were complaining about their club room being taken over by the women who were stacking baby shower presents on the two pool tables.

Reaper gave the brothers a killing glare when Ginny sighted him and made a beeline toward him.

"The first one who says something to her will be working an extra shift."

The brothers took off down the hall for the kitchen instead of going farther into the main room. From the loud grumblings coming from that direction, Reaper had no doubt that Ginny decked that room in girly shit, too.

"You're here!" Ginny enthused as she grabbed his arm. "Isn't it gorgeous?"

He couldn't flat-out lie to her with a clear conscience. "It's exactly like you said it would be."

"I know, right?" Ginny pridefully surveyed her handi-work. "Sex Piston and Killyama think Trudy's going to love it. Is it bad of me I wanted more balloons than when Lily had her baby shower?"

"Nothing's wrong with a little healthy competition." Congratulating himself on being able to keep a straight face, Reaper took a long look at what Ginny was wearing. Did the woman think he was stupid? She was wearing a dark brown animal print dress that came to her knees, with a chunky black sweater that was meant to be loose but was unable to hide the burgeoning belly she was developing.

"How long is it going to take you to get dressed?" She nudged him toward the steps.

Reaper wasn't fooled by her attempt to distract him. He had been living with her dodging and distracting him every time he tried to talk about her being pregnant for the last two and half months.

"Why do I need to change? I was going to grab something to eat and stay in our room."

"I have literally told you a thousand times that you have to keep Dalton company. He's not any happier than you. The least you could do is make it more bearable for him." Ginny voice went an octave lower. "I don't think he cares for Sex Piston."

"No shit? I can't imagine why."

Ginny gave him a glare that put his death glare to shame.

"Give me ten minutes, and I'll be back. That good enough?"

He guessed it was when Ginny gave him an air kiss on his cheek as she moved away after hearing Sex Piston yell from across the room. "Hurry up, little bitch. Trudy will be here any minute."

Grumbling to himself with no one to hear, he went up to his room with Suki to lay out clean clothes before getting in the shower. Turning the water to hot, he luxuriating in the warmth of the spray. Every fucking bone in his body hurt. He had helped load two delivery trucks with a massive order, after working on the house that he and Ginny were building. This morning they put the wooden flooring in the bedrooms upstairs.

Washing his hair, he felt the length of stubble on the side of his skull was getting longer. He needed to shave it, but he didn't have the energy. Determined for Ginny and him to be settled into the home before the baby was born was being waylaid by the wet weather and a series of mid-steps that caused multiple delays.

He'd been so distracted with his new life at home, he was surprised to see an email this afternoon regarding the investigation on the islanders' disappearances. He'd already discovered from meteorological reports that no hurricane had hit Clindale with the force Allerton had described. The discovery had him hiring two ex-military investigators to find out what happened to the islanders. So far, little had been found, and the men were now methodically going through many of Allerton's patrons to see if they played a part as well.

One of the emails had both good and bad news. What

little was left Ginny's father had been found, and he'd been the only body located in the ocean. He would tell Ginny tomorrow. He wasn't about to let her party be ruined after she had worked to make it special for T.A.

Stepping out the shower, he dried off, then went into the bedroom to dress. He gave the bed a longing glance and told Suki to stay before going back downstairs. In the time he had been taking a shower, the club room had filled with even more women, who were watching him like a hawk.

He was relieved to see more men than he expected. Calder, Dalton, Stud, Viper, Shade, and Train grouped around at the bar, looking as miserable as he felt.

Moving behind the bar, Reaper took a bottled water. "How did Lucky manage to get out of coming?"

"Prayer meeting," Razer answered, coming out of the kitchen to take a bottle of beer before he could shut the fridge door. "I volunteered to sub for him, but the lucky bastard turned me down."

"Why don't we go and hang out in the kitchen?" Reaper made the suggestion when Sex Piston and Fat Louise began talking about their experiences during childbirth.

"And leave them alone with a bar full of liquor?" Viper snorted. "That's not going to happen."

"Half of them are pregnant." Reaper wasn't ready to give up the idea of escaping.

"The others aren't. Those are the ones I'm not taking my eyes off of." Viper positioned himself in the space between the bar counter and wall, when Killyama came out of the kitchen carrying a tray of drinks.

Not put off by Viper's presence, she held the tray out for him. "Place that bottle of Effen Blood Orange on for me."

Viper's shoulders went up two inches. "No."

"You want me to put the tray down and get it myself?"

The sickly-sweet smile that Killyama gave Viper made the skin on the back of his neck crawl for his brother. Viper must have experienced the same side effect because he took the bottle of vodka off the shelf.

"None of the brothers were drinking it, anyway." Viper made the excuse for himself after Killyama disappeared into the crowd of women.

"I would have given it to her, too." Dalton gave a mock-shudder. "Train, I don't know which of you I admire most. You or Calder."

"Calder gets my vote." Train laughed from the end of the bar. "At least Killyama won't kill anyone unless they point a gun at her. All you have to do is look at Crazy Bitch the wrong way."

The men spent the next painstaking fifteen minutes having to listen to the horror stories of childbirth experiences. The stories sent his gut twisting in worry for Ginny and the child she was pretending wasn't resting below her heart.

At first, he'd mistakenly assumed she was waiting to tell him until after she knew for sure. Then, after her arm was sprained and she never mentioned birth control again, he assumed she was waiting until the perfect moment. Each day that passed, Reaper came up with a different reason until he came to the realization that he wasn't capable of figuring how Ginny's mind worked.

His best guess so far was that Ginny wasn't going to admit she was pregnant until he admitted they weren't married. The woman didn't know him at all if she thought he was going to cave. He could be just as stubborn as she, or at least until he convinced Lucky to give him permission to marry her, which, by the way that was going, Ginny would be on their third child before Lucky conceded. He told himself to be patient, he could outwait her. Time was on his side how much longer could she pretend to be pregnant before she started showing?

Jerking his thoughts away from killing a man of the cloth or ask him how far along Willa was when she started showing, Reaper tuned back to the conversation the men were having, then wished he had stayed in never-never land at hearing Viper and Razer arguing about whose wife had the worst childbirth.

"Beth had two kids during a blackout, in the middle of the night, while men were trying to kill her and breaking into her house," Razer bragged.

Viper made a slicing wave of his hand. "Winter might have had only one kid, but she nearly fucking died when that drug cartel was …."

Reaper switched off, going back to what the women were saying. At least their conversations didn't involve death.

"Did you hear the new doctor in town has two sisters?" Willa shared with the group. "One is a midwife, the other is a doula."

"Really? I didn't hear that." Trudy paused while opening a present. "Is it too late for me to use a midwife?"

"Yes, it is," Dalton provided the information, proving he wasn't the only one listening.

"When I have a baby, I plan on using a doula and a midwife," Ginny stated implacably as if it was a forgone conclusion.

"Oh … hell, you're not. Your ass will be sitting in a hospital, begging for an epidural," Reaper yelled.

The group in women went silent.

Reaper placed his hand on the counter to steady himself for the death glares sent his way from the women.

"Then it's good thing you won't have any say in the

matter." Ginny shifted on the couch to give him the cold shoulder.

"What happened to you being tenderhearted?" Reaper mocked. "You think that snatch isn't going to hurt like hell when you try to squeeze out a bowling ball?"

When the women gave Ginny expectant looks, waiting for another comeback, Reaper also prepared himself for what she would say next. Instead, she turned to Willa, but he couldn't hear what she was saying, so he looked at the brothers who were also trying to listen in.

"Ginny asked Willa if midwives give epidurals," Shade provided.

Winning that particular battle, Reaper was able to ease his guard for a sixty-second reprieve when he saw someone coming in the front door. Silently, he groaned. "Some days, it doesn't pay to get out of the fucking bed."

Viper gave a low whistle under his breath when he turned to see what Reaper was staring at.

"You're fucked." Viper sympathized, seeing the woman who walked through the door.

Reaper agreed. "Tell me something I don't know. You might as well go ahead and dig my grave."

Viper didn't argue as the woman swatted the baby foot balloon away.

Reaper started toward the door, in the hopes of getting Taylor out the door before the group of women noticed her. Moon must have said a few words to Taylor before letting her inside, and from the glitteringly angry look she was giving Reaper, she must not have liked what Moon said.

"I don't understand why Moon has to be so rude to me."

At one time, Reaper would have hastened to smooth it over. Those days were gone.

"What are you doing here?"

Taylor's expression went through a rapid-fire change. "I came to see you. I came before, a few weeks ago, and Viper told me you weren't in Treepoint."

Conscious of the room going silent, Reaper stopped moving toward her, keeping six inches between them. "We have nothing to talk about. You've wasted a trip both times."

"Let's go upstairs to one of the rooms to talk privately."

He raised his hand to stop her when she would have come closer. "You're good where you are."

"Gavin, please don't be this way. I know I hurt you when I came to the rehabilitation center, but what was I supposed to do? I was married, with my son on the way. I was confused."

"You aren't confused any longer?"

"No. Gavin, you know I love you. I'll always love you."

Reaper stared coldly at the woman who he had once thought he would marry.

The stark difference between Taylor and Ginny went far beyond appearances. Plus, there hadn't been a ring of truth in a single word Taylor said.

Dressed in a hot pink skirt and a tie-dye top, she managed to come across as both sexy and classy. Back in the day, it would have given him a hard-on at the sexual confidence Taylor was an expert at achieving.

In hindsight, Reaper could see it was the sexual challenge that had attracted him to Taylor. During the year of their engagement, the challenge had begun to dull. Seeing her now, with his mind clear of the drugs, and with Greer and Silas helping him to deal with his kidnapping, he saw the future he and Taylor would have had. They wouldn't have made it through two years of marriage, if that, and would probably have had a child dealing with the fallout.

They were too much alike, or they had been. He could see now what Ginny had been telling him; he had been running after fool's gold. Like those miners, Reaper had clung to the belief that their relationship was the real thing, because he hadn't been strong enough to kill off something Gavin had loved. With that admission, a final understanding of Rider's actions finally clicked in place, as well as the knowledge of what Reaper had to do to move forward.

"Where's your old man and kid?"

At his question, Taylor seemed taken aback. "Brandon is with Burn. We're getting a divorce. I couldn't stay with him when I realized I wasn't ever going to get over you. I married him when I thought you were dead, Gavin. You can't hold that against me. I stayed with him because I was pregnant. I wanted my marriage to work, but I can't stay with him when you have my heart, Gavin."

Reaper turned his head to see Ginny moving toward the kitchen. "Ginny, come here."

Flustered at being singled out in front of the other woman, Ginny started pulling her sweater together across her bulging middle.

Reaper took the steps necessary when she stopped short of walking directly to him. Placing a proprietary arm around her shoulders, Reaper gave Taylor an inflexible expression. "Go home. There's nothing here for you."

Reaper's aloof behavior wasn't affected by the devastation Taylor made no effort to conceal.

Catching Ginny's hand in his when she wouldn't quit restlessly stretching her sweater closed, he could see the discomfort, and the fear, in the nonchalant attitude Ginny was trying to portray.

"Who is she?" The venomous way Taylor asked the question had Ginny stiffening underneath his arm.

Reaper released her hand to smooth his hand gently over the small mound of her belly to settle the mama and baby in his arms. "She's none of your concern."

At his movement, Taylor's attitude changed. "Are you acting this way to hurt me? To pay me back for not leaving Burn when I came to see you at the rehab center? You can stop pretending, Gavin. I know the child isn't yours. We need to talk privately. Let's go upstairs where we won't be interrupted."

Taylor's rudeness had Ginny giving a shocked gasp.

Reaper arched a brow at Ginny, waiting for her deny that she was pregnant, which she had done repeatedly each time her pregnancy had been mentioned. Any plan of using the opportunity to force acknowledgment out of Ginny failed when he saw the hurt deepening in her eyes as she tried to shift away from his touch.

He tightened his arm around her shoulders, holding her in place. "You couldn't be more wrong. Taylor, when have I pretended to say or do something I didn't mean? The baby Ginny is carrying is mine, and any future children she has will be mine. She's mine, which fucking means I don't want you. No amount of us talking will change that fact. Go home to Burn and your son. There's nothing here for you in Treepoint. There never was."

"I deserve to be treated better than this from you," Taylor snapped, using a heavily ringed hand to toss her hair over her shoulder—making sure he noticed the sparkling jewel on her finger. "Do you know how I felt when I had to cancel our wedding? We didn't know if you had taken off with the money for the business, or if you were dead. Do you know how many nights I went to sleep crying over you? I held out hope until Viper found your body. Even then, I wasn't ready to let you go. Everyone kept telling me to move on, and then when I did, what happened? They found you! What did you want me to do? Leave my husband and child when you weren't in a good head place?"

Reaper moved himself and Ginny back a couple of steps

when Taylor tried to come closer. Seeing what he was doing, Taylor stopped.

"I gave us enough time for me to see if I could make my marriage with Burn last, while giving you time to get over the trauma of what happened to you. Don't send me away. Spend a couple of days with me before you decide. I love you. We can still be together, have the life we planned for, if you'd just give us another chance."

"Another chance for what? To make both of our lives miserable? I'm staying put in Treepoint. You see yourself happy living here?"

From her expression, Reaper didn't think she would be.

"You planning on walking away from your son? Burn might be willing to let you move away, but his son is a different story."

"Nothing about you has changed. It still has to be your way or the highway." Waspishly, Taylor turned her vindictiveness on Ginny. "You're nothing but a stand-in for me. You'll never replace me in his bed." Taylor gave Ginny a smug smile, her eyes sweeping over Ginny contemptuously. "Three high-class whores couldn't give him what I did for him. What I still could do when he's done paying me back for the fact I didn't divorce Burn sooner."

Taylor's gave him a suggestive smile. "I'll stay at the hotel tonight. Come by if you want me to refresh your memory."

"You did me a favor by not divorcing Burn. I'll make sure to thank him personally." Reaper's words dripped ice. "This is Ginny's party, and you weren't invited. Leave now, or I'm going to forget you have a small child."

Paling, Taylor turned hastily, and Reaper didn't miss the look of contempt she treated the room of women to as she went to the door. Raising her hand with her car keys, Taylor popped the balloon as she left.

Moon raised a questioning brow at him at the doorway. "You want me to toss her down the steps?"

"No. Leave her be. She's Burn's problem, not mine."

Reaper turned Ginny back toward the rest of the room. "I'm sorry for the interruption, ladies. There are presents left for T.A. to open. You were having a good time, so please don't let her ruin the party, which was her goal."

"We won't," Ginny said for the whole room.

Reaper noticed the sweet smile he was used to getting from her didn't reach her eyes. Reading the self-doubt, he moved his hand to the back of her hair to tug her head back. Kissing her as if he was starved for her, boldly thrusting his tongue inside her mouth, he waited until she melted against him before raising his head to give her a gentle push toward the table of presents.

Walking to the bar, Reaper watched the women resume talking as T.A. bantered back and forth with Crazy Bitch and Fat Louise over which present she should open next. Satisfied that everything was back to the party atmosphere before Taylor interrupted, he took out his cell phone and punched in Knox's number.

"What's up?" Knox answered.

"Taylor is heading to the hotel to rent a room. I want her escorted out of town."

"Any messages?"

"No message. Just get her ass out of town before I break my word never to strangle another woman."

"Can do."

Disconnecting the call, Reaper pressed another button on his phone.

"Yeah?" An irritated voice answered.

"What are you doing?"

Reaper heard a jumbled mix of voices complaining about the number of hamburgers from the other end of the phone.

"Tryin' to get my fuckin food before I have a fuckin' brain hemorrhage and die!"

"I'm at the club. I'll give you two C-notes if you're here in the next ten minutes."

Disconnecting the call, Reaper placed his phone down on the counter, then stared at Shade, who was standing behind the counter. "Give me a Jack."

Viper gave him a hesitate glace as Shade reached for the bottle of Jack Daniels. "Are you sure …?"

Viper put his hands up, backing off at lethal glare Reaper settled on him. Shade set down a thick glass on the bar and poured a generous portion of Jack. Reaper drank it in one swallow, then motioned for Shade to refill his glass.

"Keeping it coming. I've got nine minutes before Greer gets here to take the buzz off."

"Mind handing me another beer, Shade?" Stud asked from the stool next to him.

"Never mind, Shade." Sex Piston came up from behind them. "I've got a headache. I'm ready to go. Crazy Bitch is getting our coats. Let's roll."

Reaper turned to see Crazy Bitch talking to Killyama at the closet as she took her coat out, too.

"Give Stud his beer, Shade. Sex Piston, let me save you and the others the trouble. Taylor's on her way back to Ohio. She's not at the hotel."

Reaper saw the disappointment from his announcement.

"Should have let me handle that bitch. She would have gotten my message not to fuck with my girl again."

"Taylor didn't need a message from you. Mine will be waiting for her when she gets back to Ohio and finds out she's never allowed in the club there again and she has twenty-four hours to give me back the engagement ring I gave her before I was kidnapped."

Sex Piston appeared slightly modified. "You're not

thinking of giving my bitch a used engagement ring, are you?"

"No, I have another one for Ginny that she refuses to wear."

"Did it cost more or less than Ginny's?"

"Less."

"I guess that'll have to do." Sex Piston shrugged.

Reaper eyed her warily. "I guess so."

"I wouldn't have taken you for a Jack man. Probably why you're having trouble getting that ring of yours on her finger."

"How does what I prefer to drink make a difference?"

"Men who drink Jack tend to be old-fashioned, manly men."

"I don't come across as either of those to you?"

Reaper didn't know whether to take what Sex Piston was saying as an insult or a compliment.

Sex Piston swept her gaze over him from the top of his head down his body, lingering at his chest, hips, and thighs. "Fuck no. Shade, you have any ginger beer back there?"

Shade stepped back from the bar to stare at the under-the-counter refrigerator, then reached down to pull out a bottle of cold ginger beer. Seeing Shade found what she had asked for, Sex Piston went from the front of the bar to the back, then took a bottle of a dark rum from the shelf. Taking a slender glass, she poured a fourth of the glass with the ginger beer then half with the dark rum. Pushing the glass toward him, she gave him a saccharine smile. "You can thank me later."

"Excuse me."

Reaper looked over as an older woman squeezed in between him and Viper, rubbing her breast on his arm.

"Are we leaving, Sex Piston?"

"No, we're staying. He handled it."

The woman lifted heavily mascaraed eyes to his. "I told Sex Piston you would."

Reaper barely managed to prevent from gaping as the woman's eyes leered over his body.

"What'd you make for him?"

"I made him a Dark and Stormy."

"Yes, he is," she cooed. "Make me one, Sex Piston. I'm in the mood to be dangerous tonight."

The woman turned to go back to the party, making sure her other breast made contact with his arm as she left.

The men all watched Sex Piston make two more drinks.

"In case anyone else wants one," she said, giving him a wink as she walked out from behind the bar, going back to opening presents with the women.

Shaking himself out of the stunned amazement at the brazen way the older woman had acted, Reaper made sure he didn't look back to see who had gotten the second drink.

"Who was she? I've never met her before."

"You had the honor of having Sizzle make a pass at you. She's Sex Piston's mother," Stud supplied the information with smothered laughter. "You going to try the drink my wife made for you?"

The men, except for Stud, studied the mixed drink Sex Piston had poured with suspicion.

"You think it's safe to drink?" Viper joked when Reaper didn't make a move to take a drink.

"I've had one before," Dalton volunteered. "Give it a try."

Taking a few sips, Reaper had to admit the drink wasn't bad.

Viper made a few for the other brothers to try.

Reaper took one of the stools as the men stood around talking. It brought back memories of the way he used to be before he cut himself out of their lives. This time, the recollections didn't bring back the painful imagery of Memphis and Slate. Instead, it was more of an ache that he hadn't tried to fix the relationships that had been torn away from him.

Glancing up, he saw Shade studying him. "What?"

Holding his drink, Shade lifted one finger to point at him. "Haven't seen that shirt since we were in a bar in Houston. Looks good on you."

Reaper looked down at the black, long-sleeved V-neck shirt that had a white trim around the neck and down to midchest around the buttons. He had paired it with tapered black jeans and black boots.

"I still haven't replaced the clothes I had to leave behind on the island."

"Why buy more when you have plenty that Viper never got rid of? Be a waste of money, and you're going to need every penny." Shade gave a nod toward the door. "Greer's here."

Reaper gave a silent groan when Greer strutted through the room with his customary swagger. Spotting him sitting at the bar, Greer took the stool next to him. Plopping his bag of food on the bar, he began pulling out the hamburgers and fries.

"The calvary has arrived. What'd you need?"

Conscious of everyone watching, Reaper decided to wait until Greer finished eating before having him go upstairs to his room with him to talk privately.

"It can wait until you're done eating."

"I can do two things at once. What was the hurry of me getting here if you didn't need something right away?"

Reaper leaned sideways so he could lower his voice. "I took a couple drinks. I need you to fix it."

"Ah ..." Greer made no effort to lower his voice. "You done drinking for the night?"

Closing his eyes tightly, Reaper imagined the pleasure he

would get from killing Greer. If he didn't need him so badly, he would.

"Yes."

"Okay." Greer laid a hand on his arm, then slid Reaper's drink closer to him. "There you go. You got my money?"

Reaper took out his wallet and gave Greer two one-hundred-dollar bills. Greer pocketed the money and started eating as the brothers stared at Greer, dumbstruck.

Viper leaned over the bar. This time he was the one lowering his voice. "I thought you couldn't take money for using your gift?"

"You see me do anything?"

Reaper frowned at him. He hadn't felt anything when Greer touched him.

"No, I didn't." Viper furrowed his brow as if he missed something. Reaper was just as confused.

"There you go."

No longer caring who overheard, Reaper sat and watched Greer continue to eat his meal.

"I need you to fix it where I won't want another drink."

Greer cocked an eyebrow at him. "You already said you didn't want any more. What's to fix?"

"So I won't."

"Then don't." Greer shrugged, taking a drink and making a face. "What in the fuck am I drinking?"

"A Dark and Stormy," Reaper replied absentmindedly, his mind still on his problem.

"A waste of a good ginger beer and dark rum." Greer snorted.

Viper started to take the glass away, but Greer snatched it back.

"Didn't say I wouldn't drink it."

"Aren't you working?" Viper asked.

"I'm on my dinner break."

Viper narrowed his eyes on him. "You still have the rest of your shift to finish."

"You see Knox standing around? You worry about you, and I worry about me."

Reaper shook his head at Viper, trying to get Greer's attention back to what he needed done.

"I called you, so I won't want to take another drink." Patiently, Reaper reexplained. He wouldn't get anywhere if he lost his temper. "That's what I paid you for."

"What? You want me to say thank you?"

"No, I want you to do it."

"Why, when you did it for yourself." Greer gave a jut of his chin to Shade. "You got any beer behind there?"

Shade reached under the counter to get Greer a beer.

"Thankee. See? I can remember my manners." Greer twisted the top off the beer, then went back to finishing his meal.

Irritated, Reaper tried to stare Greer into doing what he wanted.

"You wanting a burger? You know I'm not into sharing my food."

"No, I want you to do what I paid you to do."

"I did. Brah, if you want to pay me just to move your glass away from you when you had—" Greer broke off to stare around the group of men around the bar, then turned his eyes back on him. "—nine others around you who could have done the same thing, who am I to argue?"

"Because they can't fix it so I won't *need* another one."

"You don't need me to give you willpower when you have plenty of it yourself. If you wanted to move that stool you're sitting on, would you ask me to lift it for you, or would you do it yourself?"

"I'd do it myself."

"If you wanted to move that pool table over there, who would you ask for help?"

Reaper swallowed hard. "Any of them."

"You already know when you can do shit for yourself, and when you need help. The only problem is you need more confidence in yourself when drinking. Any time you need me to show you, I don't mind coming, but it just seems a waste of money when you have so many people around you willing to do it for free. But that's me, I reckon."

Laughter erupted in the background as another present was opened.

Turning in his seat, Reaper watched as Ginny sat on the couch, laughing hilariously as Trudy held up a bra with "*Bite Me*" printed on the cups.

"Boy, let me ask you a question. Were you addicted to drinking and drugs before Slade kidnapped you?"

"No, I wasn't."

"Then you aren't now, unless I'm not as good as healing as you think I am. Then, if that's true, you shouldn't be wanting to call me anyway."

Reaper turned back to Greer, forgetting the brothers were listening. "I don't want to fail."

"You're not going to fail." Greer set his beer down on the counter. "You failed when Slate locked you away. Do you see any of these assholes here going anywhere?"

Reaper looked around at the men who began to circle the bar closer to him. "No."

"There you go then." Greer gave him a hard smack on his shoulders. "If these assholes ever let you down, call Ginny's brothers. Shit, there are a ton of them fuckers. 'Course none of them have my winning personality."

"Not many do." Reaper's lips curled in laughter.

"Ain't that the truth. If I could bottle myself, I'd make a fortune."

"You going to give my two hundred back?"

"Fuck no. But, to be nice, I'll give you a small piece of advice."

"Free?"

Greer made a face at him. "Of course." Wadding up his trash, he placed it back in the bag. "Don't get addicted to the burgers at the diner. I'm gonna kill that motherfucker the next time he shorts me a hamburger."

CHAPTER FORTY-SEVEN

"Do you have the next tray ready?" Ginny asked. "The one in the oven is done."

Willa hurried to the oven to take the French bread out.

Ginny wiped her hands on the dishcloth to place a trivet on the countertop. Then she went to help place the next sheet pan of bread in the oven, but Willa beat her.

"I've got it."

Shrugging at her friend wanting to help, Ginny went to the table in the kitchen and continued to make a list of supplies the club needed.

"Are there enough dishwashing tablets under the sink to get us through next month?"

Willa opened the cabinet. "Yes, the one under here is full. We're good."

Concentrating on the list, Ginny realized that Willa had stopped talking. Looking up, she saw that Willa had been staring at her. Had she said something? They were ahead of schedule for having dinner ready. She couldn't think of anything that needed to be done or anything they hadn't prepped.

"Did you need something?"

Willa walked across the room to take a seat next to her. Biting her bottom her lip as if she was hesitant to say something, she gave her a searching look. "Ginny ... I know you were raised mainly in a male household, but you and Trudy spend time together ..."

Ginny placed her pen down on the table. "What are you trying to get out?"

"Ginny, you do know you're pregnant, don't you?" Willa blurted out.

Ginny picked the pen back up. "No, I'm not."

Willa nodded to her protruding belly. "Ginny ..." Willa nodded to her belly again. "You're pregnant."

"No, I am not. Do you think three cans of coffee is enough?"

"Add one can to the list." Willa sighed in resignation, standing back up. "You know, if you need to talk, I'll be more than happy to listen."

"Thank you. You're a good friend."

Ginny was aware her friend thought she was a full-fledged cuckoo bird. She didn't care; she was determined to win her battle with Gavin. The last two and half months had both Gavin and her engaged in a battle of wills to see who would break first. She was just as adamant about getting him to realize there was a part of him hurting as he was to get her to admit she was pregnant. Internally Ginny gave a frustrated sigh. Gavin's nickname shouldn't have been Reaper it should've been Stubborn Ass. How he could be so caring, thoughtful, and protective toward her, then be a blind ass where his own welfare was concerned drove her insane. No wonder everyone in the club, Trudy, and her friends thought she was just as cuckoo as Willa.

The battle of will she had gone on longer than she expected. But with Silas's encouragement, she stuck to her guns. Her sympathy was running out the bigger her belly was getting. She was so angry at Stubborn Ass. She would've been happy if he just walked a quarter of a mile toward her, but now she was going to make him walk two.

Ginny continued working on the grocery list as she imagined Gavin walking those miles … would it be petty of her to make him walk them barefoot?

Willa started unloading the dishwasher before filling it with the lunch dishes. "How's the house going? Were you able to get the plumber out there?"

"No. He had an emergency call and rescheduled for Monday." Ginny felt the disappointment today just as keenly as she felt it yesterday. She was more than ready to get their house finished. The more they tried to rush things along, the more setbacks had come knocking on their door.

It had done nothing but freaking rain in the last two months. After they had the roof and the structure completed, they ran into one hitch after another when they'd inadvertently hired a flake to do the drywall and had to have three rooms redone. Then numerous issues with the house inspectors delaying appointments and the kitchen cabinets that she had set her heart on were on backorder. It had Ginny thinking it would be another two months before they could move in.

Ginny smiled when Lily and Beth came in the back door shaking the snow off their coats.

"I'm ready for summer," Beth complained, taking her hat off over the plastic mat by the door. Taking Lily's coat, along with hers, Beth went to hang their coats on the pegs in the pantry.

"Aren't we all," Ginny agreed glumly.

"I'm not," Lily said. "This is my favorite time of the year."

Ginny smiled, her despondency lifting. She had enjoyed

working with Lily, Beth, and Willa, all three pulling kitchen duty the same week.

Ginny finished the supply list, then volunteered to make the frosting for the cake Willa was making.

"Shade decided who's going to be promoted to fill Jewell's position at the factory?" Willa asked as she measured out the ingredients for the cake.

Ginny looked over her shoulder at Willa. "Is she tired of being the manger?"

"It's not that she's tired of being the manager; she decided to go to work for Arin. Jewell is originally from Ohio, so she's ready to move back," Willa explained.

"Shade hasn't decided," Lily volunteered the information. "He will go back to doing it full-time until he decides."

"When is she leaving?" Ginny asked casually.

"Not for a couple months. I'm dreading her leaving. I'm going to miss her."

Willa poured the batter into the cake pan. "Me, too."

The frosting ready, Ginny placed a lid over the bowl for Willa to use when the cake cooled. "Is there anything else I can help with?"

"No, thanks. I think we have it under control." Willa smiled.

"I think I'll visit Winter and Aisha before it gets dark."

Going into the main room, Ginny took her coat out of the closet, then retraced her steps back to the kitchen.

"Ginny …"

Putting on her coat, Ginny caught Lily and Beth sharing a quick glance before Lily spoke.

"I have a thicker jacket that would be … warmer, if you want it?"

"No, thanks. This one is fine. I won't be gone long if Gavin asks where I am."

Leaving through the back door, Ginny held the front of

her jacket closed. She had busted the zipper out of it yesterday when she went to the new house to be there when granite installers arrived.

The side path beside the club was free of snow and ice, as well as all the paths that led to the various houses within steps of the club. Viper was fanatical about them being cleared in case Winter came to the club or wanted to visit one of the other wives.

Reaching the parking lot, Ginny changed direction, heading toward the factory instead of Winter and Viper's house. Ginny hadn't been in the factory that often, usually when she was dropping lunch off to whoever was working in the office.

Entering the side of the building, Ginny looked around, seeing Jewell sitting behind the desk in the office. She gave a small knock on the doorframe to get Jewell's attention.

"I'm sorry to disturb you. If you have a few minutes, I'd like to talk."

Jewell gave her a preoccupied frown. "I'm busy, if it could wait."

Ginny came inside and shut the door. "I won't be long."

Jewell crossed her hands on her desk. "Go ahead."

"Don't go, Jewell," Ginny said softly. "This is your home."

"Ohio is my home. It's time to go back." Jewell got up from the desk, going to the filing cabinet to take a folder out before returning to her desk, her eyes remaining lowered.

"I know, Jewell."

The deadpan look on Jewell's face didn't fool her for a second. "What do you know? Look, Ginny, I really am busy."

"I know you're in love with Gavin."

"Then you think wrong."

"I'm not wrong. Please don't go."

Jewell's face twisted in agony before she covered her face with her hands and burst into sobs. "Does he know?"

"No. I promise Gavin has no idea."

Jewell lowered her hands, getting her emotions under control. "I'm not surprised. He never did."

"You've loved him for a long time."

"I fell in love when we were at the club in Ohio, I kept hoping Gavin would eventually fall in love with me, but then he met Taylor and got engaged. I knew it would never last—she's a spoiled bitch and I could see Gavin was getting tired of her always wanting him at her beck and call. He never gave in to her demands unless he wanted to. I think he was tired of dealing with them."

"Stay, Jewell, he doesn't have to know, and I promise I'll never mention it to him."

"Ginny, I like you, which makes this hard to say, but if I could steal him away from you, I would in a heartbeat. With there being no chance of that, I also have to admit it's going to kill a part of me when you have his child."

"Well, there's no need to rush off. I don't plan to have any children for a while. I'll tell Shade when he comes in for lunch that you're taking back your notice."

Jewell looked at her like she'd lost her mind. "If you're not pregnant, what is that?"

Ginny stretched the material tighter around her. "I've gained a few pounds, I have to admit. I'll lose it when the weather warms."

"Yes, you will," Jewell said sarcastically. "Ignore that. It doesn't matter. I'm not staying."

Ginny moved closer to Jewell's desk. "Stay, Jewell. I promise you won't regret it, but you will if you go. Give it another six months; feelings change, and you might find out your feelings for Gavin weren't what you thought they were."

"What do you mean by that?"

"Stay and find out." Ginny gave Jewell grin. "In another month our house will be done, so you won't see me as often, and despite that, how can you steal my man if you're not here? I'll see you at dinner."

Leaving Jewell's door open as she left, Ginny went outside and headed back to the club house. Seeing Gavin standing on the front porch talking to Puck as Suki ran around the yard, Ginny decided to head that way. Gavin's back was turned to the parking lot, so he didn't see her coming up the steps.

Mischievously, she shoved her hand in the snow and made a snowball. Aiming, she hit Gavin in his upper arm. When Gavin and Puck turned, startled, she burst out laughing, which sent an exuberant Suki running toward her. Knowing the dog wouldn't jump on her, she still unconsciously took a step to the side and felt herself falling. Keeping calm, Ginny threw her left shoulder back, sending her falling to the side rather than down the steep steps.

"Ginny ... are you okay?"

Her clothes didn't have time to get wet before Gavin was picking her up.

"What are you doing out here? You're supposed to be in the kitchen."

"I went to visit Winter," Ginny explained, brushing her pants down.

"Dammit, I told you not to come up these steps when it's snowing! Why did you come up the steps?" he roared at her.

Ginny kept her smile pasted on her face, despite several members of the club coming out onto the porch to see what was going on.

"Are you trying to lose my baby?" he continued to yell.

Ginny bunched her hand in a fist and punched him in the stomach. "I am not pregnant!"

Willa, Beth, and Lily slowly began backing away from the banister.

"Woman, I'm fed up with you telling me I'm not going to be a father."

"I am not pregnant!" Ginny stubbornly closed her jacket over the mound of her belly. "I am not going to be pregnant until Pastor Dean tells me I have his permission for us to be married." She left out the admission that she wanted to hear from him; there were too many eyes and ears around.

"I've told Lucky at least two dozen times, and he refuses to give it to you."

Ginny pointed a finger at chest. "Then you better figure out why!" she screeched at him. "My dad would roll over in his grave if he knew I was pregnant and not married."

"We talking about the same one who had nine children and never married any of their mothers?"

"Are you speaking ill of the dead?" Before Gavin could stop her, she pulled a hair from his head.

"Give that back."

Ginny shoved her hand underneath her top, then brought it out. "You can't have it. If you'll excuse me, I have a cake to frost." Ginny stomped her way up the rest of the stairs.

The people on the porch went to the side to keep their distance, and Ginny rolled her eyes at them. What did they think she was going to do? She was jinxing Gavin, not them.

Reaching the porch she turned to give Gavin another piece of her mind ... and found him right behind her.

Poking him again, she gave him one last warning. "You better fix this, Gavin James. I will not be shamed in front of my family. You don't want me calling Papa to come here and have a talk with you. He'll be mad enough to kick your ass if he finds out I'm pregnant."

"How's he going to kick my ass when he's six feet under?"

Ginny sucked in deep hiss of air. "I was talking about *Papa Will*. I'm calling him. Do you see what you've just done? Now I won't be able to marry you until I have his permission, too." Storming inside the house, Ginny slammed the door behind her.

Viper was the first to laugh, then Shade, then Rider.

Angrily, Reaper decided he was going inside to eat his spaghetti. Then, when he was finished, he was going to carry Ginny upstairs and fuck her brains out. He was going to show that nymph not to raise her voice at him and have the whole fucking house laughing at him.

He was brought up short when the door wouldn't budge.

"Viper, you got the key with you?"

"No. Why would I need a key when one of the brothers is always watching the door?"

"Shade? Rider?"

Both shook their heads.

"Anyone?"

"I'll go to the back door and come open the door for everyone," Lily said, going down the steps.

"I'll come with you. I don't want you to fall." Shade went down the steps after his wife.

Reaper went to the first step off the porch and sat down. Suki came running to him to plop down on his lap. Rider sat down on the porch next to him. "I thought she would have come back by now."

"No, I insulted her father. She's going to make me sit out here for a good thirty minutes. You all might as well go to the back door. As long as I'm out here, she won't let anyone open the door."

Everyone began leaving the porch, heading toward the back door.

"Might as well go, too, Puck. I'll take over the rest of the shift."

Puck didn't argue, taking off before he could change his mind.

"Lucky really isn't giving you and Ginny his permission?"

"Yes."

"Fucker knows he has you by the balls."

"Fuckwad."

Rider rubbed the tip of his boot on the step below them. "Shade got his permission."

"That's what Ginny said. I don't believe it."

"I don't either."

"You should ask Shade just to make sure," Reaper casually suggested, as if it wasn't any skin off his back if he didn't.

"I'm sure he didn't, but I'm not the one getting married to Ginny." Rider suggested just as casually. "But when you find out, let me know. Just out of curiosity, of course."

Lucky wasn't the only fuckwad in the club.

Rider's blasé attitude confirmed Reaper's sneaky suspicion why one of the reasons he hadn't married Jo was Rider would rather put his balls through a cheese grater than ask Lucky to marry Jo and be told no. If it had been any other pastor in the world, there wouldn't have been a hitch. Rider and him could have pretended to any good ol' boy. The same couldn't be said about Lucky; he was privy to the intimate details of their lives. Lucky would laugh his ass off unless they were ready to bare their soul in front of him. Shade must have come up around the problem, either Lily married Shade without Lucky's permission or Shade had blackmailed him into giving permission. Shade didn't have a soul, so third scenario wasn't an option.

"I'm sure."

"Me, too."

Reaper's shoulders slumped. "We're fucked."

Rider nodded in agreement. "Yes, we are."

CHAPTER FORTY-EIGHT

"*A*re you happy with the counters?" Ginny smoothed her hand over them. "I love them. Do you like them?" She anxiously waited for Gavin's reaction.

"I like them. I'm happy with how everything came out."

"I am, too. Now, if we can get the plumber to show, get the plumbing inspected, and get the battery installed in the garage, we can move. You think two weeks?"

Ginny was thrilled. The cabinets that had been on backorder just yesterday were now not only there but installed. As happy as she was with his surprise, she should have locked Stubborn Ass out of the club house before; they probably would have already moved into their new home.

"One thing I've learned building this house, I'd rather build five factories than one house."

Ginny walked around her kitchen, touching everything. She still couldn't believe her dream was actually coming true. The house she and Leah had spent hours on end talking about—that she worked endless hours for—was now a reality.

"I'm so happy."

Gavin gave her a searching look. "You don't sound happy."

Ginny shook herself out of the sense of doom that suddenly assailed her. "I'm just being ridiculous."

"Tell me something I don't know." Gavin gave her a wry smile that never failed to give her heart flip flops.

"My superstitious nature is coming out. Every time my life is going good, something happens to screw it all up. Last week when I went to see Myles, the other girls were there, too. I can't wait until I can invite them here."

Ginny was already imagining Trudy, Sex Piston, Fat Louise, Killyama, and Crazy Bitch hanging around her kitchen tormenting Gavin like they did Dalton.

"Don't remind me."

Ginny couldn't hold back the laughter when he shuddered at the memory.

"You have no one to blame but yourself. I told you to stay in the car."

"They had me going back to the kitchen to get them shit just so they could check out my ass."

Ginny had to smother down the laughter when he gave her an offended glance.

"It didn't help that you didn't try to make them behave. I thought women were supposed to be jealous-natured when other women act that way toward their husbands?"

"You aren't my husband."

"Legally, I am."

"Anyway," she went on, bypassing their bone of contention. Ginny wasn't about to get in the same tired argument with him. "I don't mind them looking; they just can't touch. None of them would try to steal my man."

"You're not the least bit jealous?"

Ginny heard the hint of uncertainty in his voice from across the room.

Walking toward him seductively, she saw Gavin's eyes lower to her baby bump as she sashayed to him. Reaching out, her hands went to his belt to jerk him to her.

"Why would I be jealous?" Going to her tiptoes, she licked the corner of his mouth before pulling away. "Why would you turn to another woman when I would do anything you want?"

His mouth curled in a devil-may-care smile. "Very true."

Gavin curled his palm along her jaw. "Have you forgotten to tell me something today?"

"I love you, Gavin."

No matter how many times she told him a day, she could see the uncertainty in his gaze.

He wrapped her in his arms, showing she had reassured him for the moment. "I'm pretty happy with the house myself."

Ginny smiled against his shoulder. God, she loved this stubborn man.

"Don't let your superstitions get to you. Everything is working out. The house is almost done, Allerton's case is moving along, though his lawyer managed to get a court hearing for next week, seeking bail again. Agent Collins said it'll be denied again, and he says, when he finally realizes he's not getting out, he'll come forth with the information on Clindale. Shade is still working on it, too, with the information we found out. So, hopefully, we'll get that answer soon. Everything is going our way," he reassured her.

"Shh … don't jinx us. Trudy said the same thing when I went to see Myles. But I just can't rid myself of this feeling. I even called Zoey and made a counseling session. She always helps me gain back a positive attitude."

"She give you any suggestions you could use?"

"Zoey said my insecurities could be coming from my past lives, compounded by what I've gone through, that this may be the source of my problem. She suggested I get a good psychotherapist or there's a trend where you can do it yourself with self-meditation. You can find it online and see your face and how you die in your last life. I …."

Gavin took her by the forearms and pulled her back to stare down at her. His face was formidable in its intensity. "Don't. I mean it, Ginny. Promise me?"

"I wasn't. I was just telling you what she suggested. I don't want to know how I died in a past life any more than I want to know how I'm going to die in this one."

"You're not going to die."

"Sadly, everyone does, sooner or later. Unless you're a Highlander, then you can live forever."

Gavin's expression didn't lighten at her sense of humor. "Did Freddy know how he was going to die?"

"I don't know. Silas believes he did."

"What do you believe?"

"I don't believe Freddy knew."

"Because, if he did, then your dad knew that when Leah got on the four-wheeler with him, she was going to die."

"Yes, and he knew when I switched places with Leah, his real daughter was going to die instead of me."

"You were a real daughter to him as much as Leah," he assured her.

"Would you be able to make that distinction, Gavin, if the shoe was on the other foot? If he did, it had to be a heartbreaking decision to make."

"I think your father had to make difficult decisions his whole life because of his gift. Your father was a good man. I regret I never got to meet him."

"I do, too. He would have liked you."

Gavin gave her an I'm-not-sure look before he glanced

down at his watch. "You sure you don't want to ride into town with me to fill the grocery order?"

Ginny made a face at him. "No, thanks. I'm the one who made the list. You're going to have to go to two stores to get everything. Besides, Trudy would be mad if I blew her off to go grocery shopping when I promised to go shopping with her for an outfit for Myles' baptism. We'll probably get back to the club at the same time. If I knew you were the one whose turn it was to shop, I would have taken it easy on you."

"Which is why they probably didn't tell you."

Ginny saw him glancing at his watch again.

"Go ahead and go. All my brothers are around and Trudy will be coming any minute."

"You have your phone on you?"

Ginny patted her jean pocket.

Gavin still hesitated to leave, and it was only when Silas showed up to drop off a package that he left.

"What have you been up to today?" Ginny asked, closing the windows, preparing to leave.

"Dealing with Greer. His generator is broken. It's like the one I used to have. I made the mistake of telling him that I'd broken mine down for the spare parts, and now he wants the parts to see if he can use them to fix his. The problem is I can't find the parts."

"Could the box be in the barn on the shelf where Freddy used to keep his junk?"

"Yes. Would you happen to know where it is now?"

"I threw it away."

"Why'd you throw it away?"

"Put it this way; it involved me trying to help Fynn with his science project and a dead rat."

"Enough said." Silas smiled. "The boys want to get a bite at the diner, so I might as well make a stop at the depot store on the way home. That way, they can help me load Greer's new generator in the truck for me."

"You're going to buy Greer a new generator?"

"I'd rather buy him a new generator than go to the landfill."

Ginny laughed.

Double-checking the back door, Silas and Ginny walked through her house before going outside. It was situated at the side end of the property, which had a different driveway than Silas's.

Ginny saw the gleaming metal of the car coming up the driveway. "There she is. I'll see you tomorrow," she said, locking the door.

"See you tomorrow." Silas said as he stepped off the porch and headed through the line of trees to reach his house.

Fear lanced through her when the car came to a stop and Ginny got a clear view of who was in the front seat. She slid her hand into her pocket to take out her phone to call Gavin, as she opened her mouth to yell for Silas before he was of earshot.

Soleil got out of the car. "Don't, Evangeline, I just want to talk," she said, seeing what she was doing.

"Go away. You have nothing to say that I want to hear."

"Are you sure about that? Don't you want to know what you took? Why so many people had to die because you were nothing but a little brat?" she spat.

Ginny hesitated. She wanted to hear what her mother had to say. Once she called out for Silas, and contacted Gavin, however, Soleil might refuse to tell her the information she wanted. Could she convince her to reveal what had happened to the islanders? Ginny wasn't willing to take the chance she would never find out. Soleil was no threat to her; Allerton was in prison.

"Why are you here? You're not here for my benefit—you just made that obvious."

Soleil stepped away from her car to walk toward the porch. "You made a deal with the FBI to keep your fake husband out of prison; I want you to do the same for me."

"In return, what do I get?"

"Answers, Evangeline. Isn't that what you want?"

Ginny put her phone back in her pocket and took out the key to the house. Unlocking the front door, Ginny opened it and gave mocking bow. "Welcome to my humble abode."

"Quit acting like your bitch of a sister. It doesn't suit you."

Ginny tightened her lips at the way Soleil talked about Trudy. There was a big difference when Sex Piston and the others called each other a bitch and when Soleil used the term.

Closing the door after them, Ginny had no intention of letting Trudy anywhere near their *mother*.

Taking her phone out of her pocket, she texted Trudy that she was going to have to cancel their shopping trip, then set the phone on the counter. Her sister was going to be furious, but Ginny would rather chance that than Trudy's safety.

"The FBI wants me to turn myself in to find out what information I have on Gabriel."

"I'm surprised you didn't stay on Sherguevil Island."

"I'm not safe there. Gabriel won't take a chance I won't tell the FBI what I know."

"Doesn't sound like you don't have much of a choice but to cooperate with the FBI."

"I don't if I want to stay alive. I want you to get a promise from them that I will be placed in witness protection. I'd be killed the first night in prison. I want their assurance that I won't have to appear in court, and I'll be given a new identity, one where I won't have to work, either."

Ginny lifted an eyebrow at her. "If I try to negotiate a deal with the FBI on your behalf, what do I get in return?"

Soleil slipped her hand into her pocket, and Ginny stiffened in fear, moving her hand protectively over her stomach.

Ginny stared at Soleil's hand curiously. She was holding a diamond-encrusted brooch. Soleil opened it and Ginny saw a tiny image of a beautiful woman whom she recognized.

"Oh God." Ginny put her hand to her mouth, images flashing through her mind.

"Ahh … so you *do* remember."

Ginny lifted her eyes from the beautiful brooch. "How do you have it?" She could have saved herself from asking the question, the memories coming back as the words left her lips. Ginny put her hand to her chest. "She pinned it on me. I didn't steal the brooch; she gave it to me because she knew he was going to kill her." Ginny narrowed her eyes on her mother. "I didn't swim my way back. You went on Sherguevil that night. You must have seen me climbing down off the boat and picked me out of the water."

Soleil handed her the broach. "It was late, and Jasper was frantic looking for you. When I went to Manny's home, and he wasn't there, his mother confessed where they were. When the children came running back to the village, they told me you had gone with them and where Manny had hidden you. By the time I made it to dock, Gyi's boat had left to go back to Sherguevil.

"It took me a while to get one of the men to let me take his boat of without him. I was on my way to Sherguevil when I found you swimming a few feet offshore."

Ginny placed the brooch in her pocket, unable to look at it any longer. "I'm surprised you didn't let me drown."

"I might not have been the perfect mother, but despite what you think of me, I am not capable of filicide."

Soleil's eyes dropped to her protruding belly.

"I think you're more than capable of anything you set your mind to," Ginny said in disgust, her hand going to protectively cover her stomach. "What happened to the islanders on Clindale?"

"I don't know."

"I don't believe you."

"That is irrelevant. Gabriel picked and chose what to tell me. Clindale, he chose not to."

"Why did he kill Jasper?"

"The islanders disappeared when Jasper was sent to work on another island. When he came back, he wanted his curiosity appeased. He didn't buy the hurricane story any more than your husband did."

"Allerton killed Jasper."

"Among many others." Soleil nodded toward the phone that she had left on the counter. "You can shut the recorder off now. That should be enough to get me the deal I want."

Ginny picked up the phone, clicking off the recording. "Give me your phone number. I'll call you after I talk to one of the agents."

"Which agent are you working with? Are you sure they have enough power to get me the deal I want?"

Ginny shrugged carelessly. "I guess we'll find out, won't we?" Shoving the phone in her pocket, Ginny stared distastefully at the woman who had given birth to two women who were nothing like her.

Walking to the extra-large window, Ginny looked out to the woods.

"I'm not a terrible person."

"I have to disagree with that."

"I saved your life, at my own personal expense."

Turning away from the window, Ginny gave her a mocking smile that didn't reach her eyes. "I blamed myself for my actions that day that ruined Trudy's life. You didn't help me escape to save me or Trudy—you did it for your own greedy purpose."

"I—"

"Don't bother. The one part of my story that was the truth was the DNA test, Soleil. Trudy and I are half-sisters. Jasper wasn't my father. You were lovers with Allerton. He didn't know, did he?"

"No. He would have killed me if he had known. He was fanatical about not having children."

"Gotta love men. He was fanatical, just not enough to use a condom." Ginny laughed without mirth. "I bet you were scared shitless when I started favoring him rather than Jasper. Trudy showed me our grandmother's pictures of us as babies. Trudy always looked like you from birth on. My hair was browner, and with me being out in the sun, I favored Allerton more. Sadly for you, my hair didn't start to get lighter until after I was four."

Soleil began to look uncomfortable.

"Did Jasper know?"

"No. I didn't intend to have an affair; Jasper and I were happy. Then I met Gabriel; he wasn't like any man I had met before. He has a vision, one that Jasper would never be able to see. I didn't see it at first either, but the more time I spent with him I realized he was right. You have to have power to accomplish any good."

Ginny was sickened by her mother being brainwashed by Allerton.

"Allerton used you to gain control of Jasper. You were exactly the type of woman Allerton was determined *not* to have a child with. The only reason you didn't let me drown was because you wanted to make damn sure if he ever developed a fatherly bone in his body, you could produce me. You two were made for each other."

Unable to remain in the room with her for another

second, Ginny went to open the door. "I'll call you after I hear from the FBI. It may take a couple of days."

"What's the agent's name, so if he calls, I'll know?"

"I'll give you the name. If anyone calls you before I do, then you know they aren't with the FBI."

As Soleil went to the door, she lowered her eyes to her belly. "Do you know if you're having a boy or a girl?"

"No," Ginny lied. "In case you're interested, Trudy had a boy." Without waiting for Soleil to respond, Ginny scornfully started for the door.

"Ginny, wait. There's something else I have for you."

CHAPTER FORTY-NINE

"You going to stay and help me get the generator hooked up?" Greer made no move to touch the new machine that he bugged Silas to buy for him.

Silas directed Matthew and Isaac to help him unbox the generator, which was twice the size of the one that broke. The rest of his brothers decided to take Fynn to Walmart when he complained all his socks had holes in them.

"Tate and Dustin can't help you hook it up?" Silas broke down the empty box, placing it in Greer's recycling bin.

"You see either of them here?"

Silas had two options: get the machine running or listen to Greer complain for the next twenty minutes. Silas figured it would be easier to just hook it up and save himself the twenty minutes.

Making sure the machine was level, Silas put his finger on the switch when the mountain rocked.

"What in the fuck was that?" Greer yelled.

Greer, Silas, and his brothers ran from the side of Greer's house to the front yard. Silas had never heard an explosion like that before, unless the highway was blasting to widen a road or bring down a large boulder to keep it from falling into the road.

"It sounded like it came from your land." Greer placed his hand over his eyes to shade them from the sun.

Silas stared at his property, afraid to admit he had the same thought. When a plume of smoke came rising above the tree, Silas and his brothers began running for his truck. "Greer, call the fire department!"

His cousin had his phone to his ear when Greer put a foot to his bumper and hauled himself up into the bed of Silas' truck.

Silas was speeding down the short road when he heard Greer yell from the back, "Slow down. Tate and Dustin are coming."

At the base of the driveway, Silas barely stopped long enough for his other cousins to jump into the bed. Hitting the paved road with squealing tires, Silas slammed on the gas. All his brothers were accounted for, but Ginny ... She had left, hadn't she?

Silas jerked his eyes to Isaac's. His brother's expression was ashen.

His heart pounded as smoke billowed down from the mountain to the road. Turning the last curve that put him within sight of his property, he started praying ... then drove straight into hell.

Viper went behind the bar to pour himself a whiskey. "You want one Shade? Rider?"

"I'll take one," Shade said, grabbing a stool.

"Rider?"

"Pour me one." Rider placed the cue on the pool table, walking to the bar. "No fun playing by yourself."

"You cleaned everyone out on payday." Viper took a sip of his drink, hearing a loud noise from outside.

Setting the glass on the top of the bar, the men stared at each other.

"You hear something?" Looking at the glass, he saw the whiskey in his glass jumping at the same time as the liquor bottles started clinking together on the shelf.

"A car wreck?" Rider guessed.

Jesus slammed the door open. "Viper, there was an explosion somewhere on the mountain. I hear the fire trucks coming this way."

Viper, Shade, and Rider ran outside to look off the porch as the only two firetrucks in Treepoint flew past, followed by an ambulance with the lights on, hot on its tail, then Knox's Bronco rounding the corner, catching up fast.

Viper reached for his phone, pressing Knox's number. "What happened?" he asked.

Disconnecting the call, he started issuing orders. "Call all the brothers; we have to go. Shade, Rider, get what you think we'll need. There's been an explosion."

Shade was already sending the mass text to get the brothers on their bikes as they started running down the steps.

Viper was the first one to get his leg over his seat.

"Where was the explosion?" Shade asked, getting on his bike.

"The Colemans'. Shade, there's a casualty."

Reaper pressed the button to close the hatch of the Escalade. Sniffing the air, he smelled smoke. Many of the mountain people burned off their brush or excess trash.

Settled in the front seat, he took out his phone and saw he

had missed over twenty-four calls. Looking at his phone, realized he must have accidently put his phone on silent. Making sure none had been from Ginny, he called Viper.

"What's—"

Reaper jumped at Viper's shout coming from the other end.

"Where in the fuck have you been!"

"I was at the store. What in the fuck is wrong?"

"I thought you were dead!" Viper's voice broke. "There's been an explosion at Silas's property. Go to the hospital. I'm on my way."

Reaper had already started the car after hearing "go the hospital." He peeled out of the store parking lot, driving the five miles to the hospital at breakneck speed.

Parking the Escalade, he was sick at the thought of Silas or one of Ginny's brother being hurt. He had called Ginny twice to see if she was still shopping with Trudy or if she was already at the hospital. Thinking he should call the club to see if she was there and to tell her to stay put until he could come get her, he parked the car and decided he'd call after he found out the news.

The automatic door slid open when he walked in, allowing him into the emergency room. He was heading for the desk when he saw all of Ginny's brothers and the Porters standing out in the long hallway.

Reaper slowed as they turned to face them. All their faces and clothes were covered in dark soot. However, it was their expressions that had him not wanting to take another step.

Silas didn't give him a choice. As he walked to meet him, Reaper knew it wasn't going to be good.

"What happened?" Reaper managed to croak out, his throat so tight that the words barely sounded.

"There was an explosion at your and Ginny's house."

Reaper felt a numbness washing over him, as if preparing him for the next words.

"That's okay as long as nobody's been hurt. I'll get the brothers clearing—"

"Reaper," Silas stopped him. "Ginny was in the house when it exploded."

"No." Reaper shook his head. "Ginny's with Trudy. She's terrible about answering her phone."

"She was inside the house. Greer and I were the ones who pulled her out."

"I want to see her." Reaper went toward the door the men were standing in front of.

Silas grabbed his arm. "They'll come and get us when they're ready. They had to call for a specialist."

"For what?"

"Her body is burned over eighty percent. She's been shot. Ginny's brain dead."

"No, she isn't."

"Reaper, they're waiting for the other doctor to come in. If there isn't brain activity, they want to shut off the machine."

"You're not fucking taking her off the machine!" he shouted, taking a step back from Silas.

Greer was leaning against the wall. Walking toward him, Reaper grabbed his shirt. "Fix her."

"I tried. There's nothing left." Greer's face was already haggard. "Her spirit was already gone when we got there."

"Try again," Reaper pleaded. "Greer, she's carrying my baby … Please, I'm begging you."

"I would if I could."

"I'll pay whatever you want—Viper will give me some money … Anything you want. All you have to do is ask." Tears coursed down his cheeks, but Reaper didn't care. He couldn't survive without Ginny. She was his anchor.

"Reaper, I can't help ... There's only one person who can save her, and I'm not him."

"Don't you fucking dare to turn Ginny's machine off!" he shouted, turning in the direction of the door.

"Where are you going?" Silas called after him.

Reaper took off as if the hounds of hell were after him. Running to the Escalade, he then sped out of the exit, passing Dalton and Trudy's car as they entered the parking lot. They honked the horn at him, but he didn't stop. Reaper couldn't. He didn't have any time to spare. He had to talk to the only man who could save Ginny's life, and he wasn't going to take no for an answer.

CHAPTER FIFTY

Turning the radio off, Ginny slid out of Moses' car, then shut the door. Her brother wouldn't be happy that she had taken his car without his permission. She would have to get Gavin to drive her to drop it off.

Lacking the energy to go up the front steps, she walked up the back path.

Ginny opened the kitchen door and came to a stop at seeing Willa, Lily, Winter, and Beth sitting at the kitchen table, crying their eyes out. Meanwhile, Puck and Jesus were staring at her as if they were looking at a ghost.

"Willa, what's wrong?" Ginny rushed forward, dropping the two bags of maternity clothes she had bought to the floor to comfort her crying friend.

Hearing her voice, the women jumped up from the table, running toward her to crush her in their arms.

"Willa!" Ginny tried to gain control of the chaotic situation. "Please, tell me what's wrong. You're scaring me."

"There was an explosion ... Yours and Gavin's house has burned to the ground."

Ginny felt like she was going to faint.

Jesus went to the table and slid out a chair for her sit down on. Ginny sank down into it.

Her beautiful house ... gone.

"Ginny ... we ... we ...," Willa stuttered. "They found a woman inside. Silas and everyone thinks it's you."

Shocked, Ginny couldn't believe what she was hearing. "I need to call Gavin ... Silas." Ginny took her phone out, calling Gavin, her pulse going faster when he didn't answer.

Disconnecting the call, Ginny then called Silas. She wanted to burst into tears at the sound of his voice.

"Silas!"

"Ginny, where are you? Everyone thinks you're here in the hospital on death's door."

"I know ... I'm at the club. I just found out. Is Gavin there? He isn't answering his phone."

"He was here, then ran out. I don't know where he is. Trudy is here. She wants to speak with you."

"Ginny!"

"Trudy, I'm fine. It was just a horrible mistake. I'm fine," Ginny kept repeating until she was able to calm her sister.

"Do you have any idea who was at your house when it exploded?"

Ginny didn't want to tell Trudy over the phone.

"Trudy, I have to find Gavin. When I find him, I'll come to the hospital. I shouldn't be long."

Ginny disconnected the phone and tried calling Gavin again. Still no answer.

"Does anyone have any idea where Gavin is? He's not at the hospital. I need to go to the hospital in case he goes back there."

Willa grabbed her coat off the back of her chair. "I'll drive you. I don't want you driving when you're this upset."

Ginny didn't want to take the time to argue, so she

hurried after Willa to her car. In the car, Ginny crossed her arms, shivering.

"I'll turn the heat on and warm the seats," Willa said, flicking a series of buttons on the dashboard.

"Thank you."

"Who do you think it was?" Willa asked as they hit the bottom of the hill, coming to stop light.

"My mother. She came to see me. I thought Soleil had left. She must have come back and I'd already left."

The light turned green.

"I'm sorry for your loss."

Ginny turned her head toward Willa. "Don't be. It wasn't much of a loss."

Ginny caught sight of Gavin running into the church.

"Drive back! I just saw Gavin."

Willa turned around, pulling into the parking lot.

Ginny opened the door and got out.

"I'll call everyone and tell them you found him," Willa called out as Ginny shut the door.

Wary of the slick sidewalk, Ginny walked as fast as she could to the church entrance. Inside, Ginny went to Pastor's Dean's office. Seeing it was empty, she was about to go toward the kitchen when she heard a voice coming from the chapel.

As she drew closer, Ginny heard Gavin. "I don't deserve her, but I'm begging You, anyway. I swore I would never beg to You again. You undo what You've done, I will praise Your name every day for the rest of my life."

Ginny saw where Gavin was as she came into the chapel. He was kneeling in front of the statue of Jesus on the platform where Pastor Dean gave his sermons. The room, other than Gavin's voice, was eerily still.

"I love her. She's having my child. Take my life for theirs. I was too stupid to appreciate what I had. Is that why You took them away from me? I wasn't even brave enough to tell her I love her. Why would she love me after the filth I did?"

Ginny couldn't bear it anymore. She went to his side, dropping to her knees to place her arms around him.

"Gavin … I'm here … It was just a terrible mistake."

Reaper abruptly raised his head. When she saw his face ravaged with grief, she leaned into him. Turning around to sit, she pulled his head to her chest and began slowly rocking him.

"I'm here … I never left you … I could never leave you … ever. I love you."

Gavin's heartrending sobs tore at her heart.

"I thought I lost you and the baby."

"Your son is fine. Snug as a bug in a rug," she crooned, continuing to rock him.

"I love you."

"I love you, wild man."

"I spent nine and a half years in what I considered hell. It took me one hour thinking I lost you forever to find out what true hell was. Every minute, every second I spent in that hole was worth it to have you. I would do it over a hundred times over if that's what I have to do to deserve you.

"God didn't punish me by making me suffer through the years; every single thing was preparing me to love you, and I will cherish you for the rest of my life."

Ginny wiped her tears away when she gasped in awe. "Gavin … look."

R eaper raised his head, and he saw the woman he loved more than breathing holding out her hand. Placing his hand in hers, Reaper realized what she was staring at so reverently.

The statue of Jesus caught the sun's rays as it lowered in the sky, and as it did, the statue glowed in an ethereal light. Their linked hands were covered in the light spreading across their arms.

Before today, Reaper would have said it was a trick of the light. Now Reaper knew, without a doubt, what they were being given ... a blessing.

Reaper reverently lowered his head, accepting the healing power of God's and Ginny's love. The lighting, the blessing he was being given, cut with the skill and finesse of a laser to where he needed it the most—Gavin's heart and soul, which had been locked behind the steel door of Reaper's heart.

The steel door opened, and the light targeted the soul buried beneath years of pain and humiliation. It barely stirred as the pure light of God's and Ginny's love lightened the darkness, then it began slowly opening like a flower unfurling in the first rays of sun. Still, the frightened soul fought to remain hidden, afraid. Reaper intuitively understood why.

While he would always need God's and Ginny's love, he had to love himself.

Reaper concentrated and reached down with an imaginary hand, pulling Gavin out of the ashes and into the bright light of his and Ginny's love and into God's loving arms.

Opening his eyes, Gavin found himself staring at his and Ginny's intertwined hands as the bright light faded away, returning to its home—heaven.

"Did that just happen?" Ginny asked shakily.

"Yes, it did." Gavin would never doubt love again.

A movement had Ginny and him looking to see Paster Dean standing in the aisle. Behind him were Willa, Viper, Silas, Trudy ... everyone who was important in his life was there to share his new beginning.

Pastor Dean spoke as he walked down the aisle toward

them, the others following after about him. "Mathew 5:15-16: *Let your light shine before men, that they may see your good works, and glorify your Father who is in heaven.* Thank you, Father, for letting us witness your miracle. We all are truly blessed."

Gavin stood, helping Ginny to her feet. They immediately found themselves in the middle of a circle that would offer them a lifetime of love and support to draw on in times of need and give back when others needed the same.

Gavin lay his hand on Ginny's belly. "This isn't the miracle God has given me. He gave me one the day you were born, a second when you told me you loved me, a third when my son was created, and today ... when He carried me home."

CHAPTER FIFTY-ONE

Gavin made sure his shirt was neatly tucked into the waistband of his pants before he entered the diner. Striding to the counter, he didn't sit down, just stood there until Marty noticed him as he waited on the customers.

Seeing that he wasn't taking a seat, Marty rumbled over to him with his notepad and pen at the ready. "What in the fuck do you want?"

"I love Ginny very much. I promise to love and cherish her each day. I am going to marry Ginny if she will have me. May I have your blessing?"

Marty's eyes crinkled at the corners, and his jowls wobbled as if he didn't know what to say.

"You going to keep staying away when she comes to the diner?"

"Yes."

"Then you have my blessing ... fuckwad."

G avin knocked on Silas's door.

Silas opened the door with a friendly smile. "Why did you knock? Come on in."

Gavin stepped inside, seeing all Ginny's brothers were there for their Sunday dinner. They were lounging in the living room.

Silas looked at him curiously as he stood there formally.

"I love Ginny, and I know how much Ginny loves you. If I can convince her to marry me, I will no longer have one brother but eight. I promise Ginny won't never need for anything, and I promise to provide for her and any children we may have to the best of my abilities. May I ask Ginny to marry me?"

Silas looked to each of his brothers, receiving their nods, before he walked toward Gavin and held out his hand. "You have our blessing. Welcome to the family, brother."

Ginny's brothers all shook his hand in the order they were born. After Fynn's handshake, Gavin excused himself and went outside. With Suki following, he walked across the property until he came to a fenced-off area. Unlatching the gate, he walked in until he knelt at the grave of Ginny's father.

"Freddy, my name is Gavin James. I'm in love with your daughter. I don't deserve Ginny. I'll never deserve Ginny. You raised a wonderful daughter.

"One of my biggest regrets is that I never had the opportunity to meet you. Ginny talks about you every day, as well as Leah. She keeps both of you in her heart. The lessons you taught her will be passed down to our children. I only pray I have the ability to be as good a father as you were. I can't receive your blessing in person, but I pray the blessing we are able to receive is you watching over us until one day we are able to meet in person."

Gavin stood to look down at the grave. "You're going to have a grandson, your first one. We plan to give him your given name. Rest in peace, Freddy."

Gavin took three steps to the side, kneeling down he a laid of bouquet of flowers on the small grave with a pink headstone. "Leah, my name is Gavin. I'm in love with your sister. She talks about you at least three or four times a day. How you loved to count the stars, and played make-believe, and dreamed of living next to each other. I'm sorry your hopes and dreams were never fulfilled in this lifetime."

Reaper stared at the two graves in the graveyard. Some of the markers so old, the inspiration so faded with time, they couldn't be read anymore. The small gravestone marking Ginny's sister tore at his heart.

Bending forward he plucked a clump of dead grass from the mound of Leah's grave. His jaw clenched at the strength of emotions he was feeling.

"Little Angel, I hope you find the joy and happiness in your next lifetime, like I found in mine."

Rising to his feet, Gavin turned toward the gate to see Silas standing with one foot on the bottom rail.

"I heard what you said to them. It was nice. Dad and Leah were crazy over Ginny. They would both be happy you found her."

"We found each other." Gavin came through the gate, making sure to latch it closed.

"I have to correct you about one thing, though. You did meet my father." Silas patted Suki's head as they walked.

"I would have remembered if I had." Gavin frowned, racking his memory from when he first came to Treepoint.

"It was right before he died. You even have his signature." Silas bent down to pick up a stick, throwing it for Suki.

Gavin stopped, looking at Silas. "He was the silent

investor who put up the money to build the factory and the club."

Silas took the stick from Suki, then threw it farther. "Yes." Silas reached into his back pocket and pulled out an old envelope. "There is a reason you couldn't find where Ginny's deed to her part of the mountain was. It was because it had never been put in her name."

Gavin tore the envelope open. Reading the document, he began laughing. If he hadn't believed that Freddy could foretell the future before, he did now.

The deed had been made out to Gavin and Evangeline James.

Dalton opened the door with a surprised look on his face.

"May I speak with Trudy?"

Dalton looked down at the bouquet of flowers in his hands. "Are you sure you want to come in? They're all in there."

"I'm ... sure." Gavin lied, preferring to do another tour in Afghanistan than face the group of women in the living room.

They stopped talking when he walked in.

Making a beeline for Trudy, he handed her the roses. "Trudy, I love Evangeline. I promise to love and cherish her every day. I promise she will never feel invisible again. I also promise to let her have one slumber party a month.

"Viper and I were never blessed with a sister, but if Evangeline consents to marry me, Viper and I both welcome you into our family as our sister with open hearts and arms. May I have your blessing to marry your sister?"

Trudy motioned to the side table. "Killyama, hand me a tissue. I give you my bless—"

"Not so fast, hot shot." Sex Piston picked up the tissue box, tossing the whole box at Trudy. "What do we get out of you marrying Ginny? She's like a sister to us; where're our fucking flowers?"

Gavin reached into his suit pocket and pulled out an envelope. "In the envelope are four gift certificates to King's restaurant. Each certificate has enough money to take your whole family out for steak dinners and dessert. Ginny told me how much you like eating out. I thought you might like a steak versus flowers."

"You thought right." Crazy Bitch jerked the envelope out of Sex Piston's hand, dividing the certificates among them.

"Ladies, may I have your blessing?"

Sex Piston opened her arms wide. "Come to mama!"

Gavin stepped forward to be hugged by Sex Piston, Crazy Bitch, Fat Louise, and lastly by Killyama. Trudy stood up when it was her turn, her eyes twinkling in merriment. Placing a kiss on his cheek, she hugged him before releasing him.

"Make her happy, Gavin. Evangeline has never wanted roses or champagne. From the moment Evangeline drew her first breath, she's only wanted one thing—to be loved."

"I can do that."

Escaping, Gavin hurried past Dalton.

"Ginny called and told them I was coming, didn't she?"

"About five minutes before you got here," Dalton confirmed. "Show off," Dalton muttered, holding his hand out. "I thought I'd never see the day that those she-cats could be tamed."

Gavin reached into his pocket, taking out four pieces of paper and giving them to Dalton.

Dalton laughed, looking through the cell phone numbers

scrawled under their names that the bitches had given him. "At least Trudy—"

"Forgot one." Gavin reached into his pocket and took another slip of paper.

Gavin knocked on the heavy wooden door.

"Gavin, come in. You're right on time."

Gavin waited until Pastor Dean was seated behind his desk. "I came to ask for your permission to marry Ginny. I understand where I went wrong when I spoke to you before. You're not only Ginny's pastor and friend, but the man who mentored her and gave her peace and a kind ear when she needed it most in her life. As her pastor, I am asking you to consent to our marriage. And as a friend, I'm asking you to perform our wedding ceremony, if I get your permission."

Gavin held his breath, waiting for Pastor Dean's verdict.

Coming out from behind the desk, the pastor held out his hand. "As Ginny's pastor, she has my permission to marry you. As your friend, I would be proud to marry you and Ginny." Then his smile widened. "And as a brother, I want to say you finally got it fucking right."

Reaper smoothed the sleeves of his suit before he knocked on the door. Nervously, he ran a hand around the back of his bare neck, still getting used to having all of his hair cut off. *It'll grow back,* he consoled himself. He needed to make a good impression to the man inside.

"Hi, Gavin." Lily smiled at him from the doorway. "How are you doing today?"

"Good. How are you?"

Shade's wife's beautiful violet eyes shined with mirth.

"Taking advantage of the boys being over at Razer's, and the men babysitting Mae while Rachel and I fix lunch. Come inside. The men are upstairs in Mae's room."

Waving him inside, Gavin went into the kitchen to greet and hug Shade's stepmother. Waiting until Rachel had her welcoming tears under control, he went upstairs following Lily's directions. Silently, he stood in the doorway and a tiny Mae played hostess to the men who were sitting on the floor. Mae was having a pretend tea party and the men were sipping out of plastic cups as the little girl pour imaginary tea from a teapot.

Reaper cleared his throat to let them know he was there. Shade jumped to his feet, while Will stayed seated.

"Sorry to interrupt the party. Will, may I have a word with you?"

"Shade, help me up. My knees aren't what they used to be."

Reaper entered the feminine room, going to Will's other side to take Will's other arm.

Once Will was standing, Shade went to pick up Mae when she started crying. It never failed to move him when he saw Shade holding his daughter. He was an excellent father to his sons, but Mae held Shade's heart in her tiny palm. Soothing his daughter in a low voice, Shade went to the side of the room to pick up a book to sit on a white rocking chair and began reading to her.

Returning his attention to Will he cleared his throat again.

"I appreciate you and Rachel for coming."

"Were the one's happy to get a free holiday. Thanks for offering to put us up at the hotel, but Shade wanted us to stay with him."

Nodding. Reaper started to clear his throat again and

stopped himself. Lowering his pride in front of Shade, he got to the point of why he bought first class tickets for them to come to Treepoint.

"I would have flown to Florida, but I didn't want to leave Ginny."

"Understandable. It worked out. Rachel was ready for a visit with the grandkids. What was so important you wanted to talk to me about. You want me to invest in another business?"

"No. I want to ask if I can have your permission to marry Ginny. She considers you a second father to her, and I would be honored if you'll allow me to marry her."

The hardnose ex-sheriff's face turned soft.

"Son, I can't think of another man who I'd give my permission to. She's a handful," he warned.

Reaper smiled. "I've heard that."

"How many times has she locked you out?

"Twice so far."

Will gave him a considering look. "I expected more. Show's you've got a good head on your shoulders." Chuckling, Will gave him a pat on his shoulder. "I've got to go tell Rachel you're getting married. You staying for dinner?"

Reaper turned to Shade to see him nodding.

"I'd like that. Thank you."

"I'll go tell Rachel."

Left alone, Shade laid the sleeping child in her crib.

"How many more do you have to ask?"

Reaper made a face. "One more."

Leaving the room, Shade left the door half open.

"You going to tell the brothers you caught me playing tea party?"

Pausing at the head of the steps, Reaper gave Shade a speculative gaze.

"You going to tell the other brothers Ginny asked you how to get me to let her touch my dick?"

"No. How'd you know?"

Reaper laughed. "Took me a while to figure it out."

"How did you? She swore me to secrecy."

Reaper rolled his eyes at him.

"She might have, but Ginny tells Trudy everything, and *she* can be bought."

"Hello?"

"Hammer, this is Reaper."

"You finally getting around to me?"

Walking around the back yard, Reaper stared up the bedroom window. The curtain was closed but the window was open, and he could hear Ginny's soft voice spilling out as she sang.

"I saved the best for last," he said in a low voice, not wanting his voice to carry.

"You want to call me back? We must have a bad connection."

"Don't hang up, you heard me right."

From the breathing on the other end, Reaper knew Hammer was listening.

"I want to thank you for getting me out of that hellhole. More importantly, I want to thank you for being there for Ginny before I was. Brother, without you I wouldn't have the future I'm asking you for. Can I marry Ginny?"

"Brother."

Reaper could hear the pity in his voice.

"She's all yours."

CHAPTER FIFTY-TWO

The restaurant looked different when it wasn't busy. Ginny smiled at the waitress who saw her coming in the door.

"I'm sorry. The restaurant doesn't open for dinner for another hour," the waitress explained as she walked nearer to her.

Ginny didn't lose her smile. "I'm not here to eat. I'd like to speak with King, if he's not busy?"

"Are you here about a job?"

"Yes," Ginny lied.

"We're not hiring. I can give you an application, and he can call you when there's an opening."

"I will only take a moment of his time."

The waitress gave in. "I've been there," the woman said. "I was at wit's end before he hired me. He's in his office. Go through that room, and his office is across the hall from the kitchen entrance. If he asks who let you in, tell him it was Tara. I can't stand that bitch."

"Got it, thanks."

Giving her a thumbs-up, the woman disappeared, probably afraid to be caught talking, Ginny assumed.

Walking through the restaurant, she found King's office door. Knocking, she waited until she heard the smoky voice giving her permission to enter. The office was quite a bit larger than she expected. The man she was there to see was sitting behind an imposing desk, and from his facial expression, he didn't want to be interrupted.

"Hello, I'm Ginny—"

"I know who you are. I've been to the club several times when you've been there. How may I help you?"

"I was hoping you could spare a few minutes of your time. I would like to talk with you."

"Go ahead. I have a few minutes."

Ginny closed the door before walking toward his desk.

King raised an imposing brow as he motioned for her to take the chair in front of his desk.

Not wanting to waste the man's time, Ginny got to the point. "I would like you to convey a message to a friend of yours."

"Exactly who would that friend be?"

"Desmond Beck," Ginny answered.

"What makes you think I'm friends with him?"

"Penni, Shade's—"

"Sadly, I know who Penni is," King interrupted her. "What's the message?"

"Thank him for saving my life. My mother came to the home I was building and gave me two things that will ensure the man who wanted me dead will never get out of jail. My mother would have never given me the evidence I needed if she'd had a choice. Mr. Beck must have taken that choice out of her hands.

"I heard the announcement today on the news that

565

Desmond has taken over Angels World Rescue. I sincerely hope that he serves those in need to a significantly higher standard than Gabriel Allerton did, but I'm not counting on any members in that organization to ever do the right thing.

"Since he saved my life, I'm giving him a heads-up. The walls of secrecy that AWR has been hiding behind are going to be exposed. I'm sure with the information he gave me, Mr. Beck already has his ducks in a row, but being he saved my life, I figured it was the polite thing to do."

Ginny rose from the chair. "He should also give serious consideration to changing the name. AWR is definitely a misnomer."

"I'm curious." King rested his elbows on the desk to link his fingers together. "Why didn't you call him yourself? I'm sure he would have taken a call from you."

"Shade advised me that I should make you aware of the situation. If Mr. Beck believes that by saving my life—by ensuring I got the information to convict Allerton—Gavin and I will play nice and won't go after the charity he's now in control of, I'm afraid he's very much mistaken. The next time he or any of his men steps on my property, we'll take it as a direct threat and act accordingly."

Just before she shut the door to his office, she offered, "Have a good evening, King, and tell Evie I said hi."

Ginny stood behind the curtain, waiting for her intro. From where she was standing, she couldn't be seen, but she was able see the thousands of people standing in the stadium and the huge screens that would televise the performers.

"Nervous?"

Ginny felt Gavin move closer to her, sliding his arms around her waist.

"No."

Ginny told her husband the truth. She wasn't nervous or frightened, and she should be both. She had never hoped to reach this level of fame, to perform on this international stage for Mouth2Mouth.

Kaden had been asked to perform at the massive event to highlight the charity that Sawyer and he had founded to combat violence against women.

"I should be, but I'm not. You going to regret marrying a woman who's about to instigate a national investigation?"

"I will never regret marrying you. It took me too long to get you to say yes."

"Wild man, you never needed a piece of paper, legal or illegal, to know I belong to you."

"A man needs his peace of mind," he countered.

"Do you have it now?"

"Nymph, you and peace of mind don't belong in the same sentence."

Her name being introduced had her hand going to Gavin's that was laying across her waist. "I hope I do the song justice."

Kissing her cheek, he removed his arms from around her to give her butt a hard pat to get her moving. She heard his voice as she walked onto the stage. "You're the only who can."

She was the only no-name singer performing among twenty-five of the most famous artists in the world. Without Kaden and Sawyer's help, she wouldn't have had a chance in hell of even getting a ticket to attend the event; the proceeds were going to help victims of violence across the world.

Walking to the microphone, Ginny heard the music begin to play. She was singing "Hero" by Mariah Carey.

As the words came out of her mouth, she saw Kaden give a nod to the producer. She looked up at one the screens that televised the stage. The image of her singing on the stage switched to a video; it showed a beautiful woman being beaten mercilessly.

Ginny's gaze transferred to the man who had a front row seat, next to his son.

Markoff and Alek Lukin were guests of honor.

Realizing who they were watching being beaten mercilessly garnered two different reactions. Alek got up and tried to take his father's frail arm to get him to leave. Markoff jerked his hand free, remaining seated.

On screen, Ivan Pavlov kicked Aanya again as she lay on the floor of the boat before going into another room. A second later, there was a slight movement as a small child scooted out from under the bed to crawl toward Aanya, moving her hair away from her face. The child tried to help Aanya to her feet, but she wasn't strong enough. Aanya used the side of the bed to raise herself into a sitting position.

Ginny looked at the terrified Evangeline crying as the beautiful woman, despite being beaten mercilessly, cupped the little girl's cheek to stop her from crying. When that didn't work, Aanya took off the diamond-encrusted brooch, pinning it to the thin shirt that the little girl was wearing.

Pointing at another door, Aanya was silently telling the child to leave. The little girl was shaking her head, but Aanya pushed the little girl toward the door. Little Evangeline was still crying as the door closed behind her, and as it closed, Ivan came back into the room, his face retaining the same fury as when he had left.

Bending down, he lifted Aanya's struggling body to her feet by her neck. As Aanya's body went limp in Ivan's hands, Ginny's hand went to her neck and pulled on the necklace tucked under her cream-colored blouse.

Singing the last words of the song, the screen cut to Ivan and Aanya standing on the balcony on their palace grounds. As the camera panned in, it was easy to see the woman next to Ivan, while just as beautiful, was not Aanya.

As Ginny sang the final bars of the song, the screen switched back to display her standing on stage. The crowd sat in silence looking at the screen and seeing Ginny's glistening tears and the camera zoomed in on the scalloped-shaped brooch, exposing Aanya's royal insignia that matched the ones on Alek's and Markoff's chests.

The camera panned over to Markoff, who slowly rose to his feet, tears on his face. Staring at Ginny, he bowed his head in acknowledgment, then turned to his guards to usher him out of the coliseum with Alek trying to talk to his father, whose bodyguards repeatedly kept shoving him away until his guards forced him back to the end of the procession.

Ginny finished the song and replaced the microphone. As she began walking off the stage and to the curtain, a sound of clapping could be heard, slowly swelling higher and higher until the whole coliseum was on their feet.

Walking behind the curtain, she went straight to the arms that Gavin held out to her.

Gavin held Ginny in his arms as she cried. Tonight was the only other time Ginny had been willing to watch the video that her mother had given to Ginny before her death. Gavin had watched it the same number of times. Both times, he had thanked God for how close he had come to losing the woman he loved more than life.

"Aanya told me to run and hide, Gavin."

"I know, baby."

"She saved my life."

"You would have survived."

Ginny lifted her face from his chest. "How do you know?"

"Because that's what heroes do."

CHAPTER FIFTY-THREE

Ginny's arms went out for Gavin to lift her off the small jetty that had transported them from the yacht to Clindale Island. She'd been fighting back tears since this morning when she woke to see where they had stopped during the night.

"I told you I would bring you back." Grinning at her, he set her feet on the new dock.

"Are you sure this is okay?" Ginny asked tearfully. "They have to hate me …."

"Ginny, look at them. It's because of you they were able to come home, that their families have been reunited. Allerton loaded them on two ships, telling everyone the island was in the direct path of the storm, and each ship was going to different islands. It was just luck of the draw that my investigators found one of the islanders. Do you know how many islands I paid for them to go to? When they found the first hundred people, we never expected to find the rest of them a hundred miles away. It was pure luck."

"No, it wasn't. It was divine intervention. I've never wished ill will on anyone in my life, but I do Allerton."

"Wish him dead as much as you want any other time, but not today. Today is about us, them, and the rest of our family. Deal?"

"Deal."

Placing her hand in the crook of his arm, he smiled down at her. "Are you finally ready to marry me?"

"Technically, we've been married twice before," she argued.

"Are you finally agreeing the first one was legal?"

"I'm not going there." Ginny laughed, taking the bouquet of flowers from Trudy as Dalton placed her down on the deck behind them.

She hugged her sister tearfully. "We're home, Trudy. We're home."

Trudy hugged her close, her eyes filled with tears. "It's just as beautiful as I remember."

Dalton gave them handkerchiefs. "I thought these may come in handy today."

Wiping her cheeks, Ginny turned back to the island when the children began singing. Their beautiful voices were low, reverent.

"That's our signal," Trudy said, moving in front of her and Gavin to take Dalton's arm as they began walking down the dock to the island.

Ginny took Gavin's arm to follow behind them. As they got closer, she squeezed the bouquet of flowers holding Gavin's arm tighter to keep from falling down. The children were singing "Over the Rainbow" by Israel Kamakawiwo'ole.

"Do you like it? I had trouble picking."

"I couldn't have picked better myself," she managed to get out.

Walking through the line of villagers was the most beautiful moment of her life, and she'd had so many over the last five months; the small wedding she and Gavin had in Lucky's office with only Willa as a witness, him holding her in his arms as he told her he'd asked everyone she loved for permission to marry her, and after the baby was born and old enough to travel, he had a special place where he wanted to them to take their forever vows.

"Gavin, I don't need a second wedding, if you want us to keep it private."

"I want to make this one special. You won't have to do anything. I have all the details for today, and I'll let you pick out the next one in twenty years."

Gavin had kept his word for planning this wedding. He asked for her preferences for colors and food, but he kept the location, her dress, and the song a secret.

As they walked the path that she could walk in her sleep, the villagers walked behind them, while continuing to sing.

Passing the village, she saw the effort that had been taken to restore the island and the villagers' way of life. Viper, Gavin, and Willa had created a foundation with the help of Manny's brother, who guided them to rebuild Clindale, including a new school and assistance to build the life they had before. Manny's sister was taking the courses to become the new teacher; the foundation provided monetary help and tools, but all the decisions were the islanders'.

Outside hands had destroyed this island; they weren't needed to put Clindale back together. They could do that for themselves. This beautiful island had survived despite Allerton, and they would grow stronger and flourish for generations to come.

Diamond was making sure that Allerton paid for what he'd done. Justice had finally caught up with him, and his finances were now in shambles. There was nothing left of his once vast wealth.

Picking up the front of her dress, Ginny began to climb the trail that led to the base of the waterfall. Every step of the way, she held Gavin's hand, as she would continue to do for the rest of their lives. Reaching the waterfall's basin, the area was already filled with their guests waiting for them. Those who hadn't joined them on the yacht had flown into Sherguevil Island and were staying at the resort, which Desmond Beck now ran along with the foundation.

Desmond had quickly cleaned house and removed the members who'd supported Allerton. Under Desmond's new direction, Sherguevil Island was a thriving vacation spot where charities and donors could meet for the benefit of the foundation and its causes.

Ginny took Desmond Beck being completely philanthropic with a grain of salt, but she trusted Diamond and Gavin to make sure he would be held accountable for any actions they considered shady.

The singing stopped when they entered the clearing. Pausing by a woman, Ginny released Gavin's arm to take her son. Placing a kiss on his forehead, she handed her wiggling son to Gavin.

"Go ahead. I'll be there in a second."

Snuggling Freddy to his chest, Gavin went to take his place in front of Paster Dean, who was waiting to perform their ceremony.

"Thank you for taking such good care of Freddy this morning. I really appreciate it," Ginny said.

Jewell's standoffish attitude didn't prevent her from reaching out to hug her.

Pulling back, Ginny gave her a warm smile. "Gavin told me used your vacation to come here and help him plan the wedding. You've done a beautiful job."

"You never told him I was in love with him."

Genny's heart cried for what Jewell was going through. "I told you I wouldn't."

Jewell shrugged. "A lot of people say they won't do things. Doesn't mean they won't."

Her gaze sharpened on her. "When Gavin asked me to watch Freddy this morning and keep him during your honeymoon, he said you asked for me specifically, despite Trudy and Willa offering. Why did you want me to be the one to watch him?"

"Because you would give your life to protect Gavin's son."

A flash of unimaginable pain flash crossed Jewell's face before it she could hide it behind the cool mask she normally wore.

Ginny reached out to hug Jewell again. "I swear, Jewell, there is a man meant just for you," Ginny whispered to her as she pulled back to give her a mischievous smile. "Who knows? You could meet him tonight at the party."

Moving away from Jewell, Ginny took a few steps to the man who was waiting to escort her to Gavin. Hooking her arm through Will's, they moved through the parted crowd to take her place beside Gavin.

Paster Dean cleared his throat as he began the ceremony. "We have all gathered here to witness the end of Gavin and Ginny's search for the special someone who makes them whole. This is a celebration for these two souls being reunited, as God meant for them to be. Gavin, you may speak your vows."

Gavin handed Freddy over to Viper, who was standing by his side before he turned to face her. "Ginny, there have been times in my life when I felt God had turned his back on me. I'm ashamed to admit I didn't understand He had given me His greatest gift—you. When most couples fall in love and marry, their love often evaporates over time like a glass full of water placed out in the sun until the water evaporates. That's why soul mates have to constantly fight to be reunited with the other to refill the love that was lost. I pledge to refill the glass each and every day with my love so, at the end of our life together, there will be enough to overfill into the universe to light the way for you to find the eternity our love deserves."

Breaking his gaze from hers, Gavin looked at the people surrounding them. "No matter how many lifetimes I've lived before, this will be the most special, because this is the one that I have all of you in my life. Not only did God bless me with Ginny, but He blessed me with each one of you."

Gavin turned back to face her. "Ginny, I promise never to let you walk alone again, to be the shoulder that you can lean on in troubled times, and unconditionally love you despite how many times you're angry enough to lock me out. You will never be invisible to me. You will be the reason I strive to be a better man and father. To be the man who deserves your love and the eternity that will be waiting when our time on earth is done."

Ginny had to swallow back tears several times during Gavin's speech.

"Ginny," Paster Dean prompted her to give her vows.

"Gavin," Ginny began shakily, "God never turned His back on me. It was me who turned my back on Him, I'm also ashamed to admit. Instead of punishing me, He gave me His greatest gift—you. I spent most of my life feeling as if I was expendable. With your love, I feel as if each beat of my heart and every breath I take is just as important to you as my last ones were. I don't know how this lifetime will end, but I do know you've already given me enough love so that even if my heart doesn't beat again, and I don't take another breath, I won't have to search in another lifetime. With you, I've already found eternity.

"Gavin, I promise, you'll never walk alone again. I'll be the shoulder to lean on in troubled times and love you unconditionally, especially when you've done something that makes me angry enough to lock you out. I will never take your love for granted and will strive to be the wife and mother you and our children deserve. I love you, and I promise to fill the glass with enough love for you that, when you try to pour yours, it will spill enough that everyone we love can share in our happiness with us."

Paster Dean began speaking when she finished her vows. "Marriage is never an easy path to follow. Gavin, are you willing to make this commitment before God, and before those who have gathered here to provide witness?"

"Yes, I am."

"You may place the token of your love on her finger."

Ginny had to blink back tears at his firm resolution as he placed the ring on her finger.

"Ginny, are you willing to make this commitment before God, and before those who have gathered here to provide witness?"

"Yes, I am." Her voice was just as firm as Gavin's had been.

"You may place the token of your love on his finger."

Ginny took the ring from Trudy, who had been holding it for safekeeping, to place the ring on his finger.

Paster Dean nodded as he continued to speak. "As your journey into your new lives begins, shed the pain of the journey of your search for each other."

A soft song began playing from a cassette that Jewell must have set up to the side. Ginny began moving toward one side of the waterfall as Gavin began going to the other side. One at a time, Ginny removed her shoes as she walked toward the incline. At the base of the waterfall, she unbuttoned the full skirt of her wedding gown and lay her bouquet on the ground before climbing up the mountain in her white one-piece swimsuit. Reaching the top of the waterfall, Gavin grabbed her hand, pulling her up the last step.

The music stopped, and Lucky began speaking again, his

voice echoing over the sounds of the water cascading down. "As you jump, cast the fears and doubts aside to the wind as you, Ginny, and you, Gavin, dive into a future with all of our and God's blessings."

Holding hands, they took a flying leap into the air to splash down into the water in the middle of a circle of flowers. Laughing when her head surfaced, she circled her arms around Gavin's neck.

"I pronounce you man and wife," Paster Dean said loudly over the cheers and claps. "Gavin, you may kiss your bride."

Ginny felt as if she was still falling when Gavin kissed her. Breaking the kiss, her hand went to his jaw. "You'll always be mine now," she said with her whole heart in her eyes.

"I didn't need to marry you to know that." Placing his hand over hers, Gavin linked their fingers together. "I knew that the first time I looked into your eyes."

"You fooled me then, if that's true," she teased. "You see anything else?"

"I saw the road to salvation, which seemed like a neverending ride ahead."

Ginny grew serious. "Are you there yet?"

Gavin nodded. "The day I thought you were dying, and I thought it would take a miracle to save you. I didn't realize then that I had already been blessed with a miracle."

"You had?"

"I didn't have to ride to search for my salvation; it was within reach the whole time. It was there any time you were near. You'll always be my salvation, Ginny. A salvation I don't deserve, but I'll spend the last of my life making sure I do."

If Gavin thought she was his salvation, she wasn't going to try to dissuade him. Her gladiator had fought for his salvation, and even if she had been the one killed on that day instead of Leah, Gavin would have come out of the darkness he'd been thrust into. That's what gladiators did—they fought to survive against all odds—and he won despite the insurmountable odds to be here with her in this moment in time. She wasn't naïve enough not expect there wouldn't be battles ahead in their future, but she was sure that when the battles came their way, he would never have to fight alone again. She was going to make sure of that.

Of course, she had no say if any future gladiators fighting alongside of him would be boys or girls.

EPILOGUE
TEN YEARS LATER...

Gavin sat at the picnic table, feeding his new baby girl, who they'd brought to Viper's house to show off. Winter and Viper had thrown a picnic just for little baby Leah.

Glancing over at the brothers and their wives playing football with their children on the huge lawn, his eyes then went to his other daughter who he was in charge of watching.

Keira was Ginny's daughter, that was for sure. She was a two-and-a-half-year-old, walking, talking bundle of energy. Ginny and he had to always be within touching distance of her or she would slip away. They could barely keep track of her in the house, much less when they were out. He felt as if she was in the danger zone, and she was an accident just waiting to happen. He didn't trust that, with all the children running around, he could keep a good eye on her. So, he came prepared, bringing a huge inflatable-like playpen that gave her plenty of space to play in with all her toys and a child's leash wrapped around her waist.

Before he'd had children and had seen parents using them, he had given them condescending glances, thinking how terrible they were. That was before Keira. Now he knew better. She was a living, breathing accident waiting to happen, and he was exhausted. God had given them a son who acted like perfect angel, then He had slammed them with Keira.

When he loaded the playpen in the car, Ginny had shaken her head at him. "It's not going to work."

"It's going to fucking work. You'll see."

The playpen and the leash would work, he had thought confidently. Both items would ensure Keira stayed within his eyesight the whole time they were at Viper's. Ginny would be the one seeing who was right.

"Why is she in there?" one of Rider's sons asked as he stood on the outside of the pen, staring down at Keira.

"She can be a handful, like her mom, that's why," he told the ten-year old boy. "Why aren't you playing with the others, Crux?"

Crux's bushy brows didn't move from his hard little expression he kept on Keira. "I think she wants to be free."

"She's fine," Gavin assured him, seeing Keira was perfectly content with her blocks and books. He didn't care for the way Rider's son was constantly staring at his daughter anytime she was around. "Now, go on and play with the rest of the kids." Reaper shooed him off with a wave of his hand.

"Whatever," Crux grumbled, his eyes finally leaving Keira's to give Gavin a look his father had given him many times before.

It took everything Gavin had to let that slide as he watched the boy drag his feet off.

Going back to Leah with her now empty bottle, he raised her onto his shoulder and began burping her. It was too late for him to realize his mistake, forgetting the burp bib on his shoulder to catch the spit up.

"Shit." The white goo going down his shoulder had him grabbing some wipes.

"Need some help?" Ginny asked with a smile, taking Leah from him so he could clean himself up. "Gavin …" She suddenly paused. "Where's Keira?"

"What do you mean?" he asked, wiping up the last of the spit. "She's right ther—GODDAMMIT, KEIRA!"

The playpen was empty, and the leash that had been around her waist was now tied around the big bunny on the inside.

Instantly, his instincts kicked in. His eyes did a quick sweep of the area trying to find her. Viper and the brothers immediately started searching, while the women rounded the other children to keep them within sight. His heart was in his throat when he realized she wasn't in Viper's yard, and he started running down to the parking lot.

"God, please don't do this to me. Please, God, don't let her go to the road …."

Seeing the road was empty, he looked up the side of the hill where the long flight of steps were, his eyes going wide when he saw Keira crawling up the top of the stone steps.

Keira went to stand. Seeing him below, she then started to squeal proudly. "I did it!" She jumped. "I did i—"

Even though Gavin had already taken off running the second his eyes saw her climbing, he held back his yell, not wanting to startle her into falling. Rider, at the end of the porch, came to the bannister and saw what was happening. He started running at the same time. Seeing Rider running startled Keira, and she started to tumble over.

Reaper heard Ginny scream behind him as he raced up the steps, expecting to see Keira come tumbling down the stone steps. Looking upward, he saw Crux take a flying leap off the porch to land on his feet, catching Keira as she fell forward. Reaper didn't stop breathing, waiting for the two of them to come falling down at the force that Keira's body hit the boy.

Crux planted his feet on the step as he managed to hold his balance, keeping the two of them from falling. Holding Keira tightly, Crux turned and started carrying her down the steps to meet him.

"Thank you," he wheezed out, trying to get air back into his lungs, holding his arms out for Keira. Then he narrowed his eyes into slits when Crux didn't appear to want to give him back his daughter.

"You're welcome." Crux shrugged after Gavin had to pry her out of his hands. "You should really keep a better eye on her next time."

"I'll keep that in mind," he gritted through his teeth.

Rider's son was clearly smart enough to start walking away.

Ginny tried her best not to laugh as she waited at the bottom of the steps with Leah. "I told you that wasn't going to work."

"No," Gavin grumbled, this time to his wife, as he held Keira to him tightly, walking back down the steps that Viper should bulldoze. "The playpen and leash would work on a normal child. Just not yours."

Ginny shook her head, still wearing a smile. "I wasn't talking about the playpen."

"Oh." Gavin's eyes went back to slits, watching Crux fist-bump the man who used to be the biggest manwhore in the club, understanding what Ginny meant. "I don't give a flying flip"—he tried not to cuss around Keira, as she was starting to repeat words—"what your stars say. That boy is not ending up with my daughter. If I keep his as—butt away from her, he'll get distracted by other girls, just like his father."

"Gladiator"—Ginny reached up to touch his cheek softly, giving him a pitying look—"the stars don't write themselves … destiny does. That's one battle you're not going to win."

EPILOGUE
SIX MONTHS LATER...

"Want another hit?"

Reaper took the tiny stub that Greer left for him, crossing one ankle over the other as he listened to Silas and Greer continue their arguing over Greer giving Silas his goat back that had escaped a week ago.

"I want her back, Greer. I drove to Tennessee to buy that goat two weeks ago. I'm not going back for another one. I'll give you another one, but you can't have Josie."

"The kids are already attached to her. You should have made sure she was tied off good so she couldn't take off."

Silas narrowed his eyes on him. "Pretty damn convenient that she got loose when the boys and I went to town for lunch."

"Are you accusing *moi*?"

"Yes!"

"That's not a very cousinly thing to say."

"What should I say, then?"

"Cousin, since them youngins are attached, you should buy another one for yourself."

The sound of motorcycles could be heard in the night air.

Turning in the canvas chair, Reaper saw a motorcycle pull up to Silas's truck. When the light flicked off, he could see a shadowy figure coming toward them. He moved his hand away from his gun when Viper came within the glow of the campfire.

"I thought I would join you guys." Viper's voice was hesitant as he lifted what was in his hand. "I brought beer."

The three men looked at Gavin for his reaction, leaving it to him whether Viper stayed or left.

Reaper held his hand out. "Give me one. I hope it's colder than the ones Greer brought."

"Why's everyone busting my balls tonight?" Greer complained as he reached into his pocket to bring out his plastic baggie. Opening it, he took out another joint to light. "You sons of bitches don't deserve the treat I'm going to give you tonight, but I'll share anyway. It's the cousin thing to do." Lifting the joint, he took a hit before he started passing it around.

Reaper took a hit. "Damn, Greer, you've been holding out. This one is different."

"Damn right. This is the one I only light on special occasions. We celebrating tonight, boys. I don't have to bring the beers anymore, and I can tell the youngins they can keep Nan."

"I didn't say you could keep my goat!" Silas protested.

"The night's still young. By the time this joint is finished, Nan will be the newest member of my family."

One Month Later...

Reaper was setting up the chairs as Silas made the fire when Viper parked his SUV next to Silas's truck. Looking toward the truck, he saw Viper get out the vehicle as the passenger door opened and Shade got out. Both men went to the back seat, Viper getting the beer and Shade carrying an extra chair.

Viper put the beer in the cooler, while Shade stayed on the outskirts of the camp.

"Lily and Penni are driving me nuts. I could use a break. You mind if I join you?"

Reaper reached out and took the chair from him to set it up. "Have a seat." He motioned at the chair. "Greer you bring the good stuff?"

"You know it."

Another Month Later...

Twisting the top of his beer, Reaper saw Viper's SUV pulling off the road to park next to Silas's truck. Taking a drink, he raised his eyebrow when not just the two front doors opened, but the back door opened as well. Viper and Shade got out of the driver's and passenger's, each man carrying something different.

Shade and Viper walked into the camp as Rider stopped; he was holding a gigantic bag Reaper recognized from the diner.

"It's Jo's time of the month. Save me."

Twenty-Two Years Later...

Reaper remained standing at the rock as Silas poured water from a thermos to douse the fire as the line of vehicles pulled out, leaving Greer, Silas, and him alone.

Staring out at the dark sky, he let Greer put the last of the chairs in the back of the truck.

Staring down at the rock, he didn't need a light to see how many marks had been carved into the surface. He had years of seeing it in the daylight to know the massive weight the stone carried.

All of the original Last Riders spent their Friday nights here. They no longer needed to make new marks on the stone, coming mainly now to have time together alone and let the young bloods have their fun without them being present. It was the next generation's time to become the leaders, and the original group to fade into the background. Their kids had been raised with the values that counted the most, and if they needed help, the originals would still be around to lend a helping hand. That was what parents did, and Reaper was proud to say most of them didn't need any guidance. They were making their own way in this world, and there wasn't a one of them who wouldn't give their life for the other.

"You comin', boy?"

Reaper grinned at Greer still calling him boy. "You need my help getting in the truck?" he joked.

"Kiss my effin' ass," Greer snorted.

Laying his hand on the rock, Reaper then made his way to the truck.

The rock was still standing and so was he.

READING ORDER

www.ingramcontent.com/pod-product-compliance
Lightning Source LLC
Chambersburg PA
CBHW030740030726
47497CB00001B/70